STOLEN KISS

"You are foolish, Miss Howard, to flirt with such a man," Alistair drawled. "He is only too willing to take advantage of young ladies such as yourself."

His cynical tone brought a flush to Verity's cheeks.

"Don't be ridiculous, Major," she flared. "I could have handled the Prince. Perhaps I was a bit reckless to accompany him into the gardens, but I am sure he is a perfect gentleman and would not have forced me against my will."

"If it is stolen kisses you want as an added fillip to the evening, it would be a shame to deny you," Alistair answered provocatively, now thoroughly convinced after her ridiculous statement that the girl was nothing but a sensation seeker.

He caught her in his arms and pressed a brutal kiss upon her lips, his mouth contemptuous and hard.

His strong hands easily subdued her efforts to escape. His caress softened, roaming seductively over her hair and throat.

She felt herself surrendering to his expert handling . . .

False Promises

BY VIOLET HAMILTON

ZEBRA BOOKS
KENSINGTON PUBLISHING CORP.

ZEBRA BOOKS

are published by

Kensington Publishing Corp.
475 Park Avenue South
New York, NY 10016

First printing: September, 1988

Printed in the United States of America

Also by Violet Hamilton:

Sweet Pretender
The Hidden Heart
An Officer's Alliance

Chapter One

Lightly patting her mare, Lily, and kissing her nose, Verity laughed as the horse neighed her approval. They had enjoyed a splendid run across the green Devon acres which surrounded Woodley, the Howard estate overlooking the sea. The early May morning was cloudless with sunshine dappling the woods and fields. The morning reflected Verity's high spirits. Oh, it was good to be home, away from the artificial constrictions of Bath and the confines of the proper seminary in which she had finished her education just a few months previously. She ran swiftly across the stable yard and through the kitchen garden, entering the gabled manor from the servants' quarters, anticipating a bath and her morning chocolate. Bessie, their fat jolly cook who had been with the family since Verity was a baby, chuckled a greeting to the girl as she stole an apple tart from the tray cooling on the table, and Verity continued on her way, munching at the pastry. She skipped through the green baize door and made her way across the slate-floored entrance hall toward the stairway which rose sturdily to the upper stories. As she prepared to mount toward her bedroom, her stepfather hailed her from the entrance to the library.

"Ah, Verity, back from your ride. Could I beg a moment of your time, my dear?" he asked, looking at the radiant picture she made in her green velvet riding habit, her titian hair curling wildly about her high-boned cheeks, touched with the glow of exercise. By gad, she was a lovely piece, he thought, looking with appreciation at his stepdaughter. Of average height but reed slim, her costume accented her elegant figure just blossoming into womanhood. Dark lashes framed her large hazel eyes tilted enticingly in her creamy oval face. She glowed with youth and heatlh, inciting Sir Anthony, not for the first time, to images of her in his bed. No longer a schoolgirl but a woman to stir a man's passions, her innocence a provocation to a jaded man who had had his fill of shop-worn beauties.

She turned reluctantly and faced her stepfather. Try as she might she could not like her mother's new husband no matter how diligently he tried to win her favor. There was too much of the dandy in him, with his high-starched shirt points, overly padded shoulders in the tightly fitted coats he affected. His silvery blond hair, thinning somewhat as he entered his late forties, was combed into the latest mode and he wore

8

an inordinate amount of jewelry, fobs and rings in profusion. He was not ill-looking, being well set up, almost sleek, with pale blue eyes set a bit too closely together and a light in them which appeared greedy. She realized that his spurious charm had completely enslaved her mother, but Verity thought him a mountebank.

"Oh, must it be this minute, Sir Anthony. I yearn to remove some of this dirt and change into my morning gown," she pleaded, eager to postpone any discussion.

"This will not take long, my dear," he insisted silkily, but obviously determined, indicating the door of the library with a careless hand.

Sighing, Verity walked by him into the room, and across to the long leaded windows which fronted the terrace, trying to put as much distance between them as possible. She felt her skin prickle at his gaze, wondering why she should react so strongly. Turning, she looked at him questioningly.

"And what is this urgent matter which cannot wait?" she asked haughtily. Then, as if to remind him of their relationship, "Where is mother?"

"Poor Kitty was not feeling quite the thing this morning so I prevailed upon her to stay in bed," he replied suavely, watching his stepdaughter in a manner she found vaguely disturbing.

"Oh, I must go up to her immediately and see if I can be of some comfort," Verity insisted, happy for an excuse to leave her stepfather. She walked to the door, eager to escape.

"Agnes is watching out for her, and it is best she not be bothered," he explained, interrupting her progress with a hand on her arm. Verity barely repressed a shudder at his touch, and wondered why he smiled in that odious fashion. Could he suspect she found him loathesome?

"I wanted to talk to you about your mother, Verity. I know you are expecting her to chaperone you for your come-out in London this season but I fear it is beyond her to undertake such a chore just now, with her indifferent health. Unfortunately you have no proper female relation who can substitute for her, so I think you must suffer the postponement. I know it is a disappointment to you, my dear, for like all young females you must be thinking of catching a husband," he drawled, keeping her arm within his grasp, his eyes roaming over her with a look that was far from fatherly. "And, of course, we would miss you intolerably about the place."

Verity, uncomfortable under his look, felt some surprise at this news, and wondered if this change of plans had been instigated by Sir Anthony. She had never believed her mother's health fragile and said so, frankly. "I had no idea that mother was not feeling up to snuff. But naturally her well-being must be my first concern. I am not such an unnatural daughter that I would put my own enjoyment before my mother's comfort," she explained, and then felt annoyed at his implication. "And I am not hanging out for a husband, Sir Anthony," she reproved him,

10

looking at him with some disdain.

"Well, that is good news. We would not want to lose you so soon to some downy-faced stripling, who could not possibly appreciate you," Sir Anthony smiled wolfishly, running his hand up her arm to her cheek and pinching it. Verity jerked away from him, not liking his innuendos nor the look he passed over her.

Well aware of her distaste, an ugly gleam appeared for a moment beneath his hooded eyes, but her rejection only seemed to amuse him. He enjoyed her shrinking, and the intimacy of their position, but Verity not so naive that she did not recognize his rather lewd look, gave him a scornful glance and remained silent.

"You know, my dear, you are a very uncommon type, and you must not rush into marriage without enjoying some of the delights which can be yours," he insinuated, implying some lecherous intent which Verity had no difficulty in translating.

She decided that this unpleasant conversation had gone on long enough.

"I do not know what you mean, Sir Anthony, and I am quite sure you should not refine too much on my future. Unless, of course, this is just an evidence of your fatherly interest," she replied naughtily, knowing that he would dislike being reminded of their relationship. Really, the man was a cad, and his attempts to fix his interest on her rather ridiculous.

Such was Sir Anthony's consequence that he

could not believe she did not welcome his attentions, although that jibe about fatherly interest brought a flush of anger to his pale face. Ignoring her rebuff, and her attempts to shrug off his restraining hand, he tightened his grasp, drawing her into a close embrace.

Verity could not believe this was happening to her. Had the man no conscience? He was trying to seduce her. If it had not been so repulsive, the idea would be laughable. She stood stiff and rigid, sensing that a struggle would only arouse him to further excesses.

"Let me show you how exciting a grown man's admiration can be, Verity," he said, and putting action to his words, tried to put a kiss on her averted lips. Appalled, she gasped and hit out at him, which seemed to bring him great satisfaction.

Panting with the stimulation of her lithe young body in such close proximity, the slight fragrance of her stirring his senses, he lost all control and tried again to raise her rigid face to his. "You are too delectable to be the object of some bumbling lad's furtive gropings. You should be introduced to the joys of the bedroom by an experienced man. I can give you what you need, Verity," he insisted, now almost beside himself.

Shocked and revolted, Verity smothered a scream and kicked out at him, her riding boot colliding with his shin. He gave a shout of pain and rage and bent to rub the offended member. She stepped away from him and, not allowing her fear to show, laughed.

"Really, Sir Anthony, you are making a cake of yourself. You must be jug bitten. What makes you think I would entertain your disgusting proposals with delight," she said, looking at him with scorn. Oh, he did look amusing, hot and disheveled, quite overcome by passion. She noticed too that the lines of dissipation on his face had deepened, giving him the look of a satyr. What conceit he had.

"You little devil!" he sputtered, now lost to all propriety in the face of her scorn. "But I will get my own back. There will be plenty of opportunity. And do not think you can hide behind your mother's skirts. She would never believe that I would prefer your untried charms to her own."

Verity realized tardily that her rebuffs only whetted his appetite. She dared not show her fright and abhorrence for he would only be stimulated by such a reaction. Her only defense was ridicule.

"You are a buffoon, sir," she jeered. "I would never succumb to a man whose shirt points are so starched he can barely turn his head. Try your wiles on some more susceptible girl. If this is an example of your fatherly interest in my welfare, let me tell you I find it most peculiar."

Sir Anthony flushed and made as if to clutch her again, but decided against further attempts to compel her. How dare the chit laugh at him. She would rue the day she had treated him like a doddering old fool. He was in the prime of life and well experienced in luring reluctant females. He must have her, but he would have to go slowly. Still the chase was exciting and the finale all the more to be savored—for ultimately he *would* win. He licked his lips in a manner Verity found nauseating, and she turned away, anxious to conclude this distressing incident.

"You protest too much, Verity. I think you will change your mind and become more amenable. I have it in my power to force you but I would much prefer you to come willingly to my arms. Soon you will be begging for my kisses," he said complacently.

"That is a conclusion only your conceit entertains. Actually, I find you pathetic, an old man trying to renew his youth with a young girl. Well, sir, you will have to find some other object for your lecherous desires. And my mother might not be as gullible as you think. Then you would find your comfortable billet here endangered, I vow," she warned, aware that he might indeed be intimidated by this threat. For she doubted he cared for her mother as much as his good life here at Woodley. "We will forget this incident, sir, but do not attempt such silly gropings again," she advised, and opened the door, pretending not to hear his parting words.

"That's right, my dear, escape for the moment, but remember you are at my mercy," he whispered as she vanished with an indignant whirl of her skirts.

He looked at the closed door which she had slammed with a resounding force, his anger now dissipated. He settled the offending shirt points and chuckled evilly. A sprightly filly, Verity. Just what he needed to relieve the tedium of this dull marriage to a fading beauty.

Lady Maxwell had offered him a refuge when his resources had dwindled to a precarious state. He had previously tried his luck with a plump young merchant's daughter in Bath but her canny father had not been impressed with this suave fortune hunter and had denied his suit. So he was forced to look elsewhere and had immediately transferred his attentions to Mrs. Howard, who had been taken with his polished address and title. But she was a disappointing bed partner and he craved a younger woman. The village offered little diversion, besides which, why should he seek release abroad when this delectable girl was under his roof? No, Verity might struggle but in the end she would be his. If she were foolish enough to confide in her mother, he could counter that lady's complaints by explaining that the wench had tempted him, made the overtures.

In his complacency Sir Anthony was not bothered by the immorality of seducing his stepdaughter. He thought her fortunate to be introduced to love-making by one with his expertise. Such was the man's conceit that her attempts to ridicule him, which had initially angered him, now seemed just a ploy to spur him on.

Yes, before many days had passed he would be enjoying Verity's slim firm body in his bed. In contemplation of such an outcome, his good humor was restored, and he sat back in the leather chair behind the mahogany desk to dream of what lay ahead.

Verity, in a confusion of rage and disgust, rushed up the stairs to her bedroom, all the serenity of her morning ride banished. She supposed she should look in on her ailing mother but the thought of facing that deluded woman now was more than she could bear.

What was she to do? Despite her brave attempts to fob off Sir Anthony with laughter she sensed with dread that she was powerless to keep him at bay forever. She paced back and forth, wondering how to deal with this unexpected dilemma. What a bounder the man was. Verity had disliked her stepfather from the beginning, although she had never been able to put a name to her repugnance.

Verity's father, a bluff hard riding squire, had died unexpectedly on the hunting field while still in the full vigor of life. He had left his sixteen-year-old daughter and his wife in the care of his twenty-year-old son, Charley, a lighthearted lad intent on a military career. Mrs. Howard, as she was then, had felt unable to accept the burdens of the estate, and Charley, much occupied with his commission in the Life Guards, purchased after some argument from his timid mother, had little interest in the rent roll which supplied him with a generous competence. He rarely came home, spending his leaves sampling the

16

offerings of London, so tempting to a personable young man with money to pay for them.

The estate was managed by their old baliff, Adam Wunsch, a dependable gruff countryman whose honesty and devotion to the Howards was deep rooted. But Mrs. Howard had felt the need of a husband and when she met Sir Anthony in Bath's Pump Room had immediately succumbed to his smooth address and courtly attentions. She had welcomed his suit and accepted him, feeling herself privileged to have won such an enviable husband.

Charley had raised no objections, realizing that his mother needed the protection of a man and unwilling to spare time from his own career to offer her his own company. Sir Anthony had been wise enough to enlist Charley's support, and since that young man's inclination was to take the easiest way, there had been no obstacle. Verity had not been consulted, still in school and unable to voice just why she felt Sir Anthony unsuitable. He had virtually ignored her on her holidays and only now, when she was entering womanhood, had he appeared to notice she was no longer a hobbledehoy schoolgirl.

On her arrival home some weeks ago, she had noticed his altered attitude but put it down to her new status. Until today she had believed his attentions had been an attempt to win her approval in a fatherly manner. How wrong, how naive she had been. She knew that her only recourse was to seek

Charley's help when that young officer returned home in a few days on his last leave before joining his regiment. Now that Napoleon had escaped from Elba, the possibility of a huge battle loomed on the continent, and Charley would be eager to try his spurs. Would he listen to her, believe her? And what if he left her to the mercies of Sir Anthony?

She suspected she would gain little comfort from her mother. Sir Anthony would talk her around to believing just what he wanted her to believe. Charley had always been their mother's favorite and Verity was wise enough to know that her mother, a languid woman whose charms were fast fading, would not accept her daughter as a rival to her own attractions. And Verity could not be so cruel as to endanger her mother's precarious happiness if her health was in truth failing and her worry over Charley's coming danger oversetting her.

No, she must deal with this on her own. She gave a passing thought to her childhood companion, Denis Montgomery, whom she suspected was on the verge of tendering her a proposal. Verity liked Denis, but felt for him none of the emotion she sensed should be the love of a wife for a husband. In their childhood escapades she had always taken the lead, and in this, the gravest problem of her young life, she could not rely on Denis to shield her from Sir Anthony. If only her father had lived. But there was no use repining. Verity had always faced up to reality. She had more than her share of courage and spirit and she would not be cowed by Sir Anthony. Somehow she would contrive to best him, and without causing her poor mother needless anguish. Charley would just have to cope with Sir Anthony, warn him that he would countenance no liberties with his sister. With that dubious comfort, Verity rang for her maid, determined to put the late encounter from her mind.

Chapter Two

"No, Denis, that is not the answer. I cannot marry you. You are my dearest friend, but you know it will not do." Verity Howard faced the young man who was regarding her so eagerly as they sat on a knoll overlooking Lyme Bay.

They both wore riding clothes, and their horses were tethered to a nearby tree, while the pair idled on a grassy hummock. Beyond them tossed the roiled gray sea of the English Channel, giving lie to what had promised to be a bright early May morning. Above them, clouds massed, temporarily blocking out the weak sun.

Denis reached across and took Verity's hand, looking into her dark-fringed hazel eyes with a passion of sincerity. "I know you think mother would disapprove but I can talk her around, and if what you tell me is true, you badly need protection. You, may not love me now, but you would in time, once we were married. I would do all in my power . . ." His voice dwindled as he saw her shake her head. How lovely and desirable she was with the breeze stirring her titian hair, softly waved about her oval cheeks, outlining her high cheekbones and providing a perfect foil for her haunting eyes.

Denis Montgomery had never known a time when he had not loved Verity, since the days when they were both in leading strings. But now that she had returned from her seminary in Bath, his childhood affection had deepened into a more mature emotion. He could not believe she did not return his love. And this latest trouble was even more evidence of how much she needed his support.

Verity patted his hand affectionately, and then released it. She loathed hurting her childhood friend but she could not agree that marriage was the answer to her present problem. And she cared too much for him to use him so.

"Charley is coming home soon. I will confide in him and he will know what to do," she reassured the troubled young man. She looked at him with a wistful smile. He was such a dear lad, but much as she cared for him, his tentative kisses had not stirred her beyond a pleasant comfort. Not that he was unattractive with his shock of blond hair, his deep gray eyes, and a physique which though still gangly gave promise of strength and virility. Only his mouth, drawn repressively tight in his eagerness to persuade her, showed weakness. He rushed into speech, mistaking her hesitation.

22

"If what you say is true about your stepfather pressing disgusting attentions upon you, you must not wait for Charley but tell your mother," he urged.

"I cannot do that. She would be loath to believe me and, even if she did, would not dare to challenge her husband. She is much too timid," Verity explained, sighing as she thought of her vulnerable weak-willed mother.

"She should never have married him. Anthony Maxwell is a cad and an opportunist," Denis blurted out, furious at Verity's acceptance of how powerless Lady Maxwell was to shield her daughter from her husband's lechery.

"Mother needed a husband. She could not cope with the estate, and Charley is determined on his military career. Now that a battle is imminent he would never resign his commission," Verity explained, excusing both her mother and brother with a kindly compassion. "I will just have to manage somehow."

"But you needn't manage. I can handle Sir Anthony if you will only give me the right, as your husband," Denis said, his cheeks flushing with urgency.

Verity smiled at his persuasive words, but just shook her head again. "It will not do, Denis. I do not feel that way about you, and it would not be fair to you, as well as giving your mother great pain. She has her eye on Anne Sedgewick for you, a very suitable match, for she has a tidy fortune. And you are still dependent on your mother. You would not like to be cut off without a penny," she reminded him. Denis had not reached his majority, and in his youthful enthusiasm did not realize how this restricted his actions.

"You surely do not think I am a damn fortune hunter," he protested.

"No, but you would not want to hurt your mother, go against her wishes, and for a wife who does not return your love," Verity explained carefully. Although only two years younger than Denis she felt ages older, almost maternal as she smiled at him, grateful for his suggestion but unwilling to take this method of solving her dilemma.

"Are you sure you have not mistaken Sir Anthony's advances for a natural fatherly interest?" Denis asked in some desperation.

"He is always taking advantage of the opportunity to touch me, and last night he cornered me in the upstairs gallery and tried to kiss me. It was horrible," Verity remembered, shuddering as she thought of her stepfather's groping hands and wet mouth.

"He must be a monster, to try to force a young girl, and one who is entitled to his every consideration," Denis blustered, but Verity was beginning to wonder if he really believed her story.

"I do not encourage him, Denis," she responded sharply, suddenly weary of trying to explain her situation to her childhood playmate. If Denis did not believe her, who would, for her stepfather was very careful to behave circumspectly when anyone was watching.

"Of course not," Denis agreed, but looking at Verity, could not help but understand Sir Anthony's preference for her fresh charms over the faded beauty that he had married for reasons other than sincere love, he was convinced. Verity was enough to tempt the devil himself, he concluded, watching her slight breasts rise in agitation as she protested her innocence. Underneath that haunting fragility lay a wealth of passion which Denis, far from experienced, barely understood, but recognized vaguely as an inducement to any man.

Shaking his unease off he asked, "When will Charley arrive?"

"We expect him any day. The Life Guards have already received their marching orders and will be off to Brussels within a fortnight. He can only take a few days' leave before embarking. How I wish he was not so set on this campaign. I have a presentiment of tragedy," Verity confided, her eyes shadowed as she thought of her brother about to embark into danger.

"Nonsense. He will be fine. It's a famous regiment, and he must be proud as a peacock to have been accepted. The commission cost a pretty penny, I vow," Denis reassured her, hoping to distract her from her worries.

"Yes, and Sir Anthony was not a bit pleased that Charley has come into his money and can do as he wishes," Verity remarked. "The estate is his, of course, and Charley is also my guardian, so Sir Anthony is powerless to prevent him from doing as

25

he wants, although he objected strenuously."

"Charley will settle your stepfather, never fear, and you must simply take every precaution not to be alone with Sir Anthony until you can confide your fears in your brother," Denis said, although he doubted that Charley, a likely lad but hardly the determined defender he would have wished, could prevent Sir Anthony from fulfilling his fell designs. How damnable that Verity would not accept his proposal. Before he had rashly offered it he had hesitated, knowing how much his formidable mother would object, and resigned to an elopement. But now Verity had refused his offer, no matter how deeply she needed his protection. He felt balked and frustrated by her rejection, but knew he could not move her. She had always been a stubborn girl, even when they were children, always the leader in their adventures. He and Charley had sometimes unwillingly but inevitably followed her into escapades for which she had nobly accepted the responsibility when they were caught. She had a courage unusual in a girl.

Tossing off her cares, Verity rose. "Oh, well, I will contrive, I suspect. And do not think I am not grateful for your offer, Denis, but I fear we should not suit. You would not wish to go from your mother's leading strings to mine, and you are far too young to think of marriage to such a managing female as I am," she laughed, coaxing him into a better humor.

Reluctantly he had to acknowledge that she had

26

made a touch. But he doubted he would ever feel for any female what he felt for Verity. She was so lovely, and so unattainable. He smiled back at her, unable to resist her efforts to placate him. He offered her his hand and she rose, signifying she must ride home. But as he mounted her on the frisky mare she adored, she leaned over and kissed him gently on the cheek. "Thank you, Denis, you are a dear. We will come about, you'll see," and then with a laugh she spurred her horse away, leaving him to catch up as best he might.

Later, in her room, Verity could not shake off the unease she felt. Normally, her ride blew away depression and doubt but today that remedy for her malaise had not proved effective. As she changed from her riding habit into a buttercup yellow muslin frock, a bit shabby but still presentable, she looked around the bedroom which had been hers from childhood and suddenly it seemed strange to her. The sprigged cotton hangings on the tester, the matching slipper chair by the fire, the bookcase which held her riding cups, a cherished music box, the clouded glass paperweight, and other mementos of her girlhood did not comfort her as they usually did. When she had returned from school after Christmas she had joyfully embraced these reminders of happier days when her bluff cheerful father had been alive.

She had enjoyed a remarkably happy childhood. She and Charley, often accompanied by Denis, had roamed the Devon hills, exploring and delighting in country pursuits, returning to the Elizabethan manor house which had been in Howard hands for generations. Her father's untimely death on the hunting field when she was sixteen had been the first intimation that those halcyon days were lost forever.

Charley had come home from Eton bent on pursuing a military career, uninterested in his inheritance—those green fields and the old house which was so dear to her. And her mother, moping and distracted, had offered little solace to the bereft girl who had always been her father's favorite. Then, suddenly, just before Christmas, Mrs. Howard had married Sir Anthony, whom she had met at Bath, where she had gone to take the waters and visit her daughter at school there.

From the beginning, Verity had sensed something havey-cavey about him, not just because he had replaced her beloved father, but because of some inherent quality of unctuous insincerity which she thought hid a selfish opportunistic desire to do himself well. He flattered her mother and treated Charley in a hearty man-of-the-world manner which soothed that young man's ego and kept the domestic peace, but underneath his bonhomie Verity was convinced her instincts were correct. Sir Anthony wanted to wrest as much money from the small estate as possible, to satisfy his expensive tastes. Lately she suspected he was unfaithful to her mother, but he kept his libertine propensities well disguised.

At first he had virtually ignored Verity, behaving

in an offhand manner which implied he had no time for a schoolgirl. However, since her return from Bath his attitude had altered subtly. Her innocence shielded her from his obvious intent, but his interview in the library and last night's attempt had made his feelings quite unmistakable. In his conceit, he believed she would not deny him. Verity had made her disgust and repulsion known to him in no uncertain terms but that had served only to whet his appetite. He had apparently found her rejection an exciting challenge.

As she paced around her room, she wondered anew at her mother's acceptance of this sly self-indulgent man, such a contrast to her late lovable father. Verity realized vaguely that her mother needed a man, the prestige of capturing a seemingly attractive husband who adored her. It was a role Sir Anthony played to the hilt. How could she tell Lady Maxwell that he was actually a lecherous villain who had designs on her own daughter? It would destroy her. Verity loved her mother and could not cause her such unhappiness.

As she paced back and forth reliving with a shudder her last encounter with Sir Anthony, she paused finally by her door, noticing with horror that the key to her chamber was missing. Hurriedly, she scrambled about searching for the missing key, but it was nowhere to be found. Could her stepfather have taken the key to prevent her from locking her door against his intrusion? Verity knew very little about what went on between a man and a woman in the marriage bed, but she knew enough from her more knowledgeable and sniggering schoolmates to understand what he would have in mind. Never, never would she submit to such a violation. In great perturbation she rang for a maid. Perhaps Agnes had the key.

The housemaid, when she arrived, expressed surprise. "Oh, no, Miss Verity. I have not seen the key. It must be about somewhere," she assured, eyeing her mistress in a peculiar way.

Could the servants have noticed Sir Anthony's lewd advances toward her, Verity wondered? Finally dismissing Agnes with what she hoped was a careless indifference to the missing key, she braced her shoulders. There was no one to whom she could turn. Both of Verity's parents had been only children so there was no shelter available from relatives. Only Charley could save her now, she felt with a sense of impending horror. He must come soon. He must.

That evening at the dinner table she watched with increasing trepidation as her stepfather dipped deep into the wine. He appeared in a most jovial mood, teasing Lady Maxwell and filled with satisfaction over the day. He informed them when the last covers were removed that he had that morning dismissed their old baliff, Adam Wunsch, who had directed the estate since long before Mr. Howard's death.

"Oh, dear, Anthony," Lady Maxwell protested weakly, "Do you think that was wise? Adam has been here for ages past, and is most trustworthy, you know."

"High time the old fool was pensioned off," Sir Anthony responded. "You have no need of him now, my dear, as I am perfectly competent to manage affairs. I am sure Charley will agree it is best to keep on top of things here while he is serving his country. We want to keep the boy's inheritance in good shape for him, don't we?" Sir Anthony cleverly used the argument most likely to quell his wife's objections, for she would sacrifice much for Charley.

Verity could not restrain her dismay. "But mother, Adam is well up to the work. I don't think he wants to retire. We cannot be so unkind as to deprive him of his responsibilities. He is honest and devoted," she argued, looking at her stepfather searchingly. He dropped his eyes before her accusing stare but smiled silkily, not showing his anger.

"Come, come, Verity, what does a young woman know of these matters. Best leave business to your elders, my dear. I have the estate well in hand, and will do a bang-up job. I rather suspect that the old man has been feathering his own nest at our expense. Much better to relieve him of his duties. He will keep the cottage, of course." Sir Anthony, toying with his wineglass, tossed aside her objections easily, implying she was but a silly chit who had no cause to question wiser and older heads.

"I think Charley will protest," Verity continued stubbornly.

"Perhaps Anthony is right, Verity. We women know little of these things. Best leave it to him. I have every confidence in you, my darling." Lady Maxwell turned to her husband, her pale face glowing with affection. Really, Verity was too impulsive, she thought, speaking out so boldly about the estate, which really did not concern her.

Verity, thankful that her own small jointure was closely protected by her father's foresight, bit her lips to keep from retorting. But she determined to let Charley know of this latest incursion of their stepfather's. She would persuade him to rehire Adam and she would visit the old man herself to make sure that he lacked for nothing. Suddenly she could bear to sit here no longer and listen to Sir Anthony ingenuously pay court to her mother, flattering her insincerely, and soothing any objections she might make to his plans. Could not her mother see what kind of man he was or did she deliberately close her eyes to his schemes, hoping to keep the peace?

"If you will excuse me, mother. I have a slight headache. I think I will retire to my room." Verity rose, hardly waiting for her mother's assent.

"What a shame, dear girl. Perhaps I will look in on you later to make sure you are feeling better," her stepfather said, his blatant look promising more than an inquiry about her health.

Once outside the dining room, Verity rushed up the stairs to her bedroom, which she now knew offered her little permanent sanctuary. What could she do? If she undressed and retired she would be inviting the very visit she prayed to avoid. And now that the key was missing she could not lock her door against the unwelcome intruder. Suddenly she had an idea. She would sleep this night in Charley's room. It must have a lock and was distant enough from her chamber to offer her some safety. Charley, when he was home, slept in the farthest ends of the house, having a suite of rooms which ensured him a modicum of privacy.

Scurrying about the room she prepared for bed, and quietly crept from her room and down the long hall to Charley's rooms. Once inside her brother's bedroom, she turned the key in the lock, and gave a long sigh of relief. Sir Anthony could not approach her here, and even if he should discover where she had gone, he could not gain admittance. Snuggling under the counterpane she doused her candle and within minutes drifted off to sleep.

Chapter Three

For the next few days Verity managed to keep her distance from her stepfather. He had not been able to quiz her about her empty bedchamber, and if he suspected that she had found a refuge, he did not mention it at mealtime, which was the only occasion they had to meet. He did ask her the morning after her supposed headache where she had disappeared to when he had visited her bedroom. She was amazed at his blatancy, but answered blithely.

"Oh, I stepped out into the gardens for some air to relieve my aching head. I dislike taking powders and the air quite banished by headache. Thank you so much for your concern," she assured him, looking at him guilelessly. She doubted how long her evasive tactics would succeed, but if only she could elude him until Charley arrived, all would be well.

Over the next few days she spent a great deal of time outdoors, riding her mare down to the cove, keeping all the time a wary eye out for her stepfather, who preferred to make his tours of the estate in a horse and pony cart. She did find time to visit their old baliff, Adam Wunsch, whose budget of news was most unquieting.

The old man, hearty of complexion, with thinning white hair covering his round head, and a stoop to his shoulders, still had the strong constitution of a countryman. He welcomed her gruffly.

"Well, now, Miss Verity, heard the news, have you? Have you come to comfort an old codger?" He indicated a chair in his humble kitchen, which looked neat and tidy. The cottage had been his home for forty years, and since his wife's death a few years ago, he had managed on his own, and very handily.

"I can hardly believe Sir Anthony has done such a thing," Verity fumed.

"Well, my dear. It's his right. I don't know what Master Charley will say, but now that he is going off to fight that devil Napoleon I suppose he has other matters to concern him." The old man sighed. "I've served your family man and boy these sixty years, and perhaps I am beyond it." His old eyes took in with pleasure the pretty picture Verity made, despite her shabby riding costume, the sun striking through the window and lighting up her titian hair.

"Nonsense, Adam. You know every blade of grass and every furrow in the field. Sir Anthony has a fell purpose in retiring you. Charley will never stand for it," Verity argued, determined to see her old friend restored to his duties. She crumbled the scone he had insisted on offering her with a dish of well-sugared tea.

"Don't get yourself in a pucker now, girl. I don't want to cause trouble," Adam protested, seeing how disturbed she was, and quelling his own feelings of anger and disappointment. He feared that Miss Verity had her own troubles with the new master and he did not want to add to them. What she needed was a husband who would take her away from this isolated village. She deserved a come-out. What was her mother thinking of not to secure her daughter's future? Too bemused by that new husband of her own, and a swarmy cove he had proved to be. But Adam was too shrewd to voice his own doubts of affairs up at the manor house.

"Master Charley will be along any day now, and he will put things right, I suspect," he soothed.

"I hope so. But oh, Adam, I wish I had somewhere to go, away from Sidmouth," Verity said, her brown furrowed with worry.

"Will you not be going up to London?"

"Mother is not up to escorting me, and she has no one to whom she can entrust me, not a proper chaperone who will be willing to introduce me to the ton. I have no relatives, alas."

Verity did not know that her words confirmed her old friend's suspicions. So that was how the land lay, he thought. Sir Anthony was making improper advances toward this lovely lass. Adam felt helpless. He could not protect her, and Master Charley, her natural refuge, was not available. What a damnable

37

situation. Adam looked at the lovely girl, idly stirring her tea, her thoughts far from this humble cottage. She needed a husband.

"There's Mr. Montgomery. He's powerful fond of you, lass," Adam urged. He had known the two since they were babies and believed that their neighbor cared for Miss Verity. That would answer her problem, and put paid to Sir Anthony.

"Dear Denis has proposed to me many a time, Adam, but it wouldn't do, you know. He's a good friend, more of a brother. I want to marry a man I can love in a different way," Verity confided. Adam and his late wife, Molly, had heard her troubles for years, shielded her from deserved punishments, given her treats, and watched her grow from a hoydenish child to womanhood. She truly loved the old man.

"Sometimes love comes after the ceremony, my dear," Adam said gently.

"No, Adam, it is no answer for me. I will just have to hope that I will meet my Prince Charming before too long."

"Little chance of that, buried here in Devon. You should be in London, or one of them watering places where you would meet some eligible gents." Adam shook his head in perplexity. He wanted to help her but what could he do but offer comfort, and more tea. He leaned across the scarred oak table, scrubbed clean but bare of ornament, and filled her cup with a gnarled hand which trembled a bit.

"Oh, well, it will all turn out for the best, I am

sure," Verity said. How unfair it was to heap her problem on his shoulders, which already had much to bear. "But, Adam, I will talk to Charley about your dismissal. It's unconscionable, and we will not have it," she assured him, preparing to take her leave.

"Don't you fret no more, Miss Verity. I can take care of myself. I have a bit put by. I won't starve. And these old bones need a rest, I warrant," he calmed her.

Verity arrived home that afternoon troubled in spirit and far from satisfied with Adam's efforts to soothe her, to find Mrs. Montgomery and Denis taking tea with her mother and stepfather. Hurriedly donning a suitable gown and combing her tousled hair she joined the company in the drawing room. She tried to avoid Denis's eyes as he looked at her beseechingly when she greeted the party.

"Good afternoon, Denis, Mrs. Montgomery. How kind of you to call," Verity said, her company manners to the forefront. She wondered if Denis had come to test the truth of her confidences about Sir Anthony. If so he would be disappointed, for that gentleman displayed his most suave and fatherly manner.

"Well, Verity, you have been a stranger lately. Dashing about the countryside, and neglecting us shamefully," Sir Anthony chided, giving her a meaningful glance from beneath his eyelids. His pale blue eyes rested gloatingly upon her, for she looked especially enticing, color from her tempestuous ride glowing in her cheeks, her unusual titian hair decorously arranged and her neat elegant figure, almost too slim, attractively arrayed in a modest lilac muslin gown. He took a cup of tea to her, but she refused it with a curt shake of her head. "I have already had tea, with Adam Wunsch," she said, giving him a sharp look.

But Sir Anthony was too skilled a campaigner to exhibit his anger before company. "I do not think that was wise, my dear," was his only response, but she knew she had roused his ire. Good, she thought. He needed to know he could not have affairs entirely to his pleasure.

"Really, Verity, must you roam about the estate on that skittish mare. Not at all proper behavior," her mother fussed. Lady Maxwell found her daughter's unexplained absences very trying, not at all discreet or sensible for an unmarried girl.

"My dear Lady Maxwell, I am sure you are mindful of proprieties at all times. It is regrettable that Verity is such a trial to you," Mrs. Montgomery interjected smugly, looking at Verity with some distaste. She was a majestic figure of a woman, who always wore black although her husband had been dead more than a score of years. Today her tightly corseted bombazine figure looked even more imposing than usual, her large bosom drawn erect, her small dark beady eyes darting with barely concealed dislike over the girl she feared wanted to trap her darling boy.

"Well, Evadne, there is so little entertainment here

for Verity," Lady Maxwell fluttered, aware of her own guilt toward her daughter, and how it must appear. "I suppose I should take her to London, or at least Bath, so she should enjoy some pleasures. I am sure it is boring for her here now that she has finished her schooling."

"My dear, you know your fragile health would not stand up to the rigors of a season," Sir Anthony said mildly, giving his wife an indulgent look which did not fool Verity for a moment. Her mother's pretense of bad health was just a convenience he encouraged for his own ends. And Lady Maxwell basked in his concern. What a conniver the man was, as well as the most unmitigated cad.

"Verity prefers Devon, don't you?" Denis put in gruffly, for this was what he had feared most. That Verity would be wrested away from him, perhaps to meet some more dashing and romantic gentleman. He hated the thought of her exposed to such a temptation.

"I do love the country, although I might enjoy all the fashions and fancies of town," Verity offered, hoping her mother might be lured into action.

"Young girls today are so bold and selfish, little idea of the duty they owe to their mothers. Now Denis would never desert me, would you, dear?" Mrs. Montgomery looked dotingly on her son, who straightened up from his slouching posture and glared sulkily at her. Most of the time he found it easier not to brook his mother's dominating attempts to rule his life, but where Verity was con-

41

cerned he was prepared to make an effort.

"I have been thinking lately of joining the Army." Denis threw out the suggestion boldly. "Most girls like a man in uniform." He realized that this casual threat would annoy his mother, but it might give Verity pause, persuade her into thinking of him as more than just her old childhood friend.

"Nonsense, my boy. You would be wasted in the military, and I need you here," his mother replied firmly. "Then too a commission is costly," she added, reminding him that she controlled the purse strings.

Denis shrugged off her objections silently but looked miserable.

Verity smiled ruefully. Poor Denis. If only he would stand up to his mother, and if only her own mother would bestir herself to make some provision for Verity's future. But, of course, she did not realize what danger confronted her daughter.

Before Verity could soothe Denis out of his sulks, the company was interrupted by a bustle in the hall. Within minutes the door opened and Charley Howard entered the drawing room, resplendent in his regimentals, but looking a bit travel worn. He was a taking youth, four years older than Verity, with russet hair, now somewhat disheveled from his ride, and warm brown eyes, in feature resembling their mother although he had his father's stronger chin.

Lady Maxwell gasped, and rose trembling to her feet to embrace her son, while Sir Anthony stood aside, smiling with specious indulgence on the reunion.

After Charley had hugged his sister and greeted his stepfather with more restrained enthusiasm, he turned his attention to the Montgomerys. For Denis he offered an affectionate welcome to an old friend and childhood companion. His reception of Mrs. Montgomery was all that was polite, although Verity knew he disliked the woman, having often shared his criticism with her. However, Mrs. Montgomery at least had enough tact to know that her presence was not necessary to this family reunion, and she gathered her son up and wished them all farewell, prefacing her remarks with the hope they would see more of Charles shortly, when he had the time to spare on his brief leave. She managed to imply that any worthwhile and considerate son would not have deserted his mother for the Army, and that she herself was far more fortunate than poor Lady Maxwell.

Verity was only too happy to see the back of her. She yearned to drag Charley off immediately to confide her fears of Sir Anthony but could not be so unkind to her mother, who fussed and clucked over her son as if he had returned from the dead, instead of just London.

Sir Anthony was content to stand by and view his wife's cosseting with a false smile, but at last wearying of her transports, suggested that she allow her son time to rid himself of his travel dirt.

"And how long will you be with us, Charley?" he

43

asked in a hearty fashion.

"Only a week or so. We are soon to depart for Belgium and come to grips with Napoleon," Charley answered cheerfully, anticipating the coming battle with a sang froid which made Verity shudder. How eager he was to expose himself to the French guns.

"Well, we must have a long chat about the estate," Sir Anthony said. "There are several matters I should discuss with you, but time enough for that." He eyed Verity warily as he spoke.

Verity returned his stare with a look that promised retribution. She had not forgotten Adam Wunsch and her stepfather's cavalier dismissal of that old retainer, and she determined to enlist Charley's help in defense of their old baliff. Sir Anthony had not heard the last of his high-handed treatment of Adam. She knew Charley shared her affection for Adam and would not allow his banishment so summarily. Eager to get Charley to herself, she suggested she help him unpack, and steered him away from her mother's fulsome questions toward the door. Sir Anthony watched them leave with some annoyance. He was not anxious to allow them a comfortable cose.

"Come now, Verity," he protested silkily. "I know you are overjoyed to see your brother after all this time, but you must allow your mother her innings, you know. Can't be jealous, my dear."

"I have a large budget of news for my brother, Sir Anthony, and will not bore you with my prosings. Mother will not object, I am sure," Verity replied sharply, refusing to give quarter to her odious stepfather.

Charley, aware now that there were undercurrents here, patted her shoulder comfortingly, and soothed his mother. "I will see you at dinner, Mother, and tell you all you desire," he promised, putting down his teacup and wolfing a last bit of Dundee cake. "I really must change from these travel-worn clothes. Come along, Verity, I have a present for you in my cases," he teased, remembering his sister's penchant when younger for surprises.

Sir Anthony shrugged his shoulders, accepting the inevitable, and watched the pair leave the room. Turning to his wife he said cheerfully, "I know how much it means to you to have Charley home, my dear, and we must see to it he has a cheerful leave, not scarred by worries about the estate. Verity, I fear, will burden him with a lot of her uninformed views. Women should not really meddle in these affairs, I know you agree." He crossed to his wife, who was sitting behind the tea table, and gave her a comforting pat on her thin shoulders.

"You are right, of course, Anthony, but naturally Charley will want to have a report about the estate, and Verity knows so much more about it than either of us," she said. Like many timid and weak women, when Lady Maxwell grasped an idea she clung to it obstinately, and she loved her son with a passion which overrode even her concern to keep her husband happy.

Sir Anthony, no fool, realized there was no way of

moving her to support him if Charley demurred. Damn that girl. She was a constant source of annoyance, although a damned attractive one. She would not defeat him over this matter of old Adam, nor his other desires either. Sir Anthony had complete confidence in his ability to charm women, for his experience had proved his success.

He did not argue further with his wife; instead he spent his time cajoling her and assuring her that his every thought was bent on securing her comfort.

Curled on Charley's bed Verity listened to his enthusiastic views on the Army and his commanding officer, one Alistair Glendenning.

"He really is top of the trees, Verity, a veritable tiger in battle they say, and so good with the men. He fought all through the Peninsula with Wellington," Charley was saying. He paused, as if in doubt, not wanting to cast any aspersions on his hero.

"I am sure this paragon has some faults," Verity prodded, eyeing her brother with affection. He was such a dear boy, so loyal, so eager to win his own spurs on the battlefield. She would not for the world discourage him, and it seemed unfair to blight his homecoming with her own worries.

"Well, yes," Charley admitted, rummaging in his travel-stained luggage, and not meeting Verity's eyes. "He's a very devil with women. Had to transfer from the Hussar's to Uxbridge's regiment because he was embroiled in some scandal. But it has nothing to do with his prowess on the battlefield. Women do confuse things so," he concluded naively.

Verity despised men of this type, rakes who took their pleasure where they would, uncaring of the heartache they caused, and so indifferent to the women whom they used. Just such a one was Sir Anthony and she had quite enough of him.

"Is he not married, this Major Glendenning then?" Verity asked.

"No, he says women are for amusement only. He will not be leg-shackled by some eager female," Charley explained airily.

"I can imagine. But enough of him. Charley, several really troubling events have occurred here since your last visit. Sir Anthony has dismissed Adam Wunsch, and taken over the management of the estate himself," she said soberly.

Charley looked up from his unpacking to meet his sister's worried gaze. "Oh, Verity, you must be wrong. We cannot do without Adam. He has been here for a donkey's age, knows everything, and I trust him implicitly."

"Well, believe me, he has been given his congé, and it suits Sir Anthony to have affairs in his own hands. You must insist that Adam be reinstated, Charley. I do not trust Sir Anthony, and he has no experience in running an estate. The tenants will not take to him, I know."

"You seem to have taken our stepfather in dislike, Verity," Charley said, disturbed. "But he seems an unexceptional chap to me, and goodness knows, mother could never cope without him."

"If it is unexceptional to try to seduce your sister, I can only believe you have been influenced by your new commanding officer to believe that all women are unchaste and available," Verity blurted out angrily, forgetting that she had meant to bring up Sir Anthony's advances toward her more subtly.

"My God, Verity. Are you saying he has made overtures to you, a young girl entitled to his protection?" Charley exclaimed aghast.

"Well, his idea of protection is not mine. He cornered me in the gallery a few nights ago and kissed me and made very improper suggestions," Verity said baldly, impatient with her brother's attempts to deny her accusations. "In fact, I have been forced to sleep in your room, because the key which locks my chamber has mysteriously vanished."

"I cannot believe it. Are you sure you have not mistaken his attentions for fatherly affection?" Charley asked.

"There is nothing paternal in Sir Anthony's feelings toward me, and Charley, you must face him with what he plans. I am afraid when you leave he will force me."

"It's dastardly. He must be mad. I thought he loved Mother. You have not told her of his attempts?" Charley asked, embarrassed as well as shocked by this view of their stepfather.

"Of course not. You know she would not believe

it; besides it would give her great unhappiness. Poor Mama, she is not too capable," Verity replied. "What will you do, Charley?"

"Well, I will challenge the fellow. If he knows you have disclosed his evil intent to me, that will stop any further unpleasantness, I am sure. And I will deal with this matter of Adam Wunsch, too," he declared. Shaking off the uneasiness he felt, and his feeling of helpless disbelief, he turned to more pleasant matters. "Here is a bauble I brought you from London. I hope it cheers you up, a bit. You must prevail on mother to let you have your come-out while I am away. Then you will find some lucky fellow to wed you, and all this will be but a nasty dream."

No doubt Sir Anthony did find her attractive, Charley mused, looking at his sister. She had grown up and become a very appealing young woman.

Taking the gold locket he handed her, she rose and kissed him with gratitude. "Thank you, Charley. It is lovely. Oh, it is good that you are home, for I missed you exceedingly. I know you love the Army but sometimes I wish you had not joined. Especially now with the war on again," she confided, her emotions in tumult.

He grinned at her disarmingly, hiding his own disquiet. "I do enjoy the Army, and would not miss the coming engagement for anything. But you were right to tell me about your fears, Verity. That's what brothers are for, to protect their sisters."

She should not be worrying over Sir Anthony and the estate, Charley reflected protectively, but enjoying all the pleasures to which a young well-born girl was entitled. He would insist his mother see to her come-out, and once away from Devon she would soon forget her situation with Sir Anthony. How could he accuse his stepfather of such unnatural behavior? Somehow he must assure her safety before he left home. What a damnable coil, and what a blight it cast on his leave, which he had anticipated with such enjoyment. Still, it was not Verity's fault and he must do what he could to help her.

Charley was an uncomplicated young man, still largely innocent, even after partaking of the dissipations London offered a comely young man with money in his pocket. He had no knowledge of the lecherous ways of more sophisticated fellows and little understanding of the passions a woman could arouse. He had a faint glimmering of the lusts a certain type of female inspired, but surely Verity was not of that company. It could not be true. She had mistaken the man. He desperately hoped that was the case, but knowing his forthright sister, who looked at life much more honestly than he did, he doubted that she had imagined Sir Anthony's aim. Somehow he would protect her, he vowed, but he could not postpone his departure.

Inclined to put as good a face on events as possible, Charley tried to shrug off Verity's problem—time enough to worry about the matter later when he could examine it at his leisure. Life had offered Charley few obstacles, and although he was an upstanding, dependable officer and brother, he had little experience in dealing with men of Sir Anthony's stamp. He would need all his resources to emerge creditably in the uncomfortable interview which could not be long postponed.

Chapter Four

Confiding her fears of Sir Anthony's intentions toward her should have relieved Verity's mind, but somehow she did not think Charley took her seriously. That evening at dinner her stepfather behaved with perfect propriety toward her, saving his warm endearments and cajolery for her mother, who basked under his attentions. Looking at Sir Anthony playing the role of a devoted husband, Verity could scarcely believe herself that he was other than he seemed. His sleek face with its light blue eyes showed none of the lechery which she had experienced. Had he thought better of trying to seduce her? She did not trust him, but was powerless to expose him.

After dinner the four adjourned to the drawing room, where the men enjoyed their port, a departure, for normally Sir Anthony stayed alone in the dining room and left Verity and her mother to their own devices, dipping deep into his bottle. Tonight he displayed his full charm, deferring to Charley about the estate, and asking him about his regiment, always sure to destract her brother, for he dearly loved Army life.

"Why do you think that the battle will be fought in Belgium, my boy?" Sir Anthony asked jovially.

"Well, the French consider Belgium their possession, the kingpin of their new empire, and alas, the Bruxellois prefer Napoleon to the Allies and are not too eager to be independent. Wellington is now in Brussels and is attempting to marshal his forces. Too worrying that most of his regulars have been dispatched to America and he will have to depend on raw troops, like me. I have never fought a battle!" Charley admitted modestly, but obviously with no fear that he would acquit himself without distinction.

His mother sighed, running fond eyes over her son. "Oh, my boy. I will worry so."

"Come now, Kitty, you must not be in such a taking. Young Charles will not want to hear your vaporings," Sir Anthony chided.

"I quite understand my mother's fears, Sir Anthony, for I understand it will be a fierce engagement," Charley said coldly. "This is Napoleon's last throw of the dice and he will spare nothing to defeat us, but the Iron Duke will triumph." He did not like his stepfather reproving his mother for her natural concern. Gad, but the fellow was a cold fish. He could not imagine Sir Anthony expending enough effort to force Verity into bed. Damn the man. If what his sister had told him was the truth, and he had never questioned her honesty before, he was a clever rogue, able to dissemble so easily. Charley knew little of his new stepfather. Lady Maxwell had been his wife barely a year and during that time Charley had been so occupied with his new regimental duties he had spent little time at home. His first reaction had been favorable, relief that his mother had found a husband for she was not a woman who could manage on her own, but now he was beginning to have doubts, not entirely founded on Verity's shocking tale.

"I do hope you will be careful," Lady Maxwell said timidly, "I understand cavalry regiments are always in the thick of the fight."

"Not to worry, mother," Charley reassured her, not liking all this talk of danger. After all soldiers expected some peril. He only hoped he would acquit himself well. "Uxbridge, our commander, is a fine fellow, a great tactician. He will lead us through."

"Isn't he the man who deserted his wife and ran off with Wellington's sister-in-law? Quite a man for the ladies, I understand," Sir Anthony said coarsely, eyeing Charley in a fashion that the young man found rather off-putting. Gentlemen did not discuss such affairs before respectable females.

"That does not affect his abilities as a commander, I think," Charley answered with a frown at his stepfather.

"Quite right, my boy. In affairs of the heart we

men are not to be trusted although they are of little moment compared to the serious business of life."

"Oh, Anthony," Lady Maxwell protested. "Have a care for poor Lady Uxbridge's children, and I am sure you cannot admire a man who would behave so. The mortification for her! You cannot condone his behaving so. I am sure you would never dream of such a thing."

"Who knows, my dear, when temptation is offered," Sir Anthony replied silkily, his eyes roaming over Verity in a suggestive manner.

"Enough of Uxbridge's behavior," Charley declared. "My only interest is in his ability to command. He was a giant on the Peninsula, my men tell me."

Sir Anthony shrugged, accepting the reproof, and as if bored with the subject, turned the conversation to the news of their neighbors, bringing Charley up to date on all the gossip. In passing he mentioned Denis Montgomery, implying that the young man would do well to follow Charley's lead and enlist in the Army to get away from his dragon of a mother.

"I believe he stays close to home in order to pursue your sister, who unfortunately does not favor his suit," Sir Anthony suggested suavely.

The conceit of the man, Verity fumed. Could he really believe she preferred his disgusting advances to Denis's dedicated affection?

"Denis is a childhood friend, more like a brother to Verity, and I only wish she could look at him in a different light," Charley said, moving restlessly in

56

his chair. He disliked all these undertones, and wished he were back in his Chelsea barracks with all those fine fellows, who thought only of marches and bivouacs, not all this silly gossip. Charley was distressingly uninterested in women and found them puzzling and difficult although he had indulged in some exploits with the traditional lightskirts, pushed into such transient enjoyments by his comrades. He respected his sister but he believed she was a rarity. Although he paid dutiful affection to his mother, he found her prosings tedious in the extreme, and her indifference to Verity annoyed him. Verity was a Trojan, a wonderful girl and his mother should do her duty and launch her into society instead of keeping her bound here in Devon. He decided to urge this course, upon her now.

"Mother, ought not you to take Verity up to London and give her a come-out?" he said. "She has been home from school since Christmas and all her friends must be tasting the delights of the ton. She deserves to join them."

"Well, dear, I had thought about it, but Anthony thinks it would be too much for me," Lady Maxwell explained, unhappy that her beloved Charley might criticize her.

"Yes, my boy. We need Verity here, to console us with her bright presence," Sir Anthony joined the lists. He did not want the chit going off to London to desport herself with the bucks of the town when he could enjoy her in uninterrupted bliss.

"Well, find someone to launch her then. It's what

she deserves," Charley persisted stubbornly.

"I am too worried about you, Charley, right now, to think of all that. When you return perhaps," his mother complained tearfully. "Oh, I wish you had not joined the Army. While we were at peace it was different, but now you are going off to fight, I am so afraid."

Charley, weary of his mother's lamentations, reassured her brusquely. "Never fear, Mother, I will be fine. It's what I chose and what I've been trained for. No, no more of this tragic talk. Sir Anthony, I will see you tomorrow in the library to discuss the estate matters, which must be settled to my satisfaction before I leave. I have had a long day traveling and crave my bed. Coming, Verity?" he asked his sister, eager to be away from the cloying atmosphere his mother induced and tired of Sir Anthony's efforts to engage him in scurrilous gossip.

The pair made their escape from the drawing room, and as they climbed the staircase Verity remarked, "Do you still think of Sir Anthony as a paragon, Charley?"

"I never thought that, Verity, but I did think he would make an unexceptional husband for Mother. I might be wrong," Charley conceded, his open face, usually lightened by a disarming grin, now puckered with distaste.

"The man's a mountebank and a cad, and if you are not careful he will try to rob you of your inheritance," Verity said baldly, determined that her brother should see the danger of trusting their stepfather.

"You may be right. At any rate, I will install Adam in his old post and make it clear to Sir Anthony that he must defer to him in all matters pertaining to the estate," Charley said, wearying of the problems clouding his homecoming. Despite his assurances to his mother, he was not completely sanguine about his chances in the coming fight, having been nothing but a Hyde Park soldier up till now. And he knew what the veterans thought of officers of his stamp. He hoped to prove them wrong.

"I am sorry that all this should be dampening your last leave, Charley," Verity said affectionately as she paused at her door to bid him goodnight.

"That's all right, sister. It's just a good thing I came home and relieved you of some of this trouble. I don't believe Sir Anthony will try any untoward action toward you while I am in the house, and before I leave, we will make some provision for your future. I have an idea about that." Charley returned her kiss with a brotherly smack on her forehead. "Now sleep well, puss, and no worrying. I don't want you looking hag-ridden tomorrow when we ride out," he teased, referring to the daily canter which had been one of their treats in times past.

Comforted by Charley's affection and the thought that Sir Anthony would not try to approach her with her brother under their roof, Verity slept securely for the first night in a long while. She arose to a perfect May morning, the lawns beyond the manor house green and dew-drenched in the early light. Hurriedly donning her riding habit she joined her brother in the dining room to partake of a hearty breakfast, which she had not enjoyed for some days past. In good spirits the pair rode about the estate, Charley renewing his memories of their former haunts and greeting the tenants with delight. On such a day it was impossible to be depressed, and after a heartening interview with Adam, which cheered that old man immensely, the two repaired to the house feeling much refreshed.

After luncheon, for which Sir Anthony happily was absent, Charley settled down in the estate office to go over the accounts and Verity repaired to the rose garden to read a new Jane Austen novel, protected from the cool breeze by a Norwich shawl over her light blue muslin frock. She sighed as she looked around the garden planted by her father years ago and thought wistfully how much she would miss her home if she were forced to leave it, and that brought her around to thoughts of what faced her beloved brother when he rejoined his regiment. She could only pray for his safety and hope that his eagerness to win glory would not lead him into some rash action. As she dreamed idly in the sun, she was suddenly interrupted by her stepfather, who came upon her unawares.

"Well, there you are, my girl. And I suppose you are preening yourself over prevailing upon your brother to reverse my dismissal of that damn old bailiff," Sir Anthony growled as he stood over her, menace in his every lineament.

Verity faced her accuser bravely, rising to her feet and backing away from his threatening posture. "I told you, Sir Anthony, that Charley would never stand for abandoning Adam. He trusts him."

"And you have seen to it that he does not trust me, haven't you, my little termagant." Sir Anthony's mouth curled into a sneer. "Well, you will pay for that, and for your prosy manners toward me. I want you, and I am going to have you."

Before Verity could flee he had caught her in his arms and forced her chin up, trying to press a kiss upon her resisting mouth. Verity uttered a frightened scream, but he succeeded in his plan and the feel of his wet mouth upon hers filled her with repulsion.

Before she could escape his hateful embrace he was wrested from her and knocked handily to the ground, Charley standing over him, his fists cocked and a truly menacing expression on his face.

"You miserable cur, how dare you force yourself on Verity. Get up and take your medicine," Charley growled, almost overcome with rage. He had sought Verity in the garden to tell her of his interview with their stepfather, and arrived to see the man embracing his sister as she struggled against his unwanted caresses. Until now, Charley had found it difficult to accept his sister's tale of Sir Anthony's loathsome intentions, but now he had the evidence of his own eyes.

Sir Anthony struggled to his feet, his hand passing

tenderly over his jaw where a formidable bruise was purpling. He backed away from the fury in Charley's face, trying to placate the young man. "Now, Charley, don't get in a pother. It was not as you appear to think. The chit lured me, and she's attractive, you know."

Verity sputtered with rage. Charley was not one bit mollified by Sir Anthony's assertion that this was a case of "the woman tempted me," despite Sir Anthony's worldly "we know what the ladies are like" manner.

"Don't try to gammon me, Sir Anthony. You are a cad to force your disgusting attentions on my sister. I will not allow her to remain one more minute in your vicinity. Now if you are too much of a coward to face retribution, take yourself off before I smash you to smithereens," Charley choked out the words, still beside himself with anger.

"You misunderstood . . . Charley." Sir Anthony's eyes shifted under his stepson's accusing gaze and he backed away. He would not willingly expose himself to that punishing left again. "Your mother would be most distressed to find that her darling son had attacked her husband," he whined, seeing that his efforts to explain away the disastrous encounter were having little affect.

"Get out of my sight, or I will mar that lying face of yours forever," Charley promised. He turned away from Sir Anthony in disgust and put a comforting arm around Verity's shoulders as she stood shaking and crying before him. Sir Anthony did not wait for any more argument but hurried from the garden, leaving the brother and sister alone.

"God, Verity, I reproach myself. I had no idea . . . The miserable varmint. I should have believed you," Charley soothed, taking out a handkerchief and drying his sister's tears.

"He's vile, Charley," Verity raged, "and I am afraid that when you go he will renew his efforts to seduce me. What can I do? Should we try to explain to Mother?"

"No, she's such a ninny, and completely under his thumb. There's only one thing for it. You will have to come to Brussels with me. Lots of officers are taking their wives, most of London's society is hightailing it to Brussels. Yes, that's the answer," he said decisively, his mind made up. "You will have a fine time, queening it among the fellows there. Who knows, you might even find an admirable husband to take you on and relieve me of the responsibility," he teased, trying to lighten her spirits.

"Oh, Charley, could I come with you? That would be capital. But I am not hanging out for a husband. Right now I never want to see any man but you," Verity promised, filled with disgust at the recent mauling she had received. She chided herself for her timidity. Normally, she behaved in a stout-hearted way but Sir Anthony's foul attack had overset her so that she responded in a missish manner she normally despised.

Under Charley's gentle ministrations and the

welcome news that she would accompany him to Brussels, she regained her usual optimistic demeanor. Excitedly she plied him with questions, which, seeing how quickly she recovered from her recent horrid experience, Charley happily answered. For both of them it appeared the future promised companionship and adventure, which would banish all thoughts of the odious Sir Anthony.

Chapter Five

Verity could barely restrain her excitement as they traveled through the Belgian countryside from Ostend, where their ship had landed. The low flat fields, burgeoning with green, looked their best in the misty May sunshine with lazy canals drifting beside them, so different from the Devon hills. Some of her pleasure in her first sight of a foreign land was inspired by the relief she felt in putting hundreds of miles between herself and her stepfather, but most of it came from the knowledge that she was embarking on an adventure. Her brief stay with Charley in Portsmouth before they sailed had whetted her appetite for what loomed across the Channel. The port had been filled with red-coated soldiers and gold-braided officers, many escorting fashionably gowned ladies onto packets and transports for the Continent. Few in the motley crowd appeared to fear what faced the troops in Belgium. Most of the contingent viewed the coming preparation for battle as a great spectacle, a giant festivity on foreign shores, put on for their amusement. Despite herself, Verity also caught the contagion, although occasionally she reproved herself, imagining what her dear brother had committed himself to. Many of the passengers were civilians, not one whit sobered by the specter of Napoleon's legion massing to destroy them. For the first time in years they had the chance to travel abroad and they were determined to wrest every crumb of entertainment from the opportunity.

Verity's leavetaking from Devon had been particularly trying, with Lady Maxwell bewailing her daughter's decision, her lack of gentility in following the Army, leaving her unconsoled and weeping over Charley's departure. Sir Anthony, who had explained the massive bruise on his jaw as a fall from a high-strung horse, impatiently soothed her. Secretly he was enraged at seeing his victim escape his clutches. He had tried to prevent Charley from removing her from his milieu, but could not press his objections too strongly in case Lady Maxwell should suspect his intentions.

Only the belief that Verity might find a suitable husband among the officers and ton members thronging to Brussels had calmed Lady Maxwell's complaints about her daughter's desertion at this critical juncture. After all, Charley was legally Verity's guardian, and if he insisted that he needed her companionship at this trying time, she would not be so churlish as to lament the necessity. She was much impressed with her own sacrifice, while behaving as if Verity were a veritable monster to leave her mother prey to the most odious worry. But both Charley and Verity, cleverly taking advantage of the situation, reminded her that she had her husband to support her, and Sir Anthony perforce had to agree.

Verity's last few hurried days at home had been spent administering hartshorn to her mother, and assuring her that the journey would be a great lark. She heartlessly recalled that her mother felt too unwell to chaperone her daughter at any social event during the coming summer, and that Verity's absence would happily relieve her of the necessity. Verity prevailed upon the indomitable Agnes, one of the maids, to accompany her, and this did much to calm her mother's fears about the propriety of her action. Charley had stoutly supported her through all the objections, brushing aside any demur the Maxwells felt called upon to make, and facing up to an irate Denis, who spent their last few days regarding Verity with a dismal hurt expression that young woman found very trying.

Now they were entering the capital itself, a bustling baroque town ringed by crumbling ramparts. The medieval castle of the Dukes of Brabant greeted their awed gaze, and beyond it the church of Ste. Gudule stood in Gothic splendor, the sun striking off its ancient stained glass windows. Skirting the *grande place* and the Hotel de Ville on the south side of the square, their carriage turned into the Rue Ducale, whose houses faced on the park. Verity craned her neck as they progressed down the boulevards, amazed to see so many English faces promenading in stylish splendor. The green uniforms of the Hussars cheek by jowl with the red-jacketed Guardsmen paraded in large numbers, as if in Hyde Park, pausing to greet friends and eye the lavishly gowned ladies who flirted and ogled in turn.

The rooms Charley had bespoken on one of the soberer side streets beyond the Hotel de Ville had a certain shabby gentility, which rather surprised Verity since she had expected much humbler quarters. But their landlady explained that the long French occupation, her husband's death, and economic deprivations had forced her to open her family home to guests. Madame Blancheur, a tall stout matron, displayed a certain affronted pride at the necessity of such a stratagem, but appeared to be an amiable woman, and was obviously a strict housekeeper. Agnes sniffed a bit at her own attic quarters but told Verity later that Madame kept a strict eye on her ménage and did not tolerate shoddy work. The household was scrupulously clean if a bit spartan as to furnishing, but Verity, enchanted with the strangeness of it all, delighted in the surroundings.

Once established in their lodgings Charley had little time for her, taken up immediately in his military duties, he informed her importantly. These seemed to Verity to consist of riotous evenings with his fellow officers, who were tasting the delights of Brussels to the fullest and boasting of their coming prowess, exchanging tales about the Germans who had arrived in force under the bluff commander Blucher, and generally preening themselves in their uniforms. But Verity did not complain, only too happy to hover on the fringe of all this activity, and she and Agnes made several sightseeing forays to amuse themselves. Charley, after the first few days renewing his regimental contacts, did feel some obligation to entertain his sister, and one bright morning invited her to accompany him to the races at Grammont, a favorite indulgence of many of the foreign visitors.

It was at the racetrack, crowded with officers and townspeople, that Verity caught her first glimpse of "Old Hookey," as the men called the Duke of Wellington. The savior of Europe cut a much less impressive figure than she had expected, slighter and less majestic with cold piercing blue eyes and the famous bony nose in evidence. He dressed in plain dark clothes, and was quite put in the shade by the Prince of Orange, the rejected claimant to Princess Charlotte's hand, who strutted about in a lavishly embroidered uniform, thorougly at home with his British comrades but paying little attention to his countrymen. "Slender Billy," as his compatriots called their future king, had been accused of calling the Belgians "idiots." The Prince of Orange, whose British sympathies were well known, had some reason to despise his countrymen. Most of the

Belgian officers had served under Napoleon and Billy's own father was causing all sorts of problems garrisoning the Netherlands fortresses as Wellington had requested. But Verity suspected the Iron Duke would win out, and no one could tell from his calm demeanor that he found affairs in Brussels vexing. This brief glimpse of him reassured her a great deal. Under such a commander Charley's chances appeared much brighter.

Her brother, like many of his fellow untested officers, placed great faith in the Duke, and stood in some awe of the Peninsula veterans, a great many of whom had been dispatched to America after Napoleon's defeat and were only now hurrying to rejoin the main body of the Army. Subaltern Howard reserved his chief encominums for his own commanding officer, Major Alistair Glendenning, and Verity was quite tired of hearing of this gentleman. So when Charley diffidently presented her to Glendenning, she quite expected to find him an overweening, pompous sort of man.

They were strolling casually about the grounds enjoying the warm weather, and brightly attired festive crowd, and the horses, many with their gentlemen jockeys aboard, when Charley stopped suddenly. "There's the major, by Jove." He indicated a couple crossing toward the enclosure. Verity saw a tall, chestnut-haired officer in the red jacket and white pantaloons of the Life Guards, and hanging possessively on his arm a woman of lush charms, gowned in a startling fuschia cambric dress, with an incredible ostrich-trimmed bonnet. Verity hesitated when she saw Charley meant to hail the couple. For some reason she did not want to meet the officer, but her brother had no such qualms, eager to introduce his sister to this Non-Pareil.

He dragged Verity in his wake and approached the pair. "Good afternoon, Major. Are you in luck?" he asked diffidently, eyeing the officer's companion with unabashed and naive delight.

"Ah, Howard, there you are. Kind of you to ask. I've dropped a few ponies, but nothing to signify. My luck is out, it seems," he drawled, eyeing Verity with a knowledgeable grin which made her feel undressed. What a rake the man was, conceited as she had expected, noting his bold blue eyes and swaggering stance. She supposed he had great success with women, and an equal amount of success in luring them with his practiced charm. He waited, smiling with amusement as Charley stammered the introduction.

"Verity, this is my commanding officer, Major Alistair Glendenning. Major, my sister, Verity." The young man blushed, realizing that perhaps the woman accompanying the major was not a fit companion to meet his sister. Glendenning smiled suavely, knowing full well the reason for the young man's embarrassment.

"Charmed, Miss Howard. And you have joined half of England to see us match wits with the Corsican, brave of you." Major Glendenning bowed, his tone sarcastic, implying that she was among the thrill seekers who saw the coming battle as an entertainment rather than the life-and-death struggle it might prove to be.

"Not at all, Major. I had a serious reason to accompany my brother and it does not include frivolous enjoyment," Verity answered sharply, and to her dismay felt a blush stain her creamy cheeks. She turned away from his mocking stare and looked at his companion, whom he rudely chose not to introduce.

Alistair, who had no use for respectable misses, raised his eyebrows at her reproof, but continued to smile at her in that ironic manner which caused her hackles to rise. She was conscious that her demure blue walking dress modestly faced in white muslin did not meet his standards, and tossed her head, refusing to meet his stare. The men exchanged a few more words, when they were interrupted by the cooing tones of Alistair's companion.

"Come, cher, I want to place a bet before the next race. I rather favor that spirited gray." The woman tugged fretfully at the major's arm in her impatience at the meeting.

The major patted her arm perfunctorily, staring derisively at Verity but making no attempt to introduce the woman. With a careless nod, he turned away, leaving Verity fuming with his insouciance. How could Charley admire such a man? He might have a certain attraction, but he was too cavalier in his manner, and an obvious libertine. Whatever his prowess in the field was no doubt more than equaled by his victories in the bedroom. She had no use for him, and feared his influence on Charley. Her brother sensed her dislike of his hero as they moved away.

"I shouldn't have approached Glendenning when he had that woman with him. Not a fit creature for you to meet. I apologize, Verity," he muttered, ill at ease.

"Forget it, Charley. So that is your famous leader. I found him quite unacceptable," she answered shortly, annoyed that she suspected the officer returned her opinion. She had not liked that assessing look which left her squirming with mortification. Obviously he preferred better-endowed females and was not particular about their morals.

Charley launched into a panegyric concerning the major's battle record, his leadership qualities, and his own good fortune to be commanded by such an outstanding fellow, but Verity hardly heeded his glowing words. Alistair Glendenning was not to her taste, too flamboyant, too arrogant, and, she suspected, too offhand with women. She would not be numbered among his conquests. Not that she was offered the opportunity. She had made little impact on the impressionable womanizer. Of that she was sure, determined to put him out of her mind. But throughout the day, she found herself looking for his tall figure among the many officers enjoying the racing, despising herself for her interest.

As the June days lengthened, rumors abounded

about Napoleon's triumph in Paris, his efforts to commandeer a huge force to meet his foes. The hectic pace of the pleasure seekers heightened. A few of the more timid, heeding the threats of the Bruxellois that Napoleon would soon roll up the Allies, departed hurriedly for Ostend, but most of the beau monde remained to flirt, dance, and pursue their pleasures undaunted by any fears of their eventual safety.

Wellington encouraged the gaiety, believing that a preoccupation with the social round kept the populace distracted as the suspense deepened. The French forces were on the move toward Charelroi and the Mons road, but the Duke had not yet decided where to concentrate his army. His Prussian allies pressed him for strategic deployment. Still he hesitated. His cool composure at the balls, and the giant cavalry review which Verity attended, did much to keep spirits high, but beneath the hectic social pace, the aristocratic visitors and great families of the city prepared for the worst. Napoleon was invincible, they believed, despite Wellington's proven success against the Corsican in the past.

Verity thrilled with pride as she watched Charley sweep by at the review astride his well-set-up gray. She could not restrain a sneaking admiration for his major, who looked every inch the veteran cavalry officer as he headed his sharply disciplined platoon of Life Guards. Her initial reaction to Charley's commanding officer had not softened during the days since the racetrack meeting but she had to concede he appeared a fine officer. They had met briefly at some of the larger routs, receptions, and drawing rooms which attracted the best-born officers. He continued to treat her with casual indifference as if she were a mere schoolgirl and that annoyed her, although she was not sure she wanted a different reaction. He appeared to be a great favorite with the matrons and younger married women, but ignored the respectable well-born misses who tried desperately to capture his eye. Just as she had thought, he was a womanizer who had little time for girls of her stamp. And she had heard all the gossip about his intrigue with a London lady, but he seemed impervious to the shocked whispers. Charley's admiration for Major Glendenning had not diminished and Verity hoped he would not be influenced by his idol's rakish ways.

She masked her worries about her brother's fate in the battle which could not be long postponed, although his danger was never far from her thoughts. Her concern mounted as each day passed and the tension rose. His eagerness and impetuosity were no substitute for experience. He had never fired a shot in anger. Now faced with Napoleon's veterans, how would he conduct himself? She trusted his faith in his revered major would be justified, and that Alistair Glendenning would guide Charley safely through the coming conflict.

If Verity spent more time than she wished thinking of Alistair Glendenning and pinning her hopes for Charley's survival on that enigmatic officer, the object of her thoughts had his own worries, which had little to do with the strategy and tactics of the coming battle. He had received a pleading letter from his former mistress, Olivia, Lady Bletchford, begging him to return to her. Before leaving for Belgium he had narrowly avoided a troublesome scandal involving the fetching Olivia and had been forced to take diversionary methods. She wanted to divorce her cuckolded old lord and marry Alistair, a contingency which still posed danger for him.

In the past Alistair had cleverly eluded any attempt to fall into the parson's trap with obliging ladies who had warmed his bed before realizing he took none of them seriously, but Olivia had stronger claims than many. If he survived the battle, he conceded ruefully, she could prove a definite problem. And he had tired of her, just as he had of many others. Well, he would deal with that threat if he emerged unscathed from the French guns. He had pursued a noted Belgian demimondaine since his arrival, and although he enjoyed her favors, he knew she would just as cheerfully embrace another man with full pockets.

He confided his resolution to avoid respectable women in the future to his old friend, Viscount Montague, a member of his former regiment, one afternoon as the two broached a bottle in the latter's study.

"Women are a damned nuisance. I will be glad when we march out and can forget all about them," he complained to his friend, a well-set-up black-haired officer of his own age.

"You should get shackled, Alistair, and give up all this womanizing and carousing," Ian teased, complacent in his own happiness. Lady Montague had accompanied her husband to Brussels and the pair's devotion irked Alistair at times, for he missed his comrade's company on the forays into romantic dalliance they had once enjoyed together.

He shook his head. "Now that you have become a very smug benedict you want us all to follow your lead into domesticity. I grant you that your Ariel is a pearl among women, but you took your own time about bowing to the inevitable," Alistair quipped, annoyed that the Viscount had abandoned his own youthful indiscretions so cheerfully.

Ian laughed, admitting the truth of Alistair's accusations. "I was a damned fool, but all has turned out happily. Ariel is expecting, an heir, my father hopes, but I would just as soon have a daughter," he confided.

"And you brought her to Brussels. Was that wise?" Alistair reproved. He was very fond of Lady Montague and despite his admonitions thought Ian a lucky fellow.

"She would not stay away, and I must confess, I wanted her with me. Who knows how many days we will have together," Ian confessed brusquely, reluctant to admit that he might fall in battle.

"Such gloomy talk. And you a staff officer. No need to chance a stray bullet, what?" Alistair mocked, although he knew full well Ian Montague would not hide behind a safe billet. "At least I leave no hostages to sorrow. Soldiers should not be married. There is Uxbridge, for example. A damned fine leader, but he has left his new wife in London in a family way. Careless of him," he mocked.

"So the new Lady Uxbridge is expecting already. Does not seem to have impaired his lordship's abilities in the field. Much will depend on him, you know," Ian said somberly, and the two dismissed further talk of marriage and women to recall their Peninsular days under that same Lord Uxbridge's command. They had been members of a famed Hussar regiment until Alistair had been forced to transfer to his present post because of the recent scandal over Lady Bletchford. Their military conversation was finally interrupted by the appearance of Lady Montague, determined to wrest her husband and his friend from their war talk and join her at luncheon.

"I might have known it, Alistair. Not that I am not happy to see you, but you do tend to create disturbances. What rag are you up to now?" she joked, allowing the gentleman in question to kiss her hand and give her a wicked grin. Ariel, Viscountess Montague, was a statuesque brunette of uncommon beauty, whose pregnancy was well hidden by the high-waisted silk eau de nile gown she wore. She and Alistair were old duelists and she quite enjoyed her encounters with him although she decried his libertine ways, which in the past he had tried to impose upon her to no avail.

"You do look in fine fig for an expectant mama, Ariel. Congratulations and I hope you will ask me to be a godparent," Alistair replied smoothly with a twinkle in his eys.

"Unless you mend your ways, my lad, I think that very doubtful. And I hope you have not called upon Ian here with some frightful rig in mind," she reproved him, but smiling despite herself. Alistair could always get around her, outrageous as his behavior was wont to be.

"How you misjudge me," he answered cheerfully. "Ian and I were just recalling old days and discussing the coming clash with the Corsican. I do wish Old Hookey would get down to the business, keeping us all hanging about."

"Rumor has it that he is waiting to secure the Mons road," Ian interposed, amused to see his friend and his wife at their usual tilting. "But come, we must not fall into Ariel's bad graces, Alistair. Join us for a meal."

Alistair, nothing loath to accept, agreed and the trio repaired to the dining room of the rather imposing mansion the Montagues had rented for their stay in Brussels. Their talk was of country affairs, for Alistair sensed Ariel did not want to refine on the upcoming engagement. A soldier's daughter and wife, she was not so faint-hearted as to discuss her fears about her husband's probable fate, but Alistair took her in too much affection to add to her budget of worries. However, he did confide in

79

the couple his concern over Lady Bletchford, and received the reassurance he needed.

"If you do not care for her in that way, of course you must not marry her. But Alistair, you must admit you compromised her," Ariel reproved him, remembering his liaison with that fetching lady and wondering if Alistair's heart had ever been engaged.

"She knew that marriage was never the question," he argued cheerfully. "I may be a rake, Ariel, but I am not a deceiver. I regret that she is unhappy but, in any case, I can do nothing about it now. All must wait on Napoleon. This engagement saved my muttons," he concluded blithely.

"A decent marriage would be the saving of you, Alistair," she replied sternly. "But I doubt any decent girl would have you."

"Too true. If my dear sister-in-law would produce an heir I would be most relieved and could continue to go to the devil in my own way. You two are the end. Just because you are enjoying marital bliss you want to lure us more fortunate ones into the parson's mousetrap to suffer equally. Not that I might not succumb if I could find your equal, dear Ariel," he added gallantly.

Ariel shook her head, saying ruefully, "Someday, Alistair, you will be caught, and I hope to see it."

Ian, who had been watching his wife and comrade exchanging quips, laughed at them both, then sobered. "Ariel is quite right, Alistair, and I can testify to the satisfaction of the marital bond." He gave his wife a speaking look which caused a blush to rise in her cheeks. Alistair, not unnoticing, repressed a sigh. When he visited the Montagues he sometimes yearned for such a relationship, but then admitted his chances of settling down with one woman, facing her across a dining table for the rest of his life, would undoubtedly lead him into excesses. His was not a faithful nature and he could not invisage himself shackled to a doting female forever.

"And how do you find Uxbridge? Is he the man for the job?" asked Ian, noticing that his friend appeared a bit blue deviled. Thankfully Alistair endorsed his new commander with enthusiasm and the rest of the luncheon passed with no more allusion to Alistair's romantic affairs.

Chapter Six

On June 12, news came to Wellington's headquarters that Napoleon had marched out of Paris and two days later had deployed his corps, 122,000 strong, at Beaumont, some fifty miles from Brussels. Napoleon knew his forces were outnumbered, for the Anglo-Dutch armies comprised almost twice as many men, but his strategy did not include facing the combined levies. He planned to probe their weak spot, through which he would drive and defeat each separately. Wellington, informed by his intelligence chief of the French maneuvers, decided that his enemy would try what he himself would have put in motion, a sweep around his flank to cut the Allies off from the sea, a maneuver the Corsican had employed successfully in the past. He concentrated his heavy mass of infantry west of Brussels, where he believed the attack would come, and waited.

Of some concern to the Iron Duke and many of his commanders were the Bonapartist sympathies of many of the Bruxellois. To combat this latent treachery, Wellington showed himself the very picture of British steadiness and calm indifference to their intrigues. He attended a cricket match and even had a small dalliance with Lady Frances Wedderburn-Webster, one of the beau monde, whose antics quite disgusted sober Brussels society, as did the behavior of Lady Caroline Lamb, who had followed the Army to the Belgian capital. He rejected Blucher's pleas as to his plans while reviewing his troops with serene indifference, marching the Highlanders in their bright swaying kilts, bagpipers to the fore, down the Allée Verte, followed by the Gay Gordons, and the soberer Hanoverians.

Tension was high, when on June thirteenth Sir Thomas Picton arrived to put up at the Hotel d'Angleterre and to hear the disturbing news from the Duke that he must put himself under the orders of the young, untried Prince of Orange. It did not bode well. Bonaparte had crossed the border, to the dismay of the nervous townspeople, when it was learned that the Duke and several of his divisional commanders would not be riding toward Chareloi but would instead be attending the Duchess of Richmond's ball on the evening of the fifteenth, all part of Wellington's strategy to assuage the fears of the populace.

While the ladies were choosing their gowns, and their partners ordered flowers for their various inamoratas, the French attacked at Charleroi. Still, the Iron Duke refused to order his troops to the relief of the Prussians, who were under heavy fire. He was waiting to see what Napoleon intended toward the Mons road. At headquarters many officers believed the report was a false alarm and prepared to don their dress uniforms for the ball.

Somewhat to their surprise Charley and Verity had received invitations to the Richmond ball. The Duchess was a high stickler and entertained no arrivists. Charley believed that Alistair might have secured the vouchers, for he was a great favorite with the Richmonds despite the scandal which clouded his name. Men never suffered for their immoral behavior, Verity concluded, somewhat bitterly thinking of Sir Anthony. Charley agreed reluctantly to escort her to the gala party although he was disgusted that society should be desporting itself thus on the eve of a great battle. Unable to curb his restlessness as the afternoon wore on, Charley left at last to seek out Major Glendenning, and returned within the hour in a frenzied state.

"I can't believe it. We are not yet to move. The major is attending the Duchess's ball this evening, and so is Lord Uxbridge and the Duke. How can they be so improvident?" he fumed, pacing up and down the shabby room. Verity, feeling her hands wet with perspiration, ventured to suggest that they would not be dancing if the reports of the French movements were true. She walked to the window and leaned out into the stifling air, for it was a hot and muggy day, trying to cool her fevered cheeks. There was no recourse except to wait, and looking down on the street below, she could not believe the ordinariness of the folk going about their usual business.

As Verity dressed for the ball, she could not help but echo Charley's sentiments. How foolhardy to be waltzing the hours away when a giant battle loomed just hours ahead. How could she forget, even in some momentary gaiety, that her brother would be facing French grapeshot and lances in the morning, throwing his inexperienced body against Napoleon's veterans. Well, she must not disgrace him by crying and voicing her fears. She suspected that Charley was holding on to his own nerve with the greatest difficulty and it would not help to have her wailing.

She looked at herself in the mirror with little satisfaction despite Agnes's assurances that she looked a treat. Her simple apricot silk gown, high-waisted with a modest décolletage accented by her grandmother's pearl necklace, would not show to good advantage before the lavish jewels, elegant tissues, and figured silks of London's most fashionable women. She did not realize that her glowing youth, her wide wondering eyes, had a charm which many of those same ladies would give all of their jewels, their modish gowns, to possess. But Verity had little conceit and did not rate her looks very high. Now Charley put her quite in the shade in his spanking red dress uniform of the Life Guards, his braid and buckles shining, his open lively countenance glowing with touching eagerness. She smiled at him sympathetically. She could not join in his anticipation of the battle but she would not destroy his enthusiasm for what he considered a great adventure.

Throwing a silk shawl around her finery Verity made a disgruntled moue at the mirror and turned to face her brother.

"Well, do I meet with your approval, Charley?" she asked in a teasing fashion.

"You will turn every head, and I am sure will be besieged by partners. So don't expect me to dance more than one turn with you," he said, laughing. Dancing was not Charley's forte.

"Well, thank you, brother. Let us hope I will not be forced to seek the dowagers' chairs and languish forlorn at this splendid ball. Will the Duke really be there?" Verity asked as they made their departure.

"So I hear. But I must say I think it's the outside of enough to be dancing the night away when he should be disposing his forces. But I understand Old

Hookey loves a waltz with a pretty partner," Charley grumbled.

The Richmond mansion in the Rue de la Blanchisserie blazed with light as the Howards joined the throngs waiting on the stairway to be received by the Duke and Duchess. The ballroom, which formed its own wing to the left of the hall where the hosts received their guests, was papered in a rose trellis design and banked with huge vases of roses and lilies, their scent heavy on the hot night air. French windows at the back of the hall opened onto the gardens but the air was still and close and added to the discomfort of the crowded assembly, wilting under the light of hundreds of tapers. All of Brussels society gathered in the ballroom, as well as such notables as the Prince of Orange, the Duke of Brunswick, Lord Hill and the Earl of Uxbridge with their attendant staffs, young Guardsmen and officers of all the best regiments. The glitter and shine of the brilliant uniforms outshone the crepes and silks of the ladies, who masked their anxiety with fixed smiles and a hectic gaiety.

The Duchess, born a Gordon, had prevailed upon some of the Highlanders to dance reels for her guests, and a burst of applause greeted their swirling gyrations. When the first waltz followed the blare of the pipes, the younger guests took the floor with reckless abandon, but the older members of the assembly could not completely sink their fears and huddled in small groups discussing the rumors of the battle and wondering where the Duke of Wellington was.

A bit timid in such august company, Verity wondered if any of the officers would ask her to dance after she enjoyed her initial whirl with Charley, but she need not have worried. Piqued by this new belle in their midst, Charley's comrades clustered around her, requesting her program, scrawling their names, and vying for her company. Flushed and flattered, Verity tried to accede to their pressing demands and did not at first see Major Glendenning, who easily dispersed the opposition and insisted on claiming a dance. Somehow Verity did not want to give in to the arrogant officer, but realized that Charley would expect her to receive his overtures kindly. She promised him a waltz after supper and he accepted her reluctant agreement with that mocking all-knowing smile which she found so distasteful. She hoped he realized that she had consented only because she wanted to please Charley, not because she found his attentions welcome.

She was much more intrigued by Prince Vasilii Petrov Chirnovsky, one of Tsar Alexander I's staff, who had preceded his monarch to Brussels as an observer, for the Russian troops would not be available for the battle. The Prince, a tall commanding figure in his stark white uniform ablaze with decorations, had an ardent eye and a polished manner, but his smile was warm and she thrilled to the obvious admiration in his dark Slavic gaze. Under Alistair's cynical appraisal she found herself flirting outrageously with the dashing Prince and was more than a little chagrined when Major Glendenning drawled as the Prince turned away, "You had best be wary of the Russian, my dear. He has a fearsome reputation with the ladies, I hear."

"No worse than yours, Major, I vow. Can it be that you sense a rival?" Verity responded, annoyed at his warning, and tossing her head.

"Not at all. Neither of us regard schoolgirls as fair game. But perhaps you are more experienced than I thought," Alistair replied outrageously before giving her a brief bow and crossing the room to Ariel, Lady Montague, who had just arrived with her husband. Verity, despite herself, noticed how open and sincere was the greeting he gave the dark-haired matron and wondered if she was another of his many flirts. Then she turned determinedly away, not willing to give him the satisfaction of knowing she was interested in his actions or opinion.

Alistair, greeting Ariel and Ian, cheerfully pretended not to notice Ariel's drawn face above the cream-colored jewel-crested crepe dress which successfully hid her pregnancy. Thank God he had no one who worried about his fate in the coming battle, but because he sincerely cared for Ariel he made no mention of her distress, and chaffed Ian on his staff appointment, which would keep him out of range of the guns and ensure that his glittering green Hussar's uniform would remain unsullied.

Ariel, realizing what he was about, tried to enter into their lighthearted bandiage. Ian reluctantly surrendered her to Alistair for the coming country dance, after giving his wife an affectionate smile, and the two moved into the set just forming, which included Verity and a young Guardsman.

Ariel, more intuitive than Alistair might have expected, saw him looking at the attractive young redhead with a cynical regard. She had noticed him talking to her earlier and her curiosity was aroused.

"Who is the lovely young girl at the bottom of this set, Alistair? She is quite uncommon," Ariel asked dulcetly.

"The sister of one of our officers, newly out of the schoolroom, and an irritating baggage," he answered a bit brusquely, annoyed that Ariel had caught him watching Verity.

"One of your latest flirts. For shame, Alistair. She is but a child, not up to your standard," Ariel joked. Then seeing the frown that darkened his face, she wondered if she might have trespassed.

"She is no different from most of these virginal misses on the catch for a husband," Alistair said as they came together in the set again. "Not my style, I agree. I am too wary a bird to be entangled in that kind of mesh. But her brother is a good lad."

Ariel smiled provocatively. He appeared more

91

appris than he wanted to admit. Happily married herself, Ariel wanted Alistair to abandon his rackety ways and find equal felicity, because she was convinced his current mode of life could bring him nothing but trouble.

"Ariel, you have maggots in your head. Stop trying to lead me into the parson's trap. Even if I were hanging out for a wife, that little chit would not be my choice. Underneath that prim facade lurks a veritable wanton, I am sure. And like all rakes I want a chaste bride; unfair, I admit, but nevertheless I want to make sure any heirs which are conceived are my own," he jeered, mocking her efforts to make him respectable. Ariel, reproved, shook her head and abandoned all attempts to bring him around to her way of thinking. Discussing Alistair's behavior had kept her mind from the coming danger to her husband, never far from her thoughts, but she tried to put on a good face for Ian would be disgusted if he knew how worried she was. They concluded the dance in charity with one another, for Ariel could not resist Alistair's lighthearted teasing. Perhaps it was just as well he left no sorrowing wife or fiancé when he rode out before dawn.

Verity was enjoying her first grand ball, despite the danger that hovered over the guests. She had her pick of partners and found no difficulty in living for the moment, although she knew this gaiety was but a pretense. Soon enough the dancers must face reality. Prince Chirnovsky took her down to supper, a lavish display of meats and jellies which she enjoyed immensely, their table augmented by a flushed group of revelers determined to banish the war clouds about them. She found the Prince overly attentive but did little to discourage him, her mind only partially engaged with his flirtation. It was as if they were all holding their breath, waiting for the call to arms.

It was past midnight before Wellington appeared, as stoic and unruffled as if he were strolling down Bond Street. Georgina Lennox, the Richmonds' daughter and one of the Duke's favorites, dared what few others would have, by dashing up to ask him if the rumors were true.

He looked into her drawn, pretty face and replied, "Yes, they are true. We are off tomorrow." Bystanders, hearing his low firm voice, shuddered and then returned to the dancing, hiding whatever fears they felt in the spurious pleasure of the music.

Verity had missed the Duke's arrival, for the Prince had prevailed upon her to walk on the terrace to seek a breath of air and a respite from the hot, crowded ballroom. She had not seen Charley for some time and suspected he was closeted with some comrades in the card room, whiling away the hours over a game of piquet for he disliked dancing. Distracted she barely noticed that the Prince was steadily luring her from the lighted terrace into the grounds. She looked up in surprise when he swooped, grasping her by the shoulders.

"Doushka, you are so lovely. Give me a token to carry into battle tomorrow, a kiss from your luscious lips," he appealed extravagantly, suiting his action to his words and raising her head.

Verity laughed nervously. "Really, Prince, this will not do." She struggled against the firm hands which did not release her.

"What a little charmer you are. Come, I know passion awaits beneath that prim demeanor. Let me show you the delights of love. We have so little time," he urged, his dark eyes glowing lustfully, and easily subduing her efforts to escape him.

Verity wondered how she could have come to such a pass and tried again to release herself, but the Prince would not be balked. As angry with herself as with him for allowing such liberties, she tried to explain, but before she could take any evasive measures a cool, sardonic voice interrupted them.

"I believe the lady is reluctant, Prince," Alistair suggested. He had appeared out of the dark, unnoticed by the couple.

The Prince, not at all embarrassed, explained suavely, "Miss Howard felt faint in the ballroom, and I suggested a walk in the gardens might prove efficacious."

"And an opportunity for a little dalliance, Prince. Not that I blame you, for she is a taking chit, but I believe she has had second thoughts. Also she is cutting my dance, and I cannot allow that," Alistair replied casually, but with an ugly gleam in his eye.

"We will leave it up to the lady. Perhaps she does not want to dance with you," the Prince said smoothly, unwilling to abandon his prey and eyeing his adversary with an equally baleful expression.

"Oh, she would not be so unkind as to deprive her countryman, and her brother's commanding officer, of the pleasure of her company. We are allies, Prince, only on the battlefield." Alistair straightened up, his own stance threatening.

Verity, confused and humiliated at being caught in such a compromising position by a man she detested, decided she must take a hand in events before they became too heated. Damn the major. She could have rejected the Prince's overtures without his insulting interference.

"I regret I forgot your dance, Major. Let us repair to the ballroom, by all means," she said dulcetly, biting back the words she wanted to say.

Alistair said nothing, but waited impatiently for the Prince to take his leave. The Russian hesitated, as if wanting to protest the Englishman's cavalier demands, but deciding the game not worth the candle, gave a stiff bow and turned to Verity. "Of course, madam, I will not intrude if it would cause you any displeasure. Accept my apologies," and he strode off into the night, his back rigid with anger.

"Tempestuous fellows, these Ruskies," Alistair drawled, but the look in his eye belied the casual words. "You are foolish, Miss Howard, to flirt with such a man. He is only too willing to take advantage of your search for sensation. And you are no match for a man of the Prince's stamp. He will seduce you without a thought and walk away. Were you deluded enough to believe he might make you his princess after one dance, one kiss?" Alistair asked in a cynical tone which brought a flush to Verity's cheeks.

"Don't be ridiculous, Major," she flared. "I could have handled the Prince. Perhaps I was a bit reckless to accompany him into the gardens, but I am sure he is a perfect gentleman and would not have forced me against my will."

"If it is stolen kisses you want as an added fillip to the evening, it would be a shame to deny you," Alistair answered provocatively, now thoroughly convinced after her ridiculous statement that the girl was a sensation seeker. And before she could take evasive action he caught her in his arms and pressed a brutal kiss upon her lips, his mouth contemptuous and hard as he forced her mouth open to his searching tongue. With strong hands, he easily subdued her efforts to escape. Then he hesitated, and his caress softened, roaming seductively over her cheeks and throat, overwhelming her with wild emotions.

For a moment she surrendered, her instincts winning over her conscience, and her hands creeping up around his neck, but then, recollecting where she was and her first impressions of this man, she jerked herself free. Stepping back, she slapped him soundly on the cheek, her hand stinging from the blow. "How dare you treat me so. I am not one of your doxies to be used thus," she sputtered, aware that her indignation was somewhat of a sham. She had responded to him, no doubt due to his expert handling, but she could not allow him to think she had enjoyed that disturbing kiss. Her pride would not countenance it.

Rubbing his cheek ruefully, Alistair acknowledged he had behaved badly, no matter what the provocation, but he, too, would not make excuses for his untoward behavior. Eyeing her with a cynical smile he said, "Ah, but my dear, if you behave like one you must not be surprised if I take advantage of your license. Let me warn you that if you continue in this fashion you will find yourself in similar situations and perhaps Charley will not be on hand to protect you."

The mention of Charley recalled Verity to her senses. For just a moment she had forgotten the coming battle, Charley's danger, and his reliance on this officer in the turmoil ahead. Biting her lips with vexation she realized she must apologize.

"I should not have struck you, Major, and you should not have kissed me, but the circumstances are unhappy. Despite the antipathy between us I rely on you to do your best for Charley tomorrow. He is so heedless, so raw. He has never fired a shot in anger and his impetuosity will lead him to commit every kind of excess, I know. Please do not allow him to behave recklessly," Verity pleaded, wondering how she could throw herself on this man's mercy. But for Charley's sake she would endure every humiliation.

"Your brother will do his duty, as we all will, I hope. I can make no promises as to his fate," Alistair answered curtly, then softening, for he believed she really was concerned for her brother, he turned to her. "Try not to worry. I realize it is difficult to stand by and await a doubtful outcome. I regret our passage at arms has led to mutual recriminations. Charley is a good lad, and I will do my best for him, believe me," he insisted, all mockery absent from his voice and regard. Then offering her his arm he suggested, "Now let us finish this waltz, as it may be the last time for some while that I can enjoy such pleasures." He was taking an unfair advantage of her sympathy, he knew, but the chit had broken through his defenses.

As they whirled through the throng of dancers, his arm holding her firmly, his eyes above her head held an angry but perplexed expression. She was an enigma, and one he had neither the time nor inclination to solve. His attentions should be directed at the coming battle, not trying to delve into the confusing emotions of a young girl, who no doubt was no better than she should be. The sooner she returned to her family in England, the better for them both. Charley had been a fool to give in to her pleas for excitement and romance in Brussels. She might find instead sorrow and disgrace. But he would not be the one to set her on the way to perdition. He regretted his momentary lapse of control but could not forget the taste of her lips, or the feel of her lithe young body in his arms. Battle eve excitement, he concluded, that was all it was, and it could never be more.

Chapter Seven

At the conclusion of their dance, Alistair escorted
Verity to where Charley and a few of his comrades
were clustered at one side of the ballroom. The
young men were watching the Duke of Wellington
and their commander, Uxbridge, with anticipation,
eager to see some sign they would be riding out.
They hailed Alistair enthusiastically, hoping he
would have some news. He fended off their
questions but assured them they would be off before
too long. With a brief bow and a searching look at
Verity, which she could not interpret, he was gone.
She watched his progress across the floor to where
Wellington was conferring with his cavalry commander, the Duke of Brunswick, and the Prince of
Orange, who had but recently reported from the
field. With a few words the latter two gentlemen
made their adieus, but Wellington remained. Verity
saw Alistair exchange a few words with the Duke

and Uxbridge and nod his head. He turned to look at the group around Charley and beckoned to them.

Charley, feverish with excitement, grinned happily. "Well, I guess, we are off at last." Then turning to his sister, he noticed her apprehension and pinched her pale cheek. "Don't look so Friday-faced, pet. That is no way to send your brother off to war," he reproved. His fellow officers tendered her hurried good-byes and left them alone to make their own farewells. Verity, summoning reserves of courage, tried to return her brother's smile. "Forgive me, Charley. I am not usually a watering pot. I suspect I just envy you your adventure. But do take care, won't you. You are such a one for hazarding all without counting the cost."

Charley, finally realizing that his sister was within an ace of losing her control, subdued his own impatience and bussed her soundly on the cheek, then said more soberly, "I have left a letter for Mother, and my will, back in our rooms. Just a precaution, of course, but I want you to know I have left Woodley to you. I would hate for Sir Anthony to gain control, and Mother is so under his thumb. Fortunately, the place is not entailed, or matters would be more complicated, but our solicitor, Conrad, will settle everything, if by some chance . . ." He did not put her fears into words. Charley, so young, so insouciant, had put aside any fears that he would not return trailing clouds of glory after this, his first taste of battle. But he realized that Verity had the harder part, the waiting.

He hesitated, a bit embarrassed. Then he continued, "I know I can count on you to be a stout-hearted girl, not go into a fit of vapors," he said, indicating some ladies who were crying as they desperately embraced lovers, husbands, and friends, now preparing to join their regiments.

"Well, I must not be a laggard," he insisted, giving her a final hug then saluting before he turned, eager to be off. Charley hated scenes, and Verity would not humiliate him by suggesting she was any less confident than he was of the outcome of the next hours. He had forgotten that she must be returned to their rooms and she would not remind him of his duty now when he had so much on his mind. She smiled at him one last time, and watched him as he strode across to the entrance, so valiant, so young, she thought, and then remembered that Alistair had promised to see him through. Somehow this reassured her, and before she could give in to the tears which threatened to fall, she was approached by the graceful matron she had seen earlier chatting with Alistair.

"My dear, let me introduce myself. I am Ariel, Lady Montague, and it seems we have been abandoned by our men. Ever the way when battle beckons, and I am an old campaigner. But Alistair suggested you might like some assistance in returning to your rooms. I would be pleased to take you up in my carriage," she invited, noticing how overset Verity was.

As Verity murmured her thanks and introduced

103

herself to this matron who seemed to know all about her, she noticed that the Duke had risen and accompanied Richmond from the room. The music still played for a diminishing company of dancers but most of the officers had already hurried from the assembly, intent on the battle ahead. Ladies were calling for their carriages, collecting their wraps, for the ball had lost its sparkle. Verity, murmuring her thanks for Ariel's suggestion, trailed in the wake of Lady Montague as they joined the leave-takers. In the hall, a tall dark officer approached Lady Montague. "Well, I am off, Ariel. You will be all right?" he asked anxiously, and took her into a close embrace.

"I am fine, Ian. Take care and remember you are a family man now so no heroics," Ariel quipped, amazing Verity with her control.

"Never fear. We staff officers are little more than lackeys. Have a heed to the heir, dear one," he warned, and then with a final kiss was gone. All over the hall officers were bidding good-bye to wives and sweethearts. The tone of the festivity had darkened, but the ladies did their best to see off their men with a jest and an embrace, although many clinging arms had to be ruthlessly wrenched away. Little by little the gaily caparisoned officers began their exodus, many of them to ride out in their dress uniforms with no time to change into battle dress.

Verity joined her new acquaintance in her coach and they rattled off into the night through a city astir as the dawn broke and solemn drum beats echoed through the streets. In the Place Royale all was confusion. Regiments were falling in amid gun carriages, forage wagons, commissary trains, and the neighing of plunging horses. As the troops formed up and marched down the Rue de Namur toward the Namur Gate, the Montague carriage made a perilous passage amid the engines of war. Lady Montague talked cheerfully of the ball, hoping to distract her companion and putting her own apprehensions to one side. This young girl had need of her sheltering comfort, for to her this was a frightening and new experience. As they finally arrived at Verity's door, she leaned over and gave her a brief hug.

"These will be anxious hours for you, my dear. It does not get easier, the waiting, no matter how many times you go through it, as I know only too well. Have you someone to whom you can turn, and if not, it might be best for you to accompany me home," she suggested kindly.

"Oh, thank you, Lady Montague, but my abigail, Agnes, will be waiting for me," Verity assured her, warmed by this stranger's concern.

"Well, please know that you are welcome if the waiting becomes tedious. Here is my direction," and Ariel handed her a calling card, then surprisingly kissed her gently on the cheek, and adding her farewell with a bracing smile.

Verity, heartened by the encounter, was able to meet Agnes more cheerfully, but was almost undone by that woman's woebegone face. Agnes, whose

normal mien was one of dour tolerance, had known
Charley and Verity all their lives, and she cursed the
follies of generals and the war fever of young men
who would be better employed managing their
affairs at home, but she did her best to cheer her
mistress. Under Agnes's bracing ministration,
Verity's spirits rallied and they both remembered
that Charley had always emerged from hazardous
scrapes with little or no harm. And in this, the most
perilous adventure of his young life, they must trust
in his natural ability to come out safely again. But
Verity's chief comfort was the thought of Alistair,
experienced, a veteran of many such combats, riding
by Charley's side. She accepted her maid's attempts
at consolation with a watery smile.

"I am such a ninny. Charley would be quite
disgusted. And it is most unlike me to behave in such
a faint-hearted way. You should be giving me a great
scold, Agnes. But thank you. I am much better now.
If only we did not have to endure this waiting. I must
find some task to occupy myself. I know, I will go off
to the hospitals. The surgeons will need nurses." She
stood up and, dismissing her maid's shocked demurs
at such a suggestion, prepared to dress herself for
whatever unpleasant duties lay ahead.

Wellington, who had remained at the Richmond
Ball until the last possible moment, an effort to
confound treachery, stiffen spines, and show the
flag, finally rode out of the city toward Quatre Bras

106

after a few hours' sleep at eight o'clock on the morning of June sixteenth. The French had deployed but two miles away, not yet in full force, as the Prince of Orange had informed him. But by ten o'clock Wellington realized that Napoleon had duped him and a full-scale battle was under way, the twenty thousand men of Marshal Ney's corps engaged at the crossroads against the Prince of Orange's far more slender forces. Wellington could hear the French Army shouting their huzzahs. Wellington greatly feared Napoleon would be in Brussels by the following day. By four o'clock it seemed that the Duke's worst fears would be realized, that the French would sweep all before them, and then turn and join the battle against Blucher at Ligny, where the Prussians were heavily engaged. At the critical juncture Ney received word from Napoleon that he cared little for Quatre Bras, but wished the Marshal to send a body toward Ligny. Ney, furious, for he was within an ace of routing Picton's squares, turned away in disgust.

Major Glendenning, who had been restlessly awaiting the move of Uxbridge's Life Guards to Picton's rescue, finally received word from his commander to convey a message to the Duke. He was ordered to take an officer with him, and chose Charley. The two galloped off toward the Bossu Woods, where the fighting was thick. As they neared the Guards' position, the French cavalry charged, and out of the smoke and noise rose a fierce French lancer. Charley, riding just behind Alistair, saw the

107

trooper come at his companion sideways and shot the man from his saddle just as he threw his lance, which glanced off Glendenning's shoulder.

Alistair, who had seen the enemy too late to take evasive action, looked up, shaken a bit, but said coolly enough as he reined his frenzied horse down from its plunge, "That was a near thing, Howard. You saved my muttons. Good shot, but come, we must press on."

Charley, sweating and aghast at the near tragedy, hastened to follow, admiring his fellow officer's sangfroid, and determined to emulate it. They accomplished their mission, and reached the Duke's position. There they learned that Blucher had retreated, thoroughly routed by the French but the Guards had secured Quatre Bras, after appalling losses, more than two thousand lying dead in the fields and woods around the crossroads.

At the critical moment Ney had not pursued his advantage, but toward nightfall, the Duke saw a mass of cavalry moving toward his position. Wellington ordered Uxbridge to meet them, as storm clouds hovered over the scene. The commander called upon the Light Dragons to advance, but they seemed reluctant. Finally he sent his own Life Guards into the fray. Eager to prove their commander's faith and abolish the rumors that they were mere Hyde Park soldiers, they rose furiously to the challenge, Alistair and Charley among them, and threw off the French Lancers. Wellington retired to Waterloo, knowing that tomorrow the battle would be rejoined, but not unsatisfied with the day's work.

Back in Brussels, where the noise of the guns and rockets could be clearly heard, the citizens cowered with fright. Just before dawn after the sleepless night, the Black Brunswickers arrived bearing their Duke's body to be followed by a troop of Belgiums in frightening disorder, screaming *"Les Français sont ici."* Believing the British in full retreat the population began to gather their valuables, crying and wailing, and begging for horses to transport them from town. Verity, waiting at one of the houses commandeered for a hospital, was proud to notice the British behaved better, cheered to learn that few of the cavalry had been engaged. But soon, that temporary solace was banished as the wounded from Ligny poured into town. She was hard put to swallow her revulsion at the sickening wounds, but steeled herself to do what was asked of her, joining the group of women who had never seen such carnage coolly stanching blood and puss, bandaging the dirty, moaning victims, offering water to thirsty soldiers who waited uncomplaining on the streets, and listening to the final requests of dying men. She could only hope that some charitable soul would do as much for Charley in case of need, and reminded herself that any of these men could be her brother. Almost dropping from fatigue and horror, she had little time to wonder over the fate of her brother.

That young man, well pleased with his exploits on his first taste of battle, spent the night as so many soldiers did, huddled in his cloak, for the storm had broken and was drenching the fields, miring guns and men in mud, and lowering spirits. Only Wellington seemed unaffected, reminding his staff that the deluge was a good omen, "Wellington weather," which had proved most auspicious on the Peninsula. Alistair Glendenning, accustomed to such vagaries of the elements through countless campaigns, cheered his men, conferred with his chief, and returned to tell Charley that tomorrow would see the end of the French in a bang-up battle. Ney's reluctance to move on Quatre Bras when he had the position virtually secured had turned the tide. They would put an end to Bonapart's pretensions tomorrow without fail. Charley, taking heart from his hero's confidence, could only agree. Then Alistair thoroughly embarrassed him by thanking him again for his dispatch of the French lancer. "No doubt about it, Howard, I was a goner if you had not done the job. I am in your debt. And I won't forget it," he promised his junior.

"Oh, sir, it was just a lucky hit. He came out of nowhere. I was fortunate to see him in time." He tried to treat the occurrence with the casualness he thought would be approved. Not for a thousand guineas would he let the major know he had been scared out of his wits, and that his shot was the merest lucky hit.

But Alistair, looking at him with a wry understanding, seemed to read his thoughts. "Not to worry, Howard. We all are a bit frightened when the

110

guns go, you know. The secret is not to show it. I would be very suspicious of a man who was not a bit sunk in the stomach when the charge is blown," he replied, flashing that cynical mocking grin which hinted at a world of experience Charley envied.

Heartened by his commander's bracing comments, Charley tentatively broached what concerned him, now that the first flush of the engagement had died down. "I suppose this is the most violent battle you have seen, sir, and tomorrow will not be much better," he asked, unwilling to show any apprehension, but his open face was not made for dissembling.

"It was a near thing, true. And we lost a lot of good men, but the Duke will prevail. A good soldier never anticipates what might occur on the morrow, my boy," Alistair responded bracingly, but not at all surprised by Charley's reaction.

"Oh, I will manage, I am sure. But I did just want to mention about my sister. I had to take her from our home because she was being harassed by our stepfather, the cad. I caught him trying to seduce her, and I could not leave her unprotected. If I am wounded or fall in battle, she will be alone. I am worried for her, for she must not return to Dorset and face that monster again without me beside her," Charley said, turning his pleading gaze on Alistair.

Not wanting to hear these confidences, Alistair did not know what to reply. He could hardly tell the young man that his sister might have invited such overtures, and he wondered at his own anger at the thought. But he could not allow Charley to carry such a burden into the coming day. "What do you require of me, Charley," he asked softly, unwilling to voice his cynical opinion of the girl who had stirred his own senses. Was she a wanton or an innocent as her brother believed her, a victim of a lecherous stepfather?

"I guess, sir, I just want your promise that if anything should happen to me you will look out for Verity," Charley replied soberly, watching Alistair with an anxious look as if fearing rejection. Only his real concern and apprehension for his sister would have impelled him to make such a suggestion.

"Well, I have every confidence that you will be able to protect her, but for what it is worth, I give you my word. Now stop agonizing about improbable fates. The hour is late and we had best snatch what rest we can in this infernal weather," Alistair said brusquely, gathering his cloak around him and signaling the conversation had ended.

During the night, Wellington made his dispositions, and at six o'clock in the morning rode out on his charger, Copenhagen, to inspect the troops, heartening all who saw him. The Allied army formed into squares, a human wall with spaces into between the mases for maneuvering, the right formed on La Hay Sainte, a salient facing Ney's cavalry at Hougoumont, the most vulnerable position. It was still raining and Wellington's staff, swollen to forty, noticed their chief was dressed in his civilian clothes—white breeches, a blue coat, and tasseled top boots, with a cloak thrown over all to protect him from the elements. "I never get wet when I can help it," he said. His men were not so fortunate, most of them sodden and uncomfortable, but for all that their spirits were high.

At first the battle went against the Allies despite the Guards' valiant charge, led by Uxbridge himself, but just when it appeared Wellington's forces must retreat in confusion and dreadful loss of life, Wellington noticed the French extreme right was melting away. Blucher and his Prussians had arrived at the eleventh hour. Amazingly Napoleon's Old Guard broke and took flight, but the fighting was far from over. A sporadic shell from the French lines took off Uxbridge's leg as he conferred with Wellington but his troops rallied for one more charge, Alistair and Charley to the fore. The Highlanders above La Hay Sainte rushed down, driving the French from their entrenched positions. Only the British 27th Foot did not move; they were every one dead in their square. Wellington was everywhere, unheeding of his staff's efforts to drag him back from the vanguard of the fight. "Never mind, let them fire away. The battle's won; my life is of no consequence now," he replied. The field before La Hay Sainte was awash with blood, wounded men, thrashing horses, splintered bushes and trees, bayonets upright in their mangled targets. But the retreat of the Guards had signaled the end.

Napoleon boarded his coach but was soon over-taken by the Prussians with barely time to jump on his horse and, escorted by the Red Lancers, force his way through to Charleroi.

But for Charley Howard the rout had come too late. Riding behind Alistair in a desperate charge down a hill toward La Hay Sainte, he had been struck by a shell square in the chest. Alistair saw him fall, but was too heavily engaged to come to his aid. When the French guns became silent, he reined his horse in and returned across the littered field to his subaltern's aid. Charley was a fearful sight, blood pouring from the wound in his chest, his eyes wild and unfocused. Alistair leaped from his horse, and ran to support the desperate lad.

"Charley, old man. Hold on. I will get a surgeon," Alistair soothed, appalled to discover the serious-ness of the young man's plight. A stillness had settled over the field, but sounds of dying and wounded men shattered the unearthly quiet. The ground was covered with bodies and thrashing horses, the smoke settling in a miasma of shrouded vapor.

Charley's eyes were clouding, but he managed a grimace. "No use, sir. It's all over with me," he gasped, and shuddered as a wave of pain washed over him. Alistair, shaken by his agony and cursing his powerlessness, looked about for aid, but none was forthcoming. Then he turned to the boy again, as Charley with his last ounce of strength was trying to tell him something of vast importance. Alistair tried to calm him, begging him not to exert himself,

114

but the boy would not be silenced. He was frantic to make his appeal, in the last spasms of his death rattle. As he tried to speak again, the blood gushed from his chest in a flood.

Alistair, understanding that his companion was wracked by some hideous vision, said gently, "What is it, Charley? You must try to rest, don't strain yourself," but he realized that his words went unheeded. The dying boy had to unburden himself.

"It was a grand fight, sir. I wouldn't have missed it, but I never thought it would come to this . . . that I would be taken. Still, I did my duty, didn't I?" he pleaded, his blue eyes searching Alistair's piteously.

"You were fine, Charley. The Life Guards are proud of you," Alistair insisted, his own eyes clouding as he looked at the dying boy. If only there were some help.

"But I cannot go without holding you to your promise, sir, to look after Verity. You must help her and never let her come to harm. Take care of her. She is all alone, but she thinks she can manage. She must not go back to our stepfather. He means to have her, to bring her disgrace. I cannot die and leave Verity without a protector." He choked on the blood welling up in his throat. But he took hold of himself and as his pain subsided looked wildly at Alistair, holding on for his vow. "You said I saved your life. Now you must help Verity. You will, you will, won't you?" he pleaded with frantic urgency.

Alistair, hoping only to bring him peace, hardly took in his warning about the stepfather. All he

115

wanted to do was bring the boy ease for he felt a terrible responsibility. He had told Charley's sister he would protect him, and in the heat of the battle, he had left him to fend for himself. And now it was too late. All he could do was give him that promise. His hands were wet with sweat and he tightened his grip on the shuddering body, hoping to give some relief.

"You know I will do my best for her, Charley. Be easy in your mind. No harm will come to her. You can rely on me. You have my promise," he assured him, and just in time, for the boy gave one last sigh, and said, "The pain is gone, but it is getting dark. I cannot see you, Major." After a few fraught moments, he murmured, "Remember, Verity. Protect my sister, please," and then his eyes closed and he was gone.

Alistair, who had seen many men die on battle-fields, for the first time felt tears rise to his eyes. This boy had depended on him and he had let him die. No matter that hundreds of other good men had lost their lives on this field of carnage, no matter that the defeat of Napoleon had finally been secured. The victory had been bought at a terrible cost. This brave lad, wanting glory and excitement, had been cut off in his prime, and Alistair could not prevent the haunting sense that somehow it was his fault. All around him men were groaning and crying for water, calling upon their God, but for Alistair the whole dreadful scene was centered on the boy whom he still held, the body now stiff and stark with all the

116

glowing life and eagerness dispelled in that final death throe.

Laying his burden down gently, Alistair rose warily to his feet. He had survived when so many fine young men had fallen. How ironic was fate. Charley had so much of life ahead, so much to enjoy and experience, and now he was gone, while Alistair remained. The gods were unkind. Cursing fate, Alistair looked around him at the dreadful scene and wondered if it had been worth it all. But he must not surrender to his sorrow yet. He had a bitter duty still to perform. He must get Charley's body from the field, and deliver the tragic news to the sister who had been Charley's final thought.

Dragging his horse's reins toward him, he moved the gray to his side, the animal shaking and nervous at the presence of death and the smell of blood, and hoisted Charley's inert form over the saddle. Then mounting the horse, he steadied his burden and trotted tiredly in the direction of the Brussels road.

Chapter Eight

Dark had settled over Brussels on that long June Sunday before the final guns, less than twelve miles away, had stilled. When Wellington and Blucher met soon after the hour had tolled, they decided that the Prussians would take up the pursuit of Napoleon. In the field of Waterloo more than forty-five thousand men lay killed and wounded within a three-mile-square area, fifteen thousand of them British troops. Fifty-three officers who had danced at the Duchess of Richmond's ball were killed or gravely wounded, including the gallant Sir Thomas Picton, Sir William Ponsonby, Sir Alexander Gordon, and Lord George Hay, Georgina Lennox's last partner at the famous ball.

As the carts with the wounded and dying rumbled into town, householders were convinced the Allies had lost for the Cumberland Hussars had galloped into town crying that the French were hard on their heels. But as dusk fell, the English, sitting down to dinner in their hotels facing the Park, saw a detachment of Horse Guards escorting a group of French prisoners and displaying two French eagles. By midnight the Duke of Wellington had returned to his headquarters and sat down to write his famous general order: "The field marshal takes this opportunity of returning to the Army his thanks for their conduct in the glorious action fought on the 18th instant, and he will not fail to report his sense of their conduct in the terms it deserves to their several Sovereigns." Privately, Wellington confided to his aides that he doubted the outcome would have been so glorious if he had not been there, and then he went off to visit his aide, the dying Gordon.

Major Alistair Glendenning, riding into Brussels with Charley Howard's body, hesitated wearily after he had deposited his tragic cargo at one of the hospitals, now overflowing with grievously wounded men. All along the streets he had passed more wounded, for there were not beds for all the sufferers, and the sight was piteous. He could not call on Charley's sister until he had repaired the damages of the battle, for his uniform was bloody and sweat stained, one epaulette shot off, and he had a red smear across his forehead where a ball had grazed him. Still he had no time to worry over his own fatigue and bitterness. Wellington had been successful, but at what a cost. Not even the terrible carnage at Badajos or Albuera on the Peninsula had equaled the horror of Waterloo. For the first time Alistair realized the wasteful destruction and suffering of war, which no glory or victory could lighten. He hated what faced him and felt deep personal guilt for Charley's death. The young man had admired and respected him, looked upon him as a model, and he had been unable to save him. How could he face his sister?

And what could he do? How could he redeem his promise to Charley? What recourse did the girl have, but to go home to her mother and stepfather? Was Charley right in his suspicions, that the stepfather wanted to seduce the girl, might already have done so? In the aftermath of that pitiful scene on the battlefield, Alistair had little heart to take up Charley's challenge. He had no stomach for facing a distraught and sorrowing girl, one who would blame him, and rightly, for not guarding her beloved brother. Whatever her faults she had loved her brother and her anguish would be overpowering.

Alistair knew she had trusted him to keep her brother safe, no matter how much she despised him as a man. She had made it quite clear she believed, as had Charley, that his expertise, his command, would ensure that her brother emerged alive. Alistair had lost comrades before, but the death of this worshipful boy hit him hard. For the first time in his long career, victory brought no exhilaration, only a wearying distaste and now a ghastly problem.

Remembering his last view of Verity at the ball, the feel of her artless lips beneath his own, her response, he wondered what this tragedy would do to her. Knowing he could not postpone the distressing interview much longer, and unsure of his own handling of it, he hesitated. Finally, after a bath and a change of uniform he forced himself to call upon the Montagues, hoping for some support, but fearing that he might hear more dire news. Ariel received him, pale with red-rimmed eyes, but able to give him some relief.

"Ian is resting. He received a ball in his shoulder as he was delivering a dispatch to Picton, but the surgeon says it is only a flesh wound. He will recover. We gave him some laudanum after cleaning the wound, and he is asleep now, but I cannot stay away from him long," she said after embracing Alistair. "How happy I am to see you safe, Alistair, when so many good men have been sacrificed. I know it was a tremendous victory, but at what a cost, all those men cut down in the midst of their young lives. And Napoleon has escaped yet again."

"Yes, I know. But the Prussians will overtake him and he will be made to pay for this day's work. It was the most desperate fight I have ever been in. Thank God, Ian emerged alive. Why I was spared, I will never conceive," he grimaced bitterly. "My sub-altern was not so fortunate. That is what I have come to see you about, Ariel. Now that I know that Ian has brushed through, I wonder if you can take poor Howard's sister. She is all alone in their rooms, and has no one to comfort her. I have not yet told her of her brother's death. Too much of a coward to face her, for I promised to look after him, and I failed. She will need some woman, and I would like to bring her here," Alistair pleaded, hoping that Ariel could relieve him of some of the agonizing burden. "I promised her brother, you see," he ended helplessly.

Ariel, surprised at Alistair's intense concern, for she had rarely seen him so disturbed, so worried, realized that he had lost that debonair reckless confidence which had always distinguished him no matter how grave his situation. He appeared almost a stranger, a stern sad man, so different from the careless rakish officer with whom she had laughed and joked. Had he at last faced the reality of life, not a game but a serious business which demanded commitment and faith? She pitied him, her warm heart grateful for her own happiness, rising to offer comfort to one who so badly required it.

"Of course, Alistair. Poor girl. Has she no parents or relatives to succor her?" she asked, putting her own worries behind her. She had so much to be grateful for and her compassion flowed toward the bereaved girl, whose youth and beauty had stirred her just the evening before. She knew what it meant to be bereft, for her own father had died in battle, and she had yearned to offer assistance.

123

"She has a mother and stepfather in Devon, but knows few people here in Brussels. I will make some provision for her, but I will need some help. If it were not for my promise to her brother . . ." He broke off helplessly, as if not knowing what to say or do.

"You know I have never had much to do with young respectable females—although I don't know exactly how respectable this one is. She puzzles me and she doesn't like me, for which I cannot blame her much. I have not treated her well," he confided reluctantly, half ashamed to reveal his disordered thoughts.

"Oh, Alistair, she seems a very nice, a very lovely young girl. You are such a cynic about females, distrustful and caring only for their bodies, not their minds or hearts," Ariel reproved, looking at him with pity.

"I am not sure most of them have hearts. Oh, I believe Verity honestly cared for her brother, but like most of her kind, she is on the catch for an eligible husband and does not care what methods she uses to capture one. I fear she is a flirt, even a wanton. She was flirting with that slimy Russian, Chirnovsky, and he's too wily a bird to be drawn into her net. I admit she has a certain attraction, but you know, I am not in the habit of squiring young females about," he conceded, trying to explain his doubts and distrust and becoming completely undone under Ariel's candid gaze.

"Think only of her tragedy, and what you can do

124

to relieve it. I know you have a warm heart, Alistair, under all that insouciant facade, and you must subdue your skirt-chasing instincts in this instance. I don't believe her brother quite knew what he was asking in pressing you to be her protector," Ariel answered sharply, annoyed at Alistair's heartlessness and selfishness. He looked at life and women entirely from his own convenience. Surely Verity Howard deserved better of him. She would welcome her here and keep an eye on her, shield her from Alistair's callousness. Ariel remembered when she, too, was thrown upon a cruel uncaring world, and she felt she had a debt to pay for her own happiness when so many others were suffering.

"Bring her here, Alistair. I would call upon her but I cannot leave Ian until his fever breaks," she continued, reminding him of where her duty and inclination lay.

"Thank you, Ariel. You are a real Trojan, and give Ian my best. I am so glad his wound is not more serious. He's a survivor, I guess, as I am," he concluded, somewhat ashamed under Ariel's reproof, and not wanting to incur her further disapproval.

Ariel sighed as he left her, waiting a moment before she returned to the sick room. Although her sentiments and thoughts were concentrated on her husband, she spared some time to think of the bereft girl whose only refuge was Alistair, and a chancy one at that. Of a warm-hearted and caring temperament

125

herself, Ariel had been tried by tragic events and loneliness. She yearned to offer Alistair the peace and stability she had found after a hard struggle but he made it difficult. Whatever had turned him into such a cynic and libertine was shrouded in his past, and no matter how recklessly he behaved he seemed not to count the results of his folly or prepare to change his attitude. But this girl would not be the sufferer. His charm would not put her at risk, Ariel would see to that, she vowed.

Alistair, more disturbed than he wanted to admit, by Ariel's warnings and reproof, hurried off to accomplish his distasteful task, wanting only to settle the business, although he had little faith in himself as a comforter. Charley had told him some time earlier of his direction, and as he walked slowly toward the street which housed Verity, he tried to marshal his thoughts, to find the words to tell her of her brother's death. He dreaded the recriminations and tears which would await him. For the first time in his life he was faced with a situation in which a gay quip or a careless jest would not serve, and the streets through which he walked, filled with the results of the recent battle, did nothing to improve his mood.

After a frightening and exhausting day, Verity had returned to the rooms she shared with Charley. She needed to confide her fears to Agnes, her only solace. Madame Blancheur had been no help—practical and unwilling to become involved, she had offered no comfort, absenting herself in her household duties. As the hours sped by, Verity felt an overwhelming sense of doom. Watching the scores of mutilated and dying soldiers streaming into Brussels aboard bloody carts, Verity had waited with ever increasing anxiety, searching every vehicle for her brother. Surely if he were unharmed, he would have returned by now. She had met no member of the Life Guards, and heard only appalling rumors of the charge at La Haye. She could only pray and wait. Her lovely sad eyes filled when she thought back to those last hours at the Richmond ball, to Charley's confidence and exhilaration, his conviction he was sharing a glorious adventure. But he had had no idea of what awaited him on that fearful battlefield. When Madame Blancheur announced that Verity had a caller, she knew she must steel herself for the worst news. Summoning all her composure she went down into the parlor to find Major Glendenning standing by the fireplace, and one look at his grave face confirmed her fears.

"You've come to tell me about Charley, haven't you, Major?" she asked without even greeting him, the only idea in her mind that she must know immediately what had happened to her brother.

"I am sorry, Miss Howard. I could not save him. He died bravely in that last frightful charge. All was confusion and horror and I did not see him fall, but I returned to be with him at the last. His final thoughts were of you," Alistair said diffidently. God, this was more dreadful than he had expected. Watching the girl trying to summon the courage to cope with this news. Her tears fell unheeded down her cheeks. She turned from him when he would have extended his arms for comfort, and she walked to the window, trying to grasp the tragedy. He waited, not knowing what to do.

Finally mastering her emotions, knuckling the tears from her pale cheeks, she kept her face hidden, but said softly, "He was so eager for battle, so anxious to acquit himself well. He did not understand the danger, the horror. Oh, God, if only he had not left Devon."

Uncomfortably aware that he was doing little to relieve her pain, and feeling his responsibility, Alistair tried to muster some words of comfort. "He did that and more. At Quatre Bras he saved my life, shot a French trooper who came out of nowhere. I wish he hadn't. So many better men than I fell, but I escaped, as usual, unscathed. Only the good die young, they tell us. But I was rather it was me, you must believe it. My life is not worth a farthing, and his promised so well," he said diffidently but sincerely. "It was a tremendous victory, but bought at a terrible price. I doubt if we would have won without the Duke, although it was not his finest hour," he explained, a traitorous opinion which he blurted out in mitigation. But what could he say to make the death of her brother seem acceptable? He looked at her with compassion and a certain admiration which only increased his own inadequacy. He was not the man for such a mission.

She turned then, and he met her questioning, fearful stare. "Did he suffer, Major?" she asked, clasping her hands tightly together, willing herself to accept the horror he might inflict.

"No, no. You must not dwell on that. It was mercifully quick, a ball through his chest," Alistair reassured her then cursed himself as she tried to restrain a shudder.

"You were kind to come and tell me. It has been such a long anxious day, with so many horrible experiences. I have been at the hospital, and I saw—" She broke off, remembering the wounded she had tended.

"You should not have seen such sights," Alistair protested, realizing that her imagination must be calling up frightful pictures. "I wish I was not the bearer of such news," he concluded. Then as if he could not restrain himself: "I should have been more aware, kept my eye on him," he broke off in some confusion, but his own guilt was a heavy burden. What a little soldier she was, standing there in her light blue frock so valiant, so determined not to give away to hysteria. He had not realized how lovely she was at their previous meetings. He had noticed only her youth, but looking now at her pale face and lustrous hazel eyes, he wondered why she had accompanied her brother. Surely there must be a man back in Devon who could have protected her from the sorrow and grim reality of war. She badly needed protection and, he reminded himself, he was here to give it, although he did not quite know how to present his offer.

She smiled bravely, as if sensing his uneasiness at this scene. "I am glad you came through safely, Major, and I thank you for coming to tell me about Charley. Is he still lying somewhere on that ghastly field or . . ." She hesitated to voice her question.

"No, no, you must not think I would abandon him. I brought him in to the hospital near Ste. Gudule. He will have a proper military burial. I will see to all that. Do not concern yourself with such a melancholy task now. I promised Charley I would—" He broke off suddenly, uncertain how to put his decision, and she looked at him in some wonderment.

In the fraught silence which followed his last words, Verity waited, puzzled by the major's diffidence. Surely he had done all he could. Smiling a bit tentatively, she crossed to him and gazed sorrowfully up into his clear blue eyes. "You must not worry about me, Major. I will manage some-how."

"I promised Charley to look out for you," he repeated stubbornly, as if by reiterating that vow he could somehow relieve himself of a hideous responsibility. Then, knowing he must broach the uncomfortable news Charley had given him, the fears he had had for his sister's future, he rushed into unconsidered speech. "Charley felt you must not go home to your family, your natural refuge in such circumstances. He told me—" He broke off again, aware that she was looking at him in shock and dismay.

"He told you about our stepfather. He had no right . . ." she protested, twisting her hands in humiliation and reddening under his stare.

Whatever had driven her to accompany Charley to Brussels was obviously important. Could she have been seduced by her stepfather? Did she love him, feel an unnatural passion for the man? Alistair's experience had led him to believe that most women could be persuaded if their blood was hot enough. Why should she be any different? She might appear to be chaste and respectable, but women were deceivers ever. "Have you no one to whom you can turn, no man who wants to marry you?" he asked, determined to reach a decision which would absolve him from becoming involved in a situation he felt beyond him.

Verity blushed and trembled, recalling the reason for her flight to Brussels. "There is a man, a childhood friend, but I do not feel that way about him, as a wife should feel. My stepfather—" She broke off, unwilling to confide that disgusting tale to this hard man. Then, watching his immobile waiting face, she stammered on, "When Charley came home on that last leave he realized that Sir Anthony

131

entertained lustful feelings toward me. He caught him trying to force his attentions on me," she explained, thoroughly embarrassed, but realizing she must make the matter clear.

"Surely marriage to your childhood sweetheart would solve that problem. And it might be best. Any husband is better than being alone in such a perilous position," Alistair advised, suddenly wondering why the thought of this girl in the bed of some aging rogue or some callor youth was so abhorrent to him.

"Denis has proposed, but there are problems besides my own reluctance. His mother does not approve, and he is still a minor, with no money of his own," Verity explained wondering at her artlessness in confiding in this man who appeared so unreceptive, so suspicious, so anxious to push her off onto a husband.

"Do you care at all for him?" Alistair asked bluntly, unable to help himself. Did she love this cub or feel some attraction for her lecherous stepfather despite her protests?

Hating these confidences, Verity wanted only to remove herself from his appraising eye. "Not that way, and I will not use him for a convenience, to relieve my problem. I want to marry a man I love," she explained, her sincerity apparent but not reaching Alistair, who had always denied the depths of that kind of affection.

"Love! You girls are so unrealistic. People in our circumstances rarely marry for love. Comfort, shared interests, property, heirs, those are the basis for a proper alliance," Alistair said severely. "And, of course, marriage is not for everyone, although for women it's different. And in your case I should say a necessity," he argued, annoyed at her fantasies. "I thought you were more sensible than that," he finished, feeling a recurrence of guilt at badgering her while she was trying to cope with Charley's death. But really the girl was lacking sense. What was the purpose of all this romantic silliness when she must learn to cope with life as she found it? Marriage was the answer and she had better procure a husband immediately. Somehow this sensible decision did not fill Alistair with any pleasure, although it would certainly absolve his own responsibility.

"Well, my future marriage hardly concerns you, Major. I am grateful for your concern but I will manage, I am sure," Verity answered repressively, repelled by his callous analysis of her options. He certainly was a cynical, bitter man with little sensibility, discussing these matters with her at such a time. He should be aware that her loss of Charley was all that mattered now, that and having to relay the message to her poor mother who needed her support. But how could she go home?

"Well, your immediate problem is to leave here. You cannot stay alone in these rooms." Alistair tried to marshal the practicalities and recall her to her disadvantageous position. Had she no knowledge

133

of the proprieties? Even in the aftermath of this tragedy she must take care or her reputation would be irretreivably lost, and he owed Charley some attempt to bring her around to seeing her duty.

He crossed the room to her and took her by the hands. "Listen, Verity, I know you neither like nor trust me and we have been thrown together by Charley's untimely death, but you must promise me to be sensible. Lady Montague, whom you met at the Richmond Ball and who has taken quite a fancy to you, would be a very proper chaperone for you until you recover from all this. I still think you should prevail on your childhood friend to rescue you. Even chaperoned here in Brussels you are in danger of becoming embroiled in some situation which might damage you." Alistair realized with some chagrin that he was sounding like an aging uncle, outlining the rules of proper society. Certainly he was not following his natural inclinations, which were to take her in his arms, soothe her troubles, and win her gratitude and affection, which might lead into all sorts of perilous if delightful situations. What was it about this girl that engaged him so, her uncommon type from the usual females he pursued, or her obduracy in taking his advice?

"Thank Lady Montague for her invitation. I will certainly consider it, and I am grateful to you, Major, for your interest. Now I must try to write to Mother and inform her of Charley's death, which will completely undo her. I know I should go home, but I must contrive some other answer. I cannot face my stepfather. You have been most kind and I will willingly take advantage of your offer to arrange Charley's"—she gulped, tears rising again— "Charley's funeral."

Relieved he could return to practical matters, Alistair reassured her that he would take care of all that and escort her to the obsequies. Still, he was left with a feeling of dissatisfaction and the knowledge she still did not like or trust him, but why should that bother him so? The last thing he wanted was a wailing, helpless female of tender years hanging about making untoward demands upon him. But he did not want to surrender her to her childhood sweetheart or some less eligible prospect who would coerce her into foolish behavior, like that Russian for example. She was much too appealing, too vulnerable, and might be influenced by some libertine into an irremediable course.

Craving sympathy and affection who knew whom she might respond to, and he admitted cynically, if that was her decision, he would prefer to find her in his own bed. That possibility seemed increasingly remote considering how she viewed him. Disappointing, but there were other lovelies to be consoled. Cursing his nature, Alistair made one more effort to restrain his inclinations to risk all and take her off to his quarters and relieve his own frustrations. But that would not do. He had promised Charley, and he owed him his own worthless life.

"I will return tomorrow to escort you to Lady Montague's. You can be of great assistance to her while she nurses her husband, who suffered a slight wound. That will distract you. But he will recover with care and attention, which Ariel will lovingly provide. She's a wonderful woman and can be of great support to you if you abide by her advice." Much to his own irritation, he couldn't seem to stop himself from prosing on.

"Thank you for honoring your promise to Charley, Major. I only hope this has not kept you from more important affairs. I will say good-bye now. My maid will be waiting for me, and my packing and letters," Verity said dismissively, knowing she was being churlish but wanting only to get away from this austere disapproving man who viewed her as a taxing obligation. She signaled the interview was at an end, and Alistair had no recourse but to remove his unwelcome presence.

As he strolled back to his rooms, he wondered at his unusual reaction to this disturbing girl, quite unlike the vapid misses he had met in London's fashionable drawing rooms. There was some quality about the chit which disturbed him. She had accepted her brother's death with courage and fortitude, but there was more to this stepfather affair than she admitted, and her reaction to his kisses at the ball lingered despite his effort to dismiss it. Normally, if she had been a different type, he would indeed have taken her back to his rooms and made love to her, kept her under his protection until he tired of her. What a coil, and damn Charley, poor desperate lad, for putting this burden on him. Disgusted with his feelings, Alistair settled into his quarters and broached a bottle, weary and disillusioned by his life and the thoughts of the future.

Chapter Nine

As she lay in bed that evening wakeful and
exhausted from the impact of Charley's death, and
from having composed the difficult letter to her
mother, Verity was not thinking of her own
situation, but of her brother. She spared little
thought for Alistair, who had brought her the tragic
news, but beneath her overriding sorrow lay an
unjustified anger that he had not somehow saved her
brother. Her mind throbbed with memories of
Charley. He had always been the most important
man in her life, leaving little room for other
companions, even Denis.

All the small joys and sorrows of their shared
childhood rose up to haunt her. The day that
Charley had rescued her from Farmer Anderson's
bull, plucking her from the path of the maddened
animal and scolding her in his fright for venturing
into the forbidden field to gather wildflowers. Then

there was the occasion when a pugnacious fourteen-year-old Charley had fought the village lout who had teased her, earning a black eye, and his mother's lamentations, which in no way detracted from his satisfaction in emerging from the tussle, bloody but triumphant. Then there had been the holidays when he returned from Eton, condescending in his new grandeur, but still affectionate, willing to allow her his company on long rides about the countryside and even to invite her fishing.

Often she had been the leader in their escapades but when they came to grief, he had shielded her and taken the punishment. And always he had been ready to spare hours to listen to her confidences and problems. He had realized that their mother preferred him, but this had never spoiled their relationship. He had been a splendid brother, and in this last, most troubling crisis, had come to her aid yet again, routing Sir Anthony and escorting her to Brussels.

He could not have wanted her, a constant responsibility, in this last great adventure of his life. How magnificent and carefree he had looked in the uniform he wore with such pride, and how eagerly he had gone to meet his death, caught up in all the stirring adventurous life which the military represented and never heeding the danger, the possibility his young life might be sacrificed. She could not imagine life without Charley, without his love and companionship as a bulwark between her and the troubles which had so recently darkened her womanhood. They had always been so close, never jealous or quarrelsome like so many brothers and sisters. And in his last moments his only thought had been for her, insisting on enlisting his major in the problem of her welfare.

What had caused her to listen so tamely to that man's obvious disapproval of her, his assumption he knew best how she should go on? Whatever the strange influence he exerted over her she must not surrender to it. He had no deep feelings, no real interest in her, just this burden of obligation. She acquitted him of the basest feelings under the impetus of his debt to Charley. But she sensed his disapproval of her, his judgment that she was a flirt, no better than she should be, a silly girl with even sillier delusions about the world. And he was a proven rake, a despoiler of women who used them for his own gratification. Look at how he responded to this poor woman in London who had risked all for his love, and then been spurned. She could never respect and admire such a man and whatever carnal feelings she felt toward him were only the result of the unusual aura surrounding the recent battle. He had kissed her on a whim, and then accused her of enticing him. Not the action of a man one could trust or admire. She had refused Denis because she could not offer him an abiding love; surely she was not so light-minded to be attracted to a man just because he aroused some tumultuous passion in her, which was

141

simply a physical reaction, impelled by the danger and heightened emotion of battle, the strangeness of Brussels.

No, the less she depended on Alistair Glendenning, the better she would be. There must be some resolution to her current dilemma, and perhaps Lady Montague, whose good sense and kindliness she trusted, could help her some to a decision. But how she missed Charley and mourned the loss of his presence, the thought she would never hear or see him bounding up these very stairs enthusiastically engaging her in some exciting adventure. Her poor brother. So carefree, so young, and now lost forever.

The following day Verity awoke to a numbness, an unreality, still unable to face her tragedy, but Agnes, happy to have some chore to perform, chivied her into packing, signifying her approval that Verity would soon be under the care of respectable people. She thoroughly approved of the move to the Montagues and, when Alistair arrived to escort them to their new home, viewed him with wary approval. He was wise enough to enlist her support and treated her with a dignity which completely won her confidence.

Although Agnes had been surprised that Verity's first instinct was not to return to Devon, she suspected there was a reason for her decision. She had not been unaware of the tensions in that household, the appraising looks of Sir Anthony, and having a deep-seated scorn for the lecherous, selfish intentions of men intent on satisfying their desires, had worried about her nursling. She found the Montague establishment much more to her taste than Madame Blancheur's rather come-by-chance rooms, and wanted Verity under the roof of a proper chaperone. Verity conceded that Agnes was a veritable dragon in guarding her and was full of ideas as to how she could go on.

Lady Montague's first instincts about Verity had been confirmed by the girl's manner after she joined the household. At first she had taken some heed of Alistair's inferences that Verity might in truth be a grasping creature, taking advantage of a distressing situation to further her own ends, to make a profitable alliance, and to use the Montagues as a springboard for advancement, but instead she found a fragile, tragic girl, vulnerable, well bred, well mannered, and grateful for her support. Underneath the sorrowing character she sensed an appealing young woman, not only lovely to look at, but with some inner core of strength which would guide her through this difficult time in her young life. Ariel had never forgotten what it was to be friendless and unloved, misunderstood by those who should have stood by her, betrayed by her own cousin in marriage. She was ready to make every allowance, and that included protecting the girl from Alistair, whom she seemed to have taken in some dislike. Wise, perhaps, that she had not been beguiled or deceived by his charm, and that showed her good sense, Ariel decided not without regret, but she had long learned to regard Alistair with some suspicion where women were concerned, no matter how much she held him in affection.

Her impressions were reinforced by Ian, who early took to Verity, finding her presence in the sick room soothing and distracting him from his boredom and pain. At first Verity had found the redoubtable Lord Montague quite overpowering but they soon became friends during the hours Verity helped with his nursing. Despite his impatience and irritability at his confinement, he had won her admiration by his devotion to his wife, and his stoical acceptance of his convalescence, as well as his sincere sympathy toward her own loss.

As he improved, she came to rely on his clear-sighted views and stringent opinions of the foolishness of generals and politicians. She quite enjoyed the hours spent in his chamber reading or playing chess, and responded shyly to his gentle teasing and brotherly interest in her welfare.

But Ian was not insensitive. He recognized her wariness with Alistair, and understood how she hated being under obligation to him. Knowing his insouciant friend so well he was surprised by that officer's sense of responsibility, the efficient way he had coped with Charley's funeral, a grim unreal ceremony which left Verity empty and bereft, watching her brother's coffin lowered into this alien

144

ground where so many of his comrades lay, far from the familiar green fields of Devon.

She spent many hours brooding over the grave, but that was to be expected and Ian respected her mourning. Alistair just became irritated by her preoccupation and also piqued by her attempts to avoid him. Did she still blame him for Charley's death? Perhaps, but time must banish that specter, although he still carried his own guilt for the tragedy.

As the days passed, the relationship between the two widened rather than closed, and soon Ariel made an attempt to draw Verity into some of the soberer entertainments of Brussels. Many of the English had abandoned the city and most of the serving officers and their wives had left Brussels for Paris at Wellington's request, to settle into the army of occupation.

Verity had received a pitiful, incoherent letter from her mother requesting her immediate presence, and Denis had sent his condolences and a suggestion she reconsider his proposal. He believed he had talked his mother into assenting since he refused to offer for the Sedgewick girl. Verity wrote back, putting them both off, for she would not return to Devon and expose herself to Sir Anthony. She had been appalled at her mother's suggestion that he come to escort her home, and in her terror at the idea, she had been forced to confide in Ariel, not the whole story but her plans for avoiding this prospect.

"I was hoping, dear Lady Montague, that you might help me secure a position, as a companion or governess, so that when you leave in a few weeks I will be well established," she asked somewhat timidly when Ariel asked her about her plans.

Ariel, who had been disappointed that relations between Alistair and Verity had deteriorated rather than improved during the period, was surprised. Naturally she had hoped for a happier outcome, believing that the bond of Charley's loss might have brought them together in a most satisfactory way. Both the Montagues had realized that Waterloo had affected some change in their friend, whose reckless disregard of convention, his inability to think for tomorrow, and his habit of banishing care by indulging in drink and wenching seemed to have diminished. But his attitude toward marriage or commitment had not altered, and his suspicions of Verity had increased. He noticed that often when he called now she was out riding with some of Charley's fellow officers, who had appeared as a duty but remained to be charmed by this unusual addition to the Montague household. Ariel had encouraged these outings despite Alistair's disapproval. The conventions of death, the funeral weeds and black gloves, were not so evident in Brussels as they would have been in the more rigid London society, and a little distraction, the obvious approval of respectable young men, would be consoling to Verity, she felt. It could not do Alistair any harm to see that the girl behaved very prettily too.

Chief among the claimants for Verity's company was the gallant Russian, Prince Vasilii Petrov Chirnovsky. He was a man few women could resist with his sophisticated manners and distinguishing attentions. He sent Verity flowers, took her riding, and appeared to be completely charmed by the girl. He made due obeisance to Lady Montague, too. Ariel wondered what his real intentions were. She doubted they included an honorable offer and warned Verity of her suspicions.

Ariel broached the matter tentatively, disliking to worry Verity when she was going through such an upsetting period in her life. "Verity, I would not for the world add to your burdens at this trying time, but I would be failing in my duty if I did not talk to you about Prince Chirnovsky. I know he has been quite attentive, and his manner most unexceptional, but Ian and I feel he is not to be trusted." Ariel sensed the girl had much more on her mind than she had confided, and she admired her for coping with her problems so resolutely, much as she wanted to ease her mind. Ariel herself had learned to keep her own confidences and respected that ability in others.

Verity was a trifle surprised. "But the Prince has never evidenced any but the most proper interest in me. He has been most considerate and supportive," she objected, wondering why she should take exception to Ariel's remarks. She believed her hostess would have preferred her to rely on Alistair, but her reaction to that gentleman had hardened over the past week rather than softened. Unlike the Prince, he seemed critical and questioning of her, as if expecting her to commit some outrageous faux pas. "Actually," Verity went on, eager to explain to Ariel her reasons for relying on the Prince. "He has offered to help me find some respectable employment so that I will not have to return to Devon. I am most reluctant to return home, as you know, because of my dislike and fear of my stepfather," she said candidly, hoping this would reassure Ariel without going into sordid detail.

"But what kind of employment could he secure that would be acceptable, Verity?" Ariel asked, frowning. She did not like the sound of this and Verity seemed much too eager to embrace the Prince's plan. Could she be learning to care for him? That way lay trouble, she sensed.

"The Prince has an elderly aunt in Paris who needs a companion, and he thinks that we might suit. It would answer, I am sure. After all, Ariel, kind as you have been, you cannot want to keep me indefinitely and I understand that Ian has resigned his commission to return home to manage his estates, and I know you will want your baby to be born in England. You cannot delay your departure much longer. I am just an added burden to you now. Not that I am not grateful for your care of me during this tragic time," Verity told her hostess, intent on impressing her with her gratitude but unwavering in

148

her determination not to spinelessly drift at the mercy of other people's whims.

"You know we have loved having you, and both Ian and I have grown very fond of you, Verity. I just want to be sure your future is settled before we leave. I cannot abandon you. I would like you to come back to England with us, if that would please you," Ariel suggested, hoping this would settle the matter of the Prince. She rather doubted the existence of this aunt. Then turning and taking the girl's hands in hers, she said warmly, "Can you not return to your home? I know your stepfather represents a threat, but surely your mother might shield you. I cannot believe the man is such a monster that he would force himself upon you."

Verity sighed. Why would no one believe Sir Anthony was the lecherous conceited man she knew him to be? Only Charley, who had seen with his own eyes, had realized the gravity of her situation. And just today she had received notice that Sir Anthony was en route to escort her home. She must be gone before he arrived.

"Please believe me, Ariel, that I cannot go home. And Sir Anthony is already traveling to Brussels. I must be gone before he arrives," she insisted, twisting her hands nervously and repressing a shudder which Ariel had to accept as a token of her real fear.

"It's abominable that women must submit to men's domination," Ariel declared. "You do not have to obey Sir Anthony. And I understand the manor has been left to you and your solicitor might protect you."

"He cannot protect me from Sir Anthony in my own home," Verity said sharply. "I cannot live under those conditions. And then there is my mother. I am not heartless. If she discovered Sir Anthony's intentions it would destroy her, and with the pain of Charley's death it would be more than she could stand. It's a terrible coil, but if I can go to Paris with gainful employment I can postpone the reckoning, and perhaps Sir Anthony will tire of the idea, find some more willing lady to grace his bed." She knew Ariel wanted to help, but she must direct her own life. This temporary respite had given her strength to decide matters and she would not surrender to the easiest path.

"Well, Alistair will have something to say about all this, I am sure," Ariel blurted out, then realized that perhaps her suggestion was not the most tactful. For some reason Verity resented any attempt by Alistair to aid her, and rebuffed any attempt on the Montagues' part to bring them into charity with one another.

"I am grateful to Alistair for arranging Charley's funeral and for sending me to you, but I can contrive without his arrogant assumption that he knows best for me," Verity said firmly. She would not allow that man to dictate her future. His opinion of her was insulting and wrong-headed and she did not like his implied view that she was a wanton, encouraging men to make love to her. The sooner she saw the last of him, the better. She tried to ignore the thought that by responding to his kisses at the Richmond Ball she had given every evidence to support his suspicions.

Perforce Ariel had to leave the matter there, but she decided that she would ask Ian to speak to the Prince about this opportune aunt, whose presence she doubted. And she made Verity promise not to commit herself before discussing it again with her.

The Montagues would be leaving Brussels within the fortnight, so Verity must complete her plans forthwith. And she would not apprise Alistair of her decision. Whatever debt he owed to Charley he had paid. Despite reason, she knew she not only resented his opinion of her but still felt a vague sense that somehow he could have saved her brother, a totally unfair opinion, she knew, but one she could not banish. It did not lead her to think on Alistair with any kindness, and she continued to avoid him.

Alistair himself could not banish his confused ideas about Verity, nor dispell the memory of her abandoned response to him at the Richmond Ball, much as he would have liked to forget all about it. He was not unaware of her diversionary tactics, her attempts to ostracize him, not always successful as he was a frequent guest at the Montagues. His own feelings toward the girl were a mixture of responsibility, sympathy for her plight, irritation that she could weigh so heavily on his mind, and an unwilling attraction. He wanted her in his bed, but he could not follow that inclination under the present conditions, especially considering his oath to Charley.

He did not believe her story about Sir Anthony, and he suspected her association with the Russian. Ariel did not confide in him about Verity's plan to take up employment with the Prince's aunt, but he suspected the chit had some plan to elude him and go her own way. Stubborn little fool. She had no idea of the perils that awaited her, but he would not be balked. He would have it out with her before he left for Paris himself. The British Army was gathering in the French capital now that Napoleon had been apprehended and temporarily incarcerated on a brig, *Bellerophen,* in Torquay Harbor, where the populace rowed out to see him by the thousands, to watch him take his daily promenade. At first Napoleon was greeted with jeers and catcalls but after a while many of the English saw him as somewhat of a failed romantic hero and extended their sympathy while they awaited his future disposition.

By mid-July the battlefield at Waterloo had been abandoned to the looters and crows, and the attention of Europe, both the politicians and plain people, had focused on Paris. Verity, too, had turned her mind to that city, and packed her valise, prepared to ride under Prince Chirnovsky's escort to the French capital and the new life she hoped would relieve her of both Alistair and Sir Anthony. Both those gentlemen, having little idea of her situation, descended upon the Montagues within hours of each other to find Ariel and Ian in dismay. Their guest had fled.

Chapter Ten

"I do hope your aunt will not be incommoded by my sudden arrival, Prince," Verity said as the Russian's elaborate crested coach pulled away from the Montague house toward the Namur Gate and the outskirts of Brussels. She had certainly cast her cap over the windmill with a vengeance, leaving the Montagues stealthily, because she was convinced they were opposed to her taking up this position. And the Prince had been most insistent.

"Not at all, dear lady. She will be most welcoming. And I do not think your duties will be too onerous. You will enjoy Paris," Prince Vasilii responded suavely, eyeing Verity as she sat bolt upright in the corner of the carriage. The Prince, a skilled campaigner in affairs of the heart, had been surprised at his eagerness to secure Verity for himself and had laid his plans carefully. She certainly was well worth the effort, an innocent he believed, but with the potential for great passion. Those titian curls and that full lower lip promised well, and he had been quick to take advantage of her vulnerability. Prince Vasilii was a great favorite with the women, who admired his aristocratic hauteur, his tall striking bearing, and his wealth. In his uniform, which, unlike the British officers, he wore on every occasion, he cut quite a figure in the high polished boots and long graceful coat cut with an Eastern drape, the full scarlet sleeves, the gold and silver trimmings, and the quaint belt. He did not seem to take his military duties seriously although he told Verity all that would change when he joined the Tsar's regiments in Paris. Alexander was determined to take his share of the French spoils, and the Russians always enjoyed the luxuries and sophistication of the French capital.

Verity, not so naive as the Prince believed, was well aware that his interest in her was not one solely of friendship and a sincere desire to assist her in her dilemma, but she felt she could handle him, and this offer of respectable employment appeared to be genuine. As they bowled along the road toward Paris, she attempted to quiz him about his aunt but received very little information about that lady. Her nervousness increased as his bold dark eyes roamed over her in a way she had not noticed before.

In her efforts to elude both Sir Anthony and Alistair, Verity had been forced to abandon her abigail, Agnes, a necessity she now rued exceedingly. She could hardly bring her maid to her new position as a companion and Agnes yearned to return to Devon. Verity would not have made her escape from the Montague house so quickly or so secretly if she had not received yet another hysterical letter from her mother warning her that Sir Anthony would be in Brussels within the next few days to escort her home to her grieving mother who needed her so badly.

The Prince, not unaware that Verity had some mysterious reason for not wanting to seek the natural solace of her home, had hastened to take advantage of her position. He had been quite taken aback by Ian's interest in this mythical employment the Prince had offered Verity, but had managed to brush through the interview with Lord Montague in a commendable fashion. Ian had not been convinced, but fond as he was of Verity, and as willing as Ariel to have her accompany them to England, was preoccupied with settling his own affairs in Brussels, resigning his commission, and planning to take up his estate duties, impelled to speed up arrangements because of his father, the Earl's, failing health. He was also worried about Ariel and the impending birth of the baby and wanted to travel before the journey became too arduous for her. Still he had doubts, not trusting the Russian, and well aware that many men would be tempted by Verity's unusual beauty and quality to make unwelcome advances toward her. He did not believe for one moment that Verity would succumb willingly to the Prince's advances but he knew she yearned for a refuge, and might even have hoped the Prince would offer marriage. Before he could question her on her motives, she had made her decision.

She took the opportunity to leave while the Montagues were lunching with Lord and Lady Sunderland, old friends who were also planning a Paris sojourn. Verity had sent Agnes on an errand to the milliner, and in her absence packed a few necessities, hoping the Montagues would forward her baggage to Paris when she had a direction to give them. She felt guilty and ashamed at repaying their hospitality in such a niggardly manner, for they had been more than kind to her, but she could not face Sir Anthony nor the arguments which would ensue. Also, she was not certain he could not force her to accompany him. He may have ensured legal control of her as she was still a minor. The whole prospect filled her with horror.

An added inducement to running away with the Prince was the absence of Alistair in Ghent on Army business. She knew he would prevent her from following such a course, and in a brutal way, which only strengthened her desire to thwart him. She would not allow him to control her life while he obviously disapproved of everything about her. So she had written a note to Agnes, and to the Montagues, and joined the Prince that afternoon on this dubious venture. As the miles lengthened between Brussels and their destination, her doubts surfaced again and again. But Verity, stubborn and determined to control her own destiny, would not show the craven no matter how uneasy she felt at her anomalous position in Prince Vasilii's company.

She had made her escape just hours ahead of Sir Anthony's arrival. Having settled into his hotel, he made post haste for the Montagues, smiling with anticipation at how events had fallen out to favor his seduction of Verity. She would have to accompany him home and enroute there would be plenty of opportunity for him to compel Verity into his bed. He had no doubts that once he had introduced her into the joys of his lovemaking she would prove both amenable and offer him a winter of delight. He had no qualms at all about what he planned, giving little thought to his wife, whose doting love he still encouraged although he was finding the role of devoted husband cloying in the extreme. He arrived at the Montague mansion, sleek and self-satisfied, only to find the household in an uproar.

Ariel and Ian greeted Sir Anthony with the news that Verity had left them. "This is most unfortunate, Sir Anthony," Ariel said. "Lord Montague and I were not aware that Verity had decided to take up this position as companion to Prince Chirnovsky's aunt. In fact, we had advised her against it." She eyed the girl's stepfather with inward distaste. He was not a type that appealed to her, but she showed none of her repugnance to his solitious overtures and fulsome compliments.

"Most ungrateful of the girl to run off in that ramshackle way, a nasty recompense for your kindnesses," Sir Anthony responded, taking the glass of Madeira that Ian offered him and rolling the wine smoothly in his mouth. "Well, I suppose I will just have to chase her up. She cannot be allowed to behave in such a disreputable fashion. What could she have been thinking of? I suppose her taste of high life here in Brussels made a return to staid Devon seem too tame by half." He leered in a man-of-the-world manner at Ian.

"I think you forget that Verity was in mourning for her brother," Ian said repressively, his hackles roused by this mountebank. "I would hardly say she racketed about Brussels behaving in a hoydenish way." No wonder Verity did not want to return to Devon, Ian thought. The man had a fishy eye, and if Ian did not know all of Verity's troubles in respect to Sir Anthony, he was enough of a judge of the world to have some idea of the man's proclivities. Ariel had hinted that the man's interest in his stepdaughter was more than fatherly, but he had not believed the situation was as serious as Verity had confided. In his bachelor days Ian had been a rake of some reputation, with an eye for an available woman and not averse to cuckolding dull husbands, but he had standards, and seducing virgins had not been included in his racy exploits. Still, he had no recourse but to invite the man to sit down and discuss what provisions they should make for finding Verity. But he was damned if he would invite the man to become his house guest, although it was obvious Sir Anthony was angling for an invitation.

Before the trio could resolve upon some suitable

action, Alistair strode unceremoniously into the drawing room, flanked by an agitated butler, who had been prevented from announcing him. Dismissing the major domo Ian turned to his friend, deciding that he must keep a firm grip upon events, or Ariel's drawing room would become the scene of a real turn-up. And he would not have his wife cast into a pucker.

"Well, here you are, Alistair," Ian said smoothly. "And just in time to meet Sir Anthony Maxwell, Verity's stepfather, who has fortuitously arrived from Devon." Ian introduced the two men, who bowed frigidly at one another.

"Where is Verity?" Alistair asked immediately, barely acknowledging the visitor and his hosts.

Ariel, seeing that all three men were within an ace of behaving recklessly, hurried into an explanation. "While you were in Ghent this past week, Alistair, Verity decided that she would accept a position as a companion to Prince Chirnovsky's aunt in Paris. She left rather suddenly this afternoon to take it up." She spoke calmly, hoping to minimize the effect of this news upon Alistair's temper. "Perhaps she discussed this with you?" she asked lamely.

"She did nothing of the sort, as you well know, Ariel. If she had, I would have seen to it that she changed her mind," Alistair answered, barely concealing his rage. Damn the girl. It was just as he had suspected. She had been lured into a liaison by that smooth Russian, deluded by his romantic posturings and his promise of jewels and a luxurious life. Well, she would pay a heavy price if she allowed herself to be supported by that character, and serve her right. He was tempted to wash his hands of her, but then his promise to Charley surfaced and he realized ruefully that he could not just stand aside and let that poor young man's sister enter upon a life of wanton disgrace.

"And what right do you have to interest yourself in Verity's affairs, Major Glendenning?" Sir Anthony interposed, confused by the indignation and the interference of this officer of whom he had never heard.

"The right of my promise to her brother as he was dying, a promise to see that she came to no harm," Alistair replied brusquely, not prepared to entertain any criticism from this man whose intentions he suspected were no more laudable than Prince Vasilii's. "Really, Ariel, why could you not exercise some control over the girl, who obviously hasn't the sense of a pea goose," he continued, turning on his friend, eager to blame someone beside himself for this disaster.

"I did advise her to think long and hard about this decision. I could hardly lock her in her room on bread and water, Alistair, until you had decided to take a hand in matters," Ariel said curtly, but knowing she shared some of the responsibility for this unhappy situation.

Ian, thoroughly aroused by any slur upon Ariel, and noticing that this tumultuous interview was taxing her, glared at his friend. "I will not have you

162

accuse Ariel of failing in her duties, Alistair. We were both good friends to Verity, and I must say your own attitude is churlish in the extreme. If you had exerted yourself to show a little sympathy and understanding to the girl in her sorrow she would not have been forced to rely on the company of Prince Chirnovsky, who for all we know entertains only the most honorable intentions toward her."

Alistair, realizing that Ian was in the right of it, smiled bitterly. "Ian, you have an annoying habit of being right, and I apologize if I unjustly accused Ariel of failing in her duty, but we are wasting time. We must retrieve the girl before real trouble develops, before there is a scandal. News of this elopement, as I suppose you will call it, will undoubtedly rebound throughout Brussels and Paris and then there will be no saving her reputation."

"I believe you can safely leave Verity's fate in my hands, Major. I am her natural protector," Sir Anthony interposed pompously, angry at being ignored and treated with contempt by this arrogant officer who seemed to have an inordinate interest in his prey.

Turning away from Sir Anthony in disgust, Alistair asked Ariel to call down Agnes, who might shed some light on events.

Upon the maid's entrance into the drawing room, Sir Anthony crossed to her and put a comforting arm about her shoulders. "Now, Agnes, you must help us rescue your mistress," he said. "She has foolishly embarked upon a perilous path, which will give great pain to Lady Maxwell and all her friends at home. You must help us."

Agnes, never impressed by Sir Anthony, and well aware of his activities among the village girls, sniffed, her eyes red-rimmed, and turned away from him. She spoke instead to Ariel.

"Milady, I know Miss Verity should not have left in such a shabby way, with no chaperone, but there is not an ounce of vice in the girl. She was just distraught and confused and thought that this might answer." Agnes twisted her hands, her eyes watering with tears.

"We know your first concern is for Miss Verity, Agnes. What we'd like to know is what she told you about her direction," Ariel said gently, hoping the men would not badger the poor woman and render her helpless and incoherent.

"She just said she was leaving to take up this post, and that I was to remain here as I could not accompany her, to return home with Sir Anthony when he arrived. And she thanked me prettily for my care of her." Agnes sniffled, her words muffled by her sobs.

"How long has she been gone?" Alistair asked the maid impatiently, coming to the root of the matter.

Agnes recoiled somewhat from the major's intimidating air but she was more apt to trust him than Sir Anthony, and she remembered how Charley had admired him. "Well, sir, it must have been soon after

164

lunch, for she sent me to the milliner's on an errand."

"It has just gone on four o'clock. I will try to ascertain from the butler when the coach arrived and in what direction it left the city. Someone will have seen it. That devilish man had a very vulgar equipage, all emblazoned with gold and trimmings. I will ride out now without any more delay, and when I catch up with that pair, Verity will have some explaining to do. Let us hope that is all she must reckon with," Alistair said, and bowing, strode from the room without waiting for any further discussion.

Sir Anthony sputtered to the closed door. "Now, just a minute. I must accompany the major. It is my duty," he protested, but it was obvious that he had been overwhelmed by a stronger will. He felt humiliated that he should have been treated in such a manner and before these obviously distinguished members of the ton. Sir Anthony had always prided himself on an ability to charm those members of the aristocracy with whom he came in contact, and it annoyed him that he had not appeared to advantage.

"Really, Lord and Lady Montague, I cannot think what you must believe of Verity, and such behavior. She has been properly reared, believe me. I do apologize for the chit, and she will be made to pay for her cavalier attitude," he blustered, eyeing his hosts cautiously. He must not antagonize them, although they had not seemed to welcome him very enthusiastically. He still hoped for that invitation. He wanted to be on the scene when Verity was returned repentant and ashamed. That situation could only rebound to his credit if he behaved well.

"I believe you must leave the rescue to Alistair, Sir Anthony. We will send word to your hotel when he has returned with her and then we will know how to go on," Ian said decisively. He had had quite enough of Sir Anthony, and although politeness insisted he should offer the man some refreshment, that was as far as he was prepared to go. Ariel, too, had endured enough. She looked pale, worried, and tired. He insisted that she seek her chamber and try to rest and compose herself. He would see Sir Anthony out. There was little that gentleman could do in the face of such obdurate intent on Ian's part and he reluctantly took his adieux, pleading with them to send him news immediately they had learned of Verity's whereabouts. He smiled speciously at the Montagues and left them, but once outside the door cursed roundly at the turn of events which had frustrated his fell designs. He might yet accomplish his aim but it would not be as simple as he had thought.

While Sir Anthony was grumpily tasting the amenities of a local café, trying to banish his lackluster performance in several bottles, Alistair had ridden to the Namur Gate to question the guards. He had not waited for his phaeton to be harnessed nor to pack any necessities, knowing that time was vital, and accustomed to hard riding, he expected to overtake the slower riding coach before nightfall. As he had anticipated, the Prince's equipage, of such a distinguishing appearance, had been seen by the guards some few hours previously making for the Mons road toward Paris. Fortunately the Prince's consequence demanded he journey with the full complement of outriders, making his progress quite notable.

Alistair galloped recklessly after his quarry down the road so recently the scene of hectic martial activity. Now all was quiet under the late afternoon sun, although there were still signs of the furious battle which had ended Napoleon's attempt to recapture power. As he raced along, Alistair's anger increased as he thought about Verity's rash unconsidered behavior in running off with Prince Vasilii. He had no doubts about what that rank libertine intended for the girl. She must be either a vulnerable little fool or a blatant wanton to succumb to such an obvious seducer. Not for a moment did Alistair believe in the story about the aunt, nor did he think the Prince had honorable intentions toward Verity. He had meant all along to set her up as his mistress. Why this should annoy Alistair so he refused to consider. After all, he himself had not been above such ploys in the past, especially with women of Verity's stamp, of a passionate nature and a rare appeal which stirred any man's senses. No wonder Sir Anthony was so eager to have her back.

That aging rogue had undoubtedly already sampled the goods.

Alistair, if he had been in a condition to reason sensibly, might have wondered why he cared what happened to a girl who he believed had already submitted to one seducer, and now was willing to bed another for the advantages it offered. He refused to believe she had fallen genuinely in love with the Prince, although with his striking bearing, his Slavic mystery, and his vast wealth, the man had a seemingly irresistible charm where women were concerned.

Every mile that lengthened between Brussels and his victim spurred Alistair to further wrath, most of it inspired by frustration that he had not foreseen this eventuality nor taken means to prevent it. If the maddening chit had wanted a liaison, he would have been glad to oblige, even though he could not offer her the sumptuous life-style which the Prince had at his bestowal. Once he found her he would not only render a clanging peal over her for her heedless escape but he would see to it that she behaved herself.

The confusion of his thoughts, on the one hand wanting to punish the object of his chase and the other drag her into bed and make love to her until she was thoroughly cowed, did not seem to occur to him. He had done his best for her, deposited her in a safe respectable billet, denied his own inclinations to seduce her, and this was how she repaid him for honoring his promise to her brother, by running off with this varlet. Beneath his anger lay the knowledge that his amour propre was wounded, that she had found him so unacceptable, had rejected his kisses and scorned him as a man. This escapade had brought a crisis in their affairs and he would resolve it to his own pleasure whatever her objections, he decided as he spurred his horse to further efforts.

Chapter Eleven

Alistair caught up with the Prince's coach at the L'Auberge dans le Bois, just across the French border beyond Valenciennes, as dusk was drawing in. He had realized that the Prince would not stop in the town's main hostelry if his purpose was to elude any pursuers. Then, too, a respectable establishment might look askance at a Russian noble arriving with his chère amie, if that was what Verity had become. Somehow Alistair was convinced she hadn't yet taken the fatal step with the Prince but knew that this night would seal her fate. The L'Auberge dans le Bois appeared to be a coaching inn of some distinction if not of the first quality, and the Prince's equipage was too impressive to be overlooked when it entered the environs of Valenciennes. A surly Breton farmer had given Alistair its direction, cursing and complaining at the arrogance of the outriders, and only mollified by the guinea Alistair had tossed at him for the information.

At the inn, Alistair satisfied himself that the Prince's retainers were relaxing in the public saloon, and that he could hire a horse and carriage for the return journey to Brussels. The Prince had bespoken a private parlor and at Alistair's insistence the innkeeper had escorted him to its closed door in the upper story. The host informed him that the Prince had requested that he and his companion not be disturbed, the man rolling his eyes and smirking at the information, but quickly tempering his bawdy remarks when Alistair told him the girl was a minor and he might be party to prosecution.

Outside the door he took a deep breath, trying to control his temper which had risen to an almost uncontrollable level under the landlord's unpleasant insinuations. He assumed the icy control which signified his demeanor before a battle and tried the door. It was locked. Signifying that the landlord must request entrance, he restrained his impatience and curiosity as to what was going on behind the stout oak door.

"*Monseigneur, ouvrez la porte, s'il vous plaît. J'avais la vin vous demandez,*" the boniface called.

Silence, and no response came to the landlord's request. Alistair was tempted to force the door, but then he heard footsteps and the key turning gratingly in the lock. The Prince threw open the door and stepped back hastily as Alistair brushed by him to find Verity, white-faced, standing by the fireplace. He thought for a moment a shudder of relief passed over her as she saw him but she averted her head and stared into the fire.

"What is the meaning of this interruption, sirrah. This is a private parlor," the Prince exclaimed haughtily, eyeing the intruder with a menacing look.

"Much too private, Prince. I have come to restore this lady to her natural protectors. You have no business spiriting her away from Brussels in such a clandestine way," Alistair growled. His first inclination was to come to fisticuffs with the devil but he realized his position was not advantageous. The circumstances looked suspicious, but there was yet a faint possibility he might be wrong in his assessment of the Prince's designs.

"I am escorting Miss Howard to Paris to take up a position as companion to my aunt. I believe, Major, that you have made a grievous mistake with your untimely and rough intrusion. And I cannot see that this concerns you. You will take yourself off at once," sneered the Prince in his most arrogant tone, "or I will have my lackeys remove you."

"They can try, I suppose," Alistair replied coolly, walking into the room and closing the door in the landlord's avid face. He leaned negligently against the supper table, ignoring Verity entirely.

The Prince hesitated, aware that somehow Alistair had gained the advantage. "I resent your

173

interest in my affairs, and I am not accountable to you for my actions." He frowned haughtily.

"Certainly not, Prince. I would not dream of interfering in your pursuit of whatever other lady bird takes your fancy, but this one is not for you. You may not be aware that she is a minor, and I stand in loco parentis to the girl," Alistair said cheerfully, infuriating Verity with his sangfroid. Astounded at his appearance from out of nowhere, she had at first not known what to expect, but his blithe man-to-man acceptance of the Prince's plans shocked her into protest.

"How dare you imply that there is anything disreputable in this journey, Major. The Prince has behaved like a perfect gentleman, which is more than I can say for you, bursting in here like some avenging husband, which you are certainly not," Verity sputtered, completely overlooking her own trepidations of just a few moments earlier. The pair had just finished a light supper and Verity had become increasingly uncomfortable under the Prince's suggestive remarks and hot stares. When the landlord's knock had come she had been immensely relieved, seeing it as an excuse to make her escape, but she would never admit her doubts to Alistair. How dare he place her in this humiliating position, embarrassing her in front of the Prince, who had offered her a way out of her pressing difficulties. If it had been anyone but Alistair she would have fallen on their neck with relief and

174

confided her apprehensions, but his assumption that she was some demimondaine willing to entertain vile suggestions from a man of the Prince's stamp aroused all her resistance. She would not be delivered back to Brussels by Alistair like some troublesome parcel.

"My dear Verity, I think you protest too much. Somehow I had the notion you were quite relieved at my timely arrival," he riposted, eyeing her with that mocking light which always raised her hackles. But his mouth was drawn into a tight line, which those well acquainted with him knew signified he was barely leashing his formidable temper. Normally Alistair was inclined to allow humanity to commit its own foibles without undue interference or criticism from him. But from the beginning he had found Verity maddening, inexplicable, and passionately attractive. Her efforts to rebuff him, to go her own way, to reject his more than generous offers of assistance, had aroused his worse instincts, and now her obvious preference for the Prince's tainted protection rather than his own respectable friendship had made him lose all patience with the little fool. But none of his chagrin showed in his tightly controlled expression.

"I was not relieved, and you have no right to make odious suggestions about the Prince's actions," Verity responded hotly, determined not to be cowed. Her face flushed and the look in her eye would have quelled a less obstinate man.

175

"Enough of this nonsense, my girl. Do you realize how you've distressed the Montagues? Now where is your case? Dark is coming on and I want to get back to Brussels and my dinner. I see you have had yours, so there is no reason to delay our departure," he said silkily, turning his back on the Prince and crossing to Verity's side.

"I regret causing the Montagues any discomfort for they have been very kind to me," Verity responded, raising her chin and staring balefully at her tormentor, "but I am not returning to Brussels to await my stepfather, and I see no reason to prolong this distasteful interview."

The Prince, fuming in the background, now entered the lists. "I think you have your answer, Major. The lady does not require your championship and I find your presence completely unnecessary. I do not fight with inferiors, but in your case I am willing to make an exception. If you do not take yourself off immediately I shall be compelled to render you helpless," he insisted, drawing his sword from its scabbard in a menacing fashion.

Alistair laughed, the thought of dueling with the foppish Russian filling him with unholy glee. Actually, what he wanted was to shake the varlet by the neck and land a punishing blow on that smooth, patronizing face, but although that might satisfy his basest instincts, it would not serve. Grasping Verity by the arm, he pulled her toward the door. The Prince came after him, his sword extended, and

Verity suppressed a scream. She did not want blood to be shed, although she would willingly have scratched Alistair's eyes out herself.

"Prince Vasilii, please contain yourself! I am not worth all this trouble," she cried. She smiled winsomely at the Prince.

"What is your desire, *doushka?* If you want to return to Brussels, I will, of course, escort you, but I think you would be better served continuing our journey to Paris and my aunt's chaperonage," he said, at the same time sheathing his sword. Prince Vasilii was not a coward and had faced several men on the field of honor but he felt the tawdriness of this occasion, and much as he wanted to secure Verity as his mistress, he was much too indolent to pursue the matter if it would lead to scandal or embarrassment. He had a healthy respect for his Tsar's rules of behavior, and if it came to his monarch's ears that he had engaged in a vulgar brawl with an Allied officer in a country inn over the favors of a lightskirt, it would not go well with him.

"I doubt the Prince's aunt is a reality, Verity. You would be well served if you ended up in some bawdy house after this poseur tired of you, and that will indeed be your fate if you go on with this mad escapade. Or has the Prince asked you to become his Princess?" Alistair jeered.

The Prince frowned. Such a thought had never crossed his mind. Realizing that he had lost the game temporarily he wisely decided to retire to fight another day. The lady might still become available, and even if she did not, there were other more amenable victims awaiting him in Paris.

"Of course the choice is the lady's," he conceded smoothly, bowing ironically in Alistair's direction.

Verity hesitated. The Prince's reluctance to press his aunt's claims disturbed her. Could Alistair be right and the whole ploy was to lure her into a liaison, ruin her? Damn Alistair's suspicions and damn the Prince for placing her in such a coil.

"I suppose I had best return to the Montagues, since Alistair has been dispatched on this distasteful errand, no doubt at their bequest," she agreed reluctantly. "I will absolve you of the gross plan that he has suggested, Prince, and please present my apologies to your aunt if I have incommoded her in any way." Verity surrendered with as much dignity as she could. But she was mortified to see that the Prince looked at her cynically and did not press his claims.

"I have engaged a carriage and the sooner we quit this place, the better," Alistair said, drawing Verity forcefully out the door. He spared no further word or glance for the Prince. If he had, he would have seen that the Prince's expression was an evil calculating one. He had made a bad enemy.

Within minutes a sullen and silent Verity had been bundled into the hired carriage and Alistair whipped

178

up the pair of horses from the inn's courtyard, his own horse tethered behind the equipage. Verity, hunched as far as possible from her captor, willed herself not to scream with vexation at her pitiable surrender. Now she must face the Montagues on her return and try to explain to them why she had so rudely abandoned their care, rushing off with the Prince in that hurley-burley fashion. Her natural good manners were appalled at her repaying their kindness in such an outlandish fashion. But the events of the recent weeks, ever since that dreadful interview with Sir Anthony, had overset all her previous notions of behavior, of her own ability to control her life. Then Charley's death had compounded her confusion and added a weight of sorrow and loss which had become overwhelming. What she wanted was to retreat into some refuge where none of these problems could disturb her peace. But that seemed unlikely. She must simply steel herself not to fall into a welter of self-pity and helplessness.

She would contrive to sort out her life, and would not accept any assistance from Alistair. He had proved to be no gentleman, a cad and a libertine as bad as any Russian Prince or lecherous stepfather implying she was no better than a common doxy. Remembering Sir Anthony she shuddered. She still must cope with his arrival in Brussels when she returned to the Montagues. She would not discuss that eventuality with Alistair. She did not need his sneering comments on her relationship with her stepfather added to his opinion of her immoral dealings with the Prince to complete her humiliation. He would not get a word from her.

Alistair, now that his mission had passed off with relative inconvenience, shot a troubled look at Verity huddled in her misery. For a moment compassion welled within him. Perhaps the poor girl had been misled, really was the innocent she claimed. If so he had been devilishly harsh with her. But his jealous anger could not be so easily quieted. Still, they could not continue to travel along these cursed miles in silence. And he had not told her of what awaited her in Brussels.

"Come, Verity, stop sulking. Far better that I rescued you than your stepfather, who is awaiting you in Brussels. I had the utmost difficulty in preventing him from riding pell-mell to wrest you from the Prince's arms himself. No doubt, he was not willing to share, and found himself at point non plus when he heard the news. But never fear, you will be restored to him directly," he jeered, wondering why he allowed himself to mock her so when she was obviously undone. But he could not silence those doubts which insisted that she had succumbed once to that oily bastard and might do so again.

Verity almost gasped her shock at the news but would not give Alistair the satisfaction of a reaction. Her silence infuriated him, and by the time they reached the outskirts of the city, he was in a passion of fury and other quite unworthy desires. He owed her no compunction. He had rushed headlong to rescue her from a nasty situation, had earned nothing but scorn and retribution, had antagonized an Allied officer and aristocrat which could cause him trouble, missed his dinner, and ridden his horse to a standstill. All in all he should be the one aggrieved. And he was certain the chit had lied to him. The longer she remained silent, refused to thank him for his efforts, the more convinced he was that she had deceived him, had known all along about the Prince's intentions to install her as his mistress, a much more attractive proposition than falling into Sir Anthony's bed. She had probably come to Brussels with just such a plan in mind. After all, the Prince could offer her a great deal more than that aging roué or the prospect of wedding some gullible officer with nothing but his pay to spend upon her. No doubt that was why she viewed him so unfavorably. His guilt over Charley's death, his promise to the dead young man, his natural chivalry had drawn him into this coil. Well, she had mistaken her man. He would force her to admit her indecent stratagems, and then he would wash his hands of her. Having made this sensible decision did not abate his anger and a nagging sense that he had not come to the right conclusion, despite all the evidence, dogged him.

Verity, feeling ill-used and persecuted, remained silent although her thoughts were in turmoil. She could not go back to the Montagues and face Sir Anthony. Suspecting that Ariel's hospitable nature would insist she offer Sir Anthony accommodation, Verity feared the outcome of living under the same roof for even a few days with that lecher. Why wouldn't Alistair believe her? Because she had acted in a manner to confirm all his suspicions, she admitted ruefully. But she must have time to think of an alternative plan to returning to the Montagues. Before she confronted Sir Anthony she must have a scheme that would ensure her safety. Much as she hated to appeal to Alistair, she had no choice. Steeling herself to act the poor pitiful victim, she looked at him with nervous entreaty.

"Please, Alistair, do not take me back to the Montagues. I cannot face Sir Anthony. I know you doubt me, but if we could just talk over these misunderstandings, I am sure you would see my point of view and assist me," she pleaded, turning the full force of her warm hazel eyes upon her rescuer. If she had to use a normally scorned appeal, she would, much as it irritated her to pander to his belief that he had some guardianship over her.

Wondering what she was up to, still Alistair was not proof against the panic behind her words. Just what was her fear of Sir Anthony based on, he mused? And she needn't think she could work her wiles on him, although he felt his defenses weakening before the entreaty in her voice and eyes.

By the time the carriage had turned in the Namur Gate he had made up his mind to yield to her request, although he cursed his weak-mindedness. It would be all lies and evasions, he suspected, but he would listen to her in private. Perhaps he could make her see the peril which lay in her wanton ways, her manipulation of men for her own advantage. He smiled cynically. She had certainly embroiled him in her affairs to a disastrous degree. Well, he would listen to her explanations, but she would have a job convincing him of her innocence. He nodded his agreement, but made no promises. Within moments they had turned off the Hotel de Ville toward his rooms, and Verity, coming out of her abstraction, noticed that he had granted her request. He was going to listen to her at last.

She did not like the grim expression in his dark, set face, but reassured herself that at least he was willing to hear her out. She concentrated on marshaling her arguments.

"Thank you, Alistair," she responded meekly, determined not to stir him into another rage. They drew up before an unknown gray-fronted house on a back street beyond the main city square. Alistair whistled up a hostler to take charge of the horses and helped Verity down from the carriage, his expression far from encouraging.

"For Charley's sake I am prepared to listen to your story, but I warn you, spin me no Banbury tales, for I will not be convinced by a bit of fustian," he said as he escorted her into the house.

She nodded her acquiescence, but inwardly was seething at his arrogance, his belief that she was no better than she should be, an unchaste woman whose ambitions drove her to attract men for gain. He thought her a lightskirt. She must change his opinion or she would be forced back into Sir Anthony's company with hideous results.

"These are officers' quarters, and no one would be surprised to see a woman of your stamp visiting me here, but I believe most of the residents are at dinner and you will avoid discovery," he said insultingly as they climbed the stairs to the apartment. Verity made no response, for she realized her righteous demurs would not be accepted. She was not any happier at the knowing glance Alistair's batman gave her when he opened the door.

"If you will bring me some supper, Jenkins, and some wine, you can take yourself off. I am dashed hungry, but anything will do, some meat, bread, and cheese if that is all the larder will run to," Alistair ordered, shepherding Verity into the sitting room and indicating she should sit down.

No doubt the man was used to seeing women in Alistair's rooms, and considered her of that loose company, she decided, feeling besmirched. Well, she must accept that and more if she was to persuade Alistair to help her, much as it infuriated her that she had come to this pass. She thought briefly of the Prince. Had he really intended to install her as his mistress? She would cut off her tongue before she allowed Alistair to think she was grateful for his coming headlong to her rescue, or for the implication he had made about her flight. But she was wise enough to realize that it would not assist her purpose to antagonize him further.

Alistair, disgustedly poking the fire with one booted foot, wondered just what excuses he might hear. He would not be bamboozled by her soft airs and dulcet smiles. She was a charmer, no doubt about that, but she would not take him for a flat.

"We will save these explanations of yours until after I have eaten," he growled. Then remembering his manners, he asked, "Will you join me in a bit of supper?" as Jenkins returned with a loaded tray.

Verity smiled tremulously. "No, thank you. I have dined."

"Yes, I forgot, with the noble Prince," he sneered, and then ignoring her set to satisfying his appetite. Verity watched impatiently, dreading the interview but eager to have done with what he might ask. Only the thought of Sir Anthony's wet lips and roving hands enabled her to contain herself. She would not put herself in that man's power again no matter how much disbelief and sarcasm she had to endure from Alistair.

Finishing at last, Alistair poured himself another glass of claret and turned to the girl waiting quietly in the chair by the fire across from him. The food seemed to have calmed him somewhat but his expression was not encouraging.

"Will your man disturb us?" she asked timidly.

"Not if he values his place. No, Jenkins has taken himself off to the local tavern, and we are quite alone," Alistair promised, a nuance in his voice which did not lend her much comfort.

"I know you think it brazen of me to agree to accompany you to your rooms, but really, Alistair, I am desperate. I cannot meet Sir Anthony until I have made some decision about my future. He is really a most disagreeable person. I cannot think why mother married him," she offered, hoping to soften her interlocutor.

"No doubt he has a certain appeal . . . to some women," Alistair conceded, feeling his implacable determination softening under her obvious distress. She looked so vulnerable and innocent perched nervously on the edge of the chair.

"Not to me. He is a disgusting old man with nasty ideas and no compunction about trying to seduce me under my family roof," Verity said indignantly, forgetting her resolve to argue the merits of her case without emotion.

"You are not inexperienced at misleading men, I believe. And not averse to enjoying their attentions, as I have good reason to know," he reminded her tellingly, referring to the kisses they had exchanged at the Richmond ball. He looked at her suggestively.

"I found your caresses most appealing," he mocked, enjoying her discomfort. If she was innocent why had she responded to him, whom she professed to despise, so eagerly?

"You are no gentleman, sir, to remind me of my temporary lapse from propriety. The situation was exceptional," she argued, her blushes deepening. She was only too aware that she had behaved like a wanton on that night and could not explain her own reaction.

"By God, you are a stubborn wench," Alistair growled. She was an annoyingly alluring creature, sitting there so guileless and appealing to his baser senses. He was conscious of the privacy, the intimacy of their situation, her wistful mien. The desire which he had felt from their first meeting rose hotly in his veins.

"There is, of course, one indisputable way of discovering whether you are a stranger to a man's possession," he said, his tone thick with passion. Her appeals to his understanding were swamped by a far fiercer emotion, and Sir Anthony, the Montagues, even the memory of Charley's request to watch over her, faded beneath his overmastering desire for her.

Gripping her arms, he drew her to her feet. He threw off her shawl and untied her bonnet, casting it carelessly aside. Speechless, Verity shrank within his grasp, but his arms tightened and he would not be gainsaid.

"There is only one way to deal with a chit as unreasonable and reckless as you are, my dear," he muttered, and crushed her lips beneath his. His caresses were intimately passionate as his mouth roamed over her face and neck. For weeks this girl had driven him mad with her indifference, her scorn, her preference for the company of other men. He would no longer put up with her coy pretensions.

Verity, trying to struggle free from his drugging kisses, which had now turned to an insidious assault on her senses, could feel the warmth rising within her, weakening her determination to escape from the arms which held her so strongly. Fear rode hand in hand with a strange willingness to surrender although she loathed herself and him for her reaction to this unexpected embrace.

"You are hurting me," she gasped, although his hold had become less cruel, his lips more enticing. Why was she submitting to this insulting attack? But somehow her struggles weakened under his skilled lips as they roused in her undreamed-of reactions, and insidious warmth and a treacherous desire to find some elusive satisfaction which she could not understand.

"Stop struggling. You've wanted this from the first, and now you shall have it," he murmured. His eyes gleamed as her opposition faded, and her arms crept up around his neck, her lips now welcoming the intrusion of his. Triumphantly, he lifted her off her feet and carried her into the inner room, where he threw her on the bed. Coming to her senses, Verity tried to roll away from his insistent hands, but he easily pinioned her arms. He held her immobile on the counterpane, while he deftly undressed her.

"Don't do this . . . don't . . ." but the words were lost as his lips came down on hers, stifling her protests, while he continued to loosen her garments, exposing her white body to his avid gaze. She felt trapped by a lassitude which was gradually replaced by a mounting excitement, feelings which she had never experienced before. She knew she should fight this intimate violation but she was powerless beneath his searching hands and lips. She tried ineffectually to ward off his roving hands but he brushed her feeble attempts aside and looked at her tumbled hair which spread over the pillows in disarray.

"God, you are beautiful. I can't bear that any other man has seen you like this. But now you will be mine," he muttered, his face suffused with passion.

With his knees he forced apart her legs, his hand moving down her hips to caress her in shocking ways. The violence of his movements had now siftened to a seductive pleading and she was aware of a peculiar pressure building within her.

Suddenly he was entering her. At the sudden wrenching pain, she cried out in alarm. Cursing he

189

drew back in surprise, but then, despite himself, plunged on, ignoring her cries. As he moved coaxingly, the pain lessened and to her surprise she found herself responding to his movements.

When it was over, Verity lay panting beneath him, unconscious of the tears falling down her flushed cheeks. Shuddering with the release from the terrible tension which had gripped him, Alistair looked at her with horror, only now realizing the extent of what he had done. She turned her face away.

"Go away. Leave me alone," she pleaded, covered with shame and unwilling to meet his eyes.

Remorse darkened any satisfaction he might have experienced from the seduction. He realized she was in no state to hear his apologies, and after all, what could he offer now in mitigation for his offense. He had all but raped her. In the grip of his anger and desire he had been deaf to her strangled appeals for pity. Never had he resorted to committing such an outrage. How could he have been lost to all reason and humanity! She would regard him as a veritable monster, worse even than her hideous stepfather. And she had been innocent all along.

Rising wearily from the bed, Alistair looked at the defenseless girl, who had now passed into a healing sleep. She would never forgive him. He had done the unthinkable. Restoring his clothes to some semblance of order, he bent over and covered her with a light blanket, seeing her ravaged face, those enticing limbs abandoned in sleep. Oh, God, what had possessed him? Why had he behaved in that uncontrollable mad way? There was no excuse for him, and no reparation he could make. He stumbled into the sitting room, poured himself a generous tot of brandy, and threw it down in one gulp, trying to regain his senses. But the alcohol hit his stomach with a jolt that did nothing to ease his anguish. There was only one way that he could make amends. He had no recourse. He must marry her.

———— FREE ————
BOOK CERTIFICATE

ZEBRA HOME SUBSCRIPTION SERVICE, INC.

YES! Please start my subscription to Zebra Historical Romances and send me my free Zebra Novel along with my first month's Romances. I understand that I may preview these four new Zebra Historical Romances Free for 10 days. If I'm not satisfied with them I may return the four books within 10 days and owe nothing. Otherwise I will pay just $3.50 each, a total of $14.00 (a $15.80 value—I save $1.80). Then each month I will receive the 4 newest titles as soon as they come off the press for the same 10 day Free preview and low price. I may return any shipment and I may cancel this arrangement at any time. There is no minimum number of books to buy and there are no shipping, handling or postage charges. Regardless of what I do, the **FREE** book is mine to keep.

Name _____
(Please Print)

Address _____ Apt. # _____

City _____ State _____ Zip _____

Telephone (_____) _____

Signature _____
(if under 18, parent or guardian must sign)

Terms and offer subject to change without notice.

9-88

MAIL IN THE COUPON BELOW TODAY

To get your Free **ZEBRA HISTORICAL ROMANCE** fill out the coupon below and send it in today. As soon as we receive the coupon, we'll send your first month's books to preview Free for 10 days along with your **FREE NOVEL.**

GET
FREE
GIFT

ACCEPT YOUR FREE GIFT AND EXPERIENCE MORE OF THE PASSION AND ADVENTURE YOU LIKE IN A HISTORICAL ROMANCE

Zebra Romances are the finest novels of their kind and are written with the adult woman in mind. All of our books are written by authors who really know how to weave tales of romantic adventure in the historical settings you love.

Because our readers tell us these books sell out very fast in the stores, Zebra has made arrangements for you to receive at home the four newest titles published each month. You'll never miss a title and home delivery is so convenient. With your first shipment we'll even send you a **FREE** Zebra Historical Romance as our gift just for trying our home subscription service. No obligation.

BIG SAVINGS AND FREE HOME DELIVERY

Each month, the Zebra Home Subscription Service will send you the four newest titles as soon as they are published. (We ship these books to our subscribers even before we send them to the stores.) You may preview them *Free* for 10 days. If you like them as much as we think you will, you'll pay just $3.50 each and *save $1.80 each month* off the cover price. *AND you'll also get FREE HOME DELIVERY.* There is never a charge for shipping, handling or postage and there is no minimum you must buy. If you decide not to keep any shipment, simply return it within 10 days, no questions asked, and owe nothing.

Chapter Twelve

Alistair spent a miserable night, dipping deep into the brandy bottle which availed him little ease, and finally dropped off into a restless sleep in the armchair where he had settled to brood over his misdeeds. His man found him there in the morning and hurried to restore him with a bath, shave, clean clothes, and breakfast, all of which repaired the outer man, but did nothing for his black mood. He left Verity to sleep on, steeling himself for the encounter which could not be long postponed.

The sun was well up and the morning half gone when he finally braced himself to meet her. He knocked and entered the bedroom warily, girding himself for the hysterical reproaches and vituperation he knew he deserved, but shuddered to face. But, as usual, she surprised him. She was leaning against the pillows, the bed linen pulled to her chin to hide her dishabille, but her glorious hair spread carelessly around her created an enticing picture.

Burdened with contrition, Alistair found it difficult to meet her eyes, and to his dismay felt his desire for her rising again. She looked so vulnerable, so available, he wanted to take her in his arms, but knew in that way lay madness.

"Good morning, Verity. I hope you slept well," he said coolly, then damned himself for reminding her of the night which had passed.

She looked at him with loathing, but set her chin, not willing to give him the satisfaction of seeing her shame and embarrassment.

"Under the circumstances I passed a relatively calm night. I hope you are satisfied, Major, as to my chastity now. You proved it in the most brutal way possible," she replied sharply, noting with satisfaction that his own embarrassment equaled hers. A flush rose to his cheeks, and he refused to meet her eyes.

Taken aback by her acceptance of what had happened, he rushed into unconsidered speech, "Yes, well, I lost my temper. You goaded me, by running off with that damned Russian. But you could have stopped me," he offered in excuse, knowing nothing would have prevented him, in his red-hot rage, from bedding her. However, he was willing to pay the price for his transgression, no matter how reluctantly.

"So now, what happened is my fault!" Verity replied, feeling that she had him off-balance and pleased that she could cause him some of the malaise

194

she was suffering. "I did not require you to rush after me and what you did was worse than what you accused the Prince of planning." How like him to excuse his vile behavior by putting the blame on her. When she had awakened this morning, in this strange room, and been faced with the realization of what had occurred, her first reaction had been tears and disgust, but in the hours which had passed she had decided that lamentations would serve her little. She could not return to her virginal, innocent state of yesterday and she must deal with this blow life had dealt her the best she could. She did not dwell on her first reaction to Alistair's kisses, nor her instinctive response to him, which she must hide at all costs. She would pay him back for his treatment of her if it took her last breath. He had answered Charley's trust in him with the most heinous deed a man could inflict on a woman, although she doubted he viewed his possession of her in that light.

Alistair, although he knew her words were justified, felt his own anger rising. "Well, I am prepared to marry you, which was more than Prince Vasilii was willing to do, I warrant," he blurted out. That was not the way he had planned to offer the only honorable recompense for his cruelty.

"Well, I am not prepared to marry you. Do you think I want to be tied for life to a monstrous, uncaring devil, who has wed me for expediency to remove a burden of guilt, to which you are surely entitled," she returned, furious now that he thought he could wipe out the horrors of the night with a careless offer to make an honest woman of her.

"Whether you want to marry me or not is completely irrelevant," he replied bitterly. "I have compromised you beyond all hope, ruined your reputation. I will not have that on my conscience. I cannot apologize for what I did, or return you to your former innocent state, but at least, I can offer you my protection, my name," he said austerely, turning from the picture she made, and walking across to the fireplace. He could not face the accusing look in her wide, shadowed eyes. His damnable temper! And he had not really enjoyed forcing her, bedding her in such a manner. He had planned to coax her into a response, to seduce her gently, never believing she would not be eager for the delights of his expert lovemaking. Damn the stubborn little fool. Could she not see she had no choice but to marry him? Even if he secured the Monatgues' silence over last night's miserable work, there was still Sir Anthony and the Prince. They would not be quiet about his role in that misguided adventure.

"Are you afraid I will tell your friends the Montagues just what an unprincipled rogue you are? I am sure it will come as no surprise to them to hear you have raped an innocent girl," Verity said. Anger was, in fact, replacing shame in her mind and all she wanted was to have him suffer as much as possible. The idea of a marriage under these circumstances was hideous. What chance of happiness did such a union have? Better to return to Devon and cope with

196

Sir Anthony than commit herself to a lifetime in this devil's company.

"I am not thinking of myself, although naturally I would not want to be revealed as a man who took advantage of a young woman who was entitled to my protection and care," Alistair replied, trying to retrieve the situation, but realizing that there was little hope of that. "I will take you back to the Montagues this morning and tell them I rescued you from the Prince. They need not know anything else. And I will announce our engagement. If we are wed immediately and under their aegis, there will be little gossip. The Prince does not exactly cut a heroic figure, and I doubt if he will mention last night's work when he gets to Paris. And I will handle Sir Anthony," Alistair assured her. Now that he had made the decision he would brook no opposition. The girl must have some idea of what her refusal could mean. After all, he could abandon her to her fate, but then a frightening thought darkened his mind. He blanched and clenched his hands.

"No doubt, you have not thought of the possible consequences of last night. You might have conceived my child," he said stiffly, facing her with resolution.

Verity gasped. No, she had not considered that outcome. She knew so little of how babies were conceived. That she might have to pay such a price had never entered her mind.

"Yes, I see, that has not occurred to you. Well, believe me, it might have happened. At any rate, we

197

will be married within a few days, and if that is the result of our night together, so be it," Alistair said grimly. Somehow he did not view the prospect with as much repugnance as he might have. After all, he supposed he would have to marry someday, and at least he would now have a passionate partner in his bed, even if she was not willing at first. Eventually he could lure her into a more acceptable frame of mind, and if not, he would just send her back to his home in Dorset and return to his bachelor pursuits. He would not live with a shrew, nor would he entertain a wanton under his roof. Like most of his type, Alistair did not believe men owed their wives fidelity, only respect and an outward appearance of propriety, and he was willing to grant Verity those signs of respectability.

"Listen to me, Verity," he said eagerly, crossing to the bed and taking her hands in his, ignoring her shrinking and wild-eyed gaze at him. "It will not be so bad. I am fairly plump in the pockets and can give you an enjoyable life. You will find Paris exciting, with a host of pleasures. And if I am so repugnant to you, I will not force you. This marriage can be just as you wish." He leaned over and pressed a kiss on her lips. "I can force you to yield to me again, you know. I do not want to take you in anger, but if that is the only way I can convince you, I will, and what's more, you will enjoy it this time, I promise."

His hand roved under the bed linen to seek her warm flesh, and she fought against the unwitting response her traitorous body gave. She would not submit to more of his soulless lovemaking. She wrenched herself away, barely choking down a scream, for she would not let him know how much her own shameless responses betrayed her.

"All right then, Major, I will marry you since it seems I have little recourse. But I will not allow any further intimacies," she said. He would be entitled to no rights over her body, of that she was determined.

Alistair, sensing what was passing through her mind, was content with his temporary victory, and prepared to postpone any further attempts to mollify her. He had every confidence that he could subdue her resistance once the bonds were tied. Naturally she would put up a show of timid demur to punish him, but he would get around that after a short time. His experience proved that women felt obliged to make a show of reluctance but, once they submitted, thoroughly enjoyed being introduced to the joys of the bed. Why should Verity be any different? He was wise enough not to push matters further at this delicate juncture. He rose and smiled at her with all the considerable charm at his command.

"That's a good girl. I knew you would see the sense in it. Now, we have much to do. I will send Jenkins in to you with some breakfast and your case. You will feel much more the thing after you have eaten and dressed. Then we will tool around to the Montagues and tell them our news. It will please Ariel mightily. She has always wanted me yoked," he concluded brightly, ignoring Verity's sniff of scorn.

199

Realizing that she wanted to be alone to mend her shattered senses, Alistair took himself off, aware that he had not handled the interview with any of his fabled address. Now, when it mattered so much, he could not summon the technique which had served him so successfully in the past with the recalcitrant females. Of course, in the past he had not resorted to force, he acknowledged ruefully. Damn this war, damn Charley, and damn himself, he cursed, seeing no way out of the dilemma which his own actions had induced.

Left alone to repair the ravages of the night, Verity was amazed to discover that she was hungry and the breakfast Jenkins brought was most welcome. The man's face remained stolid although she knew he must wonder at the situation. Of course, she decided cynically, he was accustomed to finding strange women in his master's rooms.

Finally she finished dressing, having some difficulty in buttoning up her plain primrose muslin gown and arranging her hair without Agnes's skilled attentions. Regarding herself in the long mirror she decided she must have more resilience than she thought, for none of the ravages of the night showed on her creamy face, although her eyes held a strange lost look she did not recognize. She only hoped that Ariel would not be too observant. Taking a deep breath and squaring her shoulders, she left the hateful chamber which had been the scene of her downfall. She was too proud to show Alistair her shame and apprehension, and when she greeted him coolly in the sitting room, his eyes flickered with admiration.

"I am quite ready to return to the Montagues now. I only hope they will not be too disgusted to receive me," she greeted him, not looking at his face but staring resolutely at his boot tops.

"Let me reassure you on that score. Any recriminations which are tendered will fall on my head. Well deserved, no doubt," Alistair replied, much too cheerfully, Verity thought. What a complete rogue he was. Obviously the seduction of an innocent girl caused him few heart burnings, and mistaking his attempt to put affairs on a normal footing, she strengthened her defenses, deciding not to spare him the contempt he deserved.

Silently she took the shawl he offered her and preceded him down the stairway to the waiting phaeton.

On the short ride to the Montagues, Verity had nothing to say, but Alistair was determined to bring her around for her own sake as much as his. One look at her contemptuous face and Ian and Ariel would guess at once what had happened between them. Slowing his horses, Alistair turned to her and said, "Come, Verity, this pose of the outraged virgin will not do unless you want the Montagues to think the worst," he chided gently. "If we tell them we are going to be married we will have to show some signs of affection."

201

"It would serve you well if I let it be known just what kind of a rogue you are," Verity blurted out, unwilling to accept any overtures from him.

"You will be the sufferer, not I, if the truth should come out," he pointed out coolly. "Unfair, I daresay, but that's the way of the world."

"No doubt in your world that is true. You yourself implied before that your scandalous attentions were somehow my fault."

"Then I spoke in haste. I am to blame. But no apologies of mine will repair the damage. For your own sake, you must try to look less as if you hated the sight of me, however true it may be," Alistair said.

"I will play the besotted bride in the company of others," Verity agreed reluctantly, seeing the sense of his remarks. "But I shan't carry on such hypocrisy in private."

Alistair, realizing that was all the concession he would win, did not press matters. "I just hope your acting talents are up to such a monumental deception. You are a formidable female, Verity, and quite terrify me with your disdain."

"Not formidable enough, I suspect. Or I would not be in this situation." Verity repressed the feeling that she was behaving churlishly. After all, she had weakened in his embrace at the crucial moment. And he had offered the only amends possible to a man of honor. Another, lesser man might have just abandoned her to whatever fate awaited a despoiled

202

lady. For a moment she wondered if she would have received his seduction of her more eagerly had it been accomplished with gentle skill and professions of love. But she quickly dismissed that thought, afraid of what her conclusion might be.

In any event their arrival at the Montagues passed off with fewer questions than she might have expected. Ariel was alone when they entered the drawing room, Ian being absent on some Army business, and she hailed their appearance with relief and few reproaches. Alistair's explanations of his wresting Verity from the Prince's escort was sketchy, but all was forgotten in the news he delivered, that he and Verity had decided to be married. As he had warned, Ariel flew into transports of joy at such a sensible resolution of their past differences and immediately began to plan the nuptials.

"It must be soon, Ariel, as I cannot delay joining my regiment in Paris. As it is, my leave has been extended beyond what the powers that be consider acceptable," Alistair warned, not, of course, mentioning his fear that Verity might be pregnant as a result of his impetuous action and that the sooner they were wed the better it would be.

Ariel, an officer's wife, quite understood that the claims of the Army must come first. "Of course, but although it must be a rushed affair, Verity is entitled to some ceremony. How fortunate that her stepfather is in Brussels and can give her away," she said guilelessly.

203

Verity was less than enthusiastic.

"I would rather Ian performed that office," she said hastily.

"As you wish. But we must apprise your stepfather of events. He was somewhat disturbed at your precipitous flight," Ariel answered dryly, remembering that gentleman's anger at Verity's escape.

"Well, I do not consider his claims to be of any account," Verity dismissed him casually. The only benefit of this hurried marriage would be her permanent deliverance from Sir Anthony's clutches.

"I will send a note to his hotel immediately. He is your guardian, Verity, is he not?"

Verity smiled a bit grimly. "No, Charley was my legal guardian, but I need no one's permission to wed. I will write my mother, of course, and notify her of my choice." Remembering Alistair's strictures, she smiled as if she could not wait to seal their union.

He responded gallantly, "It is quite flattering that you are as eager as I am to be shackled. I will approach Sir Anthony, my dear. You need not worry about his approval." Fearing that Verity had reached the limits of her ability to dissemble, Alistair took Verity's hand and bestowed on her a look of apparent besotted eagerness.

Ariel eyed the couple with a certain distrust. There was more here than she knew, but at least Alistair seemed more than willing to tie the knot. And he could not have settled on a more charming girl. She suspected that Verity would not play the role of a meek and docile wife and there should be some fireworks in this union, but she was convinced that eventually they would find the felicity which she and Ian enjoyed, if Alistair could curb his inclinations to flirt with any available female. Somehow she doubted that Verity would accept his straying with any compliance. But was the girl truly in love with the graceless scamp? Ariel wondered about the relationship but was too tactful to put her fears into words. She assumed a practical air and suggested that after her tiring time, Verity would be well to rest, after assuring Agnes as to her safety.

"Your abigail has been in quite a tizzy over your abrupt departure, my dear," Ariel explained, feeling that was safe ground.

"Poor Agnes. I must calm her down. She will be pleased to see me settled," Verity agreed, and rose to leave the room, paying little heed to Alistair's raised eyebrows at this cavalier treatment. Recollecting herself, Verity turned and said with a show of affection, "I will see you later today, I suppose, Alistair."

Althought there was much he wanted to say to her, with Ariel watching, Alistair had to be more circumspect. Still, she should not get off so easily. He raised her hand to his lips and kissed it warmly. "Of course, my dear. I will be off now to see Sir Anthony, and explain matters to Uxbridge," he informed her, giving her a speaking glance.

Forcing herself not to snatch her hand away, Verity managed a grim smile. "Good-bye for now, then." And she was gone, fleeing from his presence as if he were the devil himself, Alistair decided ruefully. But watching her straight back as she crossed the hall, he conceded she had courage. She had played her part better than he had expected. He only hoped she would not confide in Ariel the reason for this hurried wedding. He turned back to his hostess and explained. "She is a trifle overset what with all the excitement of the last few hours. She needs some time to compose herself and think of the new future which faces her."

"I hope Alistair that you intend to be a good husband," Ariel said severely, but was unable to repress a smile as she delivered her admonishment.

"Why, Ariel, I will be a veritable pattern card of a tame benedict," he replied, determined to ward off any probing by this very resolute lady who knew him only too well.

"I hope so, Alistair. I am fond of Verity and would not want to see her unhappy. She has had enough trouble."

"I am a reformed man," he assured her, his eyes mocking.

Ariel regarded him balefully.

"I am not sure I do not pity the girl, taking you on, Alistair. I wish we were going to Paris to keep an eye on events."

"You wound me, dear lady, with your lack of faith," he replied. "I will take the utmost care of her,

206

and I promise to bring her on a visit when we return to England, after the birth of your baby and before too many months have passed."

After a few more moments of chat about the arrangements for the ceremony, which would take place at the Montagues, he left to deliver his news to Sir Anthony, a task he would enjoy mightily.

Chapter Thirteen

Despite Sir Anthony's furious objections, the marriage went off happily a few days later. Alistair had seen little of Verity since delivering her to the Montagues, his time taken up with securing a license and his commander's approval, as well as making arrangements to transport them to Paris after the ceremony. He realized that Verity's role as an eager bride was not one that she could sustain for long and he did not want her to be burdened with his unwelcome presence in case she changed her mind and sought another refuge.

He need not have worried. Verity realized that she had no recourse but to enter into this loveless union. In her letters to Denis and her mother she gave no hint that she was anything but thrilled at the prospect of becoming Alistair's wife. But her emotions were in a turmoil and having to pretend to Ariel and Ian further strained her patience. Agnes's reception of her decision to wed Alistair had been relief and approval, an attitude Verity found hard to accept but she could not tell her abigail the real reason for the decision. The strain of masquerading as a loving bride was almost more than she could endure but she persevered, reluctant to tell anyone how she had been compromised. She had survived a very unpleasant interview with Sir Anthony, but Alistair had insisted on being present to shield her from the worst of her stepfather's derision and disapproval.

"I think you are making a grave error, Verity. And all this haste. Your mother will be heartbroken," Sir Anthony had said unfairly, trying to play on Verity's sympathies.

"Nonsense, Sir Anthony. She will be relieved to know that I am safely settled," had been Verity's brisk reply.

"I am considered quite an eligible parti, you know, Sir Anthony," Alistair intervened, gaining more than a little satisfaction over the pompous conceited man's disappointment at losing his prey. "You would not want Verity to make a misalliance, I am sure, or," he added wickedly, "marry without love."

"Love? Nonsense! She hardly knows you," Sir Anthony blustered.

"Time matters little to lovers." To reinforce his words, Alistair put an arm around Verity and smiled down at her, the very picture of an impatient bridegroom. "Isn't that true, my dear?" he said, tightening his grip when she tried to shrug it off.

"Mother only wants my happiness, I am sure, Sir Anthony, and I am convinced Alistair will be all that a husband should be," Verity lied through gritted teeth, glaring up at her fiancé.

Fortunately Sir Anthony was too frustrated to notice anything but the affectionate pose of the couple. He had no recourse while that grinning devil was standing by protectively but to submit to this turn of events. He hid his chagrin with difficulty, and tendered his congratulations.

He was mortified and embarrassed too by Verity's refusal to allow him to give her away to Alistair. Not that he felt the least bit fatherly toward his lovely stepdaughter, but he feared his consequence would suffer before the very society he wanted to impress at this blatant snub. On this score, however, Verity was adamant.

The rest of the wedding details concerned her less. Ariel had insisted on buying her a new costume for the ceremony, as her wedding gift, and was rather surprised at Verity's lack of interest in the shopping for this important garment. Realizing that Ariel was rather hurt by her indifference, Verity explained gently that because of Charley's death she felt any ostentatious display would be unseemly. Ariel accepted this excuse but still insisted on a new gown, one that would also serve as a traveling outfit, for the Glendennings were to leave for Paris immediately after the ceremony. In the end they settled on a mauve silk redincote style, accented with deeper lavendar ruching and a high poked bonnet faced in the darker ribbon. At first Ariel thought the color insipid but Verity's unusual hair, creamy complexion, and elegant figure gave it a style which compensated for the plainness of the design.

Only a score of guests attended the rites at the Montague mansion—a few of Charley's comrades, the British ambassador and his wife, and the Earl of Uxbridge, recovering fast from his amputated leg, who lent an air of suave approval to the occasion.

Verity's paleness and faint responses were a direct contrast to Alistair's jaunty air, and general demeanor of having secured a valued prize. Verity carefully avoided his eyes during the ceremony, and therefore missed the passionate look of satisfaction he gave her when the final words were spoken. This was not how she had expected to be wed, and she spared a wistful thought for her village church and her mother who must be moaning her absence from this most important day in her daughter's life. Just as well Lady Maxwell had not come to Brussels, Verity decided. For she would have difficulty in hiding the reason for this hurried marriage from her mother.

Receiving the best wishes of the guests and Agnes's obvious approval did little to calm her fears for the future. Surely they all could see she came to this marriage with little of the glowing enthusiasm of the usual bride, but perhaps they put her reluctance down to shyness or the tragedy of Charley's death. She felt benumbed, in a daze, hardly aware of what was going on around her, moving through the whole affair as if it were happening to someone else. But lurking behind that apathy was the knowledge that she had taken an irrevocable step which promised little happiness. She neither trusted Alistair nor believed he would make the kind of husband who would bring her happiness. And her imagination faltered at the threat of further intimacies of the kind that had forced this union. She feared that Alistair would brook no refusal when he wished to assert his marital rights and the idea of allowing him free access to her body terrified her.

His casual, if openly affectionate, manner did nothing to calm those fears. He had made it clear he considered the marriage one of expediency, demanded by honor, and in no way planned to alter his usual mode of behavior. His efforts to carry the whole business off with the sangfroid for which he was noted were no doubt due to his concern for appearances rather than any regard for her as a person. As she watched him joke with his commander and Ian, her panic rose. How could he be so sanguine, so relaxed, so affable after this farce of a wedding? But she must not let her discomfort show, and she forced a weak smile to her lips.

Finally, they were waved off in the traveling coach which Alistair had bespoken for their journey, with Agnes and Jenkins following behind in a heavily laden conveyance. The trip through the countryside to Paris would take a leisurely three days.

Alistair was not insensitive to Verity's state of

mind, but for once in his life he was unsure of how to go about putting a woman at ease, and this one his wife. Served him right, he conceded ruefully, looking at Verity's closed aloof expression as they rattled out of Brussels. She neither trusted nor liked him, cold comfort for a bridegroom. He'd have to see what he could do to change her mind . . . through the pleasures of the marriage bed.

Verity's mood of despondency increased as their carriage passed through the fields of Waterloo, where almost a month after the battle the trampled corn fields and the rotting carcasses of dead horses testified to the terrible carnage. Most of the dead had been buried in mass graves, and the looters had departed, but the evidence of the horror was still apparent. Verity shuddered as she looked from the windows of the carriage and tears rose to her eyes as she thought of Charley.

"How dreadful war is. Why do men think they will find glory in such hideous slaughter?" she said in anger and disgust, more to herself than to Alistair.

"I suppose they do not think of dying, or even being wounded, but mostly of the adventure, the comradeship, the knowledge that they are serving their country," Alistair explained, seeing for the first time how battle must appear to the loved ones of those who enlisted so carelessly and gallantly in the struggle.

"Yes, Charley never thought of the danger, only of the opportunity to grasp some honor. He was dazzled by the romance of it all, and never realized that he might not survive."

Alistair sought for some means to distract her from her tragic loss. He said gently, "Well, we will have peace now. Wellington will see to that. Napoleon is settled at last. And you will find Paris exciting, Verity." Like most soldiers he couldn't afford to think of the tragic aspects of battle, only of the job to be done. Now his attitude seemed callous, but he could see no use in dwelling on the deaths of his comrades and the inevitable results of what had occurred. They had won, at a terrible cost, but now that Napoleon's pretensions had at last been laid to rest, those who remained must get on with their lives.

"It's all very well for you to think of Paris, Alistair. You have little conscience and less sensibility, I think," Verity reproved him sharply.

Alistair looked at his wife ironically. "You persist in thinking of me as the most callous of brutes. That does not bode well for our life together as man and wife."

"You might have thought of that before you indulged in the behavior which brought us to this pass!" Verity retorted.

"My dear, I promise I shall more than make it up to you."

The gleam in his eye cast Verity into confusion. Her cheeks turned pink and she averted her face furiously. How was it that when he was so obviously in the wrong, he yet managed to put her at a disadvantage?

They stopped that evening in a luxurious hostelry near the border, where Alistair had bespoken a private parlor and bedchamber. Verity listlessy surveyed the accommodations and retired to the inner room to repair the ravages of the journey. She wished she could postpone any further discussion and climb into the huge four-poster to sleep away her unhappiness, but she realized that sanctuary was denied to her. She would have to join Alistair for supper, and then face whatever the night would bring in that same bed. She washed languidly in the fresh water which the maid brought up and turned to Agnes in relief when her abigail entered the room, hoping to gain some distraction from her thoughts.

"Is your chamber to your satisfaction, Agnes?" she asked as her maid began to brush out her hair.

"Yes, this is quite a well-appointed inn even if run by foreigners. A surly lot most of them, and they don't like us much, I vow," Agnes admitted. Her new circumstances posed problems, but she would not worry Verity with them now. Her mistress certainly did not appear to be a joyful bride, and Agnes found this puzzling, for she thought Alistair a fine, well-set-up gentleman, whom any girl might find more than acceptable. A bit of a rake, she surmised from the guarded remarks of his man, Jenkins, during the journey, but not to be faulted for that. Most gentlemen had their foibles, and he had always treated her with politeness and consideration. She had shrewdly decided that this marriage was not founded in love, but with her village practicality she

216

thought now that it was accomplished, both parties would settle down to it.

Still, the Quality had such peculiar notions, and these two appeared forever at odds with one another, a bad beginning for a life together. But Agnes, looking at Verity's shadowed face, realized her mistress was in no mood for confidences, and briskly set about her duties. Time enough to hear the real story when Miss Verity had resolved her conflicts with the major. And poor lamb, she was still grieving for Charley, and who could blame her. That the major had survived the very battle that had cost Charley his life would not favor his cause, Agnes mused with some perception.

Verity joined her husband for the fine collation he had ordered with little appetite for either food or conversation, but he would not be gainsayed, and pressed several delicacies upon her while talking lightheartedly of what they could expect to find in Paris.

"You must buy a new wardrobe, Verity, for I understand the ladies find French fashions all the crack, much more up to snuff than our English modes," he encouraged as the last covers were removed. "Here, try a bit of this wine. It will cheer you up. Now that the deed is done no more repinings, what? We cannot change the past, you know, only prepare to do better in the future." He filled her glass and said gently, "It will not be so dreadful this time, Verity. You are no longer a virgin, and it is only the first experience which is painful."

Verity was shocked at his frank words, but refused to lose her composure. "You sound as if you speak from experience at despoiling virgins," she remarked coldly.

As she rose as if eager to flee from him, he stood and grasped her by the shoulders, forcing her chin up and looking into her eyes. "I intend to be your husband in reality, Verity. There is no escaping me, and you will not find it so abhorrent, believe me. Under all that facade of propriety and disgust lies a passionate woman, who can please a man, and I intend to avail myself of what you can offer. You insist on dwelling on a regrettable experience, but it will be entirely different this time, I promise."

"I have little choice, it seems," Verity answered, struggling out of his arms and walking swiftly to the door from the parlor. In the inner chamber, she allowed Agnes to remove her dress and help her don the white batiste nightgown and peignoir which was part of her trousseau. Alistair made the coming ordeal sound so matter-of-fact. Well, he might think he could lure her into compliance with his skilled lovemaking. Her anger now thoroughly aroused, she conceded bitterly that he no doubt had faith in his prowess, and plenty of past experience to be so confident that she would be no more unwilling than his former amours. But she would not be coaxed by his beguiling ways and she was no brood mare to be bedded for her husband's satisfaction. She would remain impassive under his caresses, a fitting

218

punishment for such a libertine, she thought.

But to her shame the wedding night did not turn out the way she had planned. When Alistair joined her in the huge bed she tried to stay unresponsive as his hands roamed seductively over her body, wooing her into compliance. Despite her best intentions she found herself responding, a warm thrilling tremor igniting her body as his kisses became more insistent. Without quite knowing how it happened her arms crept around his neck and her mouth opened beneath his insistent lips. When he parted her thighs she stiffened momentarily, but he soothed her with more drugging caresses and when he entered her she felt no pain but a building pleasure which shook her whole body. She answered his demands with a mounting eagerness and they were caught up in the age-old excitement which crested at last, leaving them both spent and satisfied.

Alistair rolled over with a sated sigh and gathered her into his arms. Almost immediately he was asleep, but Verity, angry at herself as much as at her husband, removed herself from his arms with a sigh of disgust. How amenable she had been, as willing and eager as any lightskirt under his skilled lovemaking. No words had been exchanged between them during the tempestuous coupling, and Verity realized she had, after all, surrendered to the skilled expertise which had won so many other women.

She was both ashamed and disappointed that she hadn't been able to resist him, but promised that next time it would be different. She would not be used in such a fashion, to satisfy Alistair's need for a woman, any woman, to warm his bed. In the future she would make it clear to him that this marriage would be a sterile affair. She could not deny her response but never again would she allow herself to give in to the desire he so easily aroused in her. Without love or even a warm affection on either side there was no hope for a relationship founded on mere physical sensation. She hated herself and even more she despised Alistair for placing her in this position. Finally she drifted off into a healing sleep, determined that this night would not be repeated.

Chapter Fourteen

By mid-July, when Alistair and Verity arrived, Paris was crowded with the occupying troops of three nations, the peace delegates, and as many members of European society who could manage to find quarters in the defeated capital. In the Bois de Boulogne the British forces camped in startling white tents under the bower of leafy trees while the Prussians and Russians preferred to inflict themselves on the sullen populace. Wellington insisted that his men behave with politeness and circumspection, paying for all they commandeered, and following his conciliatory lead. His allies ignored such finicky notions and earned the undying hatred of the French by their brutal and gross appetites.

The Germans insisted on extracting huge indemnities from the French although Wellington pleaded for moderation, and Tzar Alexander I, completely under the influence of a spiritual medium, yearned to impose his Christian Holy Alliance principles on both the conquered and the conquering, while reacting petulantly to any disrespect for his position. The Bourbon, Louis XVIII, restored to the throne of France by the Allied armies, exacerbated events by a petty estrangement from the Iron Duke which that gentleman largely ignored. Napoleon was to be settled on St. Helena and develop his legend of a martyred savior, while his former subjects ruefully saw their dream of *égalité, fraternité, and liberté* fall under the firm authoritarian hand which would now rule them. Despite all the political maneuvering, the dashed hopes, and bitter taste of defeat, most of Paris responded to the peace with relief tempered by a certain apprehension for the future.

These emotions were shared by Verity as she and Alistair settled into commodious quarters on the faubourg Saint-Honore near the Elysée, for the few hostelries in the city were ill kept, shabby, and crowded. Relations between the newly married pair deteriorated as they took up their new life. Verity held Alistair at arm's length, and Alistair grew weary of her continued coldness. Within a week of their arrival they were ignoring each other as much as possible.

Alistair had believed that Verity would soon be won over by his skilled lovemaking and he continued to visit her bed when he felt the need. Although he could force a response from her, she never surrendered willingly to him and he soon gave up the effort in disgust, damning the girl for her stubborness. Verity decided he had discovered a more willing partner and pretended to herself that this was what she had both expected and craved, but somehow his absence left her frustrated and disappointed. In public he continued to treat her with courtesy but their few meetings in private lacked any semblance of accord.

Determined to banish the megrims which her situation had induced, Verity spent much of her time wandering about Paris, accompanied grudgingly by Agnes, who complained about the foreignness of everything and decried Gallic morals. During his years as First Consul, Napoleon had initiated impressive building plans for the capital, throwing up triumphal arches, statues, fountains, bridges, and churches, giving the once medieval city a neoclassical air which became uniquely its own. Verity found it a delightful contrast from the staid, bourgeois atmosphere of Brussels and explored its boulevards, museums, and shops with pleasure, but sightseeing did not succeed in dispelling her loneliness and unhappiness.

Much of the English entertaining centered around the Embassy, where Sir Charles Stuart reigned, having been summoned from Vienna to become the new ambassador. Lady Stuart, a formidable hostess, introduced the Glendennings to the luminaries of London society who had rushed to Paris, intent on enjoying their usual pursuits of gossiping, gambling, and flirting in a more relaxed environment. Wellington himself barely escaped the consequences of scandal by conducting a friendship with Lady Frances Wedderburn-Webster, tarnishing the Duke's image somewhat. But Fanny did not have the Duke's undivided attention. Lady Caroline Lamb, fresh from her exploits with Byron, Lady Charlotte Greville, Mrs. Arbuthnot, Lady Shelley, and other stars of the ton vied for his gallantries. Watching all these notables pursuing frivolity with a vengeance, Verity wondered if she alone stubbornly clung to her unfashionable principles. Perhaps she should abandon her strict notions and, like Alistair, enjoy what was offered. In this unfortunate mood of self-pity, estrangement, and confusion she met the one gentleman who would be delighted to join her in such dalliance.

It was at an Embassy ball that she again met Prince Vasilii Chirnovsky, who was in attendance upon Tsar Alexander during the peace conferences which engaged the various heads of state. Alistair had very properly escorted her to the party, and had led her out in the first waltz, but then had abandoned her to fetch a glass of lemonade. In all these attentions he was most punctilious if not enthusiastic. She was seated on one of the gilt chairs lining the ballroom, glad of a respite for the heat was overpowering and her new cream satin slippers pinching, when suddenly the throng parted and she looked up to meet the admiring gaze of the Prince.

"Good evening, *doushka,* what a pleasant surprise to find you in this gathering," he greeted her smoothly, bowing over her hand as if their last meeting had been of the utmost propriety. "I had expected your puritanical cavalier had dispatched you back to England after our last encounter. How delighted I am to see you gracing this assembly."

"No. He married me instead and brought me to Paris," Verity blurted out, reddening under the Prince's hot gaze. For a moment she was chagrined to meet the Prince thus, with Alistair bound to reappear at any moment and take her to task for encouraging the man. An imp of perversity made Verity smile enticingly at the Prince, knowing that her encouragement could only annoy her husband, and taking great pleasure from the thought. The Prince, for his part, seemed impervious to any awkwardness in this meeting, and immediately asked her hand for the quadrille which was just forming. Verity saw little reason to refuse.

So that when Alistair returned with the lemonade it was to find his wife gaily tripping through the movements of the dance with the very man he had hoped he had settled once and for all. It did nothing to relieve his temper to see Verity smiling and chatting in all amiability with the Russian. Damn the girl, had she no sense at all, to take up with that libertine again, knowing he was a deceiver of the worst kind! He stood against the wall watching the pair, trying to master his anger. So crowded was the floor, so pressing the Prince's attentions, that Verity did not see her irate husband staring at them with disapproval, but she was soon made aware of his displeasure when the Prince returned her to his side.

"Ah, Major, we meet again, and now you are the most fortunate *mari* of this so charming young woman," said the Prince suavely, but his pale eyes held an ugly light.

Although Alistair would have dearly loved to plant the man a facer, wiping that smirk from his bland face, he was well aware that the Prince had him at a disadvantage, for he could hardly create a scandal in the middle of the British Embassy with all the ton watching.

"Yes, it was a whirlwind courtship and wedding," he responded equably. "I could not contemplate putting the Channel between myself and Verity and so I prevailed upon her to accept my proposal. It seems we will be in Paris for some time while Wellington settles affairs."

Verity, observing them both, thought they acted rather like two wary animals circling each other to gauge a weak spot in the defenses they both had erected. Really, how stupid they were, she thought in irritation, neither willing to admit that their attitudes were insulting to her, implying she might behave in some indecorous fashion before the world.

The Prince, ignoring Alistair's explanation, took Verity's hand and bowed over it with perfect politeness, but the look in his eye was far from sedate.

"My dear madam, your presence in Paris is more than I could have hoped for. And I promise you will see a great deal of me," he offered wickedly, and then turning to Alistair threw out carelessly, "And you, too, of course, Major." Then he made his departure, crossing the ballroom to seek out an attractive brunette who greeted him enthusiastically.

"Damn the fellow. He is a complete cad. And you are not to have anything further to do with him, do you understand, Verity," Alistair growled, knowing he sounded ridiculous but unable to prevent his jealous anger from surfacing.

Varity removed his hand from her arm, where he was gripping her much too tightly. "Don't make a cake of yourself, Alistair, the Prince was only being polite. And I think you do him a grave injustice," she reproved him gaily, momentarily pleased by his reaction. But then she sobered. Of course it could not be jealousy. Alistair's consequence would suffer if his wife appeared to prefer the Prince's attentions to his own. How typical. He was not the least bit in love with her himself, but would not tolerate her fixing her interest with another. Not that the Prince, despite his obvious attractions, could lure her into imprudent action, but it would do Alistair good to feel a little unsure of her.

Before the newly married couple, who now stood glaring at each other, could continue their discussion, one of Alistair's fellow officers came up to claim a dance with Verity. She greeted him happily and went off, leaving her irate husband to fidget and fume. Alistair wondered if he was going to be hoisted with his own petard, a cukolded husband, the object of amused pity, since he had often played

227

the part of which the Prince aspired. Well, he would not have it and Verity would soon discover she could not place him in that unenviable position. She might not care for him, but she would behave—he would see to it. He could not condone a flirtatious wife, no matter how much he deserved one.

The Prince was as good as his word, and called the next afternoon at their apartments to invite Verity for a ride. She would not have accepted if she had not been furious with Alistair. The evening before, he had dragged her home from the Embassy quite early and again asserted his mastery over her, taking her with a ruthless indifference to her own wishes. That she had responded only made his possession more unwelcome. She would not be used so.

"I have a feeling, dear lady, that you would not have rushed into this so unfortunate marriage if you had trusted me more," the Prince said as he tooled his horses down the Champs Elysée, raising a wry eyebrow at Verity, who was looking most enticing in a new dress of azure blue silk, frogged over a white silk underskirt, and a matching provocative bonnet which accented her titian curls.

"But I fear I had little reason to trust you, Prince. Come—admit it. Your aunt was indeed just a ploy to lure me under your protection," Verity responded outrageously. She would not allow the Prince to think she was such a gullible fool again.

However, the Prince, a skilled fencer, would not be so easily defeated. Seeing Verity again, his former desire for her had been rekindled and this time he was not dealing with a frightened maiden, but an experienced matron. He had every confidence that he could lure her into an *affaire* which would prove a decided fillip to his weeks in Paris. And an added inducement was the notion of putting the arrogant major in his place. Still, he was too old a campaigner to reveal his tactics so soon.

"You pain me, *doushka*. I was only thinking of your welfare. I cannot believe marriage with the obstinate major was the answer to your situation. You do not love him." He observed her carefully to gauge her reaction to this statement.

"He is my husband, and I owe him my loyalty and respect, Prince," she replied piously. "But since you have not answered my question, I must continue to think the worst of you."

"Ah, I see I have my work cut out to assure you of my most respectful intentions," the Prince answered, not at all displeased by her answer. God, but she was an appealing piece with none of the simpering coyness of his usual prey. He must have her, but he would go carefully.

For the rest of their drive he behaved with great propriety, calming her suspicions and talking of the politics and fashions of Paris, charming Verity with his obvious pleasure in her company. Soothed and flattered, Verity gave little thought to what her encouragement of the Russian might provoke. Her anger with Alistair and his unwarranted suspicions tempted her to respond with more eagerness than in a soberer mood she would have considered wise, but the Prince was a tonic to her lacerated spirits. Determined to keep him off more personal topics she broached the reason for his stay in Paris.

"Are you a member of the peace conference which will now settle the fate of France, of all Europe, Prince?" she asked.

"I am an aide de camp to our Tsar, so must accompany him to many of the sessions. But I still have a great deal of leisure to pursue my own interests," he added suggestively.

Verity ignored his innuendo and persisted. "Will Russia agree to Belgium's neutrality, do you think?"

After a moment, the Prince replied shortly, "The Tsar will agree only to his Holy Alliance. He is determined to make the Allies accede to his Christian principles." He did not agree with his sovereign's rather wooly-minded ideals, but of course, he would not admit this. Why did this lovely lady want to talk politics when they could be so much more pleasurably engaged? Still, he was willing to indulge her for the moment. "The Tsar is adamant upon this Alliance and will brook no opposition, so the British had best take care," he warned, rather startling Verity with the vehemence of his measured words.

"Is there any possibility that the Holy Alliance will not be signed?" she asked, thinking that Alexander must be a strange combination of naiveté and stubborn autocracy if he persisted in pressing this idealistic plan of solving the grave problems which confronted the peacemakers.

"Your British compatriots are stubborn, but we have ways of compelling them," the Prince answered, revealing a ruthlessness and an arrogance of his own. But seeing Verity's frown, he realized he had revealed more than he intended and adroitly turned the conversation to a discussion of the barbarities of the Prussians, in which Verity could only agree.

Upon returning her to her apartment, he assured her again of his delight in her company and added that he hoped to see her at the Castlereaghs' reception that evening. She promised nothing but thanked him prettily, and tripped up the steps of the house, quite pleased with the outing and believing that she had handled the encounter with a certain sophistication. Alistair would see that he could not have matters all his own way, she thought smugly, aware of the Prince's admiring gaze as he bid her farewell.

Alistair's determination to keep Verity from renewing any friendship with Prince Chirnovsky received quite a jolt that afternoon when his commanding officer requested his presence with a demand that he make himself available to the British ambassador and Lord Castlereagh himself.

Colonel Pendleton, who had replaced the convalescing Uxbridge as leader of the Life Guards, was a far less intimidating man than Alistair's former chief, but he still expected compliance with his orders. Upon Alistair's reporting to headquarters, Pendleton had invited him into his sanctum rather brusquely.

"Stuart and Lord Castlereagh insist that you be seconded to them, Glendenning. They have a special task for you. I don't like it, but I really have no option but to agree to their demands," he explained as he indicated that Alistair be seated.

"Well, sir, I must obey orders. But I would much prefer to remain on duty with the regiment," Alistair offered.

Pendleton was a good fellow, with a fine record, but lacked the power and prestige of Uxbridge. He was a middle-aged man with thinning hair, light blue eyes, and a perpetual frown, as if wondering if his decisions were correct. As commander of the Life Guards during the occupation he would not be faulted, for he was a stickler for proper behavior but not a man to initiate events. Alistair knew that he would knuckle under to any requests the British ambassador and the Foreign Secretary might make no matter whether he approved or not.

"Yes, I can understand that. But I have promised Stuart and Castlereagh your services so you must report there immediately," Pendleton said. "I understand that you have done intelligence work before, but I decry all this spying, not at all proper for one of our officers." That a gentleman could indulge in such dirty tactics was a notion he found distasteful. Privately he scorned all this intrigue as unsuitable for a serving officer.

"Well, I must say I would prefer to be shooting at the enemy, but that option seems denied to me at present. So I must just go where I am sent and try to give satisfaction."

"Yes, well, I don't want to know about it. I only hope it won't take too long. I am very short of officers fit for duty and need you here," Pendleton grumbled before signifying that Alistair could take his leave.

Alistair, making his way on foot to the British Embassy, wondered what intelligence work could now be required of him. After all, the Frenchies were settled, although Talleyrand was still up to his tricks. Rumor had it that he and that odious Foche would be forced on the Bourbon King to ensure that peace would be secured. But Napoleon was finished as any kind of threat and it was doubtful that even the wily Talleyrand would be conspiring with his former master after Waterloo.

The last time he had been so engaged had involved the Montagues, and nearly brought Ariel to her death. Women were the very devil in these affairs, but at least this time, he had little reason to think civilians would be involved.

Thinking about women brought him around to Verity and her stubbornness in smiling upon that Russian fellow. Damn the girl. Was she doing it just to annoy him? If so, she had succeeded, he concluded ruefully, and allowed his mind to wander over the unsatisfactory relationship which his hurried marriage had provoked. Never before in his

233

casual affairs had he cared much what the lady was thinking, being only concerned that she responded eagerly to his lovemaking. In truth, Verity did respond, but only when he forced her, and he suspected she hated herself for it afterward. Why he should yearn for another reaction, he could not fathom. Damn it, the girl appeared to actually dislike him, and she was his wife, a position he had never offered to any other woman, although there had been several who had done their best to shackle him. Why did it matter so much? Was it just his conceit that was affected? Or was he in danger of falling in love with the chit, an emotion he had always sedulously avoided until now. What a turn-up that would be, to fall in love with his own wife, who despised him. Well, no good brooding about that now, when he must see what the Foreign Office boffins required of him.

He turned into the imposing entrance of the Embassy, determined to banish Verity from his mind and concentrate on the matter in hand.

On being ushered into Sir Charles Stuart's sanctum, he was surprised to see not only Lord Castlereagh, the Foreign Secretary, whom he had expected, but Wellington as well. Masking his astonishment he saluted and waited to see what this imposing trio would suggest. Castlereagh, his thin, aristocratic features showing the gravity of the situation, turned from the window and looked Alistair over with a speculative air. Indicating that Alistair should be seated, he turned to Wellington and said, "Perhaps you might explain what is required, Duke."

Alistair, turning to face the victor of Waterloo, was a bit taken back by the Iron Duke's presence at this conference. He certainly did not look like a man whose name was revered throughout Europe, respected and feared by every member of the Army. A man who rarely revealed any expression, today he appeared pensive and troubled, his normally austere expression even more accentuated above that bony nose.

"Thank you for reporting so promptly, Glendenning," Wellington said. "This matter is a bit ticklish, but General Valentine tells me you are just the man for the job, and there are some personal factors which seem to bear him out. You have worked for Valentine in the past, I understand."

Alistair nodded his head, frowning at the Duke's enigmatic remarks.

Before Wellington could continue, Sir Charles interrupted. "You won't want me in on this, Arthur. It's best I not know too much about it. I have some matters to attend to and will leave you and Robert to put the major here into the picture." On receiving Wellington's nod, he left the room hurriedly, giving Alistair a searching glance.

Wellington gave a tight-lipped smile. "These diplomats never want to face facts. And they always leave someone else to do their dirty work," he muttered, quite unlike himself. Alistair remembered that the Duke did not particularly care for Stuart, although he accorded him the respect due his position. And the Ambassador was Castlereagh's half-brother, which complicated matters.

"Charles feels that what the eye doesn't see or the ear doesn't hear, the heart need not grieve over," Castlereagh interposed wryly, "but enough of that. Let us get to the kernel."

"Em, yes. Well, you see, Glendenning, the Tsar is most anxious to have all the Allies sign this Holy Alliance of his, a damn silly piece of nonsense, but we must humor him," Wellington explained. "He's not content with a Quadruple Alliance but has some notion that all the nations should band together and govern by Christian principles. Silly fool, as if treaties were not good enough, in the usual way, but we cannot afford to antagonize him until peace is secured. And we have some reason to believe he is conniving with Louis XVIII, who wants to save Ney, a turncoat as you know." Wellington paused, as if unwilling to continue with the rather nasty news he had to deliver.

"Yes, sir, I quite understand," Alistair prompted.

"Well, the Tsar wants France to become a member of the Holy Alliance, which is ridiculous," Castlereagh interposed. "And we fear he is not above a little blackmail to get us to sign at the same time. I don't think Liverpool will consent but for now we must keep him sweet. And he is capable of stirring up the French against us, as the oppressors. To that end he is using his aide, Prince Chirnovsky"
—Castlereagh looked pointedly at Alistair—"of

whom, I believe, you have some knowledge."

"The man's a blackguard," Alistair said bluntly. How had these two learned about his encounter with the Prince, and how did they mean to use that knowledge? He was not long left in ignorance and the suggestion that he encourage the Prince's friendship with his wife was not warmly received.

"I don't like the man, and I don't want him hanging around my wife," he argued, appalled at what Castlereagh and Wellington expected of him.

"I quite see the force of your objections, Glendenning. Unfortunately the exigencies of the situation do not allow us the niceties of conduct. We must discover what the Tsar is promising Talleyrand and King Louis. I would not ask this of you if I thought there was any other way. It's a damnable coil," Wellington explained, a bit embarrassed at asking one of his officers to use his wife as bait to discover his supposed ally's plans.

In the end Alistair reluctantly agreed to the plan, on condition that he explain the situation to Verity. "I am sure she is to be trusted, and would want to help, as her brother died at Waterloo and she feels strongly about the peace."

Although Castlereagh and Wellington could not like revealing their information to another person— particularly a woman—they had no choice if they were to secure the major's cooperation. Castlereagh lacked the Duke's scruples, having used women thus before, notably Ariel Montague, but the Duke felt the ladies only complicated affairs with their insistence on propriety, and their need to be protected from the sordid details of life. They were a necessary enjoyment and could be quite fascinating, but the serious business of the world was best left in the hands of men, a belief Alistair shared.

As he took his leave, Alistair wondered just how Verity would receive this turn of events.

Chapter Fifteen

Once out of the imposing presence of the Foreign Secretary and the Duke, Alistair cursed his distasteful assignment. He wondered, too, how the pair had learned of Verity's association with the Prince. The idea that she had become an object of scurrilous gossip among the London ton flocking to Paris raised his hackles. He would not play the cuckolded husband even to serve his country.

His scruples did him little honor in a society which found liaisons of that sort quite acceptable as long as the participants observed the rules. He himself had played the game often enough, and even the Duke was rumored to have indulged in dalliance. At the moment Paris was agog over Wellington's friendship with Lady Frances Wedderburn-Webster, to whom he had written immediately following Waterloo. Lady Frances, pretty, young, and married at seventeen to a confessed libertine, seemed an unlikely object of the Duke's affections, but the fact that Lady Wellington had returned to her children, leaving her husband alone in Paris, fueled the speculation. Alistair, though accustomed to men's infidelity, put little credence in the current on dits, believing Wellington too conscious of his position to jeopardize his reputation by such behavior. Yet, there was a certain amount of evidence to support the gossip. Well, the Duke must cope with his reputation without any assistance from Alistair. He had his own domestic problems, and as he walked up the steps of his lodgings, he wondered how he was to pose his problem to his unreceptive wife.

Verity greeted him with unaccustomed amiability, conscious that she had probably been unwise to have driven out with the Prince, and hoping to hide her indiscretion from Alistair. She was sitting idly in the parlor, unable to settle, when he strode in. She glanced at his set face and wondered what had put him in such a pucker. Had he learned so soon of her drive?

"Well, Alistair, this is a surprise. I thought you were occupied with your duties for the rest of the day."

Though taken up with his thoughts, Alistair noticed that his wife was looking uncommonly fetching this afternoon. Alistair was a generous provider, well up in the current fashions, and he had insisted on Verity buying a suitable wardrobe from the smartest of Parisian modistes. He admired her taste, noting the new azure silk. Her lovely titian hair had been arranged in the latest mode, à la Greque, which emphasized her large hazel eyes and drew attention to her flawless complexion, now slightly tinged with color. No wonder the Prince found her enticing. It was all Alistair could do not to drag her into his arms and ravish her on the spot, an action not likely to be well received at this hour. He stood staring at her, wondering how he could put his news, but Verity misunderstood his silence and hurried frantically into speech.

"Are we attending the Edgecombe reception this evening? I had completely forgotten about it until this moment," she asked, figeting under his stare.

"The reception. Yes, of course. That might be wise. I have just come from a conference at the Embassy," he began, then hesitated, wondering how to explain events to her. Would she be disgusted that he was willing to allow a flirtation between her and the Prince in the service of his country? Probably. She had quite strict notions and would be appalled at Alistair allowing such license. But if he did not explain matters to her, she would find his acquiescence of her association with the Prince even more callous and cynical. Damn the Duke and damn Castlereagh for placing this burden upon him. It was infamous that he should be expected to encourage his wife to attract another man just because they feared the Tsar's machinations.

Crossing to where she sat, he looked into her eyes, which dropped before his insistent gaze. "Something has occurred, Verity, which will no doubt increase your disgust of me, if that is possible."

Anticipating hearing some tale of infidelity or worse, Verity replied brittlely, "You could not shock me with any of your peccadilloes, Alistair. After all, I do have some experience of your lecherous ways."

His lips tightened. "Can we never put that wretched night behind us? Believe me, I regret it as much as you do."

"Yes, I am sure you do, since it forced you into this disastrous marriage," Verity answered bitterly, rising to her feet and backing away from him in some trepidation.

Alistair held on to his patience with an effort.

"I do not regret our marriage, only that you view me with such contempt. Believe me, Verity, despite the circumstances, I would not have married if I had not found you to my liking."

Liking, Verity thought, a tepid emotion, and not at all what she expected from a husband. But she was behaving stupidly, she knew, and she did not wish to go on in this mean fashion. She went up to Alistair and taking his arm looked up into his troubled eyes imploringly.

"You are quite right. We must try to put the past behind us and behave in a more comfortable manner with one another. I have resented your dominance and your cavalier attitude toward our marriage, but I will strive to do better in the future," she said sincerely, hoping to see a sign in his shuttered face of something more than mere liking.

"Pendleton sent for me today," Alistair told her,

"to tell me I have been relieved of my usual duties on the request of Wellington and Castlereagh to take on a special assignment. I have done some intelligence work before, and I suppose they thought I was the man for the job, distasteful as this chore is. And it involves you, Verity."

She looked at him in amazement. This was not at all what she had expected. She had been prepared for some story of outrageous scrapes, gambling debts, if not another woman, but Alistair's sober, disturbed expression showed how off the mark she had been. "What is troubling you, Alistair, and how can I help?" she asked soothingly.

"Come, let us sit down and discuss this comfortably." He led her to the settee by the fireplace and settled next to her.

"Well, somehow my superiors have learned of your . . . well, friendship with Prince Chirnovsky and want to turn it to their own uses. It's all this political conniving. Soldiers have no business involving themselves in these diplomatic messes. But Wellington believes the Tsar plans some ploy to force the British into complying with his Holy Alliance, a nonsensical business at best, and Wellington wants us to further your association with the Prince as he is privy to all his master's plans. It's damnable, Verity, and I will refuse to cooperate if the whole notion is repugnant to you."

"The Duke expects you to countenance a liaison between the Prince and myself just to solve some of his political difficulties?" she exclaimed, shocked. "I

243

would never have expected it of him!"

"He did not put it quite like that, and he has sense enough to realize I would not be a willing partner to such a relationship. No, he only wants us to further our acquaintance with the Prince and try to find out what the Tsar intends. The Prince is his valued aide and must be privy to whatever his emperor plans against Wellington, who is convinced some such plot is afoot. It's a fine thing that allies are conspiring against one another before Napoleon has even settled at St. Helena's."

"I fear diplomats have different, and less worthy, aims than soldiers. And they are not the only ones," Verity replied, ashamed at her recent deception and her encouragement of the Prince. She would have to tell Alistair of the Russian's visit. If they were to be partners in deception, he would have to know what she had done. Girding herself to the unwelcome chore, she faced her husband, her eyes beseeching him to understand. "I have to confess Alistair, that I have just returned from a drive with the Prince, and without flattering myself, believe he does have dishonorable intentions toward me," she said, but before Alistair could reply she continued. "I went from the meanest of motives, because I knew it would anger you. I am sorry."

But Alistair did not seem angry, only saddened that their marriage had come to this. "I have been behaving like a jealous fool. But I feared you had some feeling for that mountebank."

"I care nothing for the man and would never enter

into an intrigue with him," Verity insisted, her wide hazel eyes aglow with sincerity. How dreadful if Alistair had decided that she was a light-minded female willing to flirt and dally with any personable man who encouraged her. She was not so naive that she did not understand that Parisian society, or that segment of it which fashionable Londoners accepted, was inclined to wink at liaisons as long as they were discreet, but this was a morality of which Verity deeply disapproved.

"If we are going to cooperate on discovering the Prince's intentions," she went on, "or rather his emperor's, we must agree to cry pax, to put aside our personal preferences and become partners." She smiled at Alistair, signifying that she was willing if he was to enter into a new stage in their troubled relationship.

"What a trouper you are, Verity!" He grinned disarmingly at her, relieved that she would cease casting his sins in his face, and pleased at her show of spirit in the face of the distasteful duty that lay ahead of them. "Well, my fellow conspirator, we must make some plans, especially if you think we might meet the Prince at the Edgecombe reception this evening," he suggested, taking her hand and pressing it warmly. He hesitated and then plunged into what he must learn. "Did the Prince mention the Tsar's Holy Alliance to you on this infamous ride?" he asked teasingly.

Verity sobered and wrinkled her nose in a manner which made Alistair long to kiss her. "Only in passing. But he did warn that if the British are obdurate in not signing the Alliance, the Tsar has means of compelling them. I did not know what he meant," she confided in some puzzlement.

"Ah, then Wellington's suspicions are confirmed. But what could those means be? That is what we have to discover and soon, so they can be circumvented," Alistair replied, convinced now that Wellington's fears had some substantial cause.

"What do you suggest I do? I can hardly come right out and ask him," Verity said. This task which the Duke had set them was more complicated than she had realized.

Alistair frowned, thinking of the situation and accepting an unwelcome role. "No, but I think I must alter my attitude toward the Prince, appear more congenial, and not take him in abhorrence because he is tempting my wife. A difficult job, for I can hardly stand the sight of the fellow."

Verity laughed gently, teasing him. "Yes, I think you would prefer to give him a good leveler, as Charley would say, but now that is rather out of the question." She hesitated, unsure of how her next suggestion would be received. "Alistair, I'd rather not be alone with the Prince in a compromising situation. He rather frightens me."

"Now don't be fainthearted, Verity, that is not your style. You have no trouble in putting me in my place and you must use some of that natural haughtiness with the Prince," he jibed. When she did not smile, he saw she was really worried. "But never fear, I will keep a close eye upon you, as any devoted and jealous husband should," he assured her, half seriously, for he did not like the idea of playing the role of a complaisant husband.

"Not a part with which you have had much experience, I suspect," she replied saucily. "If the Russians are up to some chicanery which involves the Duke, I will do my best to thwart them. If only to avenge Charley's death. I know he would want me to help our country in any way I can," she said seriously, aware of the dangers which confronted her, but determined to play her part in any attempt to call the Russians to account. "Charley admired the Duke so and he would have insisted I accept any assignment which would help him out of his difficulties."

"Well, just remember this is duty, not pleasure," Alistair reminded her. "And I will be on hand to see you don't embroil yourself in some heedless escapade. You are far too apt to rush carelessly into trouble."

"Oh, I will be most circumspect," Verity answered, but absentmindedly. She was trying to remember exactly what the Prince had said about this important treaty and his belief that the British would not cooperate.

Alistair wondered where would this plot lead them, and was Wellington correct in suspecting the Russians of bringing pressure upon him? Surely his reputation as the savior of Europe placed him in an unassailable position. But he did not want Verity to know how deeply he decried her involvement or his fears for her safety. She would only laugh at them. For he was coming to know his wife well enough to sense her uncommon courage and independence. In that she was far removed from the usual young girl and if her determination led her into danger, he must just see to it that she paid no price for her rashness.

They parted for once on good terms with one another to dress for the evening's entertainment. As he tied his cravat later, Alistair brooded over their interview. Had he been wise to keep the affair on a lighthearted footing, unwilling to confide that he cared too much for her to allow her to take on this chore? Wellington had offered him little choice for as an officer he had to obey orders, but he could have refused to allow Verity to become involved. Alistair had always scorned deep emotions, preferring to keep matters on a casual level, but loath as he was to admit it, he couldn't bear to think of Verity in danger. He'd have to keep a careful eye on the situation and make sure matters never got out of hand.

If Alistair was prey to conflicting emotions, Verity was scarcely less so. She had made up her mind to treat her husband with a blithe indifference, and now he had overset her intentions by offering a breezy friendship which did not quite accord with her own feelings. She found his very presence disturbing and, she wondered about her helpless responses to his lovemaking. Was she in truth a wanton whose physical needs were answered so pleasurably by Alistair that his possession of her clouded all else? Or could he have become so important to her that she craved his undivided love?

Laughing a bit cynically, Verity reminded herself that Alistair was a noted womanizer, unable to settle on any woman's charms to the exclusion of another. She would do well to remember his reputation and not yearn for a relationship she could never have. But at least now, they could rub along without any friction, a great improvement, even if this friendly partnership was much less than what she dreamed of. She was no longer an idealistic girl, expecting a lifetime of love and devotion. She must simply manage with what she had, even if it fell short of her daydreams. Other girls settled for far less, and she must steel herself to be equally accommodating, a decision she insisted was only sensible, even if it left her with a hollow sense of dissatisfaction and regret.

Casting aside her doubts and questions, she allowed Agnes to dress her in a lovely gown of cream satin with an overskirt of silver tissue, and to wind pearls in her elaborate coiffure. Viewing herself in the mirror, she had to allow that she was well girded for the challenge ahead, and had done all she could to prepare for the evening. Of a naturally resilient nature, Verity felt her spirits lift. Neither Alistair nor the Prince should expect she would tamely follow their lead. She would show them that she could determine her own fate and, with that resolution, swept out of the room to meet her husband.

Chapter Sixteen

Verity's best intentions were sorely tried almost immediately upon arriving at the Edgecombes' ball. She had been feeling pleasantly confident of her looks and her new truce with Alistair as they approached the receiving line where Lady Edgecombe, a plump rather jolly matron of middle years, greeted them roguishly.

"Ah, Major Glendenning, here you are with your charming new bride, who is in especial good looks this evening. Enjoying your honeymoon, eh?" She smiled archly.

"Yes, indeed, Lady Edgecombe, and with every reason. Is not my bride an incomparable?" he replied suavely, not one whit discomfitted by his hostess's suggestive remark.

Lady Edgecombe readily agreed. She turned to Verity. "My dear, your husband is quite right. You put us all in the shade." She hesitated and was about to say more but, seeing the press of guests behind the Glendennings, smiled vaguely and passed them on with the remark that she hoped they would enjoy themselves.

"Lady Edgecombe is such a rattle, has no more sense than a pea goose," Alistair remarked as he steered Verity toward the ballroom, just beginning to swell with the guests.

"All of London seems to have descended on Paris. But I cannot see the Prince. I am sure if he has already arrived he will hurry to claim a dance. But before he does, let us take the lady's advice and join this waltz." He swept her masterfully onto the floor.

Verity sparkled, following his lead and responding to the close clasp of his arms as he skillfully maneuvered her through the dancers. Peeping up at him through her lashes she thought, not for the first time, what a handsome man he was, especially in his dashing red dress uniform of the Life Guards. No wonder so many women had succumbed to him. An unaccustomed glow of happiness brought a flush to her cheeks and a flirtatious gleam to her wide eyes.

"Are you flirting with me, Verity?" Alistair asked softly, looking down at her. Her head with its glorious titian hair came just above his shoulders. Gad, she was a stunning woman, he thought, and he tightened his hold as they dashingly reversed on the crowded floor.

"And why not, Alistair? I must practice for the Prince, when he makes his arrival," she teased, conscious of the sensuous heat flooding through her body at the closeness of their embrace.

"Minx. It's a good thing you are a respectable married woman or who knows what you would be getting up to," Alistair warned, not entirely in jest. "I can see that I will have to keep a careful eye upon you," he continued, but she just laughed, too happy to argue with him.

But her unaccountable happiness and sense that she and Alistair had entered into a new phase of their relationship received a jolt soon after the waltz had come to an end. They were standing chatting easily with a group of Alistair's fellow officers when they were joined by a couple Verity had not noticed before. The gentleman was Count Karl Zichy, an Austrian of great wealth and reputation as one of the notable hosts of his day as well as a friend of Chancellor Metternich, as Verity later learned. But she paid little attention to the middle-aged nobleman, her eyes riveted to the lady on his arm, who was introduced as Olivia, Lady Bletchford, a stunning blonde in a revealing gown of ice blue satin and a great display of diamonds. She seemed to be on very intimate terms with Alistair, and greeted him effusively.

"Dear Alistair, I had to prevail on the Count to bring me across to meet your bride. So sudden your wedding, and all of London is astir over the news," she gushed, turning her light blue eyes meltingly on Alistair. Verity noticed that he was far from pleased with the lady's appearance and then remembered that this was the woman who had caused the scandal

253

that had forced Alistair to resign from his former regiment. He would have been ruined if Lord Uxbridge had not taken pity upon him and given him a position on his staff. Ariel Montague had mentioned the matter to Verity, excusing Alistair by implying the lady had done most of the running, and here she was obviously prepared to try again, not at all put off by Alistair's new marital status.

"There must not be a soul left in London, Olivia, since all of the ton has repaired to Paris to delight us with their company," Alistair said smoothly, bowing formally over the lady's hand, and then remembering his duty, "May I present my wife, Verity. My dear," he continued, turning to Verity, "Olivia, Lady Bletchford, is an old friend."

An old friend, indeed, Verity thought, barely restraining her anger. So this woman had lured Alistair into a disastrous liaison, and now was determined to resume their immoral relationship, if what she read in the lady's eye was any indication of her intent. Verity acknowledged the introduction coldly, earning a disapproving stare from her husband. Well, he need not think she would play a patient Griselda while he dallied with his former lover. But Lady Bletchford paid little attention to Verity; her interest was fixed on her victim.

"Do let us dance, Alistair," she cooed enticingly, "and catch up on all our news. It's an age since I have seen you."

Alistair, casting a wary glance at Verity, whose every lineament told of her disdain, cursed silently to himself. Damn, this was a coil. He had prayed that he had seen the last of Olivia when he had escorted her to her aunt's in Wiltshire, fleeing from the wrath of her aging husband, who had learned of their affair. How had she escaped from his surveillance and turned up in Paris? And Verity would not take her arrival and overtures in good part. She must have heard all the details of that past folly from Ariel, and was prepared to think the worst. Still, he could hardly refuse Olivia's request without seeming the utmost cad.

He tried to make his excuses. "I am afraid I am promised to my wife for the next set," he apologized, hoping Olivia would take the rebuff but before she could demur, Verity interrupted coolly. "Not at all, Alistair, I am sure you and Lady Bletchford have a great deal to say to one another. And here is Prince Chirnovsky, who I am sure has come to claim a dance." She smiled at the newcomer, who bowed over her hand with what Alistair thought was smarmy gallantry, and did indeed request her as a partner.

"Come now, Alistair, you must not be such a stuffy overly protective husband, not at all the thing. I am sure we can leave your little bride safely in the Prince's company," Lady Bletchford trilled, having given the Prince an all encompassing stare and summed up the situation. Alistair, inwardly fuming at the unfortunate turn of events, had no recourse but to lead Lady Bletchford onto the floor. He noticed that the Prince followed with Verity immediately but joined a set as far from Alistair and his partner as possible.

It was difficult to have much conversation as the intricacies of the dance parted the pairs frequently, and Alistair was content to have it so, distracted as he was by trying to keep an eye on Verity while answering Olivia's coy questions. Finally he surrendered to the inevitable and suggested that on the conclusion of their dance they sit the next number out so that they could converse without interruption. That suited Olivia perfectly although she was chagrined when he insisted they settle on the gilt chairs lining the ballroom, in full view of the company and of Verity. He was not going to be trapped into a secluded rendezvous with the importunate lady, no matter how hard she tried.

"Well, Olivia, I am surprised to see you here. How did you escape from Lord Bletchford? I thought he was most suspicious," Alistair said grimly, determined to learn the worst.

"My dear husband is completely incapacitated with the gout, and confined to our London house. I decided it was safe to make the journey and, of course, I was missing you dreadfully, Alistair dear," she said, laying a white hand covered with jewels on his arm. He removed it and spoke to her more harshly than he had intended.

"I am married now, Olivia, and whatever passed between us before must be forgotten. We both

256

barely avoided a ruinous scandal and any relationship between us now would only stir up all the old gossip, causing Verity pain and humiliation. I will not allow that to happen."

"Oh, Alistair, how unkind you are," she cooed, batting her eyes at him. "Here I have come all this way, mainly to see you, and you treat me so coldly. Surely your marriage, sealed in such haste, cannot mean as much to you as our former affection for one another."

Alistair refused to be drawn. "Olivia, you know that our liaison, pleasant as it was, served merely as a diversion for you, and you had no intention of it developing into a grand passion. And I think we both paid a heavy price for our indiscretion. It is over, my dear, so let it rest. What I was capable of before my marriage is not possible now, even if I was so inclined, which I am not. I would not cause my wife such distress."

"Alistair, I cannot believe you are saying these cruel words to me. I have suffered so much over your rejection and your marriage, surely you can treat me with some compassion," the lady insisted, her pouting mouth now assuming a grim, unattractive line. "I can make life very difficult for you with that simpering girl. How she caught you, heaven knows. Her birth is unexceptional, and although I daresay she has a certain unspoiled charm, you will soon grow bored with that and seek new diversions."

It was obvious that Lady Bletchford could not imagine any real rival to her own sophisticated charms, and Alistair had had enough. He had problems enough without the distraciton of Olivia Bletchford, whose charms no longer attracted him. What had he ever seen in this vapid woman who was so eager to lure him into another disastrous romantic tangle?

"It's over, Olivia," he replied curtly. "Please accept that and stop your lamentations. They do you little credit. I am sure you will soon find another poor fool with whom to cuckold your husband. Now you must excuse me. I see Lord Castlereagh has arrived and I must make my obeisances." He rose and bowed, leaving Lady Bletchford fuming and determined to take her revenge. He suspected he had made an enemy there, but in the shock of her sudden appearance just when things were going so well with Verity, he had not summoned his usual beguiling skill to soothe the irate rejected woman.

But after all, he thought, there was little more she could do to embarrass him. Meanwhile he must look after Verity, without delay. In this intention he was foiled by Castlereagh, who engaged him in a long chat, and then he could not find his wife in the press of dancers. Had she retired to have a tête-à-tête with the Prince?

She had. After their dance the Prince had insisted they sit out the next set, and since Verity had seen Alistair in intimate conversation with Lady Bletchford, admittedly in full view of the company, she consented, not without a certain trepidation. But how else was she to discover what Castlereagh and

Wellington wanted to know? The Prince, it seemed, had other aims in mind. He escorted her to one of the anterooms and settled down next to her on a convenient divan.

"Such a proper married lady—the wife of one of Wellington's gallant officers. And how do you like your new role?" the Prince asked, in what Verity thought was a sneering tone. "Does it confirm your belief in the sanctity of the connubial state?"

"Naturally, most girls of good family prefer to be respectably situated, Prince," she replied evenly. "As Mrs. Glendenning, my status is improved to what it would have been as a mere paid companion, subject to the demands and humiliations which such a position would have entailed. Do not your Russian girls of the aristocracy feel the same?" she asked sweetly. She could not resist reminding him that she had not been completely gulled by his apparent interest in establishing her in a far different role.

"Marriage is, of course, necessary to secure an heir, to cement fortunes, to settle property, but I am not thinking of what, after all, is merely practical, but of love, of passion, rarely found in the nuptial couch." He gave her a smoldering look, his dark Slavic eyes glowing with a fire which Verity, in other circumstances, might have found rather ridiculous. But she knew that tonight she must humor him. He deserved a good set-down but that would hardly further her purpose.

"Really, Prince Chirnovsky, you do say the most shocking things!" she remarked archly, feeling a

259

fool, but determined to play her role to the hilt.

"Why this formal address? You must call me Vasilii, *doushka,*" he insisted, taking her hand and moving closer to her.

"I do not think my husband would approve of that," Verity said primly.

"Ah, but your husband is a man of the world, not averse to a little dalliance himself. He is on very intimate terms with the so charming Lady Bletchford, a friendship of long standing, no doubt." He hoped to rouse Verity's jealousy, and lure her into an indignant rebuttal, which he could then counter with sympathy and insinuate himself further into her good graces.

Aware of his motives, Verity played along with him. "Oh, Vasilii, you must not be deceived by English ton manners. Few husbands and wives reveal their affection in public. Not the thing, you understand."

"Ah, the English, so cold like their detestable climate. All for war and business and little for amour." The Prince sighed theatrically.

Verity repressed an instinct to giggle at the Prince's dramatic tone. "Not at all, Vasilii, but we are not inclined to parade our emotions."

"We Slavs know how to love, and forget everything in the passion of the moment," he insisted, gazing at her with longing.

"Not everything, surely, Vasilii. What about duty? Surely you place your duty to your emperor, to your country, above all else?" From beneath her lashes, she watched him carefully.

"Of course. The Holy Father deserves my devotion, and receives it, but my nature demands that I pursue and find romance," he replied, adroitly turning the conversation back to its original theme. "Politics is no substitute for love, *doushka.*"

"Perhaps not, but politics seems to concern all of us in Paris," Verity pointed out cleverly. "It is vital that the peace be secured, that Europe be protected from another Napoleon."

"If your statesmen would agree to the Tsar's plan, his Holy Alliance, we could put this recent trouble behind us. His alliance is perhaps too visionary for you English, a nation of shopkeepers, Napoleon said, and I think he may be right," the Prince answered, annoyed that Verity was not responding to his flirtatious gambits.

"I hardly think General Wellington has the soul of a shopkeeper," she replied lightly. "He is our salvation."

"Of course, he is a great soldier, but perhaps a bit stubborn and arrogant," the Prince said impatiently. "Our Tsar has a more noble ideal, and he will prevail. But come, we must not waste our precious time together worrying over the state of Europe. Lovely ladies cannot be concerned with such matters when the other delights are offered to them."

Verity smiled. The man had a colossal ego, she thought, so confident of his charm, so certain he could beguile her into an affair. How she would like to speak her mind, but that would never do. She must find out how much the Prince really knew of the Tsar's plans to cajole Wellington into the Alliance.

"You are obviously a great support to the Tsar, so knowledgeable, so worldly. Your advice to him must be of great import," she flattered, batting her eyelashes up at him.

He was not impervious to this appeal to his conceit. He preened a bit, in what Verity privately thought a rather stupid fashion.

"I am in the Holy Father's confidence, one of his most trusted aides, that is true. And I will see to it that he achieves his aim. I have the means to compell your great Duke to comply with the Tsar's requests," he boasted, eager to display his importance to this lovely woman.

"Of course, I do not understand these matters, quite beyond my feeble powers," Verity demurred softly, "but the Duke seems to me to be a man who is not easily dissuaded when he has decided upon a course."

"Ah, but that is it, he is a man, and subject as all of us to human emotions, which can propel us into situations which threaten our good judgment— much as I am, my dear lady."

Now what did he mean by that? Verity wondered. That Wellington was apt to behave foolishly because of some uncontrollable passion for a woman? How typical of the Russians, who themselves were of unrestrained and overexuberant emotions, to think that others were of their ilk. But Verity felt she had endured enough for one interview, and gave a small moue of vexation. "Oh, dear, you are such a fascinating conversationalist, Vasilii, I have forgotten the time, and must have left my partner for the next dance wondering where I am. We must return to the ballroom." She stood, indicating that she would accept no refusal.

"Alas, I am desolate. But I am your servant in this as in all else. Perhaps we will meet again before too long and continue our interesting discussion." The Prince was satisfied that he had laid his groundwork well. She would need careful handling, this one, but he was convinced it would be worth it, and quite a blow to that insufferable major of hers to learn that his wife was not the virtuous little madam he had married.

As they returned to the ballroom, he indicated Wellington, who had just arrived and was talking intimately with Lady Frances Wedderburn-Webster in one corner of the room.

"See, your great Duke is not impervious to the charms of the ladies. I understand the luscious Lady Frances is a great favorite of his," he suggested slyly.

They were interrupted by Alistair, who claimed Verity for supper, after a perfunctory greeting to the Prince.

Verity, peeping up at her stern husband as he escorted her toward the supper table, wondered why he looked so grim. Had Lady Bletchford made him regret his marriage? Or was he angry that she had gone off with the Prince? So like a man to criticize a woman for doing exactly what she was bid. After all, if she was to discover what the Tsar had in mind, she must not rebuff the emperor's aide. Surely he saw that.

"Really, Alistair, stop glowering so. People will think you have taken me in dislike, very odd for a new bridegroom. After all, I am only following the plan we agreed upon, and you could have been a bit more courteous to the Prince.

He looked down at her and suddenly laughed. "Quite right, Verity. I am not behaving well, but this has been a trying evening. Still, let us postpone our exchange of information until we have returned to our lodgings. This is hardly the place to have any discussion. I hope you have not embroiled yourself in some outrageous situation with that fellow."

"Come, look at all those lobster patties!" Verity exclaimed, ignoring Alistair's query. "Just the thing to refresh our flagging spirits, and then a few more waltzes and we will have done our duty."

Alistair looked with amusement at his wife, who seemed in her element amid all this intrigue. He hoped that she did not find the Prince's overtures attractive despite herself.

They joined a few couples, all known to Alistair, and proceeded to give every indication of being perfectly delighted newlyweds.

Chapter Seventeen

Back in their quarters Alistair and Verity compared information about the evening, but neither mentioned the unexpected appearance of Olivia Bletchford. Alistair was reluctant to disturb the new accord which had sprung up between them resulting from the necessity of discovering the Tsar's intrigues, and Verity, although curious and resentful, hesitated to broach the topic of the voluptuous lady in case Alistair confided that he still found her attractive. They confined their conversation to the Prince's confidences about the Tsar's plans to force Wellington to sign his Holy Alliance.

"I don't quite understand what the Tsar hopes to achieve with this rather mysterious treaty," Verity said, accepting a cup of cocoa from Alistair, her white teeth biting eagerly into a sandwich as they settled down to discuss the evening.

Alistair, shrugging off his uniform jacket and

sitting down next to her on the settee, sighed in frustration. "I don't think the emperor himself really knows. He has grandiose ideas of forcing the rulers of Europe and the Orient to govern by Christian principles, all very well in theory, but grossly impractical. And Liverpool and Wellington will never agree to allowing any foreigner, no matter how altruistic, to interfere in the internal affairs of England. The whole thing is a pipe dream, but that doesn't mean the Tsar cannot stir up the populace, make England appear to be the ogre who is stalling the peace efforts. Damn nonsense, all of it," he growled, thoroughly disgusted with this Slavic mysticism.

"But if England does not sign, what about the peace? We cannot return to war," Verity argued.

"It will not come to that, but the Tsar can make matters very sticky. And Metternich is playing his games, conniving with both sides for his own ends, which are political and far from Christian," Alistair explained. "Politics are the very devil. We can throw away all the gains of the victory of Waterloo at the peace table, and I believe that is what Wellington fears."

"But these threats that the Prince makes about the Tsar's means of compelling the Duke. Could it have something to do with personal blackmail?" Verity ventured, wrinkling her forehead in perplexity.

"Personal blackmail. The Duke may not be a paragon, but I doubt he would submit to any such threat," Alistair insisted, loath to admit that his hero could be liable to any such ploy.

"The Prince made some reference to the Duke's inclination to flirt with attractive ladies. In that he is no different from most men, I suspect," Verity answered bitterly, reminded of Alistair's past and Sir Anthony's attempts upon her own person.

Alistair smiled a bit grimly, in no doubt that she was referring to his own escapades. "I cannot believe that Wellington, for all his penchant for an attractive female, would be so foolish as to give his enemies such a lever. His attentions to the fair sex have always been most open, but not serious, I am sure."

"Well, he is certainly making a cake of himself over Lady Wedderburn-Webster. I hear that he even wrote her immediately after the battle when I should think his mind would have been occupied with far different affairs," Verity responded sharply.

"I think you refine too much upon a few casual words from the Prince. He probably suspects every man of dalliance since he is so inclined that way himself." Alistair looked at Verity searchingly, realizing that he had given her every opportunity to bring up his own liaison with Olivia. But she remained silent. After a few uncomfortable moments when neither of them wanted to pursue the direction which their conversation was taking, Verity rose and signified that she wanted to retire.

"I am exhausted, and cannot think anymore this evening. Perhaps the morning will bring some enlightenment, and I suppose all we can do is to try

267

to fathom what the Prince knows of his emperor's plans. Although I don't quite see how we can wrest more information from him," she concluded in some despair, feeling thoroughly tired of the whole business.

Alistair rose and escorted her to the door. "Don't fret anymore about it tonight, Verity, and try to have a good sleep. But remember the Prince is a crafty devil, and may be using us, as we are trying to use him, for some purpose we have not yet discovered. Be careful. I hate having you subject to his blandishments. I must in truth be more possessive than I had imagined."

Verity looked at him in some surprise. Now, what did he mean—that he cared for her or just that he would entertain no man making overtures to his wife, just because she was his wife. She could not fathom the strange look he bent upon her, and she was too tired to continue this conversation which went round and round to no conclusion.

"I will see you in the morning, Verity, when perhaps we will come up with some new idea," Alistair said, implying that he would not be visiting her bed that evening. He wanted to take her in his arms and follow his inclination to make love to her, but a variety of emotions prevented him. He could not force her again, and she showed no signs of welcoming his advances. In both of them pride warred with other confused emotions and neither would make the first move to solve their dilemma or admit their growing feeling for one another.

Verity hurried from the sitting room, fearing that she might make some humiliating plea for comfort and understanding. Alistair watched her go, his eyes dark with self-mockery. Turning back to the table, he poured himself some brandy. What a damnable coil. He had entered this marriage to preserve both their reputations, but now found himself wanting more than he deserved to have from his intriguing wife. He laughed at his dilemma. He was fairly caught at last, in love with a wife who held him in disgust, while she was forced to cooperate in a conspiracy which could lure them both into deep waters. Abandoning his musing he stood up, put his unfinished glass on the table, and decided to take his own advice to Verity. He would sleep on his troubles and perhaps the morning would bring a solution.

What the morning brought was a shocking scandal. Corporal Jenkins roused his master early with a copy of the *St. James Chronicle* which drove all thoughts of his personal crisis from Alistair's mind.

A report is very prevalent in the first Parisian circles that a distinguished commander has surrendered himself captive to the beautiful wife of a military officer of high rank, in a manner to make a very serious investigation of this offense indispensable . . .

The article went on to infer that the "offense" would undoubtedly lead to a "crim con" case, in fact a divorce. There was every reason to suspect that the anonymous offender might be the Duke of Wellington, Alistair conceded. London society thrived on rumor but this item went beyond the bounds of decency. And if it was true, the Prince's innuendoes now seemed to have every basis in fact. Was this the weapon the Tsar intended to use? If so, Alistair decided, every effort must be made to thwart him.

The journal article offered a perfect excuse for Alistair to visit Verity in her boudoir. Normally, he respected her sanctuary during the daytime, and restricted his nighttime visits. But this news could not wait for niceties of behavior.

He found her sitting up in bed, looking adorably rumpled and sipping the chocolate which was her usual morning fare. Her glorious titian hair, uncombed, tumbled down her shoulders, and she wore a most fetching, and revealing, white cambric nightgown. She flushed at his entrance and drew the covers up more closely, hoping to hide her dishevelment. Agnes was fussing about, readying her mistress's clothes for the day, and Alistair dismissed her impatiently.

"Good morning, Verity. I apologize for disturbing you, but some rather startling news has just arrived which bears out our conclusions, I think. And I wanted to discuss it with you before taking any action," he said, handing her the *Chronicle* and indicating the offending article.

Verity, rather taken aback by his abrupt entrance and the appreciative gaze in his warm eyes, was too overset to take in his meaning, but she quickly settled on the article which her uncomprehending eyes at first did not grasp. Alistair's looming presence, in his brocade dressing gown, lent an intimacy to the occasion which set her pulses racing and she had difficulty concentrating on the shocking gossip which the journal reported. But she lost little time in scanning the revelations, and raised startled eyes to his.

"Could this be the threat the Prince referred to? Surely he is not responsible for this scurrilous article," she said in some confusion. She wished Alistair would not look at her so. Then, to compound her nervousness, he sat casually down on the bed, prepared to discuss the problem.

"There are plenty of eager rumor-mongers who might have relayed the latest on dits to London," he told her. "We need not lay the blame at the Tsar's or the Prince's door. But if what the *Chronicle* says is true, this may be the very weapon the Russians need to force Wellington into signing the Alliance. I must be off to confer with him, in case he has not seen this, which I doubt. Some malicious soul will have brought it to his attention. I must admit I don't relish the chore of questioning him about his dalliance with Lady Wedderburn-Webster."

"Poor Lady Wellington, immured in England with her children and having to listen to all this," Verity said, her heart touched by the affect of the scandal on the innocent party.

"If she had stayed here, and had not appeared so

271

farouche, the rumors would not have been so damning. Most of the ton have noticed Old Hookey's partiality for Lady Wedderburn-Webster. And so, it seems, has her husband. What could the Duke have been thinking of at this delicate juncture in affairs?" Alistair fulminated angrily, annoyed that his hero should be compromised.

Verity eyed him tartly. "Just what all you gentlemen think of, your own pleasures, with nary a worry for the consequences. He should have realized that his enemies would seize on such a juicy morsel to embarrass him."

"What a little Puritan you are, Verity. On the surface all propriety and severity, but underneath lies a passionate woman," he teased, leaning over and placing his hands on either side of her where she sat ensconced on a sea of pillows. "Have you no charity for us poor men, lured by your attractions into folly?" He kissed her hard on the mouth.

Verity, annoyed that she felt such a surge of warmth under this sensual assault, blushed to the roots of her hair. "This is no time for such dalliance, Alistair. We must decide how to go on," she said weakly.

"I know how I would like to go on," he said suavely, enjoying her confusion. "But you are quite right. We must decide how to deal with this imbroglio." He straightened up. "Have you any ideas?"

"Well, first, you must warn the Duke. And I forgot, in the turmoil of this latest development, to tell you what Agnes has discovered. Did you know that the Tsar's friend, Baroness Julie von Krudener, is living two doors down from us? Agnes has met her abigail. It seems the emperor visits her stealthily at night. What does that mean, I wonder?" She patted her hair and tried to put some distance between them. He was uncomfortably close to oversetting her composure and she would not give him that advantage.

"The Tsar has a reputation with women, but alas, I fear the Baroness's influence is not one of sensual delights," he explained. "She encourages him to delve into mysticism and Christian confession. His nighttime visits are confined to reading the Bible and readying his soul to meet God, I understand. She has much to answer for in pressing this Holy Alliance."

"Oh, dear. I was hoping we might find some way to hold the emperor's excesses over his head, in retaliation for his accusations and threats against Wellington, if that is what he has in mind." Verity sighed in frustration, her plans overset.

"A year ago, in Vienna, we might have tried that, but he has renounced all pleasures of the flesh in a welter of religious fervor, I believe, although he still enjoys the ladies, I vow." Alistair rose and began pacing the room. "Somehow we must find his vulnerable spot, or Wellington's whole career could be ruined."

"Could that happen, after Waterloo?" Verity asked, dismayed by the prospect of their hero's feet of clay. "He is in such high favor now."

"He will not continue to be idolized if he is accused of luring one of his officers' wives into his bed," Alistair answered frankly, disturbed by the prospect. "And even if it is just gossip, it could cause harm and political turmoil. Well, I must be off to face him with this, and meantime, you might be thinking of how to lure the Prince into an indiscretion—without succumbing to his advances, mind you. I will not be cuckolded by that womanizer or anyone, even to save Wellington."

"Really, Alistair. Do you think I am such a wanton ninny as to surrender to his immoral proposals?" she protested, pleased that he evidenced some jealousy but disgusted that he should think her so tempted by the Prince. "But I hope I am clever enough to ferret out what he and the Tsar have in mind for the Duke."

Alistair gave her a lazy smile. "You know they say rakes make the most prudish and proper husbands. I never believed it before, but I must confess I think the adage must be true. I am quite unwilling to share you, my dear, even for the sake of England."

Verity wrinkled her nose at him in reproof, but could not help but feel a thrill of excitement at his possessiveness. She wanted to believe that he was indeed coming to care for her. What a complex man he was. Underneath that insouciant, live-for-today air lurked an old-fashioned moralist. Surely his words promised a more tender emotion than just the natural desire not to have his wife become a figure of gossip and hence reflect upon his own amour propre. But for now she must continue to treat him with casual friendship rather than risk their blossoming regard for one another.

Bidding her a light farewell, Alistair went about his uncomfortable business, leaving Verity a prey to a welter of emotions, and a decision to bring matters to a climax.

Chapter Eighteen

Alistair's interview with Wellington was just as uncomfortable as he had expected. He sought out the Duke in his headquarters and was received immediately, not kept kicking his heels in an anteroom as he had anticipated. Was this an indication that the Duke took the matter of Lady Frances Wedderburn-Webster seriously? It was difficult to tell when he entered the great man's presence. Although the Duke was a man of strict propriety, with a natural hauteur in dealing with his inferiors, he could at times relax and become almost jovial in his officers' company. It was in this mood that he greeted Alistair, rising from behind a spartan desk covered with papers.

"Ha, Glendenning. You have some news to report. Thank heavens, it will distract me from these interminable reports. I suspect your news is bad for you are wearing a Friday face," Wellington said calmly, obviously not aware that his reputation had been torn to shreds by one of London's journals.

"Unfortunately, sir, I am a bearer of bad tidings. I don't quite know how to put this," Alistair replied gravely, proffering the newspaper which he had brought with him, and preparing for a storm to break over his head. "Have you seen this sheet, just arrived from London?" He waited with some anxiety while the Duke read the offending article.

Alistair watched as a ferocious frown darkened the Duke's face, his blue eyes glacial.

Placing the paper on the desk, Wellington eyed his subordinate skeptically, and then smiled a bit ruefully. "Rubbish. Surely you do not think this scandalous trash should be taken seriously. I am often the butt of such gossip. Best to ignore it, I think. Trying to refute it only lends dignity to the canard." He frowned again and then returned to the problem. "Do you have some idea that this concerns the Tsar's ploys? The emperor would never stoop to using casual gossip to further his ends."

"I only bring it to your attention because of what my wife told me of a conversation she had last evening with Prince Chirnovsky at the Edgecombe ball," he replied.

"Yes, well, continue, Major," Wellington said brusquely.

Alistair met the Duke's eyes squarely. "It was mostly hint and innuendo, but the Prince implied that he knew the Tsar had some reason to force you to accede to his wishes in the matter of the Alliance,

278

and then he made some slighting remark about your friendship for the lady."

"Don't mince matters, Glendenning. You think the Tsar might attempt to blackmail me with this gossip. I care little for his threats, and they would never hinder me from fulfilling my obligations to His Majesty."

"I never thought that, sir, but it occurred to me that this on dit could make your job a bit more difficult, and I know any rumors will fly about Paris with all kinds of embroidery. It can only cause embarrassment and tarnish your reputation as the hero of Waterloo."

"Poor Kitty. She has borne so much and this must be giving her great sorrow," Wellington answered, referring to his wife, but not apologizing or explaining whether there was any truth in the gossip. Alistair waited, hoping the Duke had some remedy to quell the scandal.

"I assure you, Glendenning, that your fear of a 'crim con' case, and all its attendant horrors is not on the cards. I am surprised that the Tsar could think that this paltry rumor could force me into unwise action. He is bound and determined to get England's signature on that high-flown Alliance, and we are in a bit of a cleft stick, for we must keep the Russians tied to some kind of treaty, although not one which would endanger His Majesty's government and its freedom to operate," Wellington mused. He said nothing about Lady Wedderburn-Webster and Alistair had not believed he would, but still the situation was grave. Wellington need not explain himself to his junior officer but he must give him some orders. He watched as the Duke walked to the window and looked out, intent on dealing with this latest problem.

Finally the Duke turned and faced Alistair, looking at him with decision. "We must have some proof that the Tsar intends to use this information to our detriment. Can you get that evidence?" he said shortly, as ever in a crisis, coming to the heart of the matter.

"I don't know, sir," Alistair admitted. "My wife is quite friendly with the Prince, as I have mentioned before, and she might be able to secure some proof. As I explained, she is most anxious to do what she can to serve her country. She feels the loss of her brother at Waterloo and wants to avenge his death. Of course, I would prefer she not be involved, but since she already knows of the machinations against you, she will not plead faintheartedness now. And she is a great admirer of yours, sir. She will do what she can."

"You are newly married, I understand, Major. It is unfortunate that your bride should become involved in this distasteful affair, but when we spoke previously, you gave me to understand she would cooperate. We must have a little more information to counter the Tsar's intrigue and I see no other way to gain it quickly," Wellington replied glumly, turning over the options in his mind. "I hate having women meddling in these affairs, but since she has signified she would not be averse to accepting the assignment, we must use the tools that are available, I suppose."

Alistair restrained his inclination to add that Wellington had brought this latest imbroglio upon himself by flirting with the lady in question.

"Perhaps Lady Wedderburn-Webster could be persuaded to return to London—or her husband, the captain, could be prevailed upon to insist that she remove herself from the public scrutiny," he suggested.

Wellington dismissed the idea impatiently. "I doubt that could be effected, and the gentleman in question is proving very intransigent. I can hardly command him to put his domestic affairs in order, you know," he added ruefully.

Alistair believed he could do just that but wondered if the Duke cared more for the lady than he was willing to admit, and the idea of abandoning her was not to his taste. He was a bit puzzled by the Duke's attitude. Was he really so fond of the female that he would endanger his own marriage, and more important, his career? If the Duke was innocent, merely the victim of particular attentions to the lady, with no carnal interest, his pride would not allow him to justify his actions, nor would he use his position as commander in chief to order Captain Wedderburn-Webster to drop proceedings, if that was what the gentleman had in mind. Wellington's character did not incline him to sue for popularity. He saw his duty and did it, without explanations or excuses. In this affair he would behave as his nature led him, Alistair concluded, making no allowances for the harm the libel, if that was what it was, might evoke. Alistair himself had been victimized by a similar situation, and so he had great sympathy for the Duke's position. How rotten if a mere casual friendship for an attractive woman could be used against the Duke by his enemies. Even if the outcome imperiled Wellington's standing at the Peace Conference, Alistair doubted that he would take steps to dispel the rumors. Could he not see the danger in this arrogant refusal to pay any attention to the journal's scurrilous outpourings?

Wellington interrupted Alistair's worried conjecture. "We are having enough difficulty with the French and Talleyrand about reparations and a constitution without any other complications. I am needed here. I cannot return to England myself, but perhaps my wife might be prevailed upon to join me here," he suggested. "The Bourbon is angry with me, too. Gave me quite a snub the other evening. However, his attitude can be explained. He hopes to prevent me from asking for clemency in the case of Ney. These Frenchies take offense easily in defeat. Louis would be wiser to seek conciliation." He appeared lost in contemplation of his various options, but then shrugged his shoulders as if shaking off the demands of state, and smiled at Alistair.

"Well, Glendenning, I am sure this is all most tiresome for you. But I think we must acquit the Tsar of any involvement in this newspaper tempest. Still, I think he is capable of any amount of intrigue and I am counting on you to discover just what he does plan. And you had better be quick about it," he ended with his usual authoritative manner. No hint of embarrassment at this discussion of his personal affairs with a junior officer marred his demeanor.

"Yes, sir. I will do my best." He saluted and left the august presence.

How to proceed was the question now, for he still thought the scandal would be turned to some account by the Russians. Could Verity lure the Prince into some indiscreet admissions, and would that be the proof which Wellington would accept? As he walked down the Champs Elysée, Alistair realized that he had entered deep waters indeed, where his expertise as a cavalry commander was of little use. The skills demanded of an officer in the field were of no help in a situation which called for crafty intelligence and knowledge of drawing room politics. If only he could seek advice from Ian Montague, but in this matter he had to keep his own counsel and hope that he might serve the Duke faithfully, assisting him to emerge from the scandal creditably. First and foremost, his concern was for Verity.

While Alistair was undergoing his awkward interview with Wellington, Verity had taken herself and Agnes off to the milliner's. She was not in need of a new bonnet but she thought she might learn whether the ton's leading lights had any knowledge of this latest attempt to discredit Wellington.

As she had expected, several ladies had gathered at the shop with the same idea in mind. It was soon apparent that the gossip about the Duke had crossed the Channel. Several ladies, whom she knew only slightly, were all agog with the scandal. Among the first to discuss the titillating topic was Lady Shelley, whom Verity had met at various functions, and who had previously enjoyed some of the Duke's attentions. Lady Shelley, from chagrin, Verity suspected, spitefully regaled the company with the latest developments in the Wedderburn-Webster affair. Verity contented herself with listening carefully, although she was tempted to tell the group that Wellington's embarrassment might lead to serious political difficulties for their country.

Watching the avid faces of Lady Shelley's audience, she wondered if these women, pillars of society, could all bear a similar airing of their private business. But Wellington had offended their unwritten code. The most shocking intrigues could be ignored as long as they were not blazoned abroad. How mean-spirited and fatuous they sounded, criticizing the very man they had idolized just days before.

The poor milliner's assistant could not distract them with the latest models, although she kept trying to lure them into purchases. The whole scene disgusted Verity. She felt, however, that any attempt on her part to interrupt Lady Shelley, would not be well received, so she continued to hold her tongue. But she remembered that Lady Shelley had been the first to go into raptures about the Duke, whom she was now castigating. "He seldom says anything worth noting," the lady complained in some disdain, "and he professes to loathe the cheering of the populace."

"But my dear, I thought you were one of his greatest admirers," another lady riposted slyly. "Could it be that you are jealous of the Duke's preference for Frances?"

"Not at all, my dear Matilda. I would not expose myself so carelessly to the opprobium of society by conducting myself in such a fast manner," Lady Shelley replied tartly. For a moment Verity thought the two women might actually come to blows. Their audience watched with eager faces as Lady Shelley flushed with chagrin, continued to shred the characters of the two participants in the juiciest scandal of the day.

They might have enjoyed the spectacle for some time if they had not been interrupted by the entrance of a dowdy middle-aged woman, with a pointed nose and a brassy blonde wig. Her arrival caused all conversation to cease until Mrs. Medford, one of Lady Shelley's bosom bows, greated the newcomer graciously.

"Good day to you, Baroness von Krudener. Are you acquainted with these ladies?"

Verity looked at the latest arrival with much

interest, making her own polite curtsy to the woman. This was supposed to be the Tsar's greatest friend, his hostess at lavish dinners who accompanied him in his carriage at the grand review. She was supposedly the spiritual mentor of the emperor and the one who had directed his mind to the Holy Alliance. He had met her in Vienna, this impoverished widow of a diplomat from an old Livonian family, and immediately came under her influence. She seemed such a gruff, tawdry creature. Verity could not see where her charm lay.

She paid little heed to the ladies clustered around the now silent Lady Shelley. She marched up to one of the saleswomen and demanded in a harsh voice, and execrable French, "I want a plain black bonnet with no frills or furbelows."

The saleswoman hurried to comply, and her erstwhile customers, eyeing the newcomer slyly, obviously found her intimidating. Verity could not wonder. What a strange creature she was—why did the Tsar find her so mesmerizing? It was rumored that she was not above taking the haughty emperor to task for his manifold sins, and insisting that he purge his soul through prayer and reading of the Scripture. Verity found her both pathetic and a bit ridiculous, but she was pleased to have seen this notable figure who was their near neighbor. She hesitated for a moment, shyness overcoming her desire to learn more about the woman, but then remembering Wellington's problem, she squared her shoulders and crossed to the Baroness.

"Good day, Baroness. I hope you will forgive my presumption, but I believe we are neighbors on the Rue Saint Honore and I wish to give you my compliments. I am Mrs. Glendenning," she said shyly, encountering a raking stare.

"Ah a *jeune fille*. I have heard of you, my child," the Baroness acknowledged mysteriously.

"How kind of you, Baroness. What a fortuitous meeting," Verity replied softly, wondering what the woman could mean.

"I can see signs of great spirituality in you, child. Do you read your Bible faithfully?"

Taken aback and stammering a bit in her embarrassment, aware that the group about Lady Shelley were watching with interest, Verity could only murmur, "Not as much as I should, Baroness."

The Baroness stared at her haughtily as if her worst suspicions were confirmed, and turned back to the bonnet the milliner was extending. Verity, aware that she had been judged and found wanting, took her dismissal with as much sangfroid as possible, and prepared to leave the presence of this formidable if fusty noblewoman. Still, she had made some contact and it might prove useful in the future. Gathering up Agnes, she hurried to make her departure from the shop, suddenly disgusted with the bevy of ladies and the peculiar Baroness. She was convinced now that whatever the truth of Wellington's relationship with Lady Frances, the gossip could be used against him in some way to the Tsar's advantage. The situation was indeed serious and

Alistair must be informed.

Walking back to her apartment, Verity pondered over her own role in all these crosscurrents of innuendo and speculation. Could she discover more from the Prince and should she make an overture, invite him to visit her and try to ferret out more of the Tsar's intentions? Did the Baroness have some part in this attempt to humiliate and blackmail the Duke? As she strolled along deep in thought, she was not at first aware of a carriage stopping nearby, when she was roused from her musings by a lilting dulcet voice.

"Ah, Mrs. Glendenning, is it not?" a lady from the splendid equipage hailed her.

Verity looked up into the speculative eyes of Lady Bletchford, who insisted on taking her up. Verity, inclined to protest, decided that politeness impelled her to accept Olivia Bletchford's invitation. Sending Agnes on her way home alone, she stepped into the carriage.

"What a happy meeting. I did so want to further our acquaintance, my dear," Lady Bletchford cooed, her rather small but brilliant blue eyes looking over Verity in an assessing manner which made that young woman vastly uncomfortable. Olivia Bletchford was dressed in the latest stare in a blue silk redincote faced in cream, and a most fetching straw poke bonnet tied with a huge matching blue ribbon. She made Verity feel the veriest dowd, but that was no doubt the reaction of most females on encountering this paragon. Verity smiled tightly, but said nothing. She was sure that this meeting was not entirely accidental and she wondered what Alistair's former paramour wanted of her.

"It was such a pleasure to meet you last evening at the Edgecombes. I am so interested in Alistair's sudden marraige. Quite a surprise to us all, for we thought him the most determined bachelor," Lady Bletchford trilled. "How did you manage it, my dear? And how did you meet? You must excuse my interest, but Alistair and I are old friends."

Verity, aware that they had been more than friends, did not quite know how to reply to the exigent lady. But she had some questions of her own, although she was loath to put them.

"My brother, who fell at Waterloo, introduced us. Alistair was his commanding officer," she said a bit curtly.

"Oh, all my sympathy, my dear. How fortunate that Alistair could console you. He is very sympathetic," Lady Bletchford agreed suggestively. "But somehow I cannot see him as a husband. He likes playing the field. Oh, that was tactless of me, to imply such a thing to his new bride."

"Not at all, Lady Bletchford. Alistair has been quite frank with me about his past lights of love," Verity answered smoothly, indicating that Alistair's libertine ways were definitely of the past. She would not be patronized by this mischief maker, who had her own motives for prying into the state of the Glendennings' marriage.

Lady Beltchford, determined to sow seeds of suspicion, ignored Verity's parry. "I would not want to offend you, my dear, but I feel I should warn you. I have had a great deal more experience of the world and men than you have, to my sorrow. And I have to confess that I found Alistair not of a constant disposition. He professed to care for me and then suddenly tired when it appeared our affair might tarnish his career. His marriage to you, I fear, was a safeguard, to protect us both," she explained smoothly, but watched Verity closely to see how she took this outrageous suggestion.

"If it gives you comfort to believe that, Lady Bletchford, I will not argue the matter. But I am sure you agree that wives have certain advantages not given to casual amours. Of course, it is not pleasant to feel you have been abandoned by one to whom you have given your affection, but that is the way of men, the wretches," Verity replied blithely. She hoped she appeared as indifferent as her words suggested, but it was only with the utmost difficulty that she restrained herself from lashing out at the woman. How dare this faithless wife insinuate that Verity was a mere convenience, that Alistair had wed her on a whim to protect himself from further trouble. Determined to hide the pangs of jealousy which Olivia Bletchford's words had inspired, Verity hurried to put an end to this interview. "If you will order your coachman, I see we are nearing my direction. It is the next turning on the right," she insisted sweetly. "So kind of you to take me up."

The lady had no recourse but to consent, although it was obvious she would have liked to continue to discuss Alistair's offenses with her rival. However, in the face of Verity's cheerful indifference to her spiteful hints, she could only retire and hope her barbed words had found some mark. The two parted politely. Verity was aware as she entered her apartment how much Lady Bletchford's confidences had disturbed her. After all, she had no evidence that Alistair found his former love's arrival on the scene unwelcome. He had made no effort to disabuse her of any suspicions and she would never ask him what he felt for the lady. But her encounter with Lady Bletchford left a decidedly sour taste in her mouth concerning her husband's sincerity.

Chapter Nineteen

The distasteful interview with Olivia Bletchford had done little to soothe Verity's general malaise. But she could not allow her personal problems to distract her from her chief concern, how to discover if the rumors concerning Wellington's interest in Lady Frances Webster could be turned to some account by the Russians. Certainly tongues were wagging, but casual gossip could not be allowed to endanger the Duke's position. She remembered the Prince's allusions and knew that somehow he intended to use this information. But she could not see how. At their apartment she was relieved to find Alistair, whose mood was somber. He had just come from Tortini's, a café on the Boulevards where some of the younger, more volatile of the British officers gathered to exchange news and escape from their far from arduous duties. He greeted her with the report of his interview and she could see that he was disturbed.

"But, Alistair, it seems so ridiculous. Surely the Duke would not be called into disgrace because of such a paltry bit of gossip," Verity tried to reassure him, unwilling to think that the hero of Waterloo could become involved in the type of typical scandal which London society found so amusing and so ephemeral.

"Your hero is no monk, and it is no secret that he admires the ladies," Alistair told her. "But this is no time to indulge in his usual flirtations. He is inclined to scoff at the business, but I am convinced there is a serious attempt here to discredit the Duke so that he will be removed, and a less skilled negotiator sent to replace him. It must not be allowed. Somehow Captain Webster must be prevented from instituting a 'crim con' bill."

"What is Captain Webster like? Do you know him?" Verity asked as she took off her bonnet and smoothed her curls.

"Come, Verity. It is such a fine day. Let us abandon all these grave matters and play truant. We might drive out to Versailles and have a picnic. You would like that, wouldn't you?" He crossed to her and looked down into her glowing hazel eyes with an expression she found hard to fathom.

"Oh, yes, Alistair! Above all things! I will just ask Agnes to arrange a picnic basket," she agreed, but did not meet his searching gaze. She had her own secrets. She did not want to ask him about Olivia, or tell him of her encounter with that lady.

Alistair sensed her reserve and frowned.

A perfect cloudless summer sky greeted them as they drove the twelve miles west of Paris toward Versailles, Louis XIV's splendid residence, now sleeping in abandoned grandeur. Napoleon had neglected the palace, the focus of so much resentment and anger from the populace. But under the bright sunshine glancing off the pretentious statues and lavish fountains, dappling the grounds, and reflected in the Grand Canal, Versailles had a rare enchantment. They picnicked in the woods near the small pavillion built by Louis XIII, enjoying the lavish repast of cold chicken and wine climaxed by ripe peaches.

Resting in the shade of a great oak after their luncheon, they seemed disinclined for speech, the somnolent mood of the warm day overtaking them. Alistair looked at the pleasant picture Verity made in her silk dress, her titian hair peeping out beneath a simple chip bonnet tied with matching ribbons. Unfortunately, he could not read her expression hidden by the parasol she held to protect her creamy complexion from the rays of the bright sun.

"I could easily fall asleep after all that food, but under the circumstances that would be very rude, I expect," he said lightly, stretching out his long legs and resting his back against the tree trunk. He looked at her quizzically.

"It's lovely here, so quiet and peaceful after the

tumult of Paris. Intrigue and gossip would be alien in this setting," Verity said, eyeing him kindly.

"But, alas, they are with us, even here." He smiled. "You asked me about Captain Webster earlier and I did not answer you. He is not quite an unknown quantity in this imbroglio. I met Bathurst at Tortini's today and he was talking about the gentleman. It seems Webster has a vast conceit. When the luscious Frances was engaged in a raging flirtation with that mountebank Byron, he laughed and told everyone that he was not jealous, because he was certain that his wife loved him to distraction. And it did not prevent him from pursuing his own amours. Those Hollands are all a faithless feckless lot, but his unjustified certainty that his wife adored him had no foundation. Byron, no gentleman, told Lady Melbourne of his dalliance with Frances, and soon the whole ton knew of it. And Byron continued to make love to Lady Webster under her husband's nose, even tried to lure her into an elopement. But eventually, the mercurial Byron's attention turned to other more available women and the affair cooled. Considering that, I don't think Webster would entertain with any complacency an affair with the Duke if his suspicions were aroused. He is now very jealous of his wife, an emotion I can quite understand," he finished provocatively.

But Verity ignored his implication, her brow furrowing as she considered his budget of information. "If Captain Webster is now inclined to be jealous, would he be amenable to persuasion over a divorce, do you think?" she asked.

"I understand he has heavy debts, another legacy of his Holland temperament, perhaps. No doubt the Tsar could make it worth his while. We have yet to discover if that is what he intends."

Verity was happy to keep the conversation to political matters and away from their personal concerns, for she was afraid of what she might reveal. This intimacy, this isolation, the seductive quality of the day, was undermining her resolution to treat Alistair in a friendly no-nonsense manner. "Today I made some beginning at that," she told him. "I met Baroness von Krudener at the milliners where I heard all the gossip. She appears to have some influence with the Tsar, I understand. And she is our near neighbor."

"Oh, let us forget all these complications for the moment. I am heartily tired of the whole mess." Alistair sat up and took Verity's chin in his hand, looking at her earnestly as she tried to evade his gaze.

"Verity, I must make you understand about Lady Bletchford. I am reluctant to discuss the whole business because it makes me look like a cad, which I fear you are only too willing to believe," he said, all levity abandoned.

"You do not have to explain anything to me, Alistair," Verity answered stiffly, remembering what the woman had implied to her not many hours past.

"Come now, admit you have some curiosity, if not jealousy about the lady," he replied whimsically, determined to tease her into some response. And he was rewarded for she blushed and then laughed a bit shamefacedly.

"Well, yes, I do admit I want to hear all the details. And I have heard the lady's story, you know. She was at great pains to tell me of your"—she hesitated, then plunged boldly on,—"your association."

"Damn, I might have known. She certainly lost no time in digging her claws in. I wish she had not come to Paris," he muttered, thoroughly irritated, and suspecting that Verity had been shocked beyond belief by Olivia's dulcet cleverness. He knew how persuasive that one could be. Well, he would have to do his best to retrieve the damage.

Verity waited, her heart pounding, but she would not reveal her perturbation. Was Alistair about to tell her that he loved Olivia Bletchford, and their marriage had been a mistake? What could she do if that was what he wanted to confide?

"Well, it's no excuse, I know, but I met her when I returned from months of battle on the Peninsula, feeling very jaded and flat. I hate to speak thus of a lady, but she did make most of the running, being bored herself with her old husband, who neglected her and could hardly have been the bed partner she desired. She had been married very young, arranged by her grasping parents, she told me, but I do not think she was averse to his wealth and position. Her family was very strapped, I understand. And she is rather attractive."

"Rather," Verity replied shortly.

298

"Somehow we drifted into an affair. She was very complaisant and available, but I did not intend to become too involved, and thought she understood that."

"Naturally," Verity said wryly.

"Well, her husband discovered that I was her lover, and determined to punish her. She pleaded with me to rescue her from his anger, and fool that I was, I felt sorry for her and regretted my role in bringing her to such a pass. In the end, I escorted her to Wiltshire, to her aunt's, so she would be out of his path, but the gossip was that we had run away together. I had to resign from the King's Dragoons and was in danger of losing my whole career. Fortunately, Napoleon and Lord Uxbridge saved me. I thought I had brushed through the whole affair with more circumspection than I deserved, but now she has tracked me down here. She did not know we had married, I believe."

"Would that make any difference?" Verity asked bitterly, and then faced up to what she feared. "If you loved her, she would not count the cost."

"But I do not love her. I know you think I am a heartless rake, incapable of any real emotion, but that is not true, and damn Olivia Bletchford for giving you a false impression of my feeling toward her."

Verity frowned, not knowing what to think of these disclosures. Was Alistair just trying to disarm her, hoping she would accept his excuses and not make a trying scene, acting the jealous vengeful wife? Well, he must be reassured. She wanted to believe Olivia meant nothing to him, but that did not mean he had transferred his affection to her, or if that was what he intended, that it was little more than a convention to serve his own ends, to lure her into a lasting love which he could enjoy without committing himself. Whatever she felt for this enigmatic charming man who had unaccountably become her husband, she was not willing to reveal herself, and put herself at his mercy.

"You refine too much on the business, Alistair. What you did before we were married is no concern of mine, although I would not fancy playing the role of a deceived wife, I admit. So you must guard your instincts when Olivia Bletchford is in your vicinity," she warned with more insistence than she wanted.

"No man would look at Olivia when he had a wife as beguiling as you, Verity," he replied.

Gently removing her parasol from her grasp, he took her in his arms and kissed her hotly. Under his skilled tutelage she responded with helpless ardor and within moments was caught up in a passion which could not be denied as his hands and lips roved over her. At last he released her.

"I was within an ace of taking you here in the forest," he admitted, rising to his feet and looking down at her with a rueful grimace.

Verity blushed and attempted to bring her rumpled clothes into some order. "I would not have let you," she said primly, but wondered if she could have prevented him, for she had been caught up in the arousal of senses which his kisses never failed to produce.

"You are safe for the moment, but I suppose we had better return to Paris before I succumb again," he suggested, smiling provocatively at her.

She busied herself with packing up the remains of their picnic and signaling that their interlude was at an end. Completely confused and overset by what had passed between them, she could not but wonder into what paths their relations were leading. She knew only that she craved Alistair's love. She wanted to trust him and rely upon him to protect her from whatever faced them in this world that was so new and sometimes frightening to her, but she would never confess her fears to him. She could not bear his rejection, and even more she feared that he would soon tire of her if she made inordinate demands or asked for more than he was ready to offer.

The pair traveled in a not uncompanionable silence back to Paris. Ahead lay more intrigue and the demands of the world, but for the moment, under the fading sunlight, they were content to leave their fate to the future.

Chapter Twenty

While Alistair and Verity were enjoying their picnic and coming to some accord, events were in train which would soon alter their temporary tranquillity. In his sumptuous quarters in the Elysée Palace, Tsar Alexander was conferring with his aide, Prince Chirnovsky, and their interview was far from conclusive. The Tsar's strange attraction to the mystic life, inspired by his relationship with the Baroness von Krudener, had begun to dissipate, inducing a querulous dissatisfaction in the emperor. He was having doubts about the efficacy of his mentor's prayers, and the Prince wondered if the Baroness's influence had waned. The Prince, whose own temperament was far more earthy, could only hail that contingency with relief. He found illogical the Tsar's emphasis on Christian principles in dealing with the wily statesmen who represented his allies, although he would never presume to criticize his monarch. Alexander did not take kindly to censure of his philosophy. Despite his handsome, commanding presence, Alexander often suffered from feelings of inadequacy and suspicion, tortured by his Romanov inheritance of moodiness and arrogance, a combination which made his subordinates tread warily.

"You have not abandoned your wishes in regard to the Holy Alliance then, Sire?" the Prince asked tentatively.

"Of course not. We must be ruled by the principles of the Alliance in all our governing," the Tsar said decisively. But then he frowned. "The English are a godless race, we all know that, but they must be persuaded to sign the Alliance if the peace of Europe will endure."

The Prince, who regarded the Alliance as just another tool to enhance the Tsar's autocratic command of his subjects, for which he did not fault him, wondered if Alexander really thought his efforts to persuade Wellington and the English contingent to his way of thinking had any chance of success. However, his own duty was clear. He must do what his master desired, no matter how foolish he thought it, or how much he doubted Alexander's motives.

"I have invited Captain Wedderburn-Webster to meet with me, to discuss this matter of the divorce. Fortunately, the English take these marital discords more seriously than we do. Not that they are moral, only jealous of their reputations. If the Duke wishes to dally with the lady, he must pay the price of his transgression. Of course, adultery is a sin," the Tsar explained pompously, unaware of the hypocrisy of his stance. He himself was not noted for his faithfulness to his Tsarina, but he was a law unto himself, and lately had abandoned licentiousness for a certain spurious Christianity. The Prince found his attitude rather ridiculous, and not one he would emulate, but he kept his ideas to himself.

The Tsar frowned and crossed himself, muttering about the sins of the flesh, but then recalled to the matter in hand, he made his decision.

"If Wellington does not surrender to my demands, it might be necessary to remove him." He offered this outrageous suggestion haughtily.

The Prince barely restrained his shock at that news. "But, Holy Father, that might mean war with the English. They would never countenance an assassination of the hero of Waterloo," he advised, thoroughly aroused by the Tsar's solution.

The Tsar tossed aside his aide's objections airily. "They would not know we are responsible. But perhaps that will not be necessary if we can persuade Captain Webster."

"Yes, of course," the Prince agreed hollowly. He watched his master warily. Could the Tsar be losing his grip on reality to consider such desperate measures? He knew the Tsar, and for that matter, he himself did not cavil at murder if it suited the situation. But murdering Wellington was a far cry from dispatching some troublesome Russian who dared to oppose his will.

"I think I must see this Englishman myself, but perhaps you will lay the groundwork. We must play on his jealousy and his conceit. I understand, too, that he has certain financial difficulties, and money may be the answer," the Tsar concluded, suddenly cheerful.

"It usually is," the Prince agreed cynically. "I will put the matter to him, then?"

He ended the audience, hoping that he had dissuaded the Tsar from more precipitate action and that the English officer would be amenable to payment. You never knew how the English would react. Look at that charming minx, Verity. On the one hand she seemed to encourage him and on the other to repulse him. Not for a moment did the Prince believe she was not tempted by his overtures. His vast experience had never led him to believe there was a woman impervious to his charms and his generosity.

The Tsar had hinted that he was impatient to return to Russia, that he wanted this Alliance signed quickly, no matter what the methods used to achieve such a resolution, but the Prince was not as eager as his master to abandon the sybaritic delights of Paris for St. Petersburg. He valued his post as the Tsar's trusted aide and would do nothing to endanger his position, but that did not mean he would happily follow his emperor's recent embrace of the sacred contemplative life for the more profane enjoyments he had previously endorsed.

That led him around again to thinking of Verity and how he could lure her into his bed. If she would not come willingly, he might enjoy coercing her. At the picture of this, an ugly lascivious light gleamed in his eyes. He had enough of the Cossack in his nature to make the idea appealing. Savoring the delights which those images evoked he, at first, did not hear the flunky who interrupted him.

"A Captain Wedderburn-Webster has called, Your Highness, and requests an audience with the Holy Father. I understand that you are to receive him first," the servant said tentatively.

"Yes, yes. Show him in here immediately," the Prince ordered briskly. He had every confidence that he could deal with this Englishman whose wife had the temerity to entice the great Duke of Wellington. In Russia they knew how to deal with erring wives, and the scourge was not unknown, nor was banishment to the wilds of the country. The English were too mealy-mouthed about such matters. But they feared scandal and any public airing of their personal affairs, so he might have difficulty persuading this one to seek redress in the courts. In his arrogance the Prince did not consider that any Englishman would put duty to his country against his personal satisfaction. But he was not so foolish to discount the English national trait, stubbornness, in confronting the man.

Captain Wedderburn-Webster, entering the room, looked puzzled at his reception. He was a well-set-up man, of an open countenance and an overweening conceit, with rather small blue eyes which looked guilelessly on the world and an assurance which was typical of his class. For this interview, and the request had puzzled him, he had dressed in the uniform of the King's Guards, an armor to bolster his pride. He did not like the Russians and could not speculate why he had been singled out for this interview. Expecting the Tsar, he was surprised to be met with the Prince.

"Good afternoon, Captain Webster. The Tsar has requested that I see you first and make some explanation which might save time. It is a delicate matter, you understand," the Prince began suavely.

"No, I do not understand, nor do I quite see the point of this interview. I have nothing to do with the negotiations for the peace treaty. You would be better advised to seek one of Castlereagh or Wellington's minions for that," he said a bit pompously, reluctant to admit that the Prince's regal air impressed him. The captain, although an accepted member of London's ton through his Holland family connections, had little experience in dealing with statesmen at a high level, and believed that all that was best left to those johnnies who conducted the nation's business. He was much more concerned with his gambling debts, affairs of honor, his frequent liaisons with the demimondaine, and his horses. In short, he was a conventional member of the rackety set which cared for little besides personal satisfaction.

"To put it bluntly, Captain, the Tsar is passionately intent upon securing Wellington's signature to the Holy Alliance and he thinks you can help us persuade the Duke," the Prince said baldly, realizing that it would be useless to approach the matter with any sophistry.

"Well, the Duke will do as he pleases, or rather as he has been instructed by His Majesty's government," Wedderburn-Webster replied, drawing himself up with an arrogance equal to the Prince's.

"I understand that, but surely the Duke's awesome reputation must be taken into account, and our investigations lead us to believe he is not sympathetic to the Holy Alliance. While you may not have any professional contact with the Duke, surely you have some personal experience of him." The Prince appeared to hesitate, but this was only to whet the man's curiosity, then he continued in an insinuating way, "I believe your wife is a particular friend of the Duke's."

The Englishman choked in anger. Now he realized the reason for this interview. The Russians wanted Frances to use her influence with the Duke. Perhaps they did not know that he and Frances were not in charity with one another and any request he might make of her would be treated with contempt. Damn it, that his wife should become the butt of every foreigner's tongue was more than he would permit.

"You forget yourself, sir. I will ignore that last statement," he blurted out, determined to preserve his dignity. These Russians had no notion of proper behavior, as he had always suspected.

"Come, Captain, let us not equivocate. We are both men of the world. You must be aware that the Duke's relationship with your wife is on every tongue in Paris, and has even been mentioned in the London journals. Whether there is truth or not in the rumors is not my concern. You will know how best to deal with your wife. But there has been some suggestion that you are considering citing the Duke for damages in a divorce, what you call a criminal conversation, I think," the Prince put the matter plainly, accepting that he could no longer mince words. "I do not think even the Duke's enviable reputation would survive such a case. But perhaps I mistake matters?" he questioned, seeing that the captain was in a passion of embarrassment and anger.

"I cannot see why my personal affairs are any of your business, sir. And I resent your insinuations," the Englishman replied, very much offended. Still, he did not deny the imputation. And he was wondering how he could turn the conversation to his own advantage. He was not a particularly perceptive man, nor overly intelligent, but he now grasped the reason for this summons to the Tsar's headquarters. "I do not see that any purpose would be served by an interview with the Emperor."

"It would be most discourteous to reject his invitation," the Prince objected blandly, hiding his anger at this breach of manners. He was aware that if the captain refused to see Alexander, his own role in this abortive discussion would be criticized severely. The Tsar was not accustomed to having his orders disobeyed, although he must make some allowances for the unreliability of the English. Could this fool not realize the honor he was so summarily and impolitely declining?

"Oh, all right. I don't suppose it signifies," the captain agreed, still smoldering from the insinuations the Prince had made and the implication that these Russians could interfere in his personal affairs, even suggesting that he turn this quarrel with his wife, a purely domestic concern, into a political gambit. Whatever Webster's fault, lack of patriotism was not among them, and he was tempted to tell the Prince and the Tsar, for that matter, to go to the devil. The strictures of London society, which put such a premium on good manners, need not be extended to these foreigners, but his own consequence prevented him from acting rudely.

The captain had seen the Tsar at various military reviews and upon social occasions, but he was quite unprepared for the emperor's imposing appearance, his charm, and his amiability.

"Good afternoon, Captain Webster. It is most agreeable of you to spare us some time. I am sure your military duties keep you busy," the Tsar greeted him affably.

"Not at all, Sire. I am honored," the captain said briefly, giving the emperor a very punctilious bow. "But I am at a loss as to why you should want to see me." He was determined not to be awed by the ruler

311

of all the Russians, although he could not repress a certain admiration for Alexander's bearing and manner.

"I realize that for an English gentleman to confide his personal affairs to foreigners is repugnant. But you must know that the estrangement between you and your wife over this affair of Wellington is a matter of open gossip," the Tsar explained without more ado.

"I have explained to your aide, the Prince here, that I do not consider it a subject of discussion," the captain replied rather pompously. Really, these Slavs had no notion of propriety. Of course, everyone knew they were an immoral lot, and despite their emperor's recent conversion to a champion of Christian principles, he was far from lily white in his own extramarital relationships. Still, the captain did not criticize him for that. He had a bluff tolerance for sexual exploits himself. But they should realize that a man did not air his marital troubles to all and sundry. It was against a gentleman's code.

"Alas, Captain, although your scruples do you honor, I am afraid that when your personal affairs become a matter of international politics, you must be persuaded to ease them a bit," the Tsar insisted, at his most unctuous. The Prince was rather surprised to see his master so obliging to this wretched fellow, whose rank did not deserve such consideration. But Alexander was prepared to sacrifice some of his hauteur in defense of his desire for this Alliance.

"To be blunt, sir, it is the most pressing desire of my life to see this Alliance be accepted by all the rulers of Europe, those sovereigns who must ensure the peace. Your Duke appears reluctant to seal the agreement and I must, of necessity, use any means on hand, to compel him. Naturally I find this distressing, but for the greater good, I am content to sacrifice my natural chivalric instincts," the Tsar explained grandiosely, giving the captain a piercing look from his soulful eyes, implying that if only all the rulers followed the principles he embraced, the world would be a far better place.

"That is all very well, Sire, but I do not understand my role in this endeavor," replied the captain, sensing that some attempt to cajole him into drastic action would be offered, but still not seeing the Tsar's drift.

"This current gossip can serve as an excuse to force the Duke to my way of thinking. If you threaten to bring a divorce action citing the Duke, endangering his reputation, he will perforce have to submit to any action which would prevent such an uncomfortable position. And I am not wrong in thinking you had probably decided to do just that even without my intercession," the Tsar continued suavely. "Naturally, a man of your own probity and distinction finds the rumors distasteful and demeaning," he finished slyly.

"Your aide, the Prince here, alluded to some such infamous bargain, but I cannot see what is in it for me," the captain said coarsely, now that the cards

313

were on the table and he realized that he need not watch his words with this imposing figure.

"I understand that you have some pressing debts, Captain Webster. Of course, we would be happy to relieve you of your obligations in return for this favor," the Tsar offered, smiling with satisfaction, sure now that he had secured his purpose.

However, the captain was not quite the easy conquest the emperor had expected. Behind his conceit and his sense of ill-usage lay a real patriotism combined with a suspicion of all foreigners. He did not like the implications that he would be paid for bringing about the downfall of the hero of Waterloo. He had a certain respect, if not liking, for the Duke, and he also realized that his own position in London society, on which he placed much importance, might be jeopardized by such an ugly action. So he hesitated.

The Tsar frowned, and the Prince, who well knew the emperor's easily aroused temper, prayed that Alexander would not ruin the whole affair by giving in to one of his famous tantrums. He decided he must intercede.

"Naturally, Captain, you are averse to threatening your commander, and might even feel it a breach of discipline, but your honor has been besmirched and you cannot be criticized for taking what means you can for redress." He thought it wiser not to refer to the money again, and only hoped the Tsar would follow his lead.

The Tsar, not liking his aide's interference, was

about to object, but then thinking better of it, turned away and walked toward the window, muttering querulously, "Well, he must do as he feels best. I am fatigued with the matter."

Thus dismissed in such a way after being so outrageously courted, the captain drew himself up and, donning an arrogant manner, made his decision known. "I will think about your offer, Sire, and make my decision."

"Thank you for coming, Captain, and listening to His Highness with such obliging patience," the Prince said, and hurried to escort the Englishman from the royal presence before the Tsar ruined matters with a display of temper and arrogance which would surely lose the day.

As the two bowed themselves from the room, the Prince wisely did not exhort the captain further, only reminding him that he would be at his disposal whenever a decision had been made. As Webster left the Palace, the Prince decided that he had done what he could but had serious doubts that the man would prove a useful tool in his emperor's plan to blackmail Wellington into the action he coveted. The Duke had a reputation for damning all interference and was not a man who would allow his personal problems to affect his political role. The Prince returned reluctantly to the Tsar, knowing he would probably earn a castigation, the blame for the whole abortive affair, but Alexander seemed to have recovered his spirits.

"Well, Vasilii, that's a good day's work done. I am

sure the maligned captain will do what we want. And Wellington will have to agree under the circumstances," he said jovially, rubbing his hands together in satisfaction.

The Prince, whose own assessment was not quite so cheerful, loathed to depress his monarch's mood but he felt he must warn him. "I hope you are right, Sire, but these English are the very devil to deal with. I believe we must consider other methods in case the Captain refuses our request," he suggested gently.

"Ah, but one way or the other the captain will oblige us. If he refuses our terms there is another use for the man. He would make an attractive victim, if Wellington were to suffer some unfortunate accident." The Tsar grinned evilly.

Oh, Lord, thought the Prince, he has not abandoned his idea of an assassination, and a plan to put the deed onto that luckless Englishman's shoulders. Did the Tsar not understand the simplest basis of the English government? A ruthless autocrat himself he did not realize that even if Wellington should be recalled or killed, another minion of George III would be dispatched to Paris with the same philosophy and orders. He must discourage his emperor from pursuing this disastrous course, but he doubted that he would be successful.

Both the Tsar and the Prince, although well schooled in diplomacy, had little real understanding of the English character, and in trying to suborn Captain Webster had greatly mistaken their man. Webster had already fought one duel over his wife's honor and was not averse to engaging in another if he thought he had cause. But like most of his compatriots, he was in awe of Wellington, and of a self-indulgent and conceited nature, he did not really believe the Duke had engaged in an intimate relationship with his wife. He did not like playing the role of a cuckolded husband, but he hesitated to approach the Duke and warn him away from Frances. He found the Russian attempts to bribe him both insulting and treacherous. He had little understanding of the implications of the Holy Alliance but he was inclined to agree that signing such a document was not in his country's best interest. Debating the matter, he decided that his best recourse was to wait upon events. He would, for the present, ignore the Russian insinuations, a decision which would soon be tested.

Chapter Twenty-One

Despite the harmony induced by their picnic at Versailles, Verity was not distracted from the question of Wellington's vulnerability to the scandal which was engaging much of Paris. If she and Alistair had not completely solved their own dilemma, their tenuous relationship had improved. But for the most part, he treated her more as a cherished sister than a beloved wife.

While she was debating her future, the present intruded with a surprising invitation from Baroness von Krudener to take tea with her. Welcoming this opportunity to discover how deep was the Baroness's influence on the Tsar and her involvement in the plot to discredit the Duke, she accepted, telling Alistair of the arrangement.

Surprisingly he was reluctant for her to accept the Baroness's invitation.

"I don't like it," he said irritably, when she

informed him of the engagement. "I don't trust the Tsar, nor his minion, the Prince, and you would be walking into a dangerous situation." He frowned, looking at her with a brooding expression she could not interpret.

Verity, puzzled by his irritation, decided that his consequence suffered because she was prepared to enter into lists against their enemies, that he might even suspect she had ulterior motives in wanting to combat the Prince. So like a man, who never believed a woman could be occupied with anything outside the domestic round. In her turn, she became exasperated.

"Really, Alistair, how are we to discover the Tsar's plans if we don't make some push to establish some intimacy with a woman who we have every reason to suspect has an inordinate influence with the emperor. If there is any danger, we are forewarned, and I cannot believe you still think the Prince has immoral intentions toward me," she protested, facing him with more confidence than she felt.

"You should not be involved in any of this. It's not suitable," he stubbornly persisted, stalking up and down the room as was his wont when he was disturbed. Watching him, Verity suppressed a smile. His pride was affronted at the thought she might affect the outcome of the matter and that he was powerless to prevent her or to take any resolute action himself.

"And don't stand there with that complacent

smile on your face," he snapped. The truth was he still entertained a vast suspicion of the Prince, and wanted to prevent any further meetings between that arrogant fellow and his wife.

"You are behaving stupidly, Alistair. This is a perfect opportunity for me to insinuate myself into the Russians' confidence. I am going to tea with the Baroness, not to some fraught interview with a bunch of villains," Verity replied gently but with determination.

"Obviously you will go whatever my objections. I can hardly restrain you," he said coldly.

"I hardly think I will be abducted or assaulted over the teacups," she soothed, turning away to write her acceptance as if that were the end of the matter. Alistair, with a muttered disclaimer, walked out of the room before he could utter any more warnings or surrender to his desire to tell her how much he cared about her safety. Believing that only his amour propre was wounded, Verity did not understand that his objections were rooted in his deep feeling for her and she dismissed his reproaches with a shrug. She was anticipating the meeting with the Baroness and was convinced she could learn a great deal about the Tsar's plans by a skillful questioning of the lady.

In this expectation she was to be disappointed. The Baroness received her in a shrouded apartment, carelessly decorated with little accommodation to comfort or artistic enjoyment. The lady herself must at one time have been attractive, but now in her fiftieth year, showed the affects of a life of dissipation and indulgence. Despite her passionate endorsement of Christian principles, Verity wondered if this was just a midlife conversion brought about by the fading of her charms. Still the Baroness put herself out to be welcoming.

"Ah, my dear, how kind of you to grant my request to visit an old woman, who endures slights and loneliness because of past transgressions. I can see you carry an aura of Christian benevolence which is most welcome," she beamed, her raddled face alight as she poured Verity tea from a handsome samovar.

"I was most interested to meet the woman who has converted His Highness, the Tsar of All the Russias, to such noble aspirations," Verity replied sweetly, determined to flatter the pathetic woman. In truth she found it difficult to believe that this aging courtesan, with her blotched complexion and obvious blond wig, could have attracted the Tsar, noted for his appreciation of beautiful women.

"Alas, I fear my prayers and exhortations are beginning to weary Alexander, although he must surely benefit from my efforts to win him away from his sinful past. He has much to atone for, but he is making a beginning," the Baroness confided.

"You mean his Holy Alliance," Verity replied boldly, coming to the point.

"Yes, he is quite adamant in his desire to persuade all the rulers of Europe to join him in seeking salvation through the godly precepts which he himself has at last embraced," the Baroness explained rather grandiloquently.

"We must wish him success, then."

The Baroness scratched her blond wig, which was pushed awry by the movement of her raddled hands. "Alas, your most noble Duke of Wellington, a very worldly man, does not completely agree."

Now we are coming to it, Verity thought. But nothing of her suspicions were evident in her dulcet tone. "I am afraid that I know little of these great affairs, Baroness."

"Nonsense. I can see you are an intelligent girl, and I understand your husband is an aide to the Duke and must be privy to all his decisions," the Baroness retorted, impatient with any game playing.

"But you know, Baroness, that men rarely discuss such weighty matters with their wives. Women are for their amusement only."

"It is your duty as a Christian woman to try to influence your husband toward an acceptance of God's work in this wicked world," the Baroness intoned.

Verity could barely suppress her amusement at the picture of her praying over Alistair, bringing him to a realization of his manifold sins and a true repentance, but she did not allow her sense of the ridiculous to show. She only nodded solemnly. Could this weird woman really believe that the peace of Europe would be gained by its rulers all sitting down and praying together? Surely she was not that naive, or was she driven by some other motive?

Remembering what she had heard of the Baroness's past, Verity had difficulty in believing that this blowsy woman exerted some mystical influence over the Tsar, who, if rumor was true, had become bored with her prognostications and prayers. And was she privy to that ruthless autocrat's conspiracy involving the Duke? Verity did not quite know how to proceed, but before she could summon up another artless question, the two were interrupted by a servant announcing a visitor. On her heels appeared Prince Chirnovsky, as surprised as Verity by this tête-à-tête over the teacups.

"Ah, Baroness, how charming of you to entertain our lovely English flower," the Prince intoned extravagantly as he bowed over his hostess's hand and gave Verity a piercing look.

"This delightful child is in search of the Christian guidance we all seek," the Baroness replied, indicating that the Prince should take a seat.

Even the Prince's urbanity was not proof against this startling explanation, but he recovered his poise quickly.

"We all seek that, dear lady, and who better to provide it?" he answered suavely, causing Verity to suspect his sincerity. Why was he attending on the Baroness? Did he have some ulterior motive? She could not accept that the Prince, with all his sophisticated manner, required tutelage in the Baroness's mystical bonds with the spiritual realm. But whatever the Prince's reasons for visiting the Baroness, he was not about to reveal them to Verity.

After a little desultory conversation, she decided it would be prudent to take her leave, as it was obvious neither the Baroness nor the Prince would reveal anything of import. She rose, drew on her gloves, and picked up her parasol.

"Thank you, Baroness, for receiving me. I hope I may call upon you again and continue our fascinating discussions," Verity thanked her hostess prettily, taking refuge from the Prince's raking stare behind polite manners.

"May I escort you to your apartment, madam?" the Prince asked, also rising.

"It is but a step, and I would not interrupt your meeting with the Baroness. No doubt I will see you at the King's levee later today," Verity replied.

"I will look forward to it, dear lady," he oozed with patent charm. He crossed the dark room to hold open the door for Verity, who felt she was being bustled out of the way, but none of her irritation was evident in the bland smile with which she rewarded him for his attentions. She sailed through the door, which closed sharply behind her, and then she hesitated. Should she try to listen to the conversation? But behind the door all she could hear was the lower murmur of voices. No, it would have to wait for another day, but she found the meeting between the two confidants of the Tsar raised several questions in her mind. Still, it would not serve her to be caught dallying here in circumstances which might raise conjecture in the pair. But she felt instinctively that the Prince's errand with the

Baroness concerned the plot against Wellington. She took her leave much exercised by this chance encounter. She must confer with Alistair.

Her intentions of confiding in her husband about the strange encounter in the Baroness's rooms were foiled by Alistair's reaction to her news that the Prince had been present at the tea party. It was evident that he thought she had arranged a tryst with the Prince under cover of the innocuous invitation tendered by the Baroness.

"I have warned you about that man. He has designs upon you. Since you ignore my warning, I can only think that you welcome his disgusting attentions," Alistair fumed as she tried to explain what she had learned.

Furious at the unjust accusations, Verity retreated immediately into a frigid displeasure. "If that is what you believe, I see no reason to continue this discussion. I refuse to dignify your ridiculous allegations with any protestations of innocence. You have a filthy mind," she responded coolly. "And now I must dress for this reception of King Louis." She finished by removing herself from his fiery gaze, angry beyond rationalization by his insinuations.

"Damn, damn, damn," Alistair cursed, watching the door through which Verity had left, restraining herself from sharply slamming it but leaving no doubt that she was as angry as he was.

Alistair hated having Verity embroiled in this messy situation. He had called on Wellington to learn the latest developments while Verity was visiting the Baroness and learned that Captain Webster had been observed entering the Palace, probably to see the Tsar, whatever that entailed. The Duke was inclined to dismiss the whole matter now that he had sent for his wife, believing that her presence would put an end to all this unsavory gossip. And he was not a man who welcomed any criticism of his actions, nor was he apt to offer excuses or explanations.

Alistair wished, not for the first time, that he could return to his straightforward military duties, but he doubted that his commander would listen to any demur on his part. He tried to warn Wellington that if the gossip was quieted, that still did not mean he was relieved from the Tsar's efforts to force him into compliance over the Alliance. But the Duke had brusquely turned away his concern. Now Verity had the bit between her teeth and, in a passion of patriotic fervor, was determined to delve into the Russian plot. He feared for her safety and her virtue. Much as he disliked the Prince, he had to admit that he was an attractive man whose suave demeanor could lure his wife into a liaison.

Donning his own mask of aloofness, Alistair escorted Verity to the levee, where she intended to pursue her investigations whether Alistair approved or not. She would show him that she was not some credulous ninny, an object of every man's flirtations and worse. He must be made to realize that he could not command her behavior when his own was certainly not above reproach. Affairs were not helped at their arrival at the Elysée by the immediate approach of Olivia Bletchford, who tripped up to them, all smiles and cajolry, soothing Alistair's ego by her flattering attention. Verity nodded coolly at the lady and turned eagerly to a young officer, a friend of Charley's, who was hovering nearby and allowed him to escort her to the refreshment table, despite Alistair's narrowed eyes. Verity knew he could hardly make a scene before these august personages. All of Paris society had turned out for the King's party and the guests were avidly watching the Duke, who arrived early and seemed his usual imperturbable self.

Verity completely charmed the young lieutenant with her sparkling conversation. As they were enjoying the champagne and lobster patties at a small intimate table in the supper room, they were approached by the Prince. Verity, reckless and unhappy, welcomed him with more fervor than usual, knowing that Alistair's eyes were upon them even while he chatted with Lady Bletchford. Soon the Prince, with adroitness, had dismissed the callow officer, and gained Verity's undivided attention.

"How beautiful you are looking this evening, *doushka,*" he murmured passionately, looking at her with an avid eye.

Verity was indeed looking a very picture of English beauty in a daringly cut gown of yellow silk, simply designed but with severe lines that accented her slim and enticing figure. Anger had given her cheeks a rosy glow and her eyes sparkled with excitement. She would show Alistair that she wasn't to be treated in this cavalier manner, forgetting for the moment the danger that the Prince posed. She thanked him gaily for his compliments and then asked boldly, "How much longer will you be in Paris, sir? I understand the Tsar is eager to return to Russia."

"As soon as the Alliance is signed we will be off, but let us not talk of such sad eventualities. We must seize the moment at hand. Come, tell me, you will miss me when I must reluctantly say farewell to you, my pigeon," he cajoled, wondering at the change in her attitude. Could she at last be ready to submit to him? He hid his excitement at the thought, but a gleam of possessive lust which Verity failed to notice shone for a moment in his dark suggestive eyes.

However, Prince Vasilii was too skilled a campaigner to reveal his strategy without preparing the ground carefully. He need only wait and play his cards adroitly. Not imperceptive when it came to women, he had noticed Olivia Bletchford working her wiles on Alistair, and he thought that gentleman not impervious to the fetching lady. He had heard the rumors, so prevalent in Paris, that at one time the pair had enjoyed a very intimate relationship and he suspected the lady was determined to continue the liaison, which suited him, too. Now, he cleverly fanned the flames of Verity's jealousy.

"I see your husband talking to Lady Bletchford, a new and very pleasant addition to the ranks of Parisian society. Do you know her well?" he asked blandly.

"Not at all well, She is a friend of Alistair's. She is very attractive, isn't she?" Verity answered, restraining any inclination to tell the Prince exactly what she did think of that lady.

"How wise of you, *doushka,* to behave in such a forebearing fashion. Jealousy is such an ineffective emotion," the Prince agreed, not deceived, as he noticed the tightening of Verity's lips and the flash of her speaking eyes. "But then you have no reason to fear a rival, for your own charms are far more subtle and alluring," he whispered in a beguiling tone which did much to soothe Verity's feelings.

Verity, tearing her gaze away from the couple, who seemed to be enjoying an intimate coze, smiled brightly at the Prince and changed the subject.

"I was quite surprised to see you at the Baroness von Krudener's today. But she is a strangely fascinating figure, don't you agree?"

"Her notions are a bit gothic, but she has an uncanny influence over the Tsar. He has become quite enamored of her psychic powers and she has certainly restrained his more intemperate behavior," the Prince responded, more frankly than Verity had expected. "Do you find her views provocative?"

"She is certainly a tonic after the petty gossip and light-minded conversation which reigns in Paris salons."

"Unfortunately, I think her influence over the Holy Father is waning. I do not think she will be accompanying him back to Russia. Still, I must commend the Baroness for what she has accomplished. She is the spirit behind the Tsar's design for his Holy Alliance."

Although he did not believe for a moment that a young, newly married matron such as his companion had any concern for affairs of state, he had rather wondered at her acceptance of the Baroness's invitation. He was more interested in why the Baroness had pursued Verity. The Baroness's tortuous thought processes worried him because she could still exert some strange power over the emperor, even though he believed that his master was becoming bored with her discipline. Still, it was prudent to keep aware of all facets of the intrigue that was such a delight to the Tsar. He was not completely sure that Alexander had abandoned his plan to do away with Wellington, a misguided and dangerous delusion which he prayed would not continue.

Before the Prince could further his design of luring Verity into a rendezvous, they were interrupted by Alistair and Lady Bletchford, the latter all smiles and ingratiating tones as she cooed a greeting at the pair.

"How serious you look, Verity. Are you discussing grave matters with the Prince?" Olivia trilled, immediately annoying Verity, who felt somehow dowdy and dull in her rival's presence. The lady was wearing magnificent pearls and an overly lavish gown of peach silk, which accented her lush blond beauty.

"Yes, Lady Bletchford. We were talking about the Tsar and his hopes for his Alliance," Verity said a bit curtly.

"How dreary, and much too complicated for me, I fear. But then I feel politics are best left to men," Olivia said, implying that any attempt to meddle in affairs of state was rather coarse and unladylike.

"I really think you care for nothing but fashions and gossip, Olivia," Alistair said sharply, earning a moue of displeasure from the lady.

"Now don't cavil, Alistair. We are much too old and dear friends to quarrel," she replied provocatively, her pale blue eyes melting as she looked at him.

"Old friends can become new enemies, sometimes," interposed the Prince, eager to stir the waters.

"Oh, not Alistair and I. We understand each other too well," Olivia said dismissively, uncertain at the tenor of the conversation.

"It's time we are leaving, Verity. We have a dinner engagement," Alistair interrupted, feeling fed up with the sparring and Olivia's innuendos.

"*Au revoir,* Prince. I have enjoyed our chat," Verity said, the amenable wife, but determined to pay back Alistair in kind.

"Perhaps you will honor me with another," the Prince said smoothly. "I would be pleased if you would ride with me in the Bois de Bolgne tomorrow—with your husband's permission, of course."

Verity, who was not inclined to accept, took

umbrage at the Prince's hint that she must seek Alistair's permission, and against her instincts, accepted immediately. "That will be lovely. I will see you tomorrow, then." She smiled as if thrilled with the prospect, ignoring Alistair's glare. Really, he was behaving like a dog in the manger, she thought, disliking his wife's interest in the Prince but brooking no criticism of his own attentions to Olivia.

As they left the levee silently, Verity decided that the temporary harmony which had prevailed since their picnic was now a thing of the past, and they were back to their former estrangement. She felt ill-used and misunderstood, as well as unloved, a situation which could only spur her toward some disastrous action.

Chapter Twenty-Two

Prince Chirnovsky had good reason to doubt that the Tsar had not abandoned his plan to seek his revenge against Wellington by violent action. The emperor, unaccustomed to meeting obstruction of his plans, had met again with the English delegation concerning the signing of the Alliance. He had instituted the display of Russian force with his grand military review of 150,000 men, 540 cannon, and 96 generals, but even this mighty maneuver had failed to impress the stubborn British with the power of the Tsar to compel all to his wishes. He saw no difficulty in his Alliance, which attempted to weld rival faiths—Orthodox, Protestant, and Catholic—into agreement. Metternich, who had hailed the bombastic document as "an empty, echoing monument," now saw it as a tool he could use to crush revolutionary plots in his own country, Austria, and believed that behind the shield of the Alliance all of the sovereigns could serve as despotic rulers of Europe.

The Tsar had already compelled the kings of Austria, Prussia, France, Sweden, Spain, Naples, and Sardinia to his way of thinking. Only the English and the Pope resisted, although most politely, but the prelate's approval was of little importance, Alexander decided. Then there was France's refusal to sign a second peace treaty which dismembered its borders. All in all the Tsar was feeling peevish and unappreciated, believing he alone of all the conquerors of Napoleon had a divine mission which was being opposed by less selfless and inspired statesmen. Unfairly he put the blame for this intransigence at Wellington's door, thinking if he removed the hero of Waterloo, all would proceed according to his wishes. A man of violent and mercurial moods, he had no conception of compromise and negotiation, taking every disagreement as a personal insult, not to be endured.

The Prince, afraid of arousing the emperor into one of his explosive tantrums, hesitated to return to the subject which the Tsar had once broached, assassinating Wellington, but he feared the idea had not left Alexander's mind. Although he could not always follow the Byzantine paths of his master's thoughts, he knew him well enough to realize that the Tsar was capable of the most outrageous ploys if his will was brooked. His machinations could easily embroil Russia in a war it was ill equipped to fight, and the Prince was astute enough, and patriotic enough, to wish to prevent this calamity. His only ally in an effort to thwart his master, without the Tsar's knowledge, was the Baroness von Krudener. Much as he disliked the woman, he had to admit that her words still had some affect on Alexander, and if she was approached gently, she might discover what he had in mind.

The Prince's fears were reinforced when he heard of a secret interview the Tsar had conducted with two Cossack thugs the emperor had summoned to his quarters. Without more ado, the Prince decided he must seek out the Baroness and implore her help, but the matter must be delicately broached. If the emperor discovered that his trusted aid was conspiring to thwart him, no matter how noble his aims, he would exile the Prince and punish him severely. For the moment, the Prince's plan to seduce Verity had to be postponed in favor of this more appalling threat. He decided to seek out the Baroness.

That lady was the object of Verity's thoughts, too. Somehow, she believed, the Baroness was the key to the problem which engaged them all. Since the King's levee, relations between Verity and her husband had deteriorated into a wary reserve, neither one wanting to make the first move to heal the breach between them. Alistair was furious that Verity continued to see the Prince after his warning, and she believed he was secretly meeting Olivia Bletchford.

At every social occasion the lady was evident, hovering over Alistair as soon as he appeared, displaying her charms and enticing him into flirtatious conversation. Her pursuit of Alistair was becoming noticeable by many of the most notorious gossips in Paris. Lady Shelley, that doyenne of rumors, had taken it upon herself to warn Verity that her husband was indulging in a dangerous dalliance, causing Verity dismay at the idea of being the cynosure of pitying eyes. If Alistair hoped to win Verity's attention and provoke her jealousy by his indulgence of Olivia Bletchford's stratagems, he mistook his wife. She was humiliated and angry that he could treat her so, make her the object of society's avid speculation, and it only hardened her maddening air of aloofness. Both of them were deeply unhappy at the course they were following but seemed powerless to prevent it.

To distract herself from her personal problems, Verity decided her only remedy was to solve the conundrum of the Tsar's plot against Wellington, although she was coming to believe it was all a figment of Alistair's imagination. In pursuit of this decision, she set out one rainy afternoon to call again upon the Baroness, who had indicated she would be pleased to welcome her young neighbor at any time. Not informing Alistair of her plan, she turned away Agnes's objections to her sallying forth alone, and set her face stubbornly toward the meeting. She would gain great pleasure from discovering the Tsar's designs and triumphantly proving to Alistair that a mere woman could circumvent the deep plots of nefarious men.

In a mood of reckless determination she arrived at the Baroness's door only to be told that lady was not at home. Not willing to abandon her plan when she had steeled herself for action, she prevailed upon the Baroness's servant to allow her to wait for her return. She paced up and down the sitting room of the dark apartment in a fever of impatience, convinced that she must not postpone her attempt to get to the bottom of this vexatious conspiracy. She had made no progress in trying to fathom what the Prince knew, and his attentions were becoming worrying. She realized he believed she found him attractive and feared that he intended to press her into some imprudent act which could only lead to more misunderstanding on Alistair's part. That is if he cared enough about what became of her, she mused bitterly. He seemed perfectly content to ignore her in favor of Olivia Bletchford and probably welcomed, by now, the distraction the Prince offered.

Where was the Baroness? Just as she had about surrendered to the impossibility of putting her decision into action, she heard steps upon the stairs, and the murmur of voices, one indisputably a male. Looking around wildly, she sought a hiding place. She did not want a stranger to interrupt her interview with the Baroness and she was not up to exchanging meaningless trivia with some unknown visitor. Finally, she retreated into the adjoining boudoir, hoping that the servant had either not told the Baroness she was waiting or perhaps thinking that she had left in despair of seeing her hostess. The two entered the room which Verity had left. She had prudently left the door to the boudoir slightly ajar, thinking that the Baroness's companion might be the Tsar himself and she would learn something of moment. But the Baroness's guest was not the emperor but Prince Chirnovsky. And he appeared to be in a state of some agitation.

"Dear lady, you must help me, and all of Russia. I greatly fear the Tsar has decided on a disastrous plot to remove the Duke of Wellington as an obstacle in achieving the resolution of his Holy Alliance," the Prince said to the Baroness as the two faced each other in the shrouded room. Verity, restraining a gasp, tiptoed closer to the door. At last she was to learn something important.

"That would be a most grievous sin which the Holy Father would spend a lifetime repenting. How can he entertain such a thought?" the Baroness replied, truly aghast at the Prince's news.

"I suspect he has instructed two men to kill the Duke and then lay the blame somehow on the luckless Captain Webster, who has every reason to detest Wellington for his interest in Lady Webster," the Prince explained shortly. "And you are the only one who might dissuade him without grave repercussions. You might hint that you have learned of his intent from your psychic visitations," the Prince suggested in rather bitter tones.

The Baroness, not assuaged by his sneering at her beliefs, responded huffily, "You are not a believer,

Prince, but you must not deride my sincerity. My powers are real and have aided the Holy Father in the past to act according to God's wish rather than indulge in his own passions. I cannot lie to him, and I have received no indication that he has entertained such wicked thoughts."

The Prince was annoyed that his adversary could retreat behind some ethical dilemma when so much was at stake. "Baroness, do you wish to see Russia involved in a bloody war, with every sovereign in Europe against her? That could easily happen and must be prevented, whatever your scruples. I am appealing to you as a court of last resort. Only you have enough influence over the Tsar to make him see that this plan is against every Christian principle he pretends to endorse."

Verity, listening with horror to the revelations, gave not a thought to her own position, an eavesdropper on matters which were of the gravest importance. She felt only a triumphant satisfaction in learning at last what she and Alistair had suspected, the danger to the Duke from the ruthless and devious Tsar. She must somehow escape from this invidious position, skulking behind closed doors and listening to such treachery. If only the Prince would leave. But then she must still face the Baroness for there was no exit from the boudoir except through the sitting room. And what if the servant remembered her arrival? In her agitation Verity moved suddenly, her arm brushing a vase standing on the dresser to the right of the door. In horror she reached out to prevent its fall, but too late, and the sound of the crash echoed loud in her ears. She stood helpless as she heard the Prince's steps approaching and remained rooted to the floor as the door flew open and he confronted her with amazement.

"Well, what a surprise. And may I ask why you are hiding here in the Baroness's boudoir?" the Prince asked silkily. Verity did not like his tone, nor the feral light which gleamed in his eyes, nor the set of his lips drawn into a menacing snarl. Never had she experienced such terror.

"I know it looks dreadfully like I was snooping, Prince, but believe me, it is all most innocent," Verity said guilelessly, trying to pass off the damning discovery as a mere jape, a silly notion of a feckless female.

"Innocent, I doubt that, my dear Verity. You have no reason but an infamous one for eavesdropping on private conversation," he sneered.

"Really, Prince, I did not hear a word. I just did not want to interrupt the Baroness in case she was holding a seance, or whatever she would call the display of her powers," Verity responded with all the hauteur she could manage. She sensed that if the Prince believed for one moment that she had heard that very revealing conversation, her chances of emerging from this confrontation safely would not amount to much.

"A good try, *doushka,* but you are not a very convincing liar. And I think you have every intention of running home to that gallant husband of yours and confiding what you have learned so that he in turn can report to Wellington. Well, you can see I could never allow that," the Prince threatened softly.

"It is most ungentlemanly of you to accuse me of lying, Prince, and I think it would be best if we ignored your threats. I have no idea what you are talking about," Verity answered bravely, wondering if she could gull him long enough to effect her escape from his daunting presence. She had never glimpsed this aspect of the Prince's formidable personality, and she did not like it. His facade of the cosmopolitan, chivalrous gentleman cloaked another temperament, pure Slavic in its cruelty and arrogance. Somehow she must dispel his suspicions and extricate herself from this situation, but watching him rather like a mouse stalked by a cat, she wondered if she would be successful.

"We will ignore your pitiful excuses, I think. Actually this untoward event may work out to my satisfaction. You have chosen the wrong man to try and dupe, my dear. I am not one of your foppish Englishmen, content with a few sweet glances. You have teased and tempted me long enough. And surely, you see, I cannot allow you to leave here," he replied smoothly, but behind the words Verity felt his barely controlled rage and a certain satisfaction that his victim was at his mercy.

"I don't know what you have in mind, sir, but I would remind you that I am not unprotected. My husband knows of my visit here, and when I do not return, he will call to make inquiries which you might have difficulty in answering," she challenged him, remembering with a frisson of despair that neither Agnes nor Alistair knew of her whereabouts. Somehow she must delay the Prince, and enlist the Baroness's aid, until help arrived.

As she was plotting her next move, the Baroness appeared in the doorway, looking somewhat surprised at seeing her visitor.

"Madame Glendenning. I had no idea you were here. Why did you not make your presence known to us?" the Baroness asked, eyeing the Prince with a questioning air but sensing the tension in the atmosphere.

"I did not want to disturb you, Baroness. I know it was wrong of me to hide away in your bedroom. It was stupid, but I thought I might be interrupting an important conference, and did not quite know how to explain my unaccountable action," Verity explained, putting on a plaintive air.

"Which you failed to do, chérie, and now you must pay the price for your *bêtise*," the Prince growled.

Turning to the Baroness, and ignoring the man looming over her, Verity protested, "The Prince believes I deliberately spied upon you, Baroness, and that is far from the truth. I did not listen to your conversation. But I must apologize and leave you to your interview. I have delayed too long and my husband is expecting me. Perhaps I could return at a more convenient time," she explained, hoping that the Baroness would allow her to leave without any more garbled explanations. She did not think the woman would connive at the Prince's scheme to restrain her against her will, but in that she had mistaken her hostess. The Baroness knew where her own best interests lay and they were not in taking up the cudgels in defense of an English-woman who had proved to be no better than she should be. Not unaware of the Prince's lewd intent toward Verity, she was neither shocked nor interested in the outcome of the affair. Dependent on the Tsar's patronage and in securing the cooperation of his aide, she was prepared only to protect her own interests, no matter who should be sacrificed in pursuit of that end. But she thought affairs could be handled in a more dignified manner. So hiding her dismay, she tried to calm matters somewhat until she could decide how to manage this dilemma.

"You must have some refreshment before you leave. It would be most rude of me to turn you away until I have learned the reason for your visit," the Baroness invited, putting a hand on the Prince's arm and giving him a warning pinch.

"Yes, of course. We are becoming overserious about this small contretemps. Let us repair to the sitting room and drink some tea." He had retreated into his normal suave manner, but Verity sensed he had not abandoned his suspicions of her. Still, she had no recourse but to obey. She preceded the pair into the sitting room with all the assurance she could mount, her back rigid, so she did not hear the muttered order the Prince gave the Baroness.

They settled down around the samovar, the Prince taking a seat on the divan next to Verity, who perched gingerly, unwilling to break the silence which had settled over the trio.

The Baroness busied herself with the tea, mixing the brew herself and muttering over the urn. Within minutes, although it seemed much longer to the apprehensive girl, the beverage was ready and Verity accepted a cup, a sudden thirst drawing her to drink the scalding tea in one great gulp. She felt exhausted, her fright fading before the casual intimacy of the routine of the tea taking. The Prince's manner had altered once again, and he set out to be as pleasant as possible, telling amusing stories about Parisian society, ably seconded by the Baroness.

Verity shook herself, feeling her eyelids droop. She was amazingly sleepy and the voices of her companions seemed to come from a distance, as if they were talking in a tunnel. Despite her best efforts she felt herself slipping away into unconsciousness, unaware that the powerful drug the Baroness had slipped into her teacup was quickly taking effect. She slid sideways, her eyelids fluttering, powerless to keep awake. For a long moment her companions regarded her silently until finally the Prince leaned over her, watching her heavy breathing with a calculating gaze mixed with a certain cruel satisfaction. He passed his hand over her face, but she made no response.

"And now that you have effected the poor girl powerless, what is your plan?" the Baroness asked, not liking the situation but thoroughly cowed by his ruthless demeanor.

"That does present a problem but not an insurmountable one. She must remain here until I can make more suitable arrangements. It would never do for the Tsar to find an insensible woman in your quarters, Baroness. He might suspect your Christian principles are merely a facade for deep designs of a more satanic nature," the Prince replied sneeringly.

"You forced this eventuality upon me, Prince, and we may have mistaken her. She might truly have heard nothing and now we are lumbered with an unconscious woman. I hope I did not give her too strong a potion," the Baroness protested bravely. She was afraid of the Prince, and felt real compunction for her role in subduing Verity. Still, she had her own welfare to consider, having throughout her long career cleverly masked her ambitions under the guise of submission. "Her husband could well appear and demand to know what has become of his wife," she warned.

"Ah, I have a remedy for that. But in the meantime, we will deposit her on your bed and hope she sleeps for some time. I do not think you need worry about the obdurate husband. He will never see her again, and no doubt, will find consolation elsewhere," the Prince assured her arrogantly with a menacing tone which caused the Baroness to stifle any protests she might have made. In case she had second thoughts, the Prince reminded her, "Your own well-being depends on your keeping silent about this day's work, in which you have played a somewhat equivocal part."

"Yes, of course," agreed the Baroness meekly. She watched the Prince pick up Verity and carry her through to the adjoining room. She was not so stupid as to jeopardize her own position by trying to rescue Verity from her folly, even if her sympathies were engaged by the girl's plight. The Prince could bring all sorts of pressure to bear upon her, and her own role in this affair ensured her silence. Whatever compassion she felt for Verity was quickly smothered under the thought of what her future might bring if her own involvement was revealed. The Prince was not a man she could challenge with impunity.

Alistair returned from his engagements quite late that afternoon and was surprised at Verity's absence. He had intended to spend a quiet dinner at home, hoping that over an intimate meal, they might resolve some of their differences. He was more than annoyed to find his wife absent and his anger recoiled on the innocent Agnes's head.

"What do you mean by letting Mrs. Glendenning wander about the streets of Paris unattended," he queried her when the hapless abigail was summoned into his presence.

"She said she would just be a short while, and I understood her errand was in the neighborhood," Agnes explained, knowing that she had been derelict. "But I could hardly insist on accompanying her, sir, when she did not require my company," Agnes justified herself, although she was beginning to share Alistair's fears for Verity's safety. "Miss Verity is a rare one for going her own way," she explained further, although she could see she was not appeasing her master.

He sighed. Useless to blame the poor abigail for Verity's absence. He knew only too well how stubborn Verity could be, and how reckless. She might have decided on some foolhardy plan to reveal the Tsar's conspiracy, hoping to solve the whole matter and then triumphantly confront him with her cleverness. He knew that he had not been exactly receptive to any explanations from Verity. On the contrary, he had rebuffed any attempts on her part for discussion of their common problem. And his jealousy had turned him into a sullen companion. At the back of his mind was the dreadful suspicion that she might have embarked on some crusade to prove her own ability to thwart the Russians, or even have decided to put an end to this charade of a marriage and return to England. But then surely she would have left an accusing letter.

As darkness drew in, his worry increased. If something had happened to her, he would never forgive himself. He toyed absently with the supper

Jenkins brought him and wondered where he could pursue his investigations into her whereabouts. He had just about decided that he must make the rounds of her various acquaintances, dreaming up some tale to explain his questions, when Jenkins announced a visitor. "A Mr. Montgomery, sir, asking for Mrs. Glendenning but I told him she was not at home."

Alistair bit back a curse. It only needed this, that Verity's childhood friend had arrived on the scene. Could this be an explanation of her disappearance? "Send him up, Jenkins. I will see him." He rose and paced impatiently around the room, wondering what Denis Montgomery could want.

Denis entered the room rather tentatively, not knowing what to expect from this stranger who had wrested Verity from him. He had arrived in Paris that morning with his protesting mother. He had wanted to make the trip alone, having been quite disturbed by Sir Anthony's curt announcement of Verity's marriage, and determined to learn for himself if she had been coerced into an unhappy union. Naturally Mrs. Montgomery had done her best to dissuade him, and when her entreaties had failed, insisted on accompanying him. Denis had finally achieved his majority a few weeks past and had come into the money his father had left him. She now had no hold over him through the purse strings but she would not easily surrender her longtime governance. She had been relieved to hear of Verity's marriage, and she tried to tell Denis that he must not come between a man and wife, but her arguments fell on deaf ears. Now he had settled her into a hotel and rushed post haste to see Verity's situation for himself. What he met was a hard-eyed man, dressed in imposing regimentals, who studied him with an unwelcoming stare, quite unnerving him.

"Yes, Montgomery. What can I do for you," Alistair asked curtly, wondering for one wild moment if the young man had come to tell him he had spirited Verity away from her demanding husband as she was too unhappy to continue the marriage. Well, he would soon disabuse him of any chivalric attempts to play the rescuing lover.

"I came to call on Verity. Perhaps she has mentioned my name to you. We are childhood friends from Devon," Denis tried to explain, rather intimidated by this haughty officer, and feeling that in his youth and callowness he cut a poor figure.

"Yes, I recognized the name. But my wife has unaccountably absented herself. I thought you might have some news of her. She left this afternoon and has not returned, most unusual." Alistair badly in need of reassurance, had revealed more of his worry than he had intended.

Denis, not understanding the seriousness of Alistair's mood, could only offer his apologies for intruding and suggest that perhaps another time might be more convenient.

"Did she expect your arrival?" Alistair asked, knowing that he was disclosing more than he meant

351

to—the troubled state of his relationship with his wife, a personal confidence he would regret—but he was unable to prevent himself.

"No. I did not apprise her of the visit. I just decided that it might be interesting to see Paris now that Napoleon has been defeated, and as long as we had made the trip, I thought I might convey my respects to Verity, er, Mrs. Glendenning," he explained weakly, feeling at a great disadvantage for he did not understand Alistair's hard, troubled expression.

"I will give her your message," Alistair promised, now eager to see the last of his unwelcome visitor. It was obvious that Denis had no news of his erring wife and he needed solitude to decide on his next move. Denis had no recourse than to bid him farewell and make his reluctant departure, feeling much dispirited by the encounter and aware that there was some suspicion in Alistair's manner.

By now Alistair was in a fever of impatience and worry, accepting that Verity's absence might have sinister overtones. He would have to make these embarrassing calls in the hope that Lady Shelley or some other matron might be able to give him an indication of where Verity had gone. As he prepared to depart on his errand, he was again interrupted by Jenkins, who entered the room with a letter on a salver.

"This just came for you, sir, by a special messenger. I thought it might be important, explaining the madam's absence," the man said sympathetically, well aware of Alistair's uneasiness and hoping to dispel it.

"Thank you, Jenkins. That will be all," Alistair dismissed the man, unable to explain that he wanted to be alone to read the message but experienceing a horrible foreboding. The letter, written on heavy blue paper, realized his worst fears.

Alistair,

Since you cannot but be aware of our estrangement, this will come as little surprise. Our marriage has proved a disaster and I can no longer endure it. I have gone to a man who cares for me and will ensure my happiness. I am sure only your pride will be affected by such a drastic decision on my part and you will feel only relief that I have taken matters into my own hands. I acquit you of blame for we are both at fault. I trust you will find happiness with a woman more suited to you in the future.

Verity

Chapter Twenty-Three

Verity came out of her drugged sleep slowly, conscious of a throbbing headache and a leaden numbness in her limbs. At first she thought she was in her bedroom at the faubourg Saint Honore and wondered why was she asleep at this time of day. But then slowly raising her aching head, she noticed that the room was a strange one, shrouded in gloom, and hazy memories of the tea party in the Baroness von Krudener's apartment returned to her. She remembered the Prince discovering her hiding in the Baroness's bedroom, and his controlled rage, then his suave insistence that she take tea before leaving.

She jerked up to a sitting position, anger forcing all her discomfort from her. They had drugged her, the two of them, sitting there all smiles and easy conversation. What a fool she had been to think they would have let her walk calmly out of the Baroness's apartment to tell of what she had learned. Despite the pounding in her head, the Prince's confidences to the Baroness were echoing in her mind. He wanted to persuade the Baroness to influnece the Tsar against any attempt to assassinate Wellington. It was as she and Alistair had suspected. There would be an attempt and the blame would be laid at the door of the hapless Captain Webster, whose jealousy of his wife was the source of all the gossip. They could not allow her to escape with such damning information, and so had drugged her and, while she was insensible, had carried her to this place. But where was she? Surely not in the Baroness's apartment, for the room was too spartan for that, and too quiet.

Slowly she rose from the bed, her body protesting at the activity. The Prince had drugged her and kidnapped her. What did he plan to do? She had a suspicion and the thought terrified her, but pushing away the frightful images, she tried to concentrate. No matter how angry Alistair was with her, he would look for her. His pride would not allow him to accept the absence of even an erring wife with equanimity. Somehow she must get away from this prison cell, for that was how she viewed it, and she must escape before the Prince returned, for she had no doubt he had not finished with her. Alistair would be bound to question him and what would he say, what specious explanation would he give?

Then she groaned. Alistair did not know she had planned to visit the Baroness nor did Agnes. Why had she been so foolhardy? The precariousness of her situation, alone and at the mercy of the Prince, returned to torment her. She dragged herself across the room, sensation returning to her heavy and unwilling legs, her head whirling with the effort. But she must walk off this lassitude and regain her wits. She must rely on her own abilities to get herself out of this hideous mess.

She could not wait for Alistair. It might be hours before he returned and found her gone. By the time he gathered his resources to look for her, it might be too late. She groaned as she paced the room, strength returning to her limbs, although her headache had not lessened under the strain of her agonized thoughts. She must banish her questions and fears and come to some resolution. For the first time she became aware of her surroundings, noting that the small room was completely dark. Either the windows were shuttered from the outside or had been boarded up, for no light penetrated the gloomy apartment. How many hours had passed since her incarceration? It must be night, for it had been late afternoon when she had been surprised at the Baroness's house.

Struggling to the window, she discovered that it was boarded from within. Beside the bed, and a small table beside it, the room held few furnishings. On a rather rickety dresser was a carafe and a glass. Suddenly aware of a raging thirst, Verity picked up the carafe, which appeared to be full of water, and sniffed it. Much as she wanted a drink, she feared the water might be drugged. How had the Baroness managed to slip whatever potion she had used into her teacup? They had all appeared to drink from the samovar. But that problem would have to wait. She must somehow effect her escape from this miserable room before the Prince returned.

She tiptoed to the door, her slippered feet making little sound across the bare boards. It was as she had feared, the door was locked, and seemed exceedingly stout, a heavy oak barrier which would not yield to any force she could exert. It had evidently been locked from the outside, and trying to peer through the keyhole, she could see nothing. Could the key be still in the lock on the outside? Shaking her head in puzzlement and trying to clear her clouded senses, she sighed despondently.

She felt faint and giddy, but she could not give in to such weakness. She returned to the bed to try to consider her options. She knew only that she could not remain here like a trussed bird to await whatever the Prince had in mind for her. There was nothing in the room she could use as a weapon. For a moment she considered standing behind the door and when the Prince returned, hitting him with some object, but aside from the water pitcher, there was nothing to serve as a weapon, and she doubted that would do the trick. Her reticule had disappeared and her shoes were soft kid, ineffective as a tool.

Despair overwhelmed her and she considered the vulnerability of her plight. Then she straightened her back, firmed her chin, and decided no use could be served by surrendering to her fears. Both Charley and Denis would have recognized her determination. She had never given in tamely to the inevitable when they had become embroiled in childish adventures. She had always been the one to somehow contrive their escape, and in this far more disastrous dilemma, she must banish her cowardice and rely on her wits to help her. She could not remain a supine victim, allowing the Prince to have his way with her. He could never allow her to return to Alistair, confess what she had learned, and expose his own role in her abduction. He had not been convinced by her guileless protestations that she had heard nothing of his conversation with the Baroness and, to protect himself, had drugged her and carried her to this lair.

She had no idea where she was but thought it must be some miles from Paris. But even if she managed to flee from this place, how would she make her way back to the city? The silence around her oppressed her. Not a sound could be heard, which only increased her apprehension. Would the Prince have left some ruffian on guard? But she dismissed that idea. Whom could he trust with such a burden? Would he allow any servant, no matter how cowed, to be privy to such knowledge, that he had abducted a woman and restrained her against her will?

Well, if there was someone on guard, she would just have to deal with that once she succeeded in getting out of this room. Then, desperation prodding her, she remembered the time when her father had locked her in her room as a punishment for

359

some misdemeanor and unwisely left the key in the lock outside. Determined to show him her willfulness, she had managed to pry the key from the lock with a hat pin and draw it under the door to unlock it from the inside. Her father, at first angry at her action, had then laughed and signed with admiration. "I pity the man who takes you to wife," he had said, facing the stubborn fourteen-year-old. She felt tears rise in her eyes at the thought of her beloved parent. If he were alive, she would never be in this wretched situation but safe in Devon with no Sir Anthony or Alistair or Prince to threaten her.

Shaking off her despair and fruitless memories, she chided herself for her timidity. Well, she must just try to see if the ruse would work again, although she had no hat pin. But then she remembered she was wearing her grandmother's pearl brooch, which had a substantial fastener. Perhaps that would do the trick.

In her eagerness to try, her shaking hands could not at first find the keyhole, but at last she succeeded in forcing the heavy pin through the opening, and by wiggling it for several minutes, suddenly released the key and heard it fall with a loud thud onto the floor outside the door.

She waited a moment, her heart thudding, expecting that if anyone was in the house, they would surely hear the noise. But after a few moments she realized that only her own frenzy had impelled such a notion.

Now she must somehow draw the key under the

door and for that she needed a piece of paper which would slide under the space between the threshold and the door itself. She looked around wildly, for there must be some paper in the room. She searched the scarred dresser, but it was empty, not even any tattered linings in the drawers.

The room was amazingly bare of any furnishings but the most primitive. She could not imagine a man of the Prince's sophisticated tastes using this place for any reason. It might be a gamekeeper's cottage or some such habitation. But such ruminations had to be postponed until she had secured the key. Aware of a strange giddiness which was clouding her reasoning, she tried to shake off the desire to collapse on the bed and seek the healing sanctuary of sleep, but she could not tamely surrender now. She must persevere.

Looking at her pale face in the spotted mirror above the dresser, her titian hair falling in tangled curls about her shoulders, she smiled grimly. She certainly had none of the appearance of a lady of fashion about her now. She looked like a raga-muffin.

Suddenly the mirror gave her an idea. Taking up the water pitcher she hit the mirror with a mighty blow, the cracking of the glass sounding like a cannon shot in her ears. Waiting to see if the sound had attracted attention, all she could hear was again the thudding of her own heart.

Carefully, she pried a jagged piece of glass from the mirror, barely noticing the blood which oozed from a cut on her finger. Taking the piece of glass over to the door, she wedged it slowly under the space between the door and the floor trying to find the key. Just as she was about ready to give up in hopeless failure, she felt an obstruction. The key! As she edged it carefully toward the opening, perspiration broke out on her forehead, and she was within an ace of fainting from the effort, but she tried not to hurry and through her urgency lose the precious key.

Finally she succeeded in drawing the vital instrument of her release into the room. Sighing with relief, she placed the key gently in the door and turned it as quietly as she could. It was stiff and reluctant, but then it clicked and the door swung open.

Her first instinct was to bolt onto the hallway, and run as quickly as she could toward safety, but she still feared a jailor, so she quieted her instincts and slipped slowly away from the door.

She waited a moment but could hear or see little. The hallway was dark and deserted. In the grim stygian atmosphere she looked frantically for the stairs. Her eyes, now becoming accustomed to the darkness, focused on the opening at the end of the small hall which led to the lower rooms. Cautiously she sidled toward them and began her descent, expecting at any moment to be halted by some ruffian.

The stairs led directly into what must be the main sitting room, as sparsely furnished as the upstairs bedroom. But across the room was a stout oak door, no doubt leading outside. She hurried to reach it only to find that it was locked and bolted with no key this time available. Sobbing with frustration she looked about. There must be another way out.

Gliding quietly across the room toward the back of the cottage, she entered the kitchen, a dank fetid room redolent with undesirable smells. But yes, there was another door and she slipped through it to find herself in what might once have been a small garden, overhung by a deep growth of menacing trees. She hesitated for a moment, then steeling herself, walked resolutely into the cover of darkness.

At least she had escaped from the Prince, if only temporarily. Now she must try to get her bearings and find some way to get back to Paris, for she could not expect that the Prince would not soon discover her escape and be hot on her heels. He could not allow her to deliver her message to Alistair or his superiors. Well, she had managed so far and she would not be so faint-hearted now as to surrender the advantage she had gained.

Alistair's first reaction on reading the startling note from Verity was not anger but a soul-shattering disappointment. He had lost her, and he was convinced her flight had been caused by his own unwillingness to confess his love for her. Whatever doubts he had had about his feeling for his wife vanished beneath the burden of his own guilt and lack of courage. He knew that if he had acted differently, wooed her gently, she might have been his. He had believed during the picnic that he had been within an ace of winning her affection.

He reread the note several times, creasing it over and over in his despair. She had not gone to Denis, her childhood friend. It could only have been the Prince who had lured her with his false gallantry and specious avowals. Of course, it was possible that the man might feel a real affection for her, but Alistair was not so far gone in misery that he believed in the Russian's sincerity. And then, there was Verity's insistence that she felt nothing for the Prince. He did not think she was capable of such deception, of hiding a love that was so overwhelming she would sacrifice reputation and all decent standards of behavior by this precipitate action. Somehow the words, which had struck him with such horror and dismay, on further perusal did not ring true. He called Agnes back to question her.

"Your mistress seems to have fled. Did she take any clothes with her?" he asked the apprehensive maid brusquely.

Agnes, who had her own ideas of the relationship between the Glendennings, answered quickly, "Of course not. I would have known if she had tried any such foolishness. I understand Mr. Denis has been here. If you suspect her, Major, of running off with him, you are greatly mistaken. She could have married Mr. Denis at any time these past few years. He was mad to have her, despite that old shrew of a mother. And Miss Verity would never throw her cap over the windmill in such a fashion," she reproved, daring Alistair to criticize her nursling.

"You are positive she did not pack a portmanteau with a journey in mind," Alistair insisted, yearning to believe the abigail but unable to accept the truth of her words.

"Of course not. She intended to go on some brief errand. She had given orders for a special collation this evening. I know she meant to return to have a quiet dinner with you, sir," Agnes soothed, seeing how unhappy the major looked. Her loyalty was to Verity, but she admired Alistair for his gallantry and past kindnesses to her. She wanted to ease his pain while reproving him for thinking such shocking thoughts about her mistress.

"Yes, well, what do you think of this note?" he asked desperately, proffering the crumpled letter to the maid. Normally he would not have exposed such an intimate revelation to a servant, but he needed Agnes's help and this was no time to consider propriety.

"That is not Miss Verity's handwriting. Someone is trying to gull you, sir, and a nasty mind it is which would impugn her good name in such a villainous way," Agnes said decisively, her eyes flashing.

"Are you sure, Agnes? If this is an attempt to deceive us, Verity is in trouble, great danger. She may have been coerced and even abducted," Alistair confided, his not inconsiderable intelligence now bearing on the problem. Verity had embroiled herself in some adventure which had caused their enemies to take drastic efforts to silence not only her, but his own suspicions. His mind settled immediately on the Prince.

"Could she have gone riding this afternoon with Prince Chirnovsky?" he asked, pacing up and down the room, wondering what could have drawn Verity into this peril.

"No, sir. She left the house on foot. Perhaps she went to call on that neighbor, the foreign lady, who is supposed to be a fortune-teller or some such," Agnes suggested, alluding in this scornful fashion to the Baroness von Krudener.

"Yes, of course. She must have gone there. I will go round immediately and put a few questions to that lady," Alistair replied decisively. He dismissed Agnes, telling her not to worry, advice he could not take himself.

The abigail, muttering to herself, left the room, her doubts and concern evident, but accustomed to accepting the peculiar attitudes of the gentry, she was somewhat mollified that Alistair had taken charge. Privately she thought the carryings-on, as she expressed it, between her mistress and the husband she had married in such haste were foolish. She knew nothing of what had impelled the marriage but she believed the two would come about with the arrival of the first baby, a practical no-nonsense approach to life which the young Glendennings could do well to emulate. But then the gentry had too much time to worry and wonder about events lesser folk had not the leisure in which to indulge.

Alistair, in a more sensible mood, would probably endorse her beliefs, but he was in no state to bring such level-headed practicality to the current situation. As he hurried down the faubourg Saint Honore to number 35, he tried to banish his fears for Verity's safety in planning his approach to the Baroness, if indeed she was involved in his wife's strange disappearance. But in the back of his mind lay a lingering guilt that his own attitude had forced this crisis upon Verity.

The late summer evening had finally darkened when Alistair arrived at the Baroness's apartment, and he hoped the lady had not left for some social occasion. Barely restraining his impatience when her servant requested his name and business, he was not inclined to pay any heed to the minion's assurances that madame was not receiving. Brushing aside the girl, he burst into the Baroness's sitting room, to find her sitting in brooding silence by the fire. Her serenity allayed his fears for the moment and raised doubts about the merit of his visit.

"Good evening, Baroness. I am Major Glendenning. We have not met, but I understand you know my wife," he said curtly.

The Baroness rose to her feet and greeted him calmly, as if the sudden arrival of a distraught military man into the sanctuary of her sitting room was not remarkable in any way.

"Indeed, Major. You seem distressed. You must turn your troubled mind to the guiding hands of the God who protects us all. He will relieve your anxieties. Alas, I fear you are a worldly man. You do not have the serenity of a true believer who is content to surrender his will to a higher power."

Alistair, a bit taken aback by the woman's coarse appearance in contrast to the sanctity of her words, remembered that she had a reputation as a seer and mystic, claiming some supernatural powers which had influenced the Tsar to abandon his licentious life. Impatient as he was to wrest whatever knowledge she might have, he brought his agitation under control with an effort and faced her with the suave cajoling manner which had always served him well with women.

"I know my invasion of your privacy is unforgivable, but you must excuse my abruptness. I believe my wife set out to visit you this afternoon. She has not returned and I hoped you could give me some news of her. With all the rag-tail and ruffians which throng the streets of Paris, I am naturally exercised as to her safety," he explained smoothly, looking about the dark cluttered room as if he expected to find Verity hiding behind some drapery or settee. It was difficult enough to discern his hostess's expression in the overly warm room, whose atmosphere filled him with a strange revulsion. In his impetuosity he had crossed to loom over the Baroness, who stared up at him, her hooded opaque eyes revealing nothing.

"Ah, yes, a devoted husband. I quite understand. My maid did mention that I had a visitor this afternoon, but she left before I returned, unfortunately. I welcome any visit from a seeker after truth," she said enigmatically, hiding behind the spurious philosophy which had served her well in the past. A skilled actress, she had half expected this questioning, but she had hoped that the Prince's methods, which he had not confided to her, would have spared her this confrontation. Still, she was not unprepared to parry the obdurate husband's demands.

"So you have not seen her?" Alistair asked, a bit chagrined at her easy explanations, not completely believing them but now knowing quite how to force any more information from the redoubtable lady. Her reference to spirituality was a cloak to hide her real emotions, he suspected, but he could hardly accuse her of lying.

"No, alas, I was not available to offer the advice she must have sought," the Baroness assured him, wondering if he would be content with her apparent easy affability. Behind the facade of calm resolution her mind scurried feverishly about. She had suggested to the Prince that this Englishman might not take his wife's sudden flight quiescently but he had overcome her objections and arrogantly informed her that he had the means to settle the matter. She must not lose her head.

"Won't you sit down and we can discuss this strange disappearance of your wife, a delightful woman, with a true nobility of soul," she invited graciously.

He impatiently took a seat on the very settee

upon which Verity had perched to indulge in that disastrous tea party of which no sign was now evident in the room. Schooling his face into an expression of hopeful expectation of comfort, he listened to the Baroness, all the while trying to probe the graven mask which hid her real thoughts.

"What makes you believe that she came to some grief upon leaving my door?" the Baroness asked boldly, deciding that the best way she could settle his suspicions was to adopt the pose of a concerned confidant.

"Just that she is a girl of established habits, not inclined to frivolously cause me worry," Alistair confided, giving her an artless smile. "We had a small disagreement, and I thought at first she was paying me out by remaining absent, and not sending word of her whereabouts, but on further consideration, I believe she would not be so vindictive, no matter the distress I caused her." He disliked playing the role of a fractious, demanding husband but he had an intuition that he might learn more by adopting this distasteful pose.

"Ah, you young impetuous husbands, so careless of your dear helpmate's contentment," the Baroness lamented with a forgiving smile.

Alistair, adopted a repentant expression, inwardly seething at the delay. He fidgeted a bit, his hands dropping to the edge of the settee, adjusting the cushions to a more comfortable position. In tugging at the recalcitrant bolsters, he dislodged a scrap of white cambric, which fluttered to the floor. With an exclamation he stooped and picked up the handkerchief. His eyes glowed suddenly with excitement. Yes, this was Verity's for a small intricately worked *V* was inscribed in one corner.

"You see, Baroness. She was here, for this is her handkerchief. How do you explain that?" he asked, his tone and stance suddenly hardening. His belief that the Baroness had lied to him was now evident, and he intended to force the truth from her. There was a mystery here of which she was a party and would tell him the truth if he had to wring it out of her. Before he could bring pressure to bear, the Baroness tried to disarm him by confessing her treachery, for she knew when she was defeated. She must avert any discovery of the Prince's real motive in abducting Verity by admitting to the lesser sin.

"Alas, Major, I must confess. The Prince and your wife used my rooms for several trysts. I know I am culpable of lending countenance to their affair, and I should not have condoned such a breach of conduct, but the Prince has the means to compel me," she disclosed with a persuasive show of reluctance. Far better that he should think his wife an adulteress than he should learn what her real purpose was in coming to the Baroness's apartment. Her Christian scruples bothered her little when it came to a question of protecting her welfare.

"I don't believe you, Baroness, much as I dislike calling a lady a liar," he replied scornfully, but he was not as successful at hiding his dismay as he hoped. The news had been a blow. The thought of Verity with the Prince revolted him.

"Of course, you can ask the Prince. He will confirm this shocking liaison," the Baroness said persuasively. She consoled herself over the lie by insisting that if Alistair caught up with the pair, her story would be true in most particulars, for the Baroness had no doubts about the Prince's intentions toward Verity, whether the lady was willing or not.

"I will do just that, but I warn you, Baroness, I have not forgiven, nor will I forget, your involvement in this disgusting affair," he warned, his eyes narrowing in anger. God, the woman was no better than a brothel keeper, admitting that she had encouraged the Prince to pursue Verity within her own home. Bowing curtly to the Baroness, whose impassive made-up face showed little emotion, he left to seek out Prince Chirnovsky.

After his departure, the Baroness brooded for a while about her own position. How would she survive this imbroglio? Alistair's threats had not moved her as much as the thought of what the Prince might do when he discovered she had betrayed him, but she had managed to emerge more creditably than she hoped. She had not revealed the Tsar's wicked purpose, and had protected her own security as well as she could. However, the Baroness, an experienced adventuress, who had surmounted adversity before, had enough perception to realize

372

that her current position was tenuous. Both the Tsar and the Prince would sacrifice her without any pangs of contrition if it was to their advantage. She must guard against their efforts even if she had to use blackmail to achieve her ends, a grievous necessity she decided piously, but she must secure her own future.

Chapter Twenty-Four

The Prince had intended to return to the cottage where he had imprisoned Verity long before this. He had expected only a few hours' delay at the most, while he made the necessary arrangements. But the Tsar inadvertently circumvented his plans. Upon the Prince's return to the Palace after delivering Verity to the cottage beyond Paris, he had been summoned into the emperor's presence by a lackey who gave the impression that his continued absence had more than annoyed Alexander. The Tsar's servants, well accustomed to his irrational rages, preferred to have the emperor's wrath fall upon those of his entourage who were able to deflect it, and the Prince had usually been among those more fortunate members. However, this time, even the Prince was to encounter difficulty in soothing Alexander's irate mood.

On entering the audience room, the Prince noticed immediately that Alexander was working himself into a huge tantrum. He tried to make his excuses.

"Please accept my apologies, Sire. Pressing business demanded my attention, and I am desolate that I was not available when your message arrived," the Prince apologized, hoping to avoid a crisis.

"Your duty is to attend me, sir, not to place your personal obligations before those of your emperor," replied the Tsar in chilling hauteur. He drew himself up to his full imposing stature, his eyes arctic as he looked at his repentant aide.

"I can only crave your indulgence, and explain my dereliction by assuring you, Sire, that the business which took me from the Palace concerned our troublesome English allies. I have reason to think that Wellington may have some knowledge of your attempts to discredit him," the Prince protested, hoping to distract the Tsar's temper by showing his zeal for the emperor's business.

"And how have you come by this information, from one of your many chère amies, Prince?" the Tsar sneered. Before the aide could explain, he continued, raising his hand to quell any demurs and looking very majestic, even though he had not fully mastered his irritation. "You know, Prince, you must abandon these purient pursuits. I think it is time you found a wife. In fact, I have a very suitable parti in mind for you. When we return to Russia I will put the matter in hand." He smiled sarcastically, knowing that the last thing the Prince wanted was a marriage of state, which would temporarily disrupt

376

his amatory adventures.

Oh, Lord, sighed the Prince to himself. Once the Tsar made up his mind that his favorite aide should embark on matrimony, there would be no changing his mind. But now was not the time to argue the matter.

"As you command, Sire," the Prince murmured impassively.

"Now I must hear more of this information you have come by, no matter how distasteful the means," the Tsar signified, relaxing a bit and indicating that the Prince could be seated. He himself dropped into a large ornate chair, which gave the impression of a throne, prepared to dispense advice and listen to what the Prince had learned. But before the two could come to grips with their problem, they were interrupted by a servant, who approached timidly, having been given instructions not to disturb the pair.

"A thousand apologies, Holy Father, but an English officer insists on admission. He desires to meet with the most gracious Prince, with your indulgence," the man insisted, tempering Alistair's furious demand and his insistence that he would interrupt the conference if he was not ushered forthwith into the royal presence.

The servant held to his well-schooled training, but he feared an outburst from his royal master which might earn him severe punishment, banishment even. But Alistair had been adamant. Surprisingly the Tsar took this outrageous news in good part.

"Show him in, this impetuous officer, sirrah," he commanded. Then, turning to the Prince, he said gleefully, "It no doubt is the vengeful Captain Webster, who, having thought over our proposal, sees the good sense in acting upon it at once. That will please you, Prince, since you disapprove of my more violent method of silencing Wellington." He grinned, implying a certain disappointment in solving his dilemma so tamely. His shock when Alistair was announced was replaced rapidly by puzzlement. He had no idea what this strange and obviously furious Englishman wanted. He knew only that it was not the man he had expected. Drawing himself up arrogantly, he ignored Alistair's sketchy obeisance, and asked in quelling tones, "What is the reason for this intrusion, sir? I don't believe I signified I wished to receive you," the Tsar said, impressing his unwanted visitor with this shocking breach of etiquette. But Alistair failed to be intimidated.

"I apologize for intruding, Sire, but I must speak with the Prince here without delay," Alistair said, with an arrogance almost equal to the emperor's.

"What is the meaning of this, Vasilii?" the emperor asked, turning with a frown to his aide. No matter how eager he was to conspire against the English, he did not like having his own officers questioned or suspected of any improprieties. He preferred to conduct his plots in a serpentine manner which would never rebound on his own head, and here this Englishman had thrust himself forward, and by his manner, would not be fobbed off with either threats or evasions. Perhaps Vasilii was correct, and despite his cleverness, some knowledge had leaked to Wellington. If that was so, whoever was responsible, including the Prince, would pay dearly for their indiscretion.

The Prince, although his expression remained impassive, was busily arranging his approach to the pointed questions he knew Alistair would ask. But his first priority was to remove the damn man from the Tsar's neighborhood. Alexander might not be concerned over the Prince's seduction of Verity, but he would prefer not to hear of it, and might even believe he should, in pursuance of his recently acquired Christian principles, insist on the Prince's restoring the erring wife to her husband. Somehow he must be prevented from learning of this day's work.

"Since Major Glendenning's business concerns me, Sire, we will not bore you with the details," the Prince interposed suavely, hoping that the emperor would not take one of his unaccountable interests in an affair which normally he would think beneath his notice.

"Perhaps your emperor is not aware of your lecherous ways, Prince," Alistair said boldly, then turning to the Tsar, still in the grip of his anger, he continued, "This varlet has abducted my wife, and I demand satisfaction. If you truly believe in the scruples you profess, Sire, you will let me bring him to account."

Alexander, who just a few minutes before had been inclined to chastise his aide for his womanizing, now defended him. He would not allow an Englishman to bring one of his nobles to task.

"You forget yourself, Major. I deeply resent your tempestuous and rude intrusion upon me with your paltry personal affairs. Your wife does not concern me, and if she prefers the Prince here to you, I am not surprised. I understand the English are poor lovers, and no doubt she found Vasilii a much more attractive proposition," the Tsar goaded Alistair, quite amused by the whole affair, his worldly instincts prompting him, for he himself had endulged in many such enjoyable dalliances.

The Tsar's casual absolution for his aide's transgressions infuriated Alistair, who had heard much of Alexander's pious if recent philosophy, but he was too skilled a tactician to lose his control.

"I am sure, Sire, you know your own subjects best, but I must protest the Prince's conduct and take appropriate action. Englishmen may be poor lovers, but they are stubborn fighters, as I am sure you have learned." His words wiped the amusement from the Tsar's face. Indeed, that sovereign had every reason to know about the English tenacity, for that quality was responsible for the uncomfortable situation in which he now found himself.

Suddenly impatient with the affair, he dismissed the trivial argument languidly with a wave of his hand.

"I find these small carnal matters of little

importance, when I have so many weighty circumstances to concern me. Vasilii, you must answer the major, but I warn you, I will have no dueling. Such egregious offenses do not interest me," he concluded grandly, signifying that two offenders must remove themselves from the royal presence.

Alistair, who found the Tsar rather ridiculous in his hypocritical pretentiousness, was only too eager to quit the audience, but he did not intend to be fobbed off by the Prince, nor was he impressed with the Tsar's haughty dismissal of his questions. Before taking his leave he decided the Tsar should be reminded of his own vulnerability.

"I doubt that His Majesty's government and its representative, the Duke of Wellington, will receive the news that a Russian officer had behaved in such a shabby fashion, insulting one of His Majesty's subjects, with indifference. The Duke is apt to view Slavic excesses with a certain contempt," he warned, and then bowed himself out before the Tsar could reply. Perforce the Prince, under his master's admonitory eye, had to accompany him.

In the anteroom Alistair faced his rival with gloves off. He would wipe that fatuous expression from the bounder's face with his fists if necessary, but then he recalled the danger to Verity and controlled his first reactions. Only by restraining his natural instincts could he learn what had happened to her.

"Well, Prince, what have you done with my wife? I think it was you who wrote that false letter informing me of Verity's flight, for it certainly wasn't Verity."

The Prince hesitated just a moment too long, wondering what Glendenning knew. He might suspect his involvement but he could not be certain. He had certainly not expected that the major would challenge him with such resolution. He had believed the man's interest was occupied elsewhere and was annoyed he had misread the situation, but that did not require he admit his part in the proceedings. After all, Alistair could not really know he was responsible, and even if he had questioned the Baroness, she was too concerned about her own future to betray him.

"I am sorry that you have mislaid your lovely wife, Major, but I fail to see why this is any business of mine," he lied suavely. "I am not so foolish as to risk my reputation by eloping with an allied officer's woman," he objected scornfully. "Prudence wars with passion and wins every time, under the circumstances. Wouldn't you agree?"

Alistair, baffled and frustrated, subdued his inclination to beat the news of Verity's disappearance from the man.

"The Baroness had confessed that you lured Verity to secret trysts in her rooms," he countered, glaring at the man, whose bland assurances did not ring true.

"Ah, yes, the Baroness, a deluded woman, I fear. I have enjoyed your wife's company on many occasions, but you accuse me falsely. Our relationship is all that is most proper," the Prince countered, hiding his worry that the Baroness might have been beguiled into revealing damning information. Still, he had no recourse but to bluff. He now heartily wished he had not abducted Verity, for the affair seemed to be rebounding disastrously on his shoulders. The Tsar would be furious if his aide embroiled him in a sordid intrigue which could endanger the Alliance. And he did not like the ugly expression in Alistair's eyes. The Prince was not a coward, but he had an inordinate pride in his position, and would do much to protect his reputation.

Alistair, far from satisfied by the man's explanation, felt balked. "Then you deny that you are at the bottom of her disappearance," he muttered, not abating his threatening mien.

"Absolutely. You must look elsewhere for your culprit, Major. And I regret exceedingly that you saw fit to involve the Tsar in your groundless accusations against me," the Prince protested convincingly, trying to shift the burden to Alistair's shoulders.

"I care little for that. And if I prove you wrong, you will have to answer not only to me but to your emperor, not an enviable position. You have not heard the last of this," he said in a menacing tone and abruptly took his departure, before he could commit the folly of smashing the Prince's bland face.

Chapter Twenty-Five

Alistair would have derived a certain grim satisfaction if he had realized how disturbed and uncertain his accusations and his warnings had left the Prince. He had escaped retribution for the moment but he was clever enough to accept the precariousness of his position. The Baroness had been coerced into revealing more than she should have, and if Alistair returned with more evidence, he would indeed be vulnerable and the Tsar would punish him for endangering the Alliance rather than for his abduction of Verity.

His was not a happy state of mind as he prepared to ride out to the secluded cottage in which he had imprisoned Verity. If he had to suffer for his villainy, he would enjoy some of the fruits of his misdeed before he faced the penalty for his rashness. But his interest in Verity had suffered a setback. She was hardly worth the candle, but she must pay for embroiling him in this undignified and perilous plot. Always the victim of his sensual appetites, this latest escapade might prove his undoing, and if so, his vengeance would rebound on the hapless girl who he believed had enticed him. He ordered his horse and rode rapidly from the Palace, hoping no one had noticed his departure.

In this hope he was deceived, for Alistair, upon leaving the Prince, had reconsidered, coolly assessing the interview. If the Prince had lied, his first response to the threat to his consequence would be to try to repair the damage, to seek out either the Baroness or Verity, wherever he had her concealed. Alistair had always preferred action to waiting upon events, and he believed that he would do well to keep a wary eye on the Prince's movements, considering that the man would think he had put Alistair's suspicions to rest, and in his arrogance could safely proceed with whatever schemes he had concerning Verity. So Alistair concealed himself behind a convenient bit of shrubbery outside the Palace Elysée and waited for the Prince's next move.

And just in time for the Prince emerged within moments and mounted his horse, galloping off into the night. Alistair decided that following him in the darkness should not be beyond his powers and rode at a safe distance, keeping his quarry in sight, hoping that his horse's hooves would not alert the Prince to his pursuer. Fortunately, on this mild September night the streets of Paris were thronged with carriages and pedestrians seeking pleasure and

Alistair was able to accomplish his purpose.

Alistair's thoughts were unhappy company to his dogged tracking as he galloped after his victim. He felt he had acquitted himself poorly in the abortive interview with the Prince. He was convinced that the Prince was lying, and he should pay the price for that deception, but a nagging fear rode with him. What if Verity had, in truth, sought the Prince's aid in escaping from her unhappy marriage? She had every reason to despise her truculent husband, who had seduced her so callously and then forced her into a sterile marriage. His temper and his pride had prevented him from making any push to mend matters, and to a girl of her innocence and sensitivity his casual treatment must have been unbearable.

And then he had embroiled her in this conspiracy, throwing her into a situation which could only increase her doubts and fears. She had stood up to him valiantly but she deserved better, a chivalrous cavalier who would protect and cherish her, and instead she had been faced with an indifferent libertine who mocked and rebuffed her efforts at companionship. How could she care for such a rake? And he had been far from clever in his assessment of this plot to discredit Wellington.

Alistair continued to disparage his efforts, his thoughts as dark as the night through which he rode toward some unknown crisis. Had he mistaken events? What would he find at the end of his ride? He was determined upon one thing. If he rescued Verity from this danger, he would sink his pride and beg for her love. He had at last faced that his life without her would be a barren unhappy journey and he must persuade her of his sincerity and his devotion. He smiled cynically at the pass to which he had come, a besotted husband in love with his own wife, and uncertain as how to woo her. Well, it would serve him right if she jeered at his avowals and turned from him in scorn. He deserved no less.

His grim thought had so occupied him that he did not realize that his pursuit of the Prince had now brought him to the outskirts of the city, and the possibility of the Prince perceiving his chase. He slowed his horse to a canter and dropped farther back, still keeping his prey within sight. Evidently the Prince, too, was preoccupied and unaware that his journey might be observed for he did not slacken his pace.

Having escaped her prison, Verity had wandered distractedly into the woods, her only hope to put as much distance between herself and her captor as possible. She had little doubt that the Prince would return before long and, when he discovered her flight, would make haste to apprehend her. She had no idea where she was, only that she was surrounded by menacing night, in some woods which seemed to have no ending. Well, she had come this far and must not lose her courage now. But her spirits were failing, and weariness threatened to overcome her. All she wanted was to fall down and sleep for hours.

Shaking off her lethargy, she struggled on, seeing no end to the mass of trees whose branches scratched her and impeded her progress. Suddenly she heard a noise behind her, the sound of a horse's whinny and a muttered curse. Oh, God, she must be nearer to the cottage than she had noticed, walking aimlessly in a circle, which had brought her around again to the vicinity of that hateful place. What could she do? She had nothing with which to defend herself.

Taking heart, she stooped and broke off a stout branch which might serve as a weapon. She would not submit without a struggle. Trying vainly to pierce the stygian darkness, she could see little, but she heard footsteps, and the creaking of the door. The Prince had returned and when he found she had escaped would search for her in the forest. Then to her surprise, she heard another horse. Had the Prince brought reinforcements or was this a rescuer?

Carefully she edged closer to the revealing noise, hesitating on the edge of the overgrown garden. A weak flare of light penetrated the gloom. Evidently the Prince had lighted a candle or lamp. The door to the cottage stood open and as she crept closer she noticed two horses tethered to a tree beside the cottage. Fear for her safety kept her rooted to the spot, but she had to know what was happening. She stood irresolute, wondering frantically what was going on in the gloomy house, so isolated, so unfriendly, beyond the clearing.

Alistair entered the cottage prepared to rescue a distraught Verity from the Prince's clutches. He fully expected to find her struggling with the varlet, but to his surprise he met a suave opponent who greeted him with aplomb.

"I rather thought I heard your horse pounding after me, Major Glendenning. You English are so precipitate," the Prince taunted him, masking his fury. When he had burst into the empty room and discovered that Verity had fled, he had been in a passion of anger, but hearing Alistair's arrival, he had quickly masked his emotion and decided to bluff through the interview. All was still not lost. He must simply persuade this fellow that he still was in control of matters.

"Where is Verity?" Alistair demanded, finding the Prince's calm acceptance of his sudden appearance rather ominous.

"Where would she be, but upstairs in the bedroom, awaiting my attentions. She will be disappointed, I fear, by your interruption of what promised to be a pleasing encounter," the Prince goaded his accuser, hoping to rouse Alistair into some violent explosion of temper which he could turn to his own advantage.

"You are lying. She would never have come with you willingly. You have forced her into some damnable situation with your false promises and scurvy lies, and you will pay to the last farthing if you have harmed a hair of her head," Alistair threatened, but a nagging doubt beset him. Could he be wrong? Could Verity have run away with the Prince because she preferred his lovemaking, his wealth, and his position to the life Alistair offered?

The Prince, sensing Alistair's doubts, was quick to capitalize on them. "No doubt it is a blow to your self-esteem, Major, but you must accept that your wife finds my lovemaking more exciting than your own rather fumbling attempts to satisfy her," the Prince jeered. He had endured quite enough from this interloper and he intended to have his revenge.

Alistair made to push past the Prince, who was barring the entrance to the stairway. "I will see for myself," he growled.

The Prince blocked his path. "I cannot allow you to embarrass the lady, my good man," he replied in a condescending tone which sent Alistair's blood boiling.

Now that his rival had challenged him, Alistair's reaction hardened into a determination to rid himself once and for all of the man. He reined in his temper to a cool assessment of his choices. While he would like to level the man with a blow, other options were available. He stepped back a pace and eyed the Prince mockingly.

"Since you do not wish to allow the lady a choice, there seems but one solution. I suspect you are a competent swordsman, Prince. Shall we put it to the test?" he asked silkily, but with menace underneath the soft words. "Unfortunately I did not bring my sword, but perhaps you can remedy that error."

"I see you have a pistol, Major," the Prince replied, not liking the turn of events, but wondering how he could handle matters. He had not dreamed that the affair would come to such a pass, and although not a coward, he was loath to fight a duel over a woman who had evidenced her dislike of him by fleeing his embraces.

Alistair smiled grimly. "Much as it would please me to put a bullet through your black heart, I cannot forget that you are supposedly an ally. I doubt that either your Tsar or the Duke would look on your murder with compunction, much as you deserve it," he concluded, astounding the Prince with his coolness. Chirnovsky hesitated in the face of this obvious fact, but by now his own temper had reached a dangerous level. From the beginning Verity had deceived and gulled him, and her husband was another twister. They would be punished.

Crossing the room to a battered chest, he removed two swords and tossed one to Alistair, who caught it smoothly.

"So be it, Major. It will give me great pleasure to teach you a lesson, and will make my coming rendezvous with your errant wife that much sweeter," he declared, baiting Alistair.

But he had mistaken his man.

Alistair thirsted for the fight, but knew that he must not allow his anger to interfere with his skill. He tested the blade, and then threw off his jacket. Facing the Prince with a steely light in his eyes, he called softly, "En garde."

Chirnovsky lunged forward, determined to make

short work of the man. But Alistair was an accomplished fencer and riposted the Prince's blow expertly.

For the next few moments the men battled furiously in the small room, hampered by the space, but each grimly determined to land the first blow. Alistair finally breached the Prince's guard and slashed his opponent's shoulder, which began to bleed heavily.

"Do you surrender, sir?" Alistair asked, not abating his attack and breathing evenly as the Prince gasped.

"Never!" Chirnovsky replied, and bent to the fight.

So engrossed were the two in their duel they did not hear the door open and Verity enter, astounded at the sight which met her eyes.

"What are you doing? Stop this senseless fight immediately! I am perfectly safe, Alistair," she called, her voice rising against the clash of steel.

But Alistair was too canny to be distracted by her unexpected arrival. With one last straining effort he succeeded in breaking through the Prince's weakening guard and disarmed him. Chirnovsky, gasping, stood waiting his enemy's final thrust, but Alistair had made his point. He picked up his opponent's sword and asked casually, "Have you had enough, then?"

The Prince, weakened from the blood which seeped through his shirt, nodded wearily, sweat standing out on his forehead. "You seem to have won, Major. But why not administer the coup de grace?" he asked. Both men ignored the girl watching them with horror.

"I would like to kill you, Prince, but alas, I must consider the ramifications of such a worthwhile solution. I don't suppose Verity would enjoy skulking about the Continent, hiding from Wellington's minions. No it would never do. We must consider our masters whatever our own desires," Alistair replied, not at all discomposed. "And, of course, I know now that you were lying about Verity's association with you."

"What has he been telling you? He drugged me and spirited me away to this wretched cottage with some fell purpose in mind. You should kill him," Verity insisted fiercely.

"I agree, my dear, it would be most satisfying, but not at all practical. Somehow, I do not think we will be bothered by the Prince in the future. Is that not true, sir?" Alistair responded, not surrendering to the almost overmastering desire to kill the man and clasp Verity in his arms.

"You seem to have settled matters to your own convenience, sir. And since the lady has given the lie to my tale I must accept your decision," the Prince responded with equal coolness. The game was lost and he must try to retrieve what he could.

"I don't know which of you is the worst villain. You, Prince, for abducting me, or you, Alistair, for believing I would go with him willingly. There is not much to choose between you," Verity protested, thoroughly angered by their apparent accord.

"I beg your pardon, Verity. I am gravely at fault, but I had some reason for my suspicions. I should have known you would not submit tamely to the Prince's disgusting ploys," Alistair turned to her, contritely, but with a certain amusement in his expression. "Come let us cry pax and see how we can solve our various problems."

"I don't know how you can contemplate even speaking to this man much less conniving with him to smooth over this disgusting action so calmly. The Prince drugged me because I heard his conversation with the Baroness about the Tsar's plan to assassinate the Duke. He could not allow me to spread the news even if the cowardly plot came to nothing. I believe he intended to do away with me, once he had . . ." Verity could not go on, shuddering as she thought of her probably fate at the Prince's hands.

Alistair, still keeping a wary eye on his erstwhile enemy, crossed to Verity and took her in his arms. "You have had a frightful experience and it is largely my fault for not trusting you. Forgive me, Verity, I have behaved badly, but you must know how much I care about you," he said, raising her chin and looking deeply into her eyes. They both ignored the Prince, facing for the first time the love which neither had been prepared to admit. "I love you, Verity, and I can only hope that in time you will return my feeling," Alistair urged with a wealth of emotion. Verity choked back a sob of relief and buried her face in his shoulder, overcome by emotion and the events of the last few hours.

"Very affecting," the Prince commented dryly, recalling the bemused pair to the dilemma before them. "And what do we do now—shake hands like gentlemen?"

"Hardly," Alistair replied shortly. Without releasing his hold on Verity, he looked at the Prince with some disgust.

Not at all put out, his adversary, trying to stanch the blood which was discoloring his shirt and obviously causing him pain, continued his explanations.

"The lady is a bit hysterical and misread my intentions, I assure you. I would not harm such a lovely one, but I could not countenance her interference in the Tsar's plans. No doubt he did make some slighting reference to Wellington's obduracy about the Alliance, but I doubt if he would commit a murder to gain his desire," he insisted. He must persuade Alistair that the Tsar's suggestion was only one of passing irritation, not a viable solution to the problem.

"The Tsar's plans do not concern me for the moment, but your designs against Verity do. She has suffered indignity and danger at your hands and I doubt very much that the emperor would receive the news of this outrage committed by one of his trusted aides against an allied officer's wife with any degree of equanimity," Alistair responded severely, knowing that the Prince would not want this night's work to be reported to the Tsar.

"It was unfortunate that I had to take such drastic measures to subdue the lady, and prevent her from spreading scurrilous tales, but I did not really mean to cause her any permanent harm," the Prince lied glibly, hoping to diffuse Alistair's anger. He did not doubt that Alistair suspected his real intentions toward Verity and would take further steps to punish him. In the passion of the moment he had created a crisis which could only rebound on his own head, causing him to suffer the full rage of the Tsar's temper. He did not blame himself, only this troublesome pair who had overset his plans. His lust for Verity had led him into this coil, and now he would not even have the pleasure of satisfying it, he admitted ruefully. Still, something would have to be retrieved. He must use whatever tools were available, lies, threats, evasions.

"I doubt that Wellington would believe your outrageous tale, if even there were some proof in it. We would be wiser to forget the whole business and admit that there were faults on both sides. I apologize for any discomfort I may have caused Madame Glendenning," he offered suavely, and bowed mockingly in Verity's direction, assuming without much hope that the two would accept this specious explanation.

Alistair did not trust the Prince for one moment, but acknowledged that it was only their word against his. He gave Verity a warning glance and replied, "I make no promises, Prince Chirnovsky, but you would do well to rue this night's work and keep your distance from us both. I will have to decide what further measures I must take to repel your nefarious efforts against the Duke, and against Verity," he warned, his tone implacable. "You will suffer one way or another for your unconscionable action, I promise you. And now I must take Verity home. She has been through a shocking trauma. Any attempt to prevent us leaving will result in an unfortunate accident to you, I promise," he threatened. His first responsibility was to carry Verity to safety. Much as he wanted to revenge himself on the Prince he had to consider her beyond all else. But he would not let the varlet escape the retribution he deserved.

"You will make such explanations to the Tsar as you see fit. And I will certainly warn the Duke of the plot against him. He will know how to deal with that, but no doubt you will suffer for this botched intrigue," Alistair predicted with some satisfaction. "We will leave you to make what amends you can. I suspect that wound is not severe enough to prevent you from riding back to Paris. I must return Verity to the city. She has suffered enough."

Helpless to prevent his adversaries from abandoning him, the Prince, giddy from his wound, watched them leave, a baleful light in his eye. But he had enough sense to heed the wisdom of Alistair's words, and for the moment could only acquiesce and worry about his own future.

Alistair, escorting Verity to his tethered horse, felt he had brushed through the mess with some adroitness, and he had even turned the crisis to good advantage for he had finally some reason to believe Verity returned his love. He was not to enjoy his triumph for long. Verity, now that the danger was past, felt a passion of fury at what had transpired. Despite her relief and fatigue she was not inclined to allow Alistair to bask smugly in the belief that he had conducted her rescue gallantly. As they covered the miles back to Paris, with Verity tucked securely in Alistair's arms on the tired horse, she battled both weariness and anger. Finally, unable to hold her peace, seeing that Alistair appeared to have regained his normal insouciance now that the danger had past, she took him to task.

"Aren't you shocked that the Prince and the Baroness used me so badly, drugging me, carrying me off to some deserted cell, and who knows what the Prince had in mind when he returned, expecting me to be tamely awaiting his pleasure?" she asked, glaring at her rescuer.

"Well, if the Prince knew you as well as I do, he would not have expected you to be awaiting his pleasure. I am sure that even if I had not ridden so frantically to your rescue, you would somehow have prevailed, escaped, and taken your vengeance on the unhappy man," Alistair replied lightly. Not for a moment would he reveal his worry over her probable fate, now that he had her safe in his arms. This was not the time to tell her of his anguish, he thought, weary and disordered as she was. But he would not wait long. He had learned his lesson.

"Umph, I see you have some faith in my ability to

manage my own life," Verity answered, not knowing whether to be pleased or disappointed that he viewed her clever escape from a potential ugly affair with so much sangfroid.

"Some faith, yes. But don't think I contemplate riding ventre à terre every other day to rescue you from some adventure which your impetuosity and your unjustified belief in your cleverness embroils you in." He laughed lightheartedly, not above teasing her a bit in hopes that it would banish any nightmares she might have about her experience.

"Not very chivalrous of you, but then I expected little praise for my courage. And the news which I learned is rather important, isn't it?" Verity pleaded, needing reassurance that her ordeal had proved of some worth.

"You are a good brave girl, and Wellington will be both astounded and appreciative of your efforts. But we will talk more of it later. You are much too tired and irritated with me to take it all in now," Alistair soothed as the outlines of the city approached.

Verity, ripe for an argument and less than satisfied with his idea of comfort, was eager to continue her tirade but she could no longer keep her eyes open and drifted off to sleep, lulled by the soothing motion of the horse. Alistair, looking down at her, smiled gently. She was a handful, but he would have her no other way. A timid, vaporing wife would not be at all to his taste. And once she had recovered from her trials, he would confess his love again and beg for hers in return. He knew he did not deserve it, but he had a faint hope which sustained him that he would receive it and, for now, was content to postpone that happy day. But first he had his duty to Wellington, and with Verity safely home again, he could allow his mind to dwell on the information she had gained at such peril to herself.

Once back at the rooms on the faubourg Saint Honore, Alistair carried Verity, who barely stirred, into the house and instructed Agnes to minister to her. He arranged for Jenkins to take his second best gray to the hideout and assist the Prince if that defeated man had not already secured his freedom, but told him not to hurry. It would do the Russian a power of good to lie on that dark drab floor and contemplate his sins, Alistair decided. It was now near midnight and he wondered about disturbing Wellington with his information, but once he had seen Verity into her bed, he believed he must not postpone the interview no matter the lateness of the hour.

Chapter Twenty-Six

Verity opened her eyes slowly, aware that she was secure in her own bed, seeing the dim light from the window gradually lightening as the sun rose. It must not be far off dawn, and the events of the tumultuous night were behind her. She snuggled down again, realizing that Alistair had shared her slumbers, although she had no remembrance of his joining her. Propping herself on one elbow, she watched him sleeping deeply. Unguarded, his tan strong face looked much more vulnerable, almost boyish, and she sighed knowing how much he had come to mean to her. Afraid he would catch her at this tender observation, she turned away, reluctant to reveal her feelings. But too late, as his eyelids opened and he grinned at her.

"What was that sigh for, I wonder. Disgust or pleasure at viewing my manly charms," he teased.

"Disgust, that you could be sleeping so innocently

after all I have endured," Verity answered sharply, a blush rising in her cheeks. "And I have a hundred questions to ask you," she insisted severely.

"A hundred. Odd, I have only one to ask you," Alistair responded, eyeing her with what she considered a very lustful look which was not unwelcome. But then his expression became grave.

"Verity, I blame myself for what you endured at the hands of the Prince. But you were foolish to visit the Baroness without giving anyone your direction. I was worried sick. Even though I did not believe the damning note that charlatan wrote saying you were tired of me and had run off with some man who could offer you a better life," he said, his voice doubtful. "And it could be true, I am a rubbishy fellow, I know, and I have treated you badly, but do not leave me," he pleaded.

Verity was astounded at his humble tone. Did Alistair really care for her? She had not quite believed him at the cottage and did not trust her instinct to throw herself in his arms and confess her own love. "I don't know you in this chastened mood, Alistair," she said, raising an eyebrow and looking at him in some surprise.

"Well, you will come to know me, and I you. We have had so many misunderstandings, so much to overcome, but I mean it, Verity. I will not let you go, even if you want to escape with that callow young fool, Denis Montgomery, who has come to Paris to rescue you from the ogre you have wed," he growled.

"Is Denis here? How kind of him. But he is foolish,

and you know I care only for his friendship. What do you mean about a note?" she asked curiously.

"It's of no importance. What matters is that I love you. I want to make up for the past, to change our marriage into a real one, with trust and companionship, and something much more. I love you, Verity, and pray that you return my love," he said, taking her in his arms and looking at her with sincerity and a strange tenseness, as if he were bracing himself for her derision.

She signed gratefully. "Oh, yes, Alistair. I love you, too, and I have, I suspect, since that first day at the races, when you behaved so abominably. As you did at the Duchess of Richmond's ball, too," she teased, remembering the ruthless kisses he had forced on her.

"Thank God. I promise, Verity, I will make you happy," he vowed, kissing her with gentle warmth, which deepened as his passion rose and his hands moved down her responsive body.

Eager as she was to experience his lovemaking, Verity was not prepared to forgive him so easily. "And there will be no more Olivia Bletchfords or other like-minded ladies. I wanted to scratch her eyes out," she confessed.

"I hoped you were as jealous as I was over the Prince," he admitted, his caresses becoming more demanding. Whatever demur she might have made was lost in the satisfying lovemaking which followed, when for the first time they were joined by more than just physical desire. Satiated and exhausted by the tempest they fell asleep again, locked in each other's arms. It was much later in the morning when they surfaced, to grin companionably at one another. Verity, no longer embarrassed or ashamed at her fervent reaction now that she was assured of his love, sighed blissfully.

"I really shouldn't complain about your vast experience, sir, when it results in such satisfactory delights for me," she said saucily, thoroughly at ease with this man who had taken over her life and offered her such unexpected devotion. "Lovely as all this is, I still want to know what Wellington decided when he heard the news of the Tsar's plot. You did inform him immediately, I hope," she asked, a bit ashamed that she had almost forgotten these grave matters in her own personal happiness.

"While you were sleeping and dreaming blissfully of me, I took myself around, late as it was, to the great man, and told him everything," Alistair assured her.

"What did he say?" she asked, her curiosity unrestrained.

"He laughed a bit grimly. After all, he is no stranger to assassination plots. But he means to thwart any plans of the Tsar in that direction. And he did tell me he had called Captain Webster in and read him a stern rebuke about consorting with the Russians. He can be quite intimidating, and I suppose he laid the man's fears to rest about any liaison with the luscious Frances. I gather that Webster had already decided against instituting a 'crim con' case, realizing that Wellington would not have behaved in such an undignified and reckless fashion. The Duchess's arrival this week will lay that canard to rest, and any lingering doubts about the Duke's guilt should be ended."

"Wellington has no intention of signing the Alliance, although he looks favorably upon cooperation among the Allies to keep the peace. He was really most forthcoming and grateful. I have great hopes of another promotion," Alistair explained with a certain complacency.

He sat up in bed and reached for his robe, then casting a quizzical look at his wife, who seemed dissatisfied with this sketchy account of events, he continued casually, "And he was most apologetic about your ordeal and profuse in his gratitude for your assistance, although he did mention that I had his sympathy in dealing with such an impetuous and disobedient wife," he finished, watching her with amusement.

"He didn't!" Verity replied in shocked tones before she realized that Alistair was being deliberately provoking. "Well, I suppose it was all worthwhile, my abduction by the Prince. What will happen to him, I wonder," she asked, watching with shy approval as Alistair rose from the bed and donned a robe to cover himself. Not that she really cared what happened to the Prince, but it would not do to let Alistair think she was completely cowed by his lovemaking, although she conceded she had given him every reason to suspect those wanton tendencies he had once decried.

"Are you concerned about the dashing Prince?" Alistair growled, not at all pleased about her enquiry. "He will be sent back to Russia forthwith, I believe, a victim of the Tsar's anger. The emperor is now inclined to put the whole blame for the conspiracy on the Prince's shoulders and he will find his life far from happy, I suspect. Serve him right and not at all the punishment that he deserves. The Baroness will receive her comeuppance, too, I believe, for the Tsar will abandon her, feeling she has served her purpose," he said angrily. "They are fortunate to be let off so easily," he informed her, evidently still resentful that the scurvy pair should be allowed to go free. He crossed the room, prepared to ring the bell for the servants. "I am devilishly hungry. You are a one for making me miss my meals, my love," he teased.

"Hah, fine thanks for all my efforts. I beg your indulgence, sir. I believe my peril last evening precluded any concern for your appetite," she responded in reproof for his apparent indifference to the danger she had suffered.

Looking at the enticing picture she made as she leaned against the nest of pillows, her face glowing, her expression softened from their lovemaking, he hesitated, and turned away from the bell pull.

"On second thought, another hunger is much more pressing," he said, grinning wickedly at her and returning to the bed.

"Alistair, you can't mean . . ." she protested

weakly, but her arms crept up around his neck and she held him close.

"Oh, but I do," he replied sternly, "And this is just a taste of the pleasures in store for us in the future."

And then there were no more arguments for a long time.

Author's Note

Although Wellington escaped assassination several times in his career, the conspirators were mostly disgruntled followers of Napoleon. Alexander I, the Tsar of Russia, brought considerable pressure to force the Duke to sign the Holy Alliance but there is no evidence that he plotted to eliminate the English opposition to his cherished treaty in such a drastic fashion. The scandal about Lady Frances Wedderburn-Webster and Wellington is a well-documented fact. The Baroness von Krudener did influence the Tsar to forsake his libertine past and embrace her Christian mysticism but he eventually tired of her. The Holy Alliance, with the Pope and the English politely refusing, was signed on September 26, 1815, and the Tsar left shortly afterward for a triumphal tour of Prussia. The Baroness did not accompany him. Captain Webster brought an action for libel against the publisher of the *St. James*

Gazette on February 16, 1816, and at the trial the Duke of Richmond testified that Wellington "was never in his life alone with Lady Webster." The captain was awarded 2,000 pounds in the London Court of Appeals. The Websters remained married, although constantly in financial difficulties until their deaths in the 1840s. They applied several times to the Duke for money but were ignored, and played no further part in his life.

LOVE'S BRIGHTEST STARS SHINE
WITH ZEBRA BOOKS!

CATALINA'S CARESS   (2202, $3.95)
by Sylvie F. Sommerfield

Catalina Carrington was determined to buy her riverboat back from the handsome gambler who'd beaten her brother at cards. But when dashing Marc Copeland named his price—three days as his mistress—Catalina swore she'd never meet his terms . . . even as she imagined the rapture a night in his arms would bring!

BELOVED EMBRACE   (2135, $3.95)
by Cassie Edwards

Leana Rutherford was terrified when the ship carrying her family from New York to Texas was attacked by savage pirates. But when she gazed upon the bold sea-bandit Brandon Seton, Leana longed to share the ecstasy she was sure sure his passionate caress would ignite!

ELUSIVE SWAN   (2061, $3.95)
by Sylvie F. Sommerfield

Just one glance from the handsome stranger in the dockside tavern in boisterous St. Augustine made Arianne tremble with excitement. But the innocent young woman was already running from one man . . . and no matter how fiercely the flames of desire burned within her, Arianne dared not submit to another!

MOONLIT MAGIC   (1941, $3.95)
by Sylvie F. Sommerfield

When she found the slick railroad negotiator Trace Cord trespassing on her property and bathing in her river, innocent Jenny Graham could barely contain her rage. But when she saw how the setting sun gilded Trace's magnificent physique, Jenny's seething fury was transformed into burning desire!

Available wherever paperbacks are sold, or order direct from the Publisher. Send cover price plus 50¢ per copy for mailing and handling to Zebra Books, Dept. 2455, 475 Park Avenue South, New York, N.Y. 10016. Residents of New York, New Jersey and Pennsylvania must include sales tax. DO NOT SEND CASH.